BORN TO LOVE YOU

Whit got up and sat on the couch beside Danielle for a moment, then stood, pulled her up, and pressed her to him. Her soft, yielding body in his arms struck liquid fire into his veins, and he knew then as he had known before that he wanted her more than anything or anyone.

For Danielle, his rock-hard body pressing in on her softness filled her with rapture. His splendid presence aroused her greatly and the spirit of the night caught her up in its dazzling promise. He had asked her to marry him. He had introduced her to his world and she felt she belonged there. That and having proved her mettle tonight with the dangerous thug on the waterfront brought her tingling with satisfaction.

She knew something then with all her heart: that when a person is faced with death, with danger, it is one of the times he or she lives in the deepest part of life. She was trembling with wanting him and their kisses were drugged. Without realizing she would say it, she told him with tears in her voice, "Take me, Whit. I don't want to wait any longer."

BOOK YOUR PLACE ON OUR WEBSITE AND MAKE THE ARABESQUE ROMANCE CONNECTION!

We've created a customized website just for our very special Arabesque readers, where you can get the inside scoop on everything that's going on with Arabesque romance novels.

When you come online, you'll have the exciting opportunity to:

- View covers of upcoming books

- Learn about our future publishing schedule (listed by publication month and author)

- Find out when your favorite authors will be visiting a city near you

- Search for and order backlist books

- Check out author bios and background information

- Send e-mail to your favorite authors

- Join us in weekly chats with authors, readers and other guests

- Get writing guidelines

- AND MUCH MORE!

Visit our website at
http://www.arabesquebooks.com

BORN TO LOVE YOU

Francine Craft

BET Publications, LLC
http://www.bet.com
http://www.arabesquebooks.com

ARABESQUE BOOKS are published by

BET Publications, LLC
c/o BET BOOKS
One BET Plaza
1900 W Place NE
Washington, DC 20018-1211

All Kensington Titles, Imprints, and Distributed Lines are available at special quantity discounts for bulk purchases for sales promotions, premiums, fund-raising, and educational or institutional use. Special book excerpts or customized printings can also be created to fit specific needs. For details, write or phone the office of the Kensington special sales manager: Kensington Publishing Corp., 850 Third Avenue, New York, NY 10022, attn: Special Sales Department, Phone: 1-800-221-2647.

First Printing: September 2003
10 9 8 7 6 5 4 3 2 1

Printed in the United States of America

*This book is dedicated to two of the most
savvy editors I've worked with:*

*Karen Thomas, senior editor, with deep appreciation
for your encouragement and your expertise.*

*Chandra Taylor, consulting editor. I am always grateful for
your expertise and your many demonstrations of excellence.*

And to:

June M. Bennett, a superior person and a wonderful friend.

*Sandra Woodard, a barrel of laughs, a romantic now
and a romantic at one hundred!*

ACKNOWLEDGMENTS

To Charlie, who stood by me one more time. Thank you so much.

To Alberta, who is a wonderful source of information and a very good friend.

I love you both dearly.

And to select members of the Montgomery County Police Department in Maryland. I greatly appreciate your courtesy, your skilled help, and your suggestions.

APRIL 2000
A DREAM BEGINS

ONE

It was happening again!

Thirty-five-year-old Danielle Ritchey crossed the Minden city line in her beige Mercury Cougar and slowed a bit. Passing a hand over her heart-shaped, honey-colored face, she reflected on how warm it was for late April, and this even at 10:00 P.M. She was late going home from her job as a detective lieutenant in the Minden, Maryland, Police Department.

The car ahead of her had books and other articles obscuring the back window and she started to wave him over, but decided not to. As she stopped behind the car for a red light on the highway, the vision came swiftly. There was no one standing beside the passenger headlight of her car, but her gift of second sight made her envision a tall man with walnut-colored skin and thick, coal-black, flat-grained, beaverlike hair. He had a broad face with high cheekbones and black olive eyes. A thrill coursed the length of her body. A widow of two years, she spent a lot of her spare time tamping down her erotic feelings, but it was no use now. The tall, sinewy man in the vision moved her—a lot. A delicious warmth spread through her.

Danielle smiled a little. This was one of the strongest visions she had ever had, and she smiled again. She was getting hot pants for a *vision*. She murmured to herself, "You're in bad shape, girl."

The vision faded and she started her car again. A deer skittered across the road in front of the car ahead of her. The driver braked sharply, causing her to slam into the back of his car as the deer plunged into the woods near the road. She and the other driver pulled onto the shoulder of the road and both got out of their cars.

She walked over to her passenger side. Striding back, a man so like the man in the vision came to her side, asking, "Are you all right?"

"I think so. Neither of us was going very fast."

"I'm Whit Steele," he told her.

She inhaled sharply. "The gospel singer?" His posters had been all over Minden that past winter.

"The same. Are you sure you're okay?" He touched her arm. "You look a little shaky."

"I'm okay. Thanks for asking."

She passed a hand over her forehead. She had slammed hard into the steering wheel, but she felt fine. The air bag hadn't activated. She examined the bumpers and found no damage, so she didn't need to call the accident squad.

"The question is, are *you* okay? I'm Danielle Ritchey— *Lieutenant* Danielle Ritchey—a detective in the Minden Police Department." She half turned to display the badge on her fanny pack.

They shook hands and Danielle thought she swooned like a teenager as his big hand covered her smaller one.

He smiled. "I'm happy to meet you, Lieutenant Ritchey." And he groaned inside thinking, *I can't tell you how happy I am to meet you. Those doelike, big, brown beautiful eyes are melting and that honey-colored, heart-shaped face is telling me things I never knew before. Talk to me, lady. Talk to me!*

"I'm glad we're both okay," she said softly, aware that only then did he let go of her hand. Her whole body felt tense with sudden joy as she turned back to her car.

A few minutes later, they still tarried, both wondering at the attraction. She noted his new burgundy Lexus. The model was one of her favorites.

Finally, he turned to her. "You're young to be a detective lieutenant."

She nodded. "We have to start somewhere. I've been with the department thirteen years. My mother was a detective. . . ."

"But she is no longer?" He didn't like the idea of her living with danger.

"She's dead," she said slowly. "Murdered. A murder never solved."

"I'm sorry."

What was wrong with her? She wanted to go into this stranger's arms and cry out her grief. Grief never properly worked through for Mona, her mother, and for Scott, her husband, who had died of leukemia two years ago. She had a feeling that this man could comfort her.

"You're kind," she murmured.

He laughed a little. "I try to be kind. Life is better that way." Danielle thought that it had been a long time since life had been really kind to her.

He drew a deep breath as he looked at the wedding ring on her finger. "Your husband is a lucky man."

She shook her head slowly. "I'm a widow of two years."

He tried to suppress a grin. "I'm sorry," he said and wondered what to say next. His heart was soaring higher than an eagle.

"Listen," he said urgently, "we're attracted and that's good, even if we don't know each other. Could I take you somewhere for a bite to eat? I've been driving here for two days to visit a friend. I once ate at a restaurant called Annie's Place. . . ."

His voice drifted off and his eyes were half closed, envisioning what? she wondered.

"Annie's Place is nice," she said. "Good food but late like this, you don't get their best. Why don't we go to my house and rustle up something simple? I'm a fair cook." What in hell was she *doing* inviting a stranger home with her? Well, she argued, he was well known and not an axe murderer.

When he was silent a moment she thought that she was

coming on to him like a groupie. This man had women coming out of his *ears*. He didn't need a small-city police detective dangling her goods at him.

But Whit was silent because he quarreled with himself. *You're going too fast. You're just getting over having your heart ripped out and thrown to the dogs. Are you some kind of glutton for emotional punishment?* But he couldn't stop himself. He had an alter ego he called Slow and Secure and another part of himself he called Full Speed Ahead. It was plain to him that Full Speed Ahead was going to win.

"Lady," he said slowly, "have you got a taker."

Her house was two miles out of Minden, set on five acres of ground. She had bought it at an estate distress price and was slowly renovating it herself.

As she inserted her key in the front door, she had a moment of panic, and thought again: *What am I doing?* But it was no use, her left brain was losing this battle and her right brain that sought and controlled joy in living held full sway. *Welcome,* she told it. As they went inside and closed the door, she felt a lurch of fear. Celebrities sometimes behaved badly, but everything about this man said he was levelheaded, caring. Appearances sometimes lied. She only knew that suddenly she'd like to be back on the highway—alone and *safe,* with nothing to fear.

"I won't stay long," he said. "I'm mostly on hiatus from singing for now so I've got time, but you need your sleep. I won't say 'beauty sleep,' because you don't need it."

"Thank you. You *are* kind."

He half closed his eyes. "And you *are* beautiful."

He wanted to kiss her somewhere. Hell, *everywhere*.

Going into her bedroom, she changed into an aquamarine silk jersey jumpsuit with a three-tiered gold chain belt that accented her narrow waistline. Dressing, she felt Whit's presence beside her as she had felt and yes, first *seen* him, on the highway. He looked the way he had looked in her vision of him just before the accident.

Danielle had had visions since she was a little girl. She rarely talked about them, but her mother and her father knew and sympathized. "They're a gift from God," her mother often said. "Use them wisely."

Back in the living room, she paused in the doorway and his eyes lingered for a moment on her body, then focused on her glowing face. He could not remember seeing anything more beautiful. Her face was gorgeous by any standard with thick, black lashes and naturally curved eyebrows. He blew a small stream of air as he studied her high cheekbones and softly curved mouth. Her satiny honey skin under the cap of curly-kinky, earth-brown, big ringlets moved him. But it was the expression on her face—warm and caring—that spurred him on.

"To the kitchen." She smiled, moving toward him. "Why don't you take off that jacket? This is unusual weather."

He quickly shucked his tan tweed jacket, which she hung in the closet, and went with her to the kitchen. "You seem to have it pretty well together. How long have you been here?"

"A year. I should have gotten more done, but I've been studying investigative manuals. The contractor is moving along nicely. I volunteer two nights a week with A Literate Minden."

They settled on and prepared grilled shrimp, green onion and cheese sandwiches with sangria wine, topped off with strawberry tarts she had made the day before. She put the food on trays and they took them back to the living room. "One day I'll get it together," she told him.

"You're not that far behind. My bedroom is always a jumble. Music," he said. "Sheet music. Cassettes. CD's. . . ."

They kept glancing at one another, but with the food consumed, they settled down. For the moment, she let the trays sit on the table.

Around 11:30 P.M. he sighed deeply and told her, "I ought to go, but . . ."

"But?" she questioned.

"I don't want to." He grinned. "I'm enjoying your company. I guess I'm lonely, but that's not the whole reason." *Don't move too fast*, he told himself. *You'll frighten her off.*

When she finally got up to remove the trays, he stood to help her. In her flat shoes, her five feet seven and a half inches seemed shorter. She was *so* conscious of his lean, well-muscled body, for a moment she couldn't get her breath.

"You work out often," she said.

"Does it show?"

"It shows. I'm kind of slothful about it, but I work out too. I've got some equipment. There's a spa in Minden. A couple in fact."

Grinning, he looked at her narrow shoulders and wonderfully rounded body with its wide hips and deeply curved buttocks. His eyes were grave, but his mind was playing havoc. He could not remember ever wanting to kiss anyone more, not even his ex-wife, Willo, who had shattered his heart.

Back in the living room, both knew they were clinging to each other and neither moved to let go.

"Tell me more about your mother."

She thought about that a long moment before the grandfather clock struck twelve.

"Mom was great. I'm an only child and Mom, Dad, and I were really close. Dad lives a couple of miles from here. Mom was a detective on Minden's police force and there's never been anything else I wanted to be. She died the year I graduated from John Jay College of Criminal Justice in New York. She never wanted me to be a policewoman."

"Too dangerous?" He certainly thought so.

She shook her head. "Being a detective is certainly not altogether safe, but many jobs are more dangerous. You've got to have a sharp mind and steel nerves to be one, but I wouldn't say it's dangerous."

He didn't agree, but he was silent. He had given a concert

in Boston the year before and the papers were full of a female detective being killed in a stakeout. He didn't mention that now.

"I've dedicated my life to finding my mother's killer," she said. "I'll never give up on that."

"Did your husband back you up on being a cop?"

"All the way."

He wasn't sure he could.

"I wish you luck," he said slowly, wanting to hold her, take away the grief that was suddenly etched on her face.

She wanted him to know what had happened to her a few hours earlier. "I *saw* you before we had the little accident tonight. Just before the fender-bender, I saw you so plainly. . . ."

"You *saw* me. . ." he began, puzzled. Then he quickly got her meaning. "You mean second sight, a psychic thing?"

"A *vision*. Please don't mock me. Sometimes I wish I didn't have it, but I do."

Silently he thought, *Anything you've got, babe, I'll take*.

"I'd never mock you," he said gently. "I *believe* it happens. Be glad you have it."

"I've been able to help a few people. The Perkins boy. I dreamed of him drowning. Reluctantly, I told his mother that and found several boys were slipping off to swim in a hazardous part of the creek. She made him stop. A friend didn't stop, however, and he died in that creek. Sighting makes you feel a bit cut off from people . . . different."

"It should be worth it to have a gift like that."

"I don't know," she said slowly, stroking her shoulders as she crossed her arms over her chest, *protecting* herself. From him?

"It's a great gift," he said.

Bitterness laced her voice and her throat felt raw as she asked him, "If it's such a great gift, *why* don't I know who killed my mother?"

Hot tears of rage filled her eyes and her body shook. It

had been thirteen years. *Thirteen years* since Mona was killed. And it was plain that her death was never going to stop hurting.

He slid over and took her in his arms, held her. Her father had been a Rock of Gibraltar when Mona had been killed. "She never knew my husband, and she never saw me graduate." She held up her right hand with the lovely garnet and diamond ring on it. "I finished college in January. She sent me this for an early graduation gift with a card that read 'Always do your best and make yourself proud.'"

She could not have stopped herself from crying if she had tried and she didn't want to try. Her heart seemed to be breaking as she told him, "Oh, God, I miss her so!"

He held her tightly, stroked her.

Time passed and as Danielle cried, some dam of grief seemed to be breaking in her body. Long years of holding back her emotions were over. She was weeping bitterly in the arms of a stranger. Scott had understood and comforted her. Her father had understood and comforted her. She knew about the five steps of grief and had done her best to go through them. Yet, it was in this man's arms that she found the faint beginning of a cessation of grief for her mother.

Finally, she pulled away a bit. "Thank you," she said softly. "I feel better now. I have a famous man in my living room and he has to console me."

"Don't mock yourself. I get the feeling you've been running away."

"I have. I didn't know it, but I have. Tell me about your concerts. People here are crazy about you and your sister, Ashley, and the Singing Steeles!"

"I'm glad and thank you for telling me. We grew up singing gospel music. Ashley and I both wanted to specialize in spirituals because we're so crazy about them. Mom and Dad are retired. Ash travels the world over. I pretty much stick to the United States."

"Scott and I were at your concert in D.C. a couple of years

back just before he died. I like any kind of music, but your voice sent me rocketing. You have a truly beautiful voice."

He nodded. "And *you* are beautiful . . ." He hesitated for a moment. "Danielle."

They seemed on the verge of a kiss, but each held back. He learned forward and kissed the top of her head as she smiled.

It came from the depths of him and he couldn't have stopped it if he had tried. "It would be magic making love to you."

He drew in a quick breath. She was going to bolt now for sure. *Idiot*, he fumed at himself.

To his surprise, she smiled slowly, then radiantly. "Whoa, tiger, but who am I kidding?"

The moment lay between them, palpably trembling the way her soft body was trembling. *I ought to go,* he thought. But he couldn't leave, and she thought about how hard it was going to be to function properly that day with little sleep.

"I want to see you again," he told her. "Have dinner with me tonight at a place of your choosing. I'll get you back early."

"I'd love that. You've been so kind and I've had to tell you that several times. You're an unusual man."

"I hope I am, if you like unusual men."

She looked obliquely at his clear, humorous black eyes that reflected his love for life. His face was square, intelligent with its big, straight nose and wickedly sensual mouth. Her eyes kept going back to that mouth.

Finally he said, "Working at the Minden Police Department, you must know Captain Jon Ryson."

"He's my boss. I know and dearly love him."

"He's one of my best friends. Great guy."

"One of the best. He tells me that one day I'll be police chief. He flatters my ego."

Leaning forward, he said gravely, "I think you'll be anything you want to be. Something tells me you've got a gift of getting to where you're headed."

During the time they'd talked she'd felt less shattered. They spent the rest of the evening in deep conversation. Still, he stayed until finally, he said, "How did it get to be four o'clock in the morning?"

She thought a moment. "Time's a monster. Unforgiving. It just keeps passing relentlessly."

Yes, he thought, *including the time that passed before I met you.* He'd never believed in love at first sight. Now, he wondered.

At fifteen after five, dawn's coral rays crept across the sky. At five-thirty, she suddenly stood up. "Do you want to see something stunning?" she asked.

"Sure."

As they rose from the couch, she took his hand and led him to the kitchen. Through the wide windows of one wall, they saw a blushing dawn, then a magnificent sunrise that spread its coral and gold rays over the countryside. She led him out to her long back porch where the fresh air caressed them. The house stood on a hill and they could see a long distance away.

He studied the scene that lay before him a long while before he said, "My God, this is beautiful. You like beauty, don't you, the same way I like beauty. One day I want you to watch the sun set and rise on the Potomac River from the cabin cruiser I'm living on at Washington's marina."

"Great. I'd love to see that."

He touched her face gently. "Do you feel better? I couldn't go away and leave you in so much pain."

"Thank you. It's been so long. Will it never be over, Whit?"

He nodded. "I think one day it will. You've dedicated your life to finding her killer, and that's good. You married and tried to move on with your life. Have faith in God, Danielle. Only by God's grace did I survive when my marriage broke up. Anything at all I can do to help, I will."

They walked back inside to the living room. "You're so sweet," she began to say.

It was happening in slow motion and both of them savored

every minute. Strangers. And she smiled inside. Potential *lovers*. Whit's heart spun with ecstasy as he pulled her into his arms. The long rays of gleeful sunrise danced and they found themselves locked together. With his rock-hard body pressed against her softness, he fought for breath. Her lips were silken and smooth, her mouth like honey and rich red wine.

He teased the corners of her mouth with his tongue, seeking to bring her every heartwarming pleasure. He could not remember a time when he had felt more at one with the world, but he did remember well the pain of a past encounter. Willo. Damn her for her betrayal that had nearly cost him his faith in love—and life.

His hot breath fanned Danielle's face and she pressed closer for a longer, deeper kiss. He groaned and cupped her face in his hands as she swayed against him, half falling before he caught her.

"Oh, my God," she whimpered. At no time in her life had she known desire the way it swept her now. The very feel of his engorged shaft was proof of his desire and filled her with awe and pure light which illuminated her brain, even as hot, nebulous clouds of passion filled her trembling body.

He wanted to cup those fabulous hips in his hands, but he knew it was too soon. He could not get close enough. She trembled wildly again, with fear or desire he couldn't tell. Her body against his filled him with desire so deep it scared him. He caught her hand and pressed it, then slowly pulled away, leaving her gasping for breath. And she wondered if he took her now, could she, *would* she stop him?

Again, he took her face in his hands. "I'll never press you," he said huskily. "I promise not to move too fast."

"Thank you," she breathed, "but I'm not helping you much in that direction. I'm sorry, but I—"

He put a finger to her lips. "Hush," he said. "You're doing everything right. We won't beat up on ourselves. We're both lonely, hurt. We can comfort each other."

She didn't want to talk. She wanted to be folded in his arms

again, thrilled in a way that she had never felt before. She and
Scott had known simple pleasure, not wild rapture like this.
He raised her hand and kissed her palm, the tip of his tongue
tracing wet lines on it. She felt she willed him to kiss her
again and this time they were slower, steadier. For the briefest
moment his spirit stormed through the portals of her body,
then eased. The leathery skin of his face felt wonderful as she
stroked him feverishly. His thick, smooth hair under her
stroking made her want to purr like a sleek cat.

For moments he laced his hand in her own, then moved to
her scalp, feeling the whorls of hair and the buttery flesh beneath. He took her shoulders in his big hands and squeezed
them softly. Her slender shoulders had borne so much pain in
her young life and he knew that if he were not torn up, he
could love her, God help him.

He laughed shakily. "I'm emotionally damaged goods."

"I thought you might be."

"Your psychic gift let you know?"

She smiled a bit. "Get this straight, Whit. My gift doesn't
let me know all about you, what you're thinking, that sort of
thing, except *sometimes* it does."

"You're perceptive, and I'd bet on that. What I'm thinking
is I wish I'd known you longer. I've never wanted to make
love to a woman the way I want to make love to you and it's
not a flash-in-the-pan kind of thing. Danielle, I think we're
headed into something deep."

She nodded. "I think we may well be."

This time he began to pull away and she let him go. Sunlight flooded the kitchen, washed over them. "How about
breakfast?" she asked.

He shook his head. "I'd better go. This is the countryside
and gossip runs amuck. I may have already compromised you
and for that I'm sorry."

"I needed you. I've led enough of a straightforward life that
if my neighbors knew I entertained someone overnight it
would be my choosing, my business."

He touched her face. "You're protecting me. Maybe I was wrong to stay, but I couldn't help it. I'll never hurt you."

She stroked his face. "You'll hurt me because people sometimes hurt each other, but you'll know because I'll tell you and you'll do whatever you can to make it better."

"You're an *old soul*."

Danielle smiled a little. "Ah, yes, an old soul, someone young who sees as deeply or nearly as deeply as a much older person. I guess I am. I'm thirty-five. That's not so young."

"I want to see you often," he said.

"Should we? We're moving so fast."

"We'll slow down. *I'll* slow down."

"It's not just you. I seem to be on fire. It's not like me."

He laughed then. "I'm *stoking* that fire and I'll just stop. We'll see each other, talk, have a few light kisses and gentle hugs. It's been a long time since I've felt I'd like to live forever."

TWO

After Whit left, Danielle stood at her kitchen windows. She felt light-headed, unreal, yet profoundly real—and wonderful! She would call in late and catch a couple of hours of sleep. There was nothing much going on at the station house. Minden was not a violent city, and except for a mobster and a couple of muscle men down from New York who were trying to set up gambling and God knows what else, the city was quiet.

She showered quickly and as the needles of warm water struck her body, she felt exhilarated. Lathering with bath oil, she scrubbed with a loofah sponge and burst a lavender gel cap into the shower water. The pleasant scent filled the room.

After drying off and smoothing on Nivea oil, she climbed into bed naked and lay there, no longer feeling sleepy. Instead, she slid into a relaxed dream state, reliving the feel of Whit's torrid kisses, and feeling a little afraid. She would see him again tonight. Her mind raced to the night ahead, and she thought then, *Fools rush in. . . .*

Her mother's death had changed her greatly. She developed a deep, primal anger and the world did not seem as wonderful a place to be. She was glad her father had been there for her and she had tried to be there for him. The love between her parents had been deep, abiding. When she married Scott, she had felt better, steadier, but life was still bleaker than she wanted it to be. Then he was gone and she grieved again.

She had developed a taste for the edge of danger. Bring on the bad guys; she knew how to handle them. Captain Jon

Ryson, her top supervisor, often spoke to her about exercising paramount care in dealing with criminals. "Their world and yours are different," he had often told her. "You're in love with life," he told her. "They are all too frequently in love with death."

Looking at him steadily, she had answered, *"Once* I was in love with life. Now I'm not so sure."

He had sighed. "Mona wouldn't want you to feel that way. She was a superb human being, a loving woman." Cocking his head a little to the side, he had offered, "Dedicate your life to your mother. You were blessed with having her for so long as she was here. She'd be so proud of you. I miss her too."

Her mind segued to blankness, then—Whitley Steele. She had heard him only once in concert and she was not remotely a groupie, but his voice and his interpretation of the spirituals had moved her. She had a couple of his CD's and a couple of his tapes. Would he invite her to go to his concert in D.C. in July? Reality got the upper hand and she laughed a little. Singers were often players. He would probably have turned to another woman by then, especially once he knew that she would not be an easy lay.

She rolled over onto her back and hugged herself. *Lord, but he was beautiful!* She closed her eyes and saw him again in all his glory. Funny, she had never sighted someone before she met them. She had not sighted her dead husband. Only on the night he had died had she known he would go. Of course, she had been driving behind Whit and could see only the back of his head. She had seen photos of him, so that might have kicked in her memory, but—she sighed—no, there had been something special, something spiritlike in that sighting. In her vision he had looked altogether somber, unlike his immediate smile upon meeting her.

Goose bumps peppered her body as she had another sudden vision of him. He stood beside her bed, in deep pain, and blood flowed down his face and over the left side of his body. She sat up quickly. "Whit?" she gasped. With a terrible moan, he said, "Dani!" It was a dream. He called her "Danielle." It was too soon for him to call her "Dani."

The vision was so *real,* her blood ran cold. Then it was gone. It had lasted longer than most of her infrequent visions. Should she call him? How could she *not* call him? She had been in her dorm room bed when her mother was killed. Mona had appeared in a vision her with terrified eyes and called her name. Just called her name and stood there looking down at her. Then Danielle had seen the blood on her mother's breasts and had screamed. Scrambling up, she had gone to the telephone and called home. "No," her father had said sleepily, "Mona said she'd be late." She was expecting to wrap up a case and told him not to wait up. He would call around and look for her. Hanging up, Danielle had gotten back into bed and lain there wide awake.

Later, she had gotten up again and paced the floor. The phone rang near midnight, two hours after she had called her father.

"You're going to need to sit down, baby," her father had said.

"What is it? Just tell me. Has one of you been hurt?" Her mind would not embrace anything more threatening.

"Your mother is dead," he had said slowly. "Hunters found her body a little while ago. I talked with Captain Ryson. Sweetheart, I'm sorry."

Sorry. Sorry. Sorry. The words rang through her head like shrill whistles from hell and she pressed her hands to her head to drive away the hounds of truth. How could Mona be dead? She had a future son-in-law to meet, future grandchildren to coddle and cuddle, and a daughter to be even more proud of. Now, she thought, *Oh, God, is it ever going to be over?*

Whit. She hardly knew him. Was something terrible going to befall him too? Was she a jinx on those who meant so much to her?

She called and he answered sleepily on the first ring.

"Whit?"

"Hello there." He seemed very pleased.

She hesitated a few moments. "Whit, I had a dream," she said, not telling him about the vision. "You were hurt. I don't want to frighten you, but please be careful. So many times things can be avoided if we're just careful."

He was silent a long moment. "Believe me, I'm a careful man, but I'll be even more careful. Thank you so much for telling me. I've been thinking about you. I'm really looking forward to seeing you tonight. Would you like to drive into D.C.?"

She drew a deep breath. "Sometime later, yes, but tonight I agreed to go to Annie's Place for a reason. There are a couple of hoodlums who hang out there that I'm keeping my eye on. . . ."

"You've got it. What's your favorite flower?"

"Roses. Gardenias. Peonies. Oh, Lord, I seem to like so many. You don't need to bring flowers."

He laughed a bit. "Sweets to the sweet. Flowers to the beautiful. Pick you up at seven o'clock. Get you back in time to get plenty of sleep. Have you gotten any sleep?"

"A little. I was thinking of . . . things." He didn't seem bothered. Maybe he didn't believe in omens and sightings. Visions.

"Whit, I . . . You *will* be careful?"

"You're thinking I'm not paying attention to your dream, but I am. I'm an artist, Danielle, and we believe in other way stations in this world as well as the more familiar ones. There's something markedly different about you and I like that, as I like you. I'll always listen to you."

She felt mollified then. She had once warned her father of a possible accident with his car and he had been more careful and had had a small accident instead of a major one. Ah, yes, she thought bitterly, her gift.

* * *

The large cabin cruiser rocked on the gentle waters of the Potomac River at the marina on D.C.'s southwest harbor. Upstream several yachts lorded over the smaller boats.

Whit had been sleeping fitfully. Now he threw back the covers and sat up. What exactly had Danielle seen in her dream? She hadn't said. Should he press her tonight? He could hardly believe his good fortune in meeting her. When she told him about sighting him on the shoulder of the road, he was moved.

He lay on his back, thinking. At thirty-eight years old, he was highly successful and growing more so. But his love life was in shambles. When Willo had walked out on him, he understood the urge to kill.

His heart was so shattered that his family and friends had been afraid for him. For the first time, death had seemed preferable to life. He had gotten up most nights and walked around town, sometimes to dangerous areas seeking to cool the heartache.

He found himself retreating into his music, and his audiences grew more enamored of him. With music, his family, and his friends he had found himself able to go on.

Now, Danielle was in his life and he wanted her, but he was terrified of the searing pain he had known such a short while ago.

Danielle.

She was a strange—he half closed his eyes—and absolutely beautiful woman.

Getting up, he made coffee, opened a package of frozen waffles, and laid thin slices of Canadian bacon on top of them in the waffle iron.

A barge's foghorn sounded. He stretched, did a couple of push-ups, and got on his treadmill.

Last night had been like a dream. His hands—in her hair, then lightly caressing her soft body—had seemed to have a life of their own. He had been very much in love with his ex-wife, Willo, but nothing he had known with Willo was like the brief time he had spent with Danielle.

Danielle Ritchey. He mouthed the words and his lips curled upward in a smile. This was like a wonderful madness taking over his being. He was completely enchanted by a woman he hardly knew. Yet he *did* know her. Did he believe in reincarnation? Had they been lovers in some past life? One thing was certain, something unusual, something out of the ordinary was going on.

Looking around, he thought about what she had said about her dream of him. Yeah, he had dreamed of her too, naked and pliant, and going wild beneath and above him. He grinned widely and felt sorry for people who didn't have extensive fantasy lives. Fantasies, he thought, could keep a person out of a lot of trouble. When there was no one left to truly cared about, he could always return to the person of a past time, or build a new dream. Now, he had Danielle and he hoped that they would last.

He would be careful. But he was always careful. It had been sweet of her to call. He would invite her over on the weekend. Would she come? He'd go easy if she came. No coming on to her like a caveman. She had been yielding in his arms, but he knew he'd have to take it slow out of respect for her feelings.

He thumped his chest like Tarzan and growled. Looking around he stared at the shelves of mystery novels. Walter Mosely. Agatha Christie. All the best mystery writers. He thought he'd have made a great cop up to and including a police commissioner. He bet Danielle was a damned good detective but, he shook his head, he still saw it as dangerous work.

On other shelves he had collections of gospel and classical music, rhythm and blues, rap and soft rock. CD's and tapes. He picked up a guitar and began strumming. He would sing later.

Whit had led a charmed life up to his breakup with his wife, Willo. Son of Frank and Caroline Steele of the Singing Steeles, he had a highly successful gospel singing sister, Ashley, and an adoptive sister, Annice, a psychologist who lived near Minden on Paradise Island. He had never known anything other than love, respect, and gentle discipline. And he was grateful because he needed every vestige of goodness he owned when the hellish throes of his breaking marriage were on him.

Laying down the guitar after a few minutes, he realized how hungry he was, got up and served himself, and poured his coffee, adding cream and sugar. He drank a couple of cups a day. He was careful about his health, but he left plenty of room for enjoyment. A sensual man, he loved the earth and was grateful to the God who had blessed him. Looking across the table, he could envision Danielle sitting across from him, and he smiled lazily. *The woman had mesmerizing eyes,* he thought. Hell, mesmerizing *eyes,* she was quintessentially *enchanting.* Merlin, the great magician, could create none better. She was a gift from God.

THREE

At the station house that morning, Danielle felt joy surge through her veins like liquid gold. She sat at a table in an interrogation room waiting for Jon Ryson and Ed Ware to come in. They were to talk with an Immigration and Naturalization agent about illegal aliens being smuggled into the country. Her cell phone rang. It was Whit.

"How're you feeling?" he asked. She blushed as heat flashed through her body.

"I . . . I'm fine," she heard herself stammering. "And you?"

"A whole lot better than usual. I feel great. Danielle," he paused a moment, "I was wondering—well, we agreed to slow our wagon down. How about inviting a couple of other people to go with us tonight?"

"Okay," she answered without hesitation, a little relieved. "Do you have anyone in mind?"

"Afraid not. I don't know anyone in Mindon except Jon Ryson and his family."

She searched her mind quickly and came up with two names. "I have a girlfriend I'd like you to meet, and I'd like you to meet my father. . . ." She frowned a bit. Was she rushing it?

"Super. I've got people I'd like you to meet, too. Just because I'm an emotional wreck doesn't mean I don't need friends."

"Right," she said lamely. "I'm sorry you were so hurt. I imagine betrayal is difficult to get over; it's a matter of trust."

He laughed harshly. "I wish I'd met you first."

"Well, we all need friends and I think you'll make a good one."

"The best. Just don't trust me in the romance department."

Her intake of breath was sharp and hard. She *wanted* friends; she had always *needed* romance. Now she said sadly, "Thanks for being so honest."

"I can do no less. See you at seven o'clock."

She rocked a bit in her swivel chair and put a hand flat on the table as Captain Jon Ryson came in. He grinned at her. "Hey there, you with the stars in your eyes," he said, laughing. "What's up, or should I say, what's going down?"

She shook her head, smiling. "I'm not sure. I met a friend of yours last night."

"Oh?"

She told him about the accident. "I took the car to the garage before I came in. There was no damage."

"Who's the friend whose name you're so reluctant to call?"

"Whit Steele."

He whistled. "Now why in the hell didn't I think to introduce you to him? I guess I've been too busy. You're his type, all right."

"He's got a type, meaning he's a player?"

Jon shook his head. "Nothing like that. He gets around and I guess he's wined and dined a few, but he's pretty levelheaded. Women sure cotton to him. I wouldn't call him a player."

She felt relieved then; she trusted Jon's judgment.

He sat smiling at her. "You look lit up and that's good. I don't mind telling you, Danielle, I've worried about you since Scott died. You've had too many losses to be so young."

She shrugged. "It's the breaks. Sometimes they go that way."

She looked at this rugged, brown, powerful man and was glad he was her friend.

Sergeant Ed Ware came through the door, giving them his usually grumpy good morning. He stopped midway between the door and the table and looked keenly at Danielle, but said nothing else.

Instead, he ran his hands over his close-cut medium brown hair and yawned. His hair and his skin were nearly the same hue and his dour expression said he trusted the world only as far as he could throw it. Forty-five years old, he had worked with Danielle since she came on the force, and he never showed the least bit of envy when she was promoted to detective lieutenant and he remained a sergeant. He thought of her as being *his* protégée as much as she was Captain Ryson's.

A young cop knocked, came in, and introduced a young, casually dressed man with him—Immigration and Naturalization Service Agent Colin Matthews. The man displayed his badge, and Jon rose and introduced them all to the agent, who accepted Jon's offer of coffee and chose a coconut doughnut. He seemed cheerful, competent, and got right down to business.

"I'm glad you could see me on such short notice," he said. "We think we're on the tail of an illegal alien smuggling ring somewhere in this area and we can't seem to get to the bottom of it. We'd appreciate all the help we can get. We've always gotten good cooperation from you here in Minden."

"We'll do what we can," Jon Ryson said. "No leads?"

"None. We've got suspicions, but they don't go anywhere. Now, where the smuggling *begins* is another story. We're getting professionals desperate to get away from war-torn African countries and they've got the money to pay someone big time to smuggle them out. Sometimes they pay in diamonds and tanzanite. So far, we've been losing them in New York, which is easy to do. We've traced a few to D.C. I don't have to tell you it's often difficult to set up as a professional when you've been smuggled in. A couple of times their fake I.D.'s and papers have been easy to spot and we've nabbed them. So far, no one's told us the whole story."

Jon nodded. "How can we help?"

The agent drew a deep breath. Keep your eyes open for *anything* that might be out of the ordinary. We don't know if they come in small or large bunches, or how they fan out. We suspect twenty to thirty people in each group. We're talking about ten to twenty thousand dollars a head here. Add it up and it could bring out the greed in a lot of people, if you do it often enough."

"Good old Dr. Greed," Jon said, "always on the job."

The agent nodded and smiled. They talked about protocol and Jon buzzed for an officer to take the agent's number. The agent then took the telephone numbers of the team members. They sat around then, chewing the fat about various INS policies.

"We're waterlogged with people," the agent said. "For a long time we've been a country that included more than excluded. Now we're paying a price. This is a top-drawer outfit we're coming onto. They've got worldwide Mafia connections. I don't have to tell you we've got our hands full. You're police people and you're interfering with their lifestyles. They're dangerous, so for God's sake, be really careful."

Danielle sat up straight. The vision this morning had warned her that Whit needed to be careful and she had duly warned him. Would he listen? He had said he would.

As soon as the meeting broke up, Danielle got on the phone with her best friend, Daphne Taylor, a high school nurse.

"Well, girlfriend, you sound like the cat that swallowed the canary. What's up?"

"Would you be interested in dinner tonight on short notice?"

"If you'll tell me why you're so happy. I'm always interested in dinner when I don't have to buy it. But first, I insist on knowing why you sound so happy."

Danielle grinned. "I don't call you Daffy for nothing. I've met a guy. We've promised to go slow. . . ."

"Whoa! *When* did you meet this dude?"

"Last night. I literally bumped into him. . . ." She licked her suddenly dry lips and felt anxious. "And, Daphne, I had a vision of him just before I rammed his bumper when a deer crossed in front of him."

"Name? Station? Maybe the vision is a good omen."

Daphne believed in her visions, listened to her.

"Name," Danielle repeated after Daphne and drew a deep breath. "Whit Steele."

"Now why does that ring a—hey, wait, not the gospel singer you nearly creamed over when we went to his concert?"

"One and the same, I'm afraid."

"Well, holy moley. You have grabbed ahold of a hunk."

"Well, I don't intend to be a fool over him. The man's got a world of women at his feet. . . ."

"Think he's a player?"

"Jon knows him and thinks he isn't."

Daphne tut-tutted. "Men always stick together. Their self-esteem is higher than ours."

"Well, if I find he is, he'll be playing on someone else's field. He's really nice, but he's got fallout from a failed marriage. He didn't say much about it, but his face looked devastated when he talked a little about it."

"You trust him already?"

"I do. He just seems on the level. After all, I want you to meet him, don't I? And I'm inviting my dad."

"Oh, well now." Daphne's voice went deep and sexy. "Anywhere Julian goes, I'm willing. You've got an ace of a dad, Danielle."

"He likes you too. A lot."

Daphne was thirty-nine to Danielle's thirty-five, but Daphne was younger than her age, and Danielle was far older. Now Daphne laughed. "You think he does?"

"I know he does, but he's hurting, too. All this time since Mom died and he's still aching. They had it all, Daffy."

"I know," Daphne breathed, thinking she would like to have it all with Julian.

"Well," Daphne added, "I was going to throw on something simple and comfortable, but now that I know your handsome dad *and* Mr. Hunk himself will be there, maybe I'll stop and do some shopping. I haven't bought anything new in a long time."

"I'm glad you're interested."

"Interested? Honey child, I'm enthralled."

Julian Welles picked up on the first ring of his phone.

"Dad?"

"My darling daughter."

"Could you have dinner tonight around seven-thirty with a man I just met, Daphne, and me?"

"Well, I'm not doing anything else and I'm always happy to see Daphne. Who is this *friend?*"

Danielle hesitated. "I just met him when my car bumped into his. . . ."

"I see." He sounded grave. "I was coming home from a poker game with my guys and I saw a new fancy car parked in the driveway behind your car. I couldn't help wondering who it belonged to."

"Dad, he's Whit Steele, the gospel singer."

"Well now, it was pretty late and we're a gossipy little burg. Listen, baby, I've never wanted anything but the best for you."

After a moment, she told him, "We stayed up until sunrise—talking." She wanted him to know what was in her heart. "We kissed—just once. Dad, the earth really does move when some people kiss you. . . ."

He laughed a little. "You don't have to tell me that, Dani. Your mother and I had that. I don't think you and Scott did, but it's always what I've wanted for you. But don't move too fast. It's usually not wise. Give it time. He leads a life so different from yours. *Ordinary* men can make the earth spin, too, when they kiss you."

"I'm on your line. What Scott and I had was good. Whit and I talked last night about taking it slow. That's why I'm inviting you and Daffy to go with us. You and Mona taught me well. I know how to take care of myself."

He was silent a moment before he said, "I know you do. I trust your judgment, honey, all the way."

She still sat at the table lost in thought when Ed Ware stuck his head in the door and asked, "You busy?"

She looked up, smiling. "Not really. What's on your mind?"

"I wondered if you'd like to ride shotgun with me. I'm feeling my age and am lonely today." Ed had a sometime girlfriend, Shelley.

"So early?"

"Don't rub it in. I was thirty-five once, a hundred years ago."

"Ed, you're forty-five. That isn't old."

"I could kiss you for that. How come you're lit up like a sky full of stars?"

"Everyone gets happy sometime."

"What's happening, baby?" He drew out the syllables of the last word.

"I wish I knew."

He cocked his head to one side. "We work together and God knows I feel like I'm the best friend you could have. What's up?" His eyes nearly closed.

Danielle was a little irritated. "What's with you today? Are you one of the high priests of the Inquisition? So I'm happy. Don't I have a right to be happy?" On the last sentence, her voice got gentle, wistful.

He rubbed his hand over his brown, stubby, coarse hair. "Well, I wasn't going to mention it, but maybe I should. I was out late, the way I often am when I can't sleep. I passed your house at three in the morning. The lights were on, and there was an extra car parked in your driveway. It wasn't Daphne's and it wasn't your dad's."

"They're not the only people I know," she said a little sharply.

"Dani, you're well thought of. Don't pick up with some

crazy clown and ruin it. Your lights were on all night. I came back by around four this morning."

Thoroughly annoyed now, she asked him, "Did you go on home then, get some sleep? Lord knows, you look beat enough now."

He looked at her thoughtfully. "Yeah, I went on home then, snatched a few hours. Don't be mad at me. I've always looked after you the way I looked after Mona, although she was a few years older than me. She was special to me, as you're special."

"I'm sorry, Ed. I didn't mean to bark at you. I'm ready to go if you are."

He grinned then. "Let's ride out Cal Catlett's way. I'm going to be in the market for a new mattress. Might as well give the hometown boy my business."

"My car won't be ready until this afternoon," she said.

"We'll take mine. I'll drive. God, it's slow around here. Come on, you hellers! Act up for Daddy; he doesn't trust it when it gets too quiet."

"Don't do it," she said, shuddering. "Mabel Land was slaughtered five months ago by her no-good husband. That's enough to last me for years. I checked. Her kid is with her sister here in Minden."

"Yeah. Dani, you keep up with things."

She nodded. "I wanted to adopt May, but her aunt wants to keep her."

They were out on the highway then, going away from Minden toward D.C. The April air was fresh, misty. "You know," she said, "it was like this the day he killed her. Came home drunk from another woman's house and she laced into him, told him she was leaving, that she was sick of him and his women."

"And the son of a bitch told the dispatcher that he was going to kill her, that she wasn't going anywhere." Ed's voice was hard with judgment.

"By the time we got there, he had done what he threatened," she said, "and turned the gun on himself." Her voice was raw with emotion.

"It's times like that when I wonder about being a detective." He slowed and turned off onto a side road. A battered old Chevy pulled out of the driveway they were headed toward and raced on, hellbent for leather. They stopped at the gate to be checked by a security guard. Ed drove a short way down to the spacious complex that held Calvin Catlett's big stone mansion and, a short distance away, his mattress factory, Southern Comfort. A rangy, reddish brown man with dark red, gray-flecked hair came swiftly to their car, crossing his extensive, well-kept grounds. Two security guards patrolled. Only one of his five tractor trailers sat on the parking lot.

"You're not coming about the trouble with Janey?" Calvin Catlett asked.

"What trouble? We just drove by on a friendly whim," Ed told him.

"It's Keith Janey. He threatened to kill me when I fired him. I just placed the call. Well, they'll be on. You guys are prompt," Calvin Catlett said jovially, his deep-set eyes squinting. "Get out, stretch. Come in and have a drink."

The two got out of the car. "Now, you know we can't drink on the job," Ed said. "I'd like to haul you in for tempting us." The men laughed heartily and gave each other the high five.

The man everybody called Cal bowed to Danielle. "You're still beautiful, Lieutenant Ritchey. Looks like something's agreeing with you. Ed here treating you right?"

"He's a nice man," she said noncommittally. She never felt quite comfortable with Cal Catlett. His gaze roamed her body as if they were lovers. The world and its women were his harem.

"If he gets out of line, you come to old Cal. I know how to set him right."

"I can handle him," she said.

Cal put his fists together, cracked his knuckles. "I'll just bet there ain't much you can't handle, missy." He cackled at his remark. "Come in and look me over. I've got some new machines in."

He didn't seem a bit bothered by Keith Janey's threats.

Danielle and Ed looked at each other and decided to go into the mattress factory. Inside, business bustled. The steel machines hummed, padded, and stitched. Cal pointed out the new stitchers. Different qualities of mattresses slid off the assembly line for final inspection, and were boxed for shipping. The place was spotless. Cal employed about fifty people.

"Course you two been here before. Every day it seems like I get more and more in love with my factory. This could be my wife if I didn't have one."

"It's something to be proud of," Danielle told him. She liked his wife, Irene, and couldn't stop thinking of his girlfriend, Annie Lusk, who owned Annie's Place. A man like Cal felt he deserved however many women he wanted.

"Thank you, ma'am. You two make a good team; you might think about getting together sometime."

Ed laughed shortly. "You mean really together?" When Cal nodded, Ed said, "She thinks I'm too old for her."

Cal looked at her. "That right?"

Danielle pursed her lips. "Let's change the subject, okay?"

Ed's laughter was tight, and she smiled at him. He meant well. There wasn't much he wouldn't do for her.

Police sirens sounded outside and Cal got up. "I didn't think you two detectives were responding to my call."

"What's the story on Janey?" Danielle asked.

"Janey's pissed because I had to fire him for drinking on the job and missing time, coming in late, that kind of thing. He pulled a gun. I faced him down and called police on my cell phone. He left."

Ed whistled. "He's a mean one. Watch your back."

"Hell, I'll have twenty-four-hour security if I have to, but I ain't scared of nobody."

Two policemen were in by then. A gruff, red-faced sergeant questioned Cal, who told him what had happened.

"He threaten you?" the sergeant asked.

"Hell, yes. Said he was going to blow my brains out, scatter them to the winds. I don't fire lightly. My people like me and I like them."

He led them all to his big office where a friendly blonde held sway as secretary and receptionist. He introduced them. The young woman, Millie, came to attention. "Could I get anyone coffee, wine, anything? I've got some great lemonade in the fridge."

"We've got to locate Janey," the sergeant said. "He's a real nut. You know we can't drink anything. Give us a description of his car."

Cal gave them a description of Janey's car and the two cops left, telling him to be careful. Cal rubbed his hands together as Millie offered them refreshments again. Danielle accepted lemonade and Ed hot, black coffee.

Finally, Danielle said, "You don't seem to be afraid. I hear Janey's bad news. He's beaten a couple of men very badly. You should watch out for him."

"He's a no-good bastard. Before I'd run scared from the likes of him, I'd scatter my own brains."

"Still," Danielle insisted, "it's wise to look out for him."

Cal laughed shortly. "I've got a gun factory at home. All legal. I'm a crack shot. He's not coming at a helpless simple-minded fool."

"Just don't get overconfident," Danielle said quietly.

Cal laughed. "Don't you worry, pretty lady," he said. "Old Cal didn't live to be nearly sixty and get himself a business like this by not knowing what he was doing."

Back in the squad car, the detectives sat for a while, discussing the threat to Cal Catlett.

"Janey's mean, with a capital M," Danielle said. "He's not too bad when he's not drinking, but when he is, he gets out of control. You remember, the last man he beat up was a friend who wouldn't press charges against him. Otherwise, he'd be in the clinker. People who are fired kill more than any other group of people."

She watched as Ed slouched back in the driver's seat and drew a small gold object from his shirt pocket. It was shaped like a cross with numerous strands of tiny gold beads strung across about two and a half inches wide making a bar.

"How pretty," Danielle said. "Are you Catholic?"

"You've known me forever. I'm not."

"You could have joined lately."

"It's an Egyptian ankh—a symbol of life."

"It's beautiful. Where did you get it?"

"New York. An Egyptian guy I know there makes them. If you really like it, I'll get you one."

"I've got so much jewelry. I'll think about it. A symbol of life," she mused.

"Dani" he said suddenly, "who is this guy you saw last night?"

"You don't know that it is a guy unless you skulked outside and waited for the person to leave."

He coughed. "I wouldn't do that but, hell, I sure wanted to. I've always looked out for you. I can't stop now."

"We'd better get back," she said slowly. "I've got a lot of paperwork to catch up on. We're in a lull and I'm glad about that, but you never can tell when things will heat up."

He nodded and turned on the ignition. The Ford Crown Victoria so favored by police departments purred to a smooth start and they pulled across the yard of Southern Comfort and out onto the side road that led to the highway.

FOUR

At home that night, Danielle soaked in warm water sprinkled with French lavender bath gel that gave lots of relaxing suds. She rubbed her flesh voluptuously with a long-handled loofah sponge and gloried in the tingling of her skin. Her exhilaration had lasted all day, but she grimaced now. It would be her luck to get ahold of a man torn up by someone else. She longed to comfort him. *Now, you listen to me,* she said to herself sternly. *You're lucky he's honest and above-board. You can see the pain on his face when he talks about his breakup. He will be a long time getting over her.*

She felt a bit crestfallen with those words, but she soon rallied and her heart danced again. Getting out of the tub after lazing fifteen minutes or so, she dried herself and looked into her bathroom's full-length mirror. *Not bad,* she thought dreamily. Far from perfect, but not bad at all. Her nipples tautened and pebbled.

She dressed carefully in a dark rose, silk-crepe dress with a color-matched sheer jacket. She took a long time selecting her best wide gold hoop earrings, and no other jewelry. She looked good; she didn't have to be vain to know that. She got her fairly large natural tan leather shoulder bag, which was specially fitted to hold a smaller gun than she usually carried. The gun could be reached without opening her bag. The bag also contained slender, strong handcuffs and some evidence bags. You just never knew. She sat down with an *Ebony* magazine to leaf through. Then she got restless and picked up a

Heart and Soul magazine. Looking at her Movado watch, her only luxury, she saw it was only a little before seven o'clock.

When her door chimes sounded, she had to restrain herself from racing to the door. Opening it, she found a grinning Whit with an armful of flowers and a box of gold foil-wrapped Godiva chocolates. Before he handed the bouquets and the chocolate to her, he hummed, "What a difference a day makes."

"How beautiful," she said, taking the flowers and putting them on the table. She held up the candy. "My favorite. You didn't have to."

"I wanted to bring more. You said these flowers were your favorites. They didn't have peonies. I'll get you some later. I just guessed you'd like the chocolates." So, she thought happily, there *was* to be a later.

"Thank you so much." There was a dozen truly gorgeous bloodred roses and a dozen exquisite gardenias. Bidding him to have a seat, she went to her kitchen and got two very large crystal vases from the cupboard. She filled them with water and quickly arranged the blossoms. Whit came into the kitchen.

"I wondered if you need help bringing the vases back into the living room."

"You're thoughtful."

"Sometimes I forget to be."

"I'll open the candy if you'd like some."

He shook his head. "I don't want to spoil my appetite."

"Then I'll wait."

Once the flowers were on the long table behind the couch and the candy between the vases, she stood in front of him as he sat on the couch. His gaze devoured her. She wasn't uncomfortable in the least; his eyes were warm, compelling.

Only then did he whistle, long and low. "I thought last night that you had mesmerizing eyes. Now that I'm leveling out a bit, I see you're altogether magic."

She laughed. "You talk a great streak. It's a good thing my head doesn't turn easily."

For a moment, he was having trouble getting his breath. Those were fabulous long legs, but they were only a part of her. He glanced at her heart-shaped face under that thick, curly-kinky, earth-brown hair, long, swanlike neck. And the *body*, oh, Lord, the body. He half closed his eyes and laughed to himself as he thought of Little Red Riding Hood and the Big Bad Wolf who had said, "The better to *see* you, my dear." He was far from a wolf, but he wanted this woman with a passion that unsettled him. Where were they headed?

He ran his tongue over dry lips as his glance caressed her narrow top, waist, wide hips, and rounded bottom. Lord, help him. She was five feet seven and a half and she had it all going on.

"You're staring at me," she teased.

"Yeah, I imagine people stare at the Taj Mahal."

"Flatterer."

Her eyes went over him casually, taking in his navy blazer, cream flannel trousers, and cream gabardine shirt. She had never dated a truly handsome man before; she thought them too spoiled, but he didn't seem to be.

He cleared his throat. "I want to tell you something." She sat on the sofa a little distance from him. "It's plain I may make a fool of myself over you, but I want to make something clear. I'm not just out to put my moves on you. Something happened when we met. You felt it."

He hesitated and she nodded. He looked a bit miserable then. "I won't lie. I feel like running. This is scaring the hell out of me. Both your husband's and your mother's deaths hurt you, but that was clean hurt. You will recover in time. Betrayal is a *dirty* hurt. It puts a knife in your gut and twists it. Can you understand that?"

"I think I can. I'll at least try. Whit?"

"Yes."

"Why don't we back away for the time being, let you get over some more of your pain? Then we can see if we want to see each other again."

"Are you a little afraid of what's happening?"

She answered immediately. "Yes, I am. I've never known anything like this before."

"I don't think waiting is an option. So quickly you go so deep with me. You're kind and you're knowing about the world. I just sense that in you. You're tender and you're warm, really warm from some deep wellspring. I want to take you in my arms and run *with* you, too, as well as run *away.* Forgive me for being so damned mixed up."

Danielle smiled. "You're forgiven. I'm pretty shaky, as I said. How long have you been all broken up?"

"Fourteen months. Think that's long enough to heal?"

She shook her head. "I'd never sit in judgment on that. Some pain takes a very long time. Like my mother. . ."

"You do understand and I thank you." He moved a bit closer and took her right hand, lifted it to his lips and lightly kissed it. Her heart lurched at the electricity between them. A trail of fire began in her heart and blazed downward. They had to stop. Yet, how *could* they stop?

"After tonight," she said slowly, gently, "perhaps we should just take a breather for a couple of months."

"Not an option," he declared adamantly. "I've got to see you. I won't touch you. You deserve the deepest kind of commitment and if I can't give it, I'll let you go. But see me, talk with me, let me at least give you small gifts. I'm drowning in my own sadness, Danielle, and you pull me out of it. I've been happy since last night. . . ."

"Are you maybe on the rebound?"

He thought a long moment. "Maybe, but somehow I don't think so."

"Yet, you're scared. I'm scared."

"Yes. You know there's a very old Austrian saying, 'Before you was coming, I was I.' Do you understand?"

"I think so. Meaning, alone, I felt like and was myself. With another, I'm not sure what or who I am."

"It comes from a psychiatrist writing about love—and lust.

Believe me, no matter how much lust I feel for you, what I'm feeling is also love."

She didn't say it then because it hurt, but Mona had spoken of that Austrian quote, had liked it. Laughing, Danielle threw back her head and he watched the lovely line of her slender brown throat. "Why are you laughing?"

"Because you make me happy too, and so I laugh because you please me. I don't think you know your own mind, but I like the thought of you loving me. Know something, Whit? I *want* to go on seeing you. I've got a light heart. I haven't had that in ages. We won't touch in a romantic way again soon, but we'll talk, meet each other's friends and have fun together. . . ." He looked at her closely then. "It's got to work because I need you and maybe you need me. God help us both!"

Out on the highway, headed toward Minden, Whit drove and they were mostly silent. He looked at the wedding ring on her left hand. It bothered him, but he sure as hell had no right to ask her to take it off. Its presence let him know she intended to hold him at bay.

They passed a wooded section of the road with a small partial clearing and in the middle sat a huge oak tree. "One hundred fifty years old," Danielle explained, "but it's said to be dying."

Daylight saving time had begun and it was nearing twilight. A man dressed in black sat propped against the tree; they could see part of him in profile.

"Someone's getting a taste of the fresh April air," Danielle said. "Let's visit the tree one day. Are you a nature lover?"

"In spades. I want to help you with your yard."

"I'll take you up on that. Whit, when you're off on hiatus from concerts what do you do?"

"Well, I keep my daily practice up. Work out with my group from time to time. I study the music I sing and it goes deeper into my soul all the time. I'll sing for you, if you'd like me to."

"You know I would."

When Danielle and Whit reached Annie's Place, her father, Julian, and her best friend, Daphne, were already seated. Julian stood up as Annie brought them to the table, telling them, "We have fabulous stuffed pork chops tonight and the best desserts we've turned out in a month of Sundays."

Danielle smiled at the heavyset, attractive, florid-skinned woman, Annie Lusk. Danielle ate there from time to time and liked the food and Annie.

Annie grinned as she looked at Whit. "I hope you don't mind my saying so if you aren't, but you look a lot like that gospel singer."

Danielle laughed. "Annie, meet Whit Steele, the gospel singer."

Annie laughed explosively and extended her hand. "Your CD's and tapes light up my house and my life. Congratulations on the last CD. It gives me a whole lot of pleasure."

"Thank you," Whit said, smiling. "I'm glad to know you like my music."

"Like isn't the word. *Love* best describes it. Welcome to my humble little place."

"It doesn't seem so humble to me. You've got a nice place here."

Annie flushed. "I hope you'll come often and I'll get you a waiter immediately."

Julian had watched the proceedings with a smile. Danielle introduced them to Whit. Julian was cordial, warm, and Daphne grinned from ear to ear. She had never met a celebrity she didn't like. Whit greeted them as if they were already friends.

True to Annie's word, the waiter came with menus and stood for their orders. After looking over the menu carefully, they all chose the stuffed pork chops, candied sweet potatoes, brown rice, spinach soufflé, and strawberry cheesecake. The waiter left and in a few minutes returned with a humongous green salad. This time each person chose a different dressing.

"No need to be sheep all the way," Daphne twitted. "I'll bet these chops are to die for."

They served themselves heavily with the delicious salad and the dressing. The waiter came and bowed. "Our main course will be a little late. Miss Annie has ordered special touches. It will be worth the wait."

"Which gives me a moment for the powder room," Danielle said. Whit got up to assist her. Julian stood as Daphne got up, saying, "I'll go with you."

As the two women crossed the floor, Julian watched the way Whit's eyes followed his daughter. The younger man's eyes were warm and a smile hovered about his mouth. The older man and his wife had had an easy time raising Danielle. In spite of being beautiful, she was levelheaded, and never gave them any trouble. Boys liked her and she liked them, but she never got out of line. Who was this gospel singer, this celebrity who seemed so smitten with Julian's daughter? What did he stand for?

For a few minutes they were silent and Julian reflected on the way the world had changed since his youth. Men bragged about being *players* now, seemed proud of the many, many women they were intimate with. *No*, he thought, *intimate wasn't the right word*. They *played* over women and left them hardened or heartbroken—or both.

Julian cleared his throat. "I understand you and Dani just met last night."

"Yes," Whit said ruefully. "You could say we ran into each other. A deer ran in front of my car and she ploughed into my bumper. Fortunately, we were both just starting up at the green light. . . ."

"I see."

Dani was thirty-five, Julian thought, and he couldn't be her keeper. She wouldn't allow it, but he took the bull by the horns. "We're a relatively small community, Mr. Steele. . . ."

"Whit, please."

"All right, Whit. We're a relatively small community." A frog was coming into his throat. "I passed along at two something this morning and a second car was in my daughter's driveway. If it was you, I hope you don't damage her reputation. She's my daughter and I want the best for her. . . ."

Whit looked at Julian steadily and felt very comfortable with him. He lifted his water glass, then set it down. "Mr. Welles, I want you to know that something is happening between Danielle and me. The kind of passion you sometimes read about." He didn't want to sound like a jerk. He told Julian about his family, his broken marriage and his heartbreak, and the older man was sympathetic. When Whit had finished, Julian was silent for a long time.

"I'm sorry, but it's all the more reason my advice for you two is to go very slow."

"Which is what we've decided to do, which is why we're here with you and Daphne instead of being alone."

"Smart move. You two seem very attracted to each other. I can only hope you'll manage to keep things in check." Julian wasn't quite of the old school, but he believed in making a man bide his time and he had taught this to Danielle.

Whit sought to reassure him. "I'll never hurt her. I'm the walking wounded and she deserves the best."

Julian asked him how long it had been since his divorce and Whit told him. Julian bit his bottom lip. "You've got plenty of time to heal. Meantime, if you two go full speed ahead and you hurt her, you'll lose something precious."

Whit looked grave. "We're not going full speed ahead. I'd die before I'd hurt her, sir."

"Be certain about it." And he wondered who had hurt whom in Whit's marriage. Whit seemed to be the salt of the earth, but the man was a gospel singer. He made his living impressing people. And he thought angrily, *I'll kill him if he hurts her.*

* * *

In the blue-, white-, and gold-colored powder room, Danielle and Daphne gave each other the high five.

"How do you like my shoes?" Danielle stuck out one foot toward Daphne to show off her tan kid-leather ankle-strap sandals.

"Oh, they're great and you look great, but . . ."

"So do you. I've always loved you in pale green. Is it new?"

Daphne groaned. "Listen, girlfriend. Clothes and everything else take a backseat to Mr. Wonderful. That man is the *finest*. A hunk made in heaven. Oo-o-o. Congratulations on landing the biggest of the big fish."

Danielle grinned. "Then I take it you like him."

"I love, love, love everything about him. He looks at you like you're the Queen of Sheba."

"Really?"

"You were with him all night long, huh? And a passionate kiss at sunrise. I predict you two are not going to be able to keep this wagon from plummeting down the mountainside."

Danielle felt sober then. "We're going to take it slow. We know we're coming on too strong. Daffy, I'm praying things work out with us. I know how crazy it is, this sudden meeting, my envisioning him."

Daphne sighed. "I never doubt your visions, but you've seen him onstage. Could you have had an idea who he was before you actually met him?"

Danielle shook her head. "There was stuff piled up in his back windows. When I pulled up behind him, I thought about stopping and telling him what I saw."

"Instead fate did it for you. Oh, you *go*, girl! You *go!*" Then she got serious. "But on the other hand, don't go too far too fast."

"Believe me, I won't. He's an honest man and he's shy of commitment. He said so in a very short while. If it doesn't work, I've loved every minute we've had. You should see the flowers and the Godiva chocolate he brought me."

"Flowers *and* candy. Oh, my!"

"Roses and gardenias. I'd like to share the candy with you."

"I'd rather have a piece of the man." Daphne laughed heartily at her joke.

"I'll just bet you would. Daffy, you like my dad a lot, don't you?"

Serious now, Daphne said, "I sure do."

"Think he's too old for you?"

"I'm thirty-nine. He's fifty-five. I don't believe in age discrimination, love. Julian is quite a guy." Her voice was low, throaty.

"You might ease into a relationship. Ask him out; don't wait for him to ask you. You're much younger, but you remind me of my mother, and those two worshipped each other. Take a chance."

Daphne sighed. "What have I got to lose?"

When the two women returned to the table, they found the men deep in conversation about gospel singing. Danielle looked from her father to Whit. What else had they talked about?

In a few minutes, the beautifully prepared and served food lined the table. Delicious odors filled the air as the waiter poured the wine. Annie had remembered that Danielle liked *warm* red wine.

At a nearby table, a middle-aged man with rough snow-white hair sat with a big plate of spaghetti—Manny Luxor. Across from him sat a tall, wiry young man. Swarthy and black-haired, he was Buck Lansing. Danielle flexed her shoulders a bit. They were Mafia hoods from New York. Only Manny was a mob *boss*. They had been around for many years, owned a big home and kept to themselves. Manny owned a car repair shop. Manny talked of opening a night-club, but never did. Manny only came down from New York from time to time. It made Danielle's head hurt just to think about them.

Annie's piped music played Luther Vandross, a serenade to lovers everywhere. Danielle looked up to find Whit's gaze on her for a deep moment, before he looked away. Daphne looked amused, happy, and Julian looked at both women. When the waiter poured fresh wine, Whit proposed a toast and they raised their glasses.

"To love, wealth, health and happiness, and time to enjoy them all!" he said.

Julian raised his eyebrows. "I like that."

"I'm paraphrasing an old Spanish proverb. We'd have all of the riches in the most perfect of all worlds." He looked a bit sad then and Danielle's heart went out to him.

They all had found their meal scrumptious. Annie had made the strawberry cheesecake and it was outstanding. Danielle chewed with small bites, the better to savor it.

They ate in silence as Manny Luxor and Buck Lansing finished their meal, paid their check, and got up. Danielle thought they slowed as they neared her table, then thought she might be mistaken. But no . . .

Three feet or oo from her, the barrel-chested Manny bowed and said, "Detective Ritchey, it's always good to see you."

What was his point? Danielle wondered. What did he want from her? But he passed on as Whit and her father studied her

"Now, I wonder what's he up to?" her father asked. "Manny Luxor is never good news."

Danielle shrugged. "Actually, it's Buck Lansing who makes my skin crawl more. I wish they'd both just get out of town and stay out."

FIVE

"It's been exactly twenty-four hours since we met," Whit mused as he drove from Annie's toward Danielle's house.

"You're a romantic," she told him.

"More now than usual. I like your dad and your friend."

"I like them, too."

"I've got people I want you to meet."

"Okay."

"You'll like my family."

"You're speeding emotionally. I may be a witch and not show it."

"And you may also be a sweetheart. I think I'm a great judge of character."

It was a clear night with great clusters of stars hanging in the sky. The moon was half full. Whit drove at moderate speed; he wasn't anxious to get Danielle home.

Suddenly, he said, "I've got a concert coming up in D.C. July eighteenth. I'm inviting you as my guest. Will you come?"

Danielle's heart skipped a beat. "I'd love to, but how can you plan so far ahead?"

"Trust me. Trust yourself. We'll do ourselves proud."

"Whit! Slow down!"

"What is it?"

"Can you turn around at that next opening? I want to check out something under that big oak tree."

Whit did as she asked and in a few minutes they had

parked and walked over to the huge tree where a man sat sprawled.

"Think he might be drunk?" Whit asked.

Moonlight lit them well enough, but Danielle took a flashlight out of her tote bag, then gave the flashlight to Whit to hold as she set her tote and purse down.

Kneeling, she felt for a pulse and found none. She felt no heartbeat. Blood ran down the man's chest. Had he been beaten? Stabbed? Shot? His face bore a tormented expression. He was very dark brown, short, with chiseled features. "I think he's dead," she said.

The old sense of dread flooded her when she was faced with a murdered body, then her detective expertise slowly came into play. Reaching into her tote, she quickly found her cell phone and called the medical examiner's office, the police department, and Adrienne, a member of her team who would call the other two team members. Then she stood up.

"My God," Whit said, "he was dead the whole time."

Danielle shook her head. "Maybe not. Maybe he was dying when we passed by earlier. I hope we couldn't have saved him."

"Don't blame yourself. We couldn't know."

Danielle sighed. "You don't want to meddle in people's lives. A lot of folks sleep under this tree. Anyway, the medical examiner will know when he died. Maybe there was nothing we could have done to help him."

Whit cupped a hand around her shoulder. "For a city this size, we don't have many murders," she said. "Ten last year. Ten too many. We have a good youth program and our kids aren't dying. I do my part in that. Six of the murders were domestic. I don't recognize this man. . . ."

In a very short while, they heard sirens. A police crime van and a police car drove over to the tree and a policeman got out. A second police vehicle stopped and two more officers got out and came over; one went to direct traffic.

"What have we got here?" one of the policemen asked.

"Afraid it's a body," Danielle answered.

A little later there were more sirens and two men from the M.E.'s office squatted beside the body, examined it. "If my experience means anything, he's kicked this world aside."

It never stopped, Danielle thought. With every body came the question: Why?

A hoot owl sounded on a sudden breeze and a lone night bird sang its mournful song.

"Any idea how long he's been dead?" Danielle asked.

The man from the M.E.'s office put a finger to his face and sighed. "I'd guess only a few hours or so. We'll have to run a liver temp study to prove exact time. The body wagon'll be along any minute now."

More sirens were in the air by the time he spoke and two more men got out of the body wagon and came over with a stretcher. The police department used a specially equipped hearse from a Minden funeral home to pick up corpses and handled them with special care to preserve evidence.

"Got us some business, Lieutenant?" one of the men asked.

"Looks like it," Danielle replied.

"Poor guy. No gun around saying he might have bumped himself off?" one of the men asked.

"No weapon found," Danielle said. She steadied her breath.

Whit looked at her and mused. She was a different woman out here. Poised. In control. He'd bet she was one of the best.

Under Danielle's supervision, fingerprints were taken from the corpse. A massive ring was removed from his finger and placed in an evidence bag. Men fanned out, searching for evidence for a short distance. Wink, the photographer, took photographs nonstop.

One of the men got wooden stakes from the squad car, drove them into the ground, and stretched the yellow crime tape. They had brought battery-operated lights.

Adrienne, a crime analyst, took even more photographs

and Matt, a fingerprint technician, opened his kit and took fingerprints.

Then the men from the funeral home hoisted the body onto the stretcher and left. "I'll check with your office early in the morning," Danielle said.

The men left, with the two policemen staying. As the siren ran a lower, more even cry, they sped away. Danielle talked with her fellow officers.

"Did either of you recognize him?" she asked.

"No," they both said.

One man shrugged. "We've got Manny Luxor running around town. Could be one of his."

Danielle shook her head. The dead man, his features frozen in death, had looked cultured, sophisticated. His clothes were expensive. He was no ordinary hood. People were killed in one town and carried to another to slow solution of the crime. By the time police knew who had been killed, the killer had had time to blend into the woodwork.

A policeman directed traffic, but a few people had already stopped on the road shoulders and walked over.

"What's going on, Officer?" an older woman asked, addressing a policeman.

"We seem to have found a man's body." The policeman was all business as he checked each person, got names, addresses.

"Someone from Minden?"

"If he is, I don't know him and none of us do."

"Where is the body?" the woman asked.

"Gone to the morgue."

Surprisingly, the woman giggled. "It could be my husband."

One of the men shushed her and they all walked away.

Danielle stood, committing the corpse's image to memory. A light fog surrounded her as she stood transfixed. She heard drums—massive rolling drums—for a few minutes. Her flesh cooled and a tremor ran the length of her body. She turned to the policemen and to Whit. The drums stopped. Coming to herself, she asked them, "Did any of you hear anything?"

She knew what their answer would be.

"No," Whit answered, staring at her strangely. "What did you hear?"

She didn't answer. The other cops said they had heard nothing. She had heard a terrible rumbling of drums, the way she had read that drums rolled in certain parts of Africa when people died. Who was this corpse? Who had he been?

"Well," one of the officers finally said, "it's been a few months. Peace can't last forever. We wouldn't have a job if it did." He laughed at his own joke.

Whit stood thinking they were all so lighthearted, as if it didn't matter much. As if dead, no one was very important anymore.

Danielle spoke to her team. "Let me have those prints and the photos early. I'll need them to have pictures run in the paper if we haven't found out who he is by ten o'clock. We'll run flyers, contact other cities, the works. I'll be going by the M.E.'s office first thing to see what turns up on the body. I guess we've done all the damage we can do."

Driving along, Whit broke their silence to say, "You seem so calm. Doesn't it shake you up? You all seemed downright lighthearted."

Danielle looked at his profile. "It's an emotional camouflage," she said. "If we got too rattled, we couldn't do our job. But you're wondering if we *care*. We care, all right."

At her house where she had left a few lights burning, he turned to her. "I'll walk you to the door."

"Okay, but I can't invite you in. I've got a rough day ahead tomorrow."

"Besides, we're a dangerous combination."

"Something like that."

"I know we've got to take it easy," he said, touching her face. "But I'm going to touch you from time to time to make sure you're still here. Good luck on your case tomorrow." She handed him her keys and he opened the door for her.

He turned then and walked down the flagstone steps, and she went inside, with the echo of the drums she had heard reverberating in light waves in her head.

SIX

As she walked to the big beige brick building that housed the medical examiner's office the next afternoon, Danielle felt quiet, thoughtful. She opened the door and walked down the corridor to the big open white room. An assistant medical examiner, Carl Key, was eating a jelly doughnut. Dressed in a wrinkled pale gray smock over his baggy white pants, he stood with his back to her at first, then turned and smiled.

"Afternoon, Detective. Thanks for getting me more business."

His sad eyes belied his easy banter. It had taken her a long time to get used to the fact that law people joked to cover their horror of murder and mayhem. Talking about it with Mona had been one thing; actually experiencing it was another.

"Listen," he said, "I've got bones to pick with you, things you'll be interested in."

"Oh?"

He rubbed his nose, then ran his hand over his coarse, gray-flecked black hair. He stepped aside and picked up a long scarf-like, beautifully colored cloth from the counter.

"I found this strapped to the body and two thousand dollars. They're locked with the other evidence. I'll send it back to you."

"It looks like a kente cloth!" she exclaimed.

"Yep. Mother Africa. The money, which you'll find is twenty hundred-dollar bills, was folded into the cloth, then taped around his chest.

"I'll need to study them."

He nodded. "I'm about to get started. Want to see me do my Y-trick?"

"Not really."

Carl referred to the Y-incision made on the body preparatory to removing and studying the organs.

There were two other bodies on tables—one, a natural-cause death they had found in a seedy section of town and one, Danielle guessed, a domestic violence victim.

Keeping up his conversation with her, Carl picked up his scalpel and began cutting his Y-incision on the man killed the night before. "He died from two gunshot wounds to the chest, close in. You'll find the tattoos from the wounds."

Danielle sighed. "We've got our work cut out for us. Hopefully, we'll find out soon who he is."

Captain Jon Ryson came in with Ed Ware, who touched Danielle's shoulder. "Jon and I decided to follow you. Sorry I went over to D.C. last night and wasn't available."

"Don't be," she said. "We got through it okay. Do you recognize him?"

"Nope. Perfect stranger. He might be a visitor." Did he look at her obliquely? Whit was a visitor.

Captain Ryson studied the naked cadaver. "He looks like an on-top-of-it diplomat. Know when he died?"

"He hadn't been dead three hours, Carl says," Danielle told him. "But he's dead now."

"A genuine stiff," Ed said.

"I hope this isn't the beginning of random murders committed on strangers," Jon muttered.

"First thing," Danielle said, "I want to go on or put someone else on TV with this man's drawing and try to find out who knows him. In line with this, I want a police artist and sculptor to make a clay model of his head. This way we'll know something. Get Lyle Lacey. He's the best sculptor I know. And I'll need Dr. Art Little to profile the killer."

"Sure thing," Carl said, saluting her. Danielle was one of his favorite people and he admired her expertise as she admired his.

"How about a doughnut, Lieutenant?" Carl said to her now.

"I'd have to get out of here to eat it," she said. "We're loaded with them at the other building. I'll get one there."

"Picky, picky." Carl grinned. "Squeamishness is *not* one of the desired attributes for a detective."

Danielle looked at him levelly and smiled. "You hoe your row; I'll hoe mine."

"Touché," Carl said.

Jon patted Carl's back. "You can be happy now. You've got another nice, dead body to work on."

"Hell," Carl came back, "I already had enough. It doesn't take much to keep me happy."

"In which case," Danielle said, pursing her lips, "we'd all better watch our backs."

"Yeah," Carl said, "wouldn't *that* make a great story?"

As a young man on the medical examiner's staff entered and the other men fell silent, Danielle reached out and touched the body. The expression on the corpse's face was anguished and it reminded her of Mona's face that not all the expert undertaker's skills had been able to erase. Murder was a dirty business, she thought. She liked being someone who made the murderer pay the price for the deed.

Very late that afternoon, in Danielle's office, she, Jon, and Ed were joined by Matt, the fingerprint technician, Adrienne, the crime analyst, and Wink, the photographer. The mood was somber. Danielle told them she had had death mask photos sent out because it could take a week or so to make a clay model of the skull if the sculptor had other jobs.

"I hope this doesn't have Manny Luxor's slimy prints all over it," Ed said.

Jon looked at him sharply. "So far, he hasn't given us any trouble, but I'd say it could start at any time. He's steering clear of D.C. right now because they've got a strong chief, but we've got a strong chief, too. Luxor's bad news.

He's got a really rough way of handling his thugs. New York is after him and he's looking for some place to lie low. Minden could be it. Nice little city. Big enough to hide in, recruit a few new hoods."

No one said anything. Jon idly tapped his desk. "I'm more worried about INS being around. Let's give them all the help we can." He answered his buzzer and said, "Okay. Send him in."

Colin Matthews came in as Jon rose. "Come in, Agent Matthews. We're working on a murder. . . ."

At Jon's bidding, Colin sat down. "That's why I'm here. I heard about the murder on the news last night. So far you haven't identified the body. . . ."

"That's right," Jon said, interested now.

"It's still very early," Colin said, "but no one's come forward to say someone close to them is missing. If it's a foreign guy, he could be connected in some way to illegal aliens being smuggled in."

Jon nodded. "The cadaver is African, could be American, but perhaps comes from somewhere else," Danielle told him. "I'll take you out to see the body. Any headway on what's going on?"

Colin thought a moment. "I'm busy trying to figure it out. We've been working on this case for a long time. Things were hot ten years ago and we thought we could nab them, but everything seemed to stop abruptly. Then we began to get rumblings about three years ago that it was starting up again.

"Whoever's handling the operation is sharp and they're running it well. I'm sure you know we have to build an airtight case. We make a false arrest and we're out millions, not to say some bureaucratic backsides won't be covered. CYA. Cover your . . ." He sounded bitter.

Danielle touched her face. "Have you thought about the mob?"

"All the time. We think they're implicated, all right. That's why we're having such a tough time. New York. Philadelphia.

Baltimore. D.C. Transporting illegal aliens is going to be the twenty-first-century Fort Knox and it got well grounded more than twenty years back. We're swamped, but we intend to do what we can."

"And we'll give you all the help we can," Jon reassured him.

Danielle thought a moment before she said, "We found a kente cloth and money strapped to the body."

"A ken-tay . . ." Colin began, then his face brightened. "Sure. I know what a kente cloth is. I've taken a lot of courses on Africa since I've been working on these cases. Maybe I can tell you the possible country of origin." Then he shrugged. "I don't want you to think I'm hotdogging it. . . ."

"It's all right," Danielle said. "I think we're going to need all the help we can get."

"Great. I'm going to be in town awhile and tomorrow another agent is joining me. Our chief thinks Minden has grown to be a hot spot for transporting illegal aliens. We think there are safe houses here and from those bases they'll spread out over the country with false I.D.'s and other papers. Some of these aliens are wealthy. Twenty thousand is nothing to them and they pay extra for additional help, like false degrees that let them get a head start. You'd be surprised how trusting some people and institutions are in this country."

Colin started to get up. "I can't tell you how much we appreciate your help here. I have a good feeling about this. Sorry about the murder. You haven't had one for quite a while. If someone will show me, I'll look at the body and the kente cloth."

Danielle sat in her larger-than-usual office and began to forage through some papers on her desk. Ed came in, sat, then lounged in a big chair in front of her desk.

"Lordy, Lord," he said. "Five more years and Mexico and I will become the lovers of the century. Happiness, come to Daddy. How can you let me go without coming with me?"

Danielle gave him a slow, friendly smile. "I like the U.S. Parts of Mexico are beautiful, but more parts of the good old U.S.A. are beautiful."

He shrugged. "Pick your poison." He was looking at her intently. "Dani, you can't get past the age part with me, can you?"

Danielle looked up sharply. "Ed, you know better. You're my friend. You'll always be my friend. We're just not meant for certain people."

His eyes were half closed as if he measured what lay between them. "I'm going to get out of line, so forgive me. A clown comes along, likely a major player, and you tumble like a load of clothes in a hot drying machine. I'm not a bad-looking guy and, God knows, you could have anything I own."

She was embarrassed now. She always was when Ed talked like this; thank heaven he seldom did it.

"If you'd waited," she said, "to have this conversation, you'd know Whit and I are putting everything on hold. You surely know me enough to know I largely play it safe. Don't you think I'm aware of the world he lives in?" Then she grew a little testy. "I can take care of myself, Ed. Believe me."

He grinned, stretched and got up, came around the desk and patted her shoulder. "That's my girl. That's my Dani talking. My levelheaded Dani. Now, let's talk about the body and what's shaping up."

Matt, Adrienne, and Wink came in and they all sat at the table. Danielle felt close to them all. They were good at what they did and they cared about victims who had somehow gotten in the way of others, bringing disaster onto themselves.

The meeting lasted over an hour. Danielle remained sitting at the table after the others had gone. Chief Wayne Kellem knocked and at her bidding came in.

"Well, Dani," he said cordially, "I'm glad to know you're handling this. Murder is a nasty business. It seems to me you always take a fresh approach to solving homicide cases.

You're a fine young woman and you're headed straight for the top. I want you to know that whatever I can do, you've got it."

"Thank you," Danielle said, feeling a lump in her throat. He was so much like her father.

His dark chocolate face was lighted now. Looking at her, he envied her father. He, Chief Kellem, had all boys. Seven. He would retire in a few years and one thing he wanted badly was to know who had killed Dani's mother, as fine a woman as he had ever known. He wanted a special place in hell reserved for her murderer.

Danielle was back at her desk, rearranging papers, when her cell phone rang. Daphne.

"Daffy, darling!"

"That's me, the quintessential darling." Daphne giggled. "I had a great time last night. Your old man came in for a slug of brandy and we talked—a lot. He's a great guy, Dani, but he's not ready for another commitment."

"Then that makes two of them," Danielle said and laughed hollowly. "I can't say give him time. It's been thirteen years. But then, *I* don't seem to hurt a lot less either. A sharp stab of anxiety sliced through her. "Maybe for some, it *never* goes away," she said. She thought about Whit and his broken marriage. She was hurt by Mona's death, but she had married and was happy for a time. Whit had been honest enough to say he was too hurt to commit. Would he always be too hurt?

SEVEN

Two days after the murder, Daphne called Danielle at her office early. "Listen, love," Daphne said, "I'm calling about us going to A Literate Minden tonight. It's all over the news about the body being found. Can you make it?"

Danielle said slowly, "I have to make it. I'm reading some of Langston Hughes's poems and some Shakespeare to my group tonight and they're expecting it. They're reading, too. I'll have to leave early, but I'll be there. Those kids have been disappointed too often."

"Yes, even our adult students have."

The women were silent then, thinking. Cal Catlett had contributed to fixing up a place for them to teach others to read, and to socialize. Most were teenagers who were dropouts or doing poorly in school, but there was a large sprinkling of adults who were able to admit they couldn't read and intended to learn.

Daphne laughed. "I ran into old Cal today and he told me he'd be by tonight. He wanted to see if we knew what we were doing."

"And of course he thinks he's the best judge in the world," Danielle said tartly.

"He's something else again. He undresses you with his eyes even in a heavy coat."

"That's the man. I wonder why Irene puts up with him."

"Because he's rich would be my guess. She's so passive, but she's a nice person. Too nice for him."

"We're gossiping."

"I know. Isn't it wonderful? Gossip lets you know that other people have troubles too."

By six forty-five that evening, Danielle had finished setting the murder investigation wheels in motion and stood on the steps of the converted building that housed A Literate Minden. Students filed by her, ebullient in their greetings.

"Lieutenant Ritchey!"

She turned to see Cal Catlett loping toward her. "Just thought I'd pay you a visit. It's been too long."

She greeted him warmly. Even if she didn't like the man, he had been very much in favor of what she and Daphne were doing here. Daphne came up behind him.

"Mr. Catlett," Daphne said, "we don't see enough of you."

He bowed. "Well, I can rectify that."

A gray and brown German police dog bounded up to stand at Cal Catlett's side. "I never see her," Danielle said about the dog, "but what I marvel at is her beauty."

The man was more touched by her compliment than he would have been had she complimented him on something about his own person.

"Yes, Girly is a great dog. She cost me a pretty penny, but she's worth it."

"Girl . . ." Danielle began. She had never known the dog's name. Cal hadn't had her long.

Cal laughed uproariously, then a mischievous expression crossed his face. "Now I know calling her Girly might offend some women libbers, but my wife says I'm a consummate male chauvinist. You ladies aren't women libbers?"

"Well," Danielle drawled, "I guess I could be called that."

"And I'm right along with her. Times have changed, Mr. Catlett," Daphne told him smoothly.

"Oh, hell's bells," Cal shot back. "Call me Cal. I insist on it. It's not like I'm that old. Fifty-eight, well set up. I can run rings around most young guys. You, too, Lieutenant Ritchey. I call you lieutenant out of respect for your uniform. Remember, now. How's the school going?"

"Very well," Danielle told him. "We can never thank you enough for helping us fix this place up. The students really like it."

"It's nothing," Cal said, looking down suddenly. "You live in a neighborhood and you do everything you can to make it better. That's always been my creed."

Inside the palc, yellow brick house where classes were held, Danielle went to her room where seven students were seated and greeted them. "Before we go to work," she said, "I'd like to introduce a guest that most of you know, Mr. Calvin Catlett. Let's give him a hand."

Cal flushed. "I'm really glad to do all I can," he told them. "I'm proud of you all. Make me cven prouder. A man doesn't know what life is until he can read and read well."

A thirteen-year-old girl's hand went up. "Yes, Melanie," Danielle said.

The girl hunched her shoulders. Being bold didn't come easy to her. "Mr. Catlett, you said a *man* doesn't know what life is until he can read and read well. What about women and girls?"

Cal threw back his head and laughed. "A little women's libber. Honey, you better get used to the real world. Now I didn't mean any harm. Women. Men. We all had better learn to read. I'm one hundred percent behind A Literate Minden ALM and all it stands for. You people have got two fine young women helping you. I hope you appreciate them."

The four grown-ups who wcre there expressed their appreciation. Danielle told them she would be leaving early, then went to the double blackboard and took up her chalk and wrote *A Literate Minden* on the board.

Daphne came into the room. "Now, it's our turn," she said, indicating her room. Cal walked over to her, and Danielle excused herself to go with them. She wanted to tell Daphne's students that they would combine with her class tonight when she left early.

In Daphne's room, there were more adult students. They warmly greeted the well-known Cal, who was on many boards of directors, including the excellent hospital Minden enjoyed. A loyal church member, he contributed to many churches, as well as to his own.

One small woman's hand went up. "I hear we've got a murder on our hands."

"Yes," Danielle said.

"I didn't expect you here tonight. Thought you'd be too busy."

"That's why I'll be leaving early. There's a lot going on."

"Who was it got killed?" the woman continued.

"We don't know yet."

"I've got a missing Uncle Paul," the same woman said. "I hope it's not him. He carouses and drinks like there's no tomorrow. My mother's always telling him someone's going to find him somewhere he don't want to be."

Danielle nodded. "Let's hope it's not your uncle. The corpse may be from overseas."

A lanky boy of seventeen said gleefully, "Intrigue! Love it! More and more I plan to be a policeman."

Danielle smiled. "We'll be happy to have you on the force. Feel free to visit anytime."

"Great!" the boy said. "I'm gonna take you up on that."

Danielle went back to her class then and Cal Catlett trailed her. "I'll just stay in here with your bunch until you leave. You mind?"

"Not at all."

Other students had come in. Danielle looked about. Checking her attendance sheet, she saw that she had fifteen students that night and surmised that Daphne had around fifteen. Minden's teachers thought highly of the work Danielle and Daphne did and frequently volunteered to help.

The rooms of the house were painted a pale blue and the

floors were kept highly polished, all with money raised from Cal, the community, and Minden's coffers. There were desks for the younger students and comfortable chairs with wide-armed writing spaces for the grown-ups.

Danielle passed out booklets of poetry from several poets. Langston Hughes. Shakespeare. Sonia Sanchez. "Look through and pick a poem you'd like to read. This is only the beginning. We'll be on this at least a month. It doesn't matter if several people pick the same poem. Sylvia, please help me pass these out."

A tall, thin girl got up, took the booklets and began to help. "Does Mr. Catlett get one?" she asked.

On the spur of the moment, Danielle told her, "He certainly does. He'll need the book to follow up."

Cal Catlett scoffed. "I don't follow; I lead. I want to read too."

The students were delighted. Danielle stood near the board to write down words that might prove difficult, then she frowned. Where was May Land tonight? May Land's mother had been killed by her father. She was missing often now.

As Danielle began to read the introductory part of a collection of Langston Hughes's poems, the door opened and a breathless young girl came in. She came directly to Danielle, saying, "Lieutenant Ritchey, I'm sorry I'm late. I wasn't planning on coming. Can I talk to you a minute?"

"Of course." Danielle looked at Cal. "Please finish reading this for me, and go on from there. I'll be back in a little while."

The students clapped as Cal assumed the leadership role. May and Danielle went to a small kitchen in the back of the house. It wasn't lost on Danielle that the fifteen-year-old looked hungrily at the bags of food being spread out on the table by one of the students. There were crackers and cheese, olives, pickles, small and not so small sandwiches—all wrapped in clear plastic.

"Have you eaten?" Danielle asked gently.

"It's all right," May answered.

Danielle partially unwrapped one of the trays and placed sandwiches and other food on a large napkin and a paper plate.

"When did you last eat?"

The girl hesitated a long while. "Yesterday morning?" Two large tears rolled down the girl's face. "I want to be with my mother," she said flatly, hollowly. She sounded terrible.

Danielle drew the frail brown girl to her bosom. "Sit down," she said. "Please talk with me. Where have you been? What have you been doing?"

At first, the girl hung her head. "I've still been staying with my mother's sister, but she's got five children of her own; she's got no place for me. I've got nobody else here."

Danielle smoothed the thick black hair, the beaded long braids and the silken brown cheeks. She had called the aunt's house several times after Mabel Land had been killed and left messages for May, who never returned them.

"I would have helped you. Why didn't you call me?"

"I couldn't. I just couldn't," the girl said in a dead voice. "You would have stopped me and I want to be with her. I only come to class because you're like my mother. . . ."

Danielle stroked the girl's back, soothing her. "Eat something now." She got a container of chocolate milk from the refrigerator and poured a cupful.

"May, I want to help you. With your aunt's permission, you can stay with me."

"No, ma'am, I couldn't. I smoke marijuana sometimes."

Danielle wasn't surprised. "You can always stop."

"I don't think so. It's the only thing that stops the pain. That, and wine."

"How much wine are you drinking a day?"

"A fifth or more."

"Where do you get the money to buy this wine?"

"It's cheap," the girl said in a barely audible voice. "I steal the money from my uncle's pockets. He's a truck driver, makes good money. My aunt works and I work helping a lady in a store stock her goods when I can. I've got a boyfriend; he wants to marry me."

"You're too young to be married. Here, sweetheart, eat up and drink the milk."

With tears drying on her face, May wiped her cheeks with the long sleeve of her dress. Danielle reached back and handed her a Kleenex, which she took and dabbed her eyes.

Danielle drew up a chair as May sat down. She patted the girl's knee. "Eat slowly now. Do you want some soup? We've got some here."

"No. This is plenty. I don't know what got into me yesterday. Yes, I do know . . ."

Danielle smiled sadly. "Eat right now. We'll talk later."

The girl and the woman sat with knees touching at the kitchen table. May nibbled very slowly at first, as if she were reluctant to eat, then faster and faster. She gulped her milk when she had finished the food.

Leaning back in her chair, May looked sad beyond the telling.

"Did something happen yesterday?" Danielle asked after a minute.

The girl took a long time answering. "I heard on TV that they found a man—killed—murdered. I don't know why, but it made me think about my mother."

"I know. I'm very sorry you have to suffer this pain."

And the girl's pain was reactivating her own, the way it had done in the beginning. Was that why she hadn't followed up with the girl as faithfully as she might have?

After fifteen minutes or so, Danielle said, "I'll need to go back out now. I want you to stay in here awhile longer. You don't have to come out at all tonight. I have to leave early, but I want you to keep in touch with me. Call me every day and I'll talk with your aunt. Give me her number."

Going back to her classroom, Danielle paused at a closed door, then opened it, switched on the light and looked inside. It was an old darkroom—windowless and nearly airless.

Danielle sometimes got the creeps when she passed it and wondered why. Closing the door, she went on.

Back in the classroom, Danielle realized how long she had been gone. She thanked Cal for filling in and as she prepared to leave, she turned the students over to Daphne. May came in and silently took a seat.

She looked a lot better, Danielle noted as she gave the girl her card. She gathered her things and left. At the door she felt compelled to look back. May blew her a kiss, which she returned.

EIGHT

A week later a puzzled Danielle stood before a mask of a head on a table in her office. She had opened the blinds and drawn them up for maximum lighting in order to study the mask. Gingerly, she touched the brown-stained clay. It was a noble head, but the anguish on the face in death had carried over. Mona's face had been anguished like that. The drumbeats she had heard the night before reverberated in her head now.

Slowly, Danielle paced the floor in front of the head. *Who was this man?* As soon as the rendering of the head had come in, she had had photographs made and flyers run and distributed. It was early, but so far, nothing.

She sighed deeply. Whit had called daily and she had spoken with him briefly, surprised at how much she looked forward to his calls. May had called twice.

"You don't need to worry about me," she'd said. "I asked my aunt and she doesn't want me to stay with you. She says I'd be a nuisance. I'll be all right, I promise. My boyfriend helps me over the humps."

Danielle had reflected testily, *And I wonder if he isn't the source of your marijuana supply.* She was very worried about the girl. She thought, *No fifteen-year-old should be dependent on her boyfriend to take care of her.* May hadn't gone into the subject of her boyfriend. Danielle wondered if he was a teenager or an older guy. Married? The negative possibilities were endless. She was going to talk with May about this.

Her cell phone rang and she answered to a happy-sounding Whit.

"How's your case coming?"

"Not too well, I'm afraid. We've got no leads. Zilch."

She touched her face and blushed because she was imagining Whit gently touching her face.

"If I know you," he said, "you give your cases your all. Jon thinks the world of you. He said when he assigns you a case, it's as if he himself were working on it."

"That's because he and Ed have trained me well. Look, if you have nothing better to do, I'm going on TV and radio today to talk up this case."

"Tell me when and I'll listen—and look."

"Okay, it's four o'clock this afternoon for the TV station and ten-thirty this morning for the radio station."

"You're taking care to get enough rest?"

"You bet," she said at first, then, "Who am I kidding? I never get enough rest when I'm on a case until we either solve it or admit we've come up against a dead end. And even then we go back over them. We haven't got any cold cases, just lukewarm ones. Compared to a lot of cities, Minden's a great place to be murdered. Great for the victim, that is. We're hell on perpetrators. Chief Kellem has put together a really good force, if I do say so."

"You sound a bit down, a little tired."

"I am."

"You're off tomorrow. I wonder if you'd let me pick you up and take you somewhere."

She thought about it a long time. "I'd be the worst of company."

"That's okay. You deserve a break. If you're there, that's all that matters."

"Thanks for saying that. You're a sweet guy."

"And a bitter one. I wish I weren't."

"You're honest about it. That matters so much."

"I'll always be honest with you."

"And I'll always be grateful. What's on your agenda? Dress? Casual clothes?"

"Casual by all means. I think you'll enjoy this."

"Are there others involved? I tend to be a loner when I'm working on a case."

"You. Me. One other person for a while. I won't answer any more questions. I don't want to spoil the surprise."

"All right. Can't I just have a hint?"

"No hints. You'll know soon enough. I'll pick you up around three o'clock."

He never talked long. He was a thoughtful guy. Danielle sat at her desk. This time last week she had been stewing in her own emotional juices. Lonely. Now, she was being pursued by someone she wasn't sure she ought to want to be pursued by. "Whit," she whispered to herself, "why couldn't you be free to come to me?"

Grace, the dispatcher, stuck her head in the door. "It was the funniest thing," she said. "First, though, are you busy?"

"Always time for you, Gracie."

The rotund, chocolate-colored woman smiled. "In that case, I'll pop in for a minute."

"Have a seat."

"No, I've been sitting all morning. A young girl came in a very short while ago, asked to see you. I buzzed but got no answer. . . ."

"I was on the phone." *With Whit, and I didn't want to get off—something that's never happened before,* she reflected.

"Well, when you didn't answer, she left hurriedly. She said she couldn't wait."

"How did she look? Upset?"

"A little. No, I'd guess a lot. She wouldn't give me her name, but she said she'd be back later."

"Thanks. I believe I know who it was."

"Okay. That's my good deed for the day. Now, I'll go out and have a brief cigarette and telling you will make up for my sin."

"You ought to stop, you know."

"Lord, how I know I ought to, but I've got the habit hard. I started at thirteen. I just thank my lucky stars it isn't marijuana."

Grace left and Danielle moved to stand again in front of the clay head. In a few minutes, she'd call May.

"I see the clay model head's come back," Jon said as he knocked and came in. "Clue me in." He studied the head carefully. "He looks like a live one. Like a diplomat. Or some ancient king."

"And now he's dead," she said softly.

"Dani," Jon said sadly, "it hits you every time, doesn't it? Every death brings it all back and we've had a lot of deaths since your mother died. Would you—"

She looked at him levelly. "Would I like to try something else? Take a leave of absence?"

"You're reading my mind."

"Not completely. I don't have to read your mind. You've said it all before. No, Jon, this is my life. It's what I want to do. I wouldn't be anywhere else, working with you and Chief Kellem, Ed, the whole gang. We've solved such a higher number of murders than police in other cities have solved. I like to think I'm at least partially responsible for that."

"You're damned right you're responsible—and largely. You don't quit, Dani. The only thing I'm afraid of is you'll burn out. It's been thirteen years since you joined the force. You came in dedicated, a green kid who had psychic powers that have helped us."

Danielle shook her head. "I don't know about the psychic powers. Sometimes they work, sometimes they're just a part of things I've seen, heard and forgotten. Jon—"

"Hey, how about my inflicting myself on you two for a few minutes?" Ed stuck his head in the door. "Oops. Forgot to knock. Too anxious."

"Come in," Danielle said. "I can tell you both this."

"Shoot," Ed said.

She hesitated a moment. "The night the man was killed, I heard drums. They sounded different—sad. Some tribes in Africa give drum rolls on the death of someone."

"And the kente cloth says he *may* be African," Jon said.

He eyed her sharply. "Keep that psychic juice flowing. It may be we're going to need all the help we can get. Why do my instincts tell me this is far more involved than some simple man being killed?"

"And why do mine tell me the same?" Danielle said.

Jon left then, saying, "Let's keep in close touch, Dani."

She nodded. "When you talk with your wife, remind her that I'll be over to broadcast around ten o'clock. I go on at ten-thirty."

"Yeah, I know. She'll be waiting." Jon's wife, Francesca, was a radio talk show host in Minden.

When Ed had placed himself in a chair, Danielle said, "My dear friend, you don't sit, you flop."

"You're just jealous because I'm so relaxed. What's the latest on the stiff?"

"Don't call him that. I have a feeling he deserves more respect."

"We all do, but do we get it? Our good friends talk about our flopping in chairs. Hold us at bay. You and I could live the high life in Mexico, Dani. Better think about it. With my pension and the money I've saved, we could really make it."

"If dysentery and drug battles let us."

"I'd cover you with silver and gold."

"I'm not that fond of jewelry. I've only got a few pieces. I've never longed for more."

"I could make you happy if you let me."

"We're the best of friends, Ed. Let's leave it that way."

He drew a deep breath and his eyes were half closed. "I'll never stop trying. Don't expect me to."

"Stop it, Ed. I'm on my way over to the radio station to talk about the man we found."

"Let me take you. I'm lonely. I need someone to talk with. Shelley's kicked me out again."

"Have you been misbehaving?"

"Good as gold. I think she knows how I feel about you."

"Grow up. Learn how to accept that we can't have everything we want. I'm no prize, believe me."

"To me, you put the Queen of Sheba to shame. Let me take you."

With a faint smile, she relented. "Okay, as long as the conversation is about Shelley and not about me."

It was six-thirty the same afternoon before Danielle was free to go by May's house. The broadcasts had gone well and she had enjoyed seeing Jon's wife, Francesca, again. The talk show host had shuddered. "So, we've got intrigue on our hands," she'd said. "Whatever we can do to help, we will."

The people at the TV station had been no less cooperative. The possible Africa connection gave them all something to build on.

She was tired now, frustrated. Why hadn't May waited for her? The neighborhood she drove through was seedy, littered. She stopped in front of a battered white-frame house with peeling paint and a trash-strewn front yard with children playing.

"Hey!" a young boy called. "Looking good, Mama!"

"Hey, yourself," Danielle answered. "How are you?"

"I'm fine. How *you?*"

"Well," she answered, "right this minute I've seen better. Is May home?"

An older girl shook her head. "She ain' here. She li'ble not t'come in soon. Jake pick her up. They go to his place."

"Is your mother home?"

The girl turned sharply and went into the house calling, "Mama, a lady he'ah want t'see you." The girl went back out and invited Danielle in.

A man entered from a back room, wearing a tank top and tight black jeans. He muttered, "You looking for my wife. She be on in a minute." He looked up in the darkened room. "Ain' you the lady cop want May?"

"Yes," Danielle answered levelly.

"John, who . . .?" The angry voice preceded the woman into the room. She stopped just inside the door. "You looking for May, ain' you? Or is she done something wrong?"

"No," Danielle answered. "I just want to talk with her a bit. I won't be long. How are you, Mrs. Shutt?"

"She . . . ah . . . in some kinda trouble?" the man asked. The woman didn't answer Danielle's greeting.

"No. Nothing like that. We keep up with children who've lost their parents."

The woman shrugged. "I ain' never goin' to let go a' th' girl. She be my blood."

"I've been thinking," Danielle said. "I could help with her while she stays here with you. I want to see her get back in school. She could help me around the house. I'll pay her well."

The small woman stood with her head to the side. "She go back to school when *she* want to. That girl's grievin' worse'n anybody I ev'a seen. She need me. And I needs her help when I c'n get it."

"Aw, Lily," the man said. "The girl do the bes' she can."

A car door slammed outside. In a moment, a key turned in the lock and May stood there. Her pale yellow face blanched. "Why, Lieutenant Ritchey."

Danielle didn't say the girl had been looking for her. "I haven't got long," Danielle said, "but I wonder if I could talk with you a few minutes."

"Sure," the woman answered for May. "It be so private, ya'll c'n go out on th' back porch."

They filed through the badly lit, greasy, dusty house and onto the small back porch. May spoke first. "Maybe you hadn't oughta come. I don't want t'cause no trouble. It was a lot of trouble for you to come here, and it's gonna make my aunt mad. She's like the dog in the manger we read about in school. She don' want me and she don' want nobody else t'have me."

The girl sounded bitter as she balled her fists by her side. They sat in rickety chairs facing each other as Danielle asked, "Why did you need to see me?"

"Was it all right I came?"

"You know it is. Come anytime. What's going on?"

The girl closed her eyes and swallowed hard. "Jake wants to marry me. That's not all, but that's what I can *tell* you. It's so hard for me to talk."

"May, do you feel *any* better about your mother?"

The girl thought a long minute, then licked her dry lips. "I didn't for the longest time. Then you started talking and I felt better. What you did a few nights ago, fixing all that food for me. And a while back you asked my aunt to let you keep me. I never had nobody since my mother died. Am I wrong, thinking you care?"

"You're not wrong, May," Danielle answered gently. "I care—a lot."

Danielle thought that this young girl and she had a link— mothers who had died too soon. *Murdered* mothers.

"Is Jake pressing you to marry him?"

"Some. He says he cares about me. You think he does?"

"I don't know because I don't know him. How old is Jake?"

"Twenty-two."

"You're much too young to marry."

"I know, but I got to get away." The girl's voice was edgy, scared. She barely spoke above a whisper. "I can't talk about it here. Can I come to your office and talk?"

"Yes, please do. Let me give you some money."

May shook her head. "Jake gave me some today. You know I work helping a lady and she pays me good. I don't need money, but thank you so much."

Danielle felt a lump in her throat. "May, if somehow your aunt could change her mind, I'd like that, but now, while you stay here, I want to see you, help you, tutor you, or when I'm busy get my friend to tutor you. I'm very fond of you. . . ."

May suddenly grinned and it was like the sun breaking from behind clouds. "I think you *love* me," the girl said, "and golly, that makes me happy."

But as suddenly as the sunshine had come, it left and as the man bellowed in another room at his wife, a fearful expression crossed May's face.

"Listen," May said, "you better leave now. Aunt Lily's not in the best of moods. Him neither. She don't mind going upside my head. I'm so glad you came and I'll come by Monday. We got to talk. Any special time?"

"Can you come by on your lunch hour?"

"Yes, ma'am. I'll see you then."

Danielle gave her a quick kiss, said good-bye to the aunt and uncle, who now sat in the living room. The aunt seemed a little friendlier as she said, "I guess it'll be okay if you come by t'see the girl from time t' time, give her money. That is, when she's here. And God knows, we all needs the money."

Out in the yard, with the aunt and uncle standing in the front doorway, Danielle glanced back. The little boy who had first greeted her came to stand in front of her, saying, "Good-bye. Don' be a stranger now!"

Laughter bubbled in Danielle's throat. He was so cute. But her thoughts and her feelings were on May. Grief and the hurt had lain on May's countenance since she had come across her, but the fear was new. Who or what was May afraid of?

NINE

Sunday afternoon Danielle walked onto the upper deck of Whit's very large white cabin cruiser, the *Sea Nymph*. Whit introduced her to the crew: Lee, the captain, a large, bluff, berry-brown man; Mark, the first mate, a thin, wiry soul who smiled a lot; and Cookie, the cook, an ebullient, big, ginger-colored woman who was also one of two bodyguards. Danielle met them easily and they made her feel welcome.

"You've been raved about," the captain said, bowing. "You live up to your notices."

Danielle blushed and glanced swiftly at Whit, who stood grinning.

"I think you'll get a dinner from your dreams." Cookie smiled broadly at her. "Especially when the master himself has prepared it. He puts my cooking in the shade."

"So much trouble," Danielle murmured. "Do I deserve all this?"

"This and more," Whit said gallantly. "Now let me give you the grand tour."

And a grand tour it was. They began on the top deck, then moved to the lower deck with its deep-cushioned heavy leather furnishings in blue, dark gold, and burgundy. Deep leather sofas and chairs were everywhere.

Danielle laughed. "I'm envious. I'm here for a day. You *live* here."

"Only for part of the time. When I'm on travel, which is

most of the time, it's rented out. Would you like to live on it for a while? We're only twenty miles from Minden."

She looked at him obliquely. "My own house is a handful, but thank you for asking. Whit, you make things sound so easy."

"Well, I don't believe in making the easy hard. Any time you want to spend a week or so, I'll check into a hotel or spend time at my parents' or one of my sisters'; so you've got no excuse. Besides . . ." He frowned. "Let's go to the cabin."

They went down another level and Danielle found herself enjoying the continuous beauty of the boat. The cabin was done in burgundy and cream—a decorator's dream. One bed was the shape of the boat's bow, the other in the shape of its stern. Large mirrors were everywhere. "Let me take your purse and your tote," Whit said.

She slid the tote and the purse off her arm and handed it to him. He held up the large polished leather bag, admiring it. She took it back and showed him what it held in its compartments: a smaller gun than she usually carried, this in a separate specially fitted compartment, cosmetics, and pages of police work in other sections. The police work filled the purse and made it heavy.

Whit shook his head and put the bags into a teakwood bureau drawer.

"Dani," he murmured as he came back to her side, "I'm so glad you're here."

They swayed toward each other, craving deep kisses and more, but they held back. Instead, their glances caressed unashamedly. He lingered over her quintessentially feminine wide-hipped, narrow-waisted form, her pert breasts pressing against the eggshell silk turtleneck blouse and her burgundy jacket. Her legs were long and sleek in the short, eggshell-colored silk skirt. And she bit her lip as she went over his wide-shouldered and slim-hipped figure, garbed in a navy T-shirt and navy Dockers with an oatmeal tweed jacket.

He came very close. "I told you when I picked you up, but

I'll say it again. You're beautiful, Dani. I wish I were free to tell you what's in my heart. I'm torn up. You know that, don't you?"

"Yes, I know."

She wondered what hell he had known. The bitterness filmed his features and his eyes were bleak.

Is that why you don't kiss me again? Hold me? She was crying out inside, *I need you. If we don't work out, I still win.*

He put his finger under her chin, tilted it. "What are you thinking? I wish I could read your mind."

"You'd be pleased," she murmured.

"You want me to kiss you. Do I see that in your eyes?"

"Yes."

"What if I can't stop? What if I have to have you? You know, I would never force you, but I might press too hard, be unwilling to take no for an answer."

"You're an alpha male. I think I can handle you. You're not a man who likes to hurt."

He smiled lopsidedly, saying, "And I don't like to *be* hurt."

"But you were."

"*Devastated*. Dani, I know most pain ends sometime. The question is when?"

She reached up and touched his face as his hot breath fanned her face. "You can talk to me about it. I'm a good listener."

"I can tell you are." They were standing so close and every cell of Danielle's body wanted, *craved* him.

She shook her head. "This is our second time being alone and we're steaming the waterways, burning up the cabin. We're quite a pair."

He sighed deeply. "I won't let us move ahead too fast, Dani. You've got a right to a man who's free and clear, in emotions as well as matrimonially. Just bear with me. See me from time to time."

Was he pulling away? Giving up? Tears were forming behind her lids. She touched his face lightly with her lips. "I trust you, Whit. We're one day short of a week knowing each other, but I've known you in my heart forever."

His body hurt with wanting to crush her to him, but he was all control as he said levelly, "I'm going to settle you in the living space with music while I put the finishing touches on dinner."

"Let me help you."

He shook his head. "No, this dinner is all mine. I'm even going to serve. The men ate earlier. At sunset we're taking off down the river. Would you like that?"

Danielle gave a happy cry. "I'd love it."

"Okay, we'll put the show on the road."

He settled her on the lower deck in the living area with *Heart and Soul*, *Ebony*, *Black Enterprise*, and other magazines.

"What kind of music do you like?" he asked.

"My tastes scan the world," she answered. "Gospel has come to be a favorite. I love African drums. . . ." She hesitated, thinking of the drums she had heard the night of the murder. Mona had loved classical music. "And I like classical music, too. Do you?"

"I've got quite a collection. Name your favorite."

Without hesitation, she chose Mona's favorite: Gustav Mahler's beloved Fifth Symphony, a favorite when she was in college.

He grinned. "The adagietto from that?"

"Yes," she murmured. "Would you play that? And anything from you and the Singing Steeles—and your sister, Ashley."

"Coming up. I've got a great recording of just the adagietto. You're going to be listening here until morning. What would you like to drink?"

"White wine, please. Any kind of white wine, although I'm fond of chardonnay."

"Ever tasted muscadine wine? My father makes it."

"Yes, I have. It's about my favorite. My grandmother used to make it."

"Then I'll get you some." As he turned she asked him, "Who taught you to cook?"

"Dad's the cook in our family. My mother is a very good cook, but he outdistances her."

"What are we having?"

"It's a surprise. I'm vain enough to think you'll like it. Look, I feel as if I'm shepherding you. Feel free to walk around. Enjoy the boat. The men are drooling over you. Behind your back, they kept giving me the A-OK sign."

"I'm glad," she said. "I'd hate it if they didn't."

When Whit left, Danielle leaned back onto the glove-leather sofa and relaxed completely. She hadn't realized how tired she was. She knew she worked too hard, but something drove her. For a moment or so she leafed through a magazine, then got up and looked out the porthole at the rippling sunlit Potomac and the brilliant sunlight streaming in. Sunset would be spectacular.

Whit went to the galley and came back with the wine on a small silver tray with a white damask napkin. "Something smells delicious," she told him.

"And it had better be as good as it smells," he said. "I've taken hints as to what you like when we've talked on the phone. You said you love cherry cheesecake. . . ."

"You didn't make . . ." She laughed happily. "Tell me you didn't go to all that trouble."

"Guilty. I make the best. The rest of the dishes are my secret."

"I'd leave happy with the cheesecake alone."

His big hand touched hers as she held the wineglass and a jolt of electricity flashed through them both. She felt the wine bubbling in her throat from constriction. Why did life need to be like this? She and Whit were different from others. Why couldn't they hold, caress, yes, make love to each other? When was too soon too soon?

But the boundaries of convention exerted their hold on them both. She wished violently for a country in the South Sea where they could be together at a time of *their* choosing. She smiled then, because in those countries, there were other problems she wouldn't be comfortable with.

"Whit?" She was suddenly alert.

He started. "Yes."

"You were staring at me."

He was sober then. "I want to remember every detail of you. I have a couple of things to tell you later, Dani, by way of explanation and by way of a schedule for me."

When he came to announce dinner, Danielle was lost in the magnificent rumbling thunder of African drums. "I just found that tape yesterday," he said. "I thought you'd like it."

On impulse, she kissed him on the corner of his mouth and heard him draw a deep breath. Then the drums were quiet and the otherworldly opulence of the adagietto from Mahler's Fifth Symphony flooded the room.

The music flowed into the dining area, where a magnificent table of cream damask, Waterford crystal, and cream Royal Doulton china with broad navy and gold bands was set. It was one of the loveliest sets she had seen and it reminded her that she was on one social level; he was on another. The table had been surrounded by screens when they had gone through earlier. There was a lovely centerpiece of lilies and maidenhair fern.

Dinner began with giant shrimp and a special hot tomato sauce. Delicious. When they had finished, he cleared the dishes, refusing to let her help. "You're looking a little less tired. I want to keep you that way."

The main course was lobster and filet mignon, with dishes of potato-onion-cheese casserole, baby lima beans, and asparagus. A big garden salad with thinly sliced tomatoes and blue-cheese dressing pampered her taste buds with crisp delight. Hot homemade rolls were covered in a silver bread basket.

"My uppity friends tell me never to serve white wine with beef," Whit said, "but the more down-to-earth ones agree that chardonnay goes with anything."

As they ate slowly, savoring each dish, Danielle exclaimed, "Lord, I didn't realize I was starved."

"I would have served you snacks, but I wanted all your appetite for the meal."

"You're a wonderful cook," she told him.

"I'm glad you think so. Do you like to cook?"

"When I've got enough time. It's funny, both our fathers are the cooks in the family. Julian packs a wallop in the kitchen, but he's got nothing on you."

When they finally got to dessert he asked if she preferred to eat it later.

"What I'd prefer," she said, "is to taste mine now then you take it and I'll finish it later. No cherry cheesecake is safe around me."

After Whit had taken the dessert dishes and put them in the refrigerator for later eating, they stood in the galley where food was prepared, with her admiring the stainless steel setting. Then, they moved back to the living area and sat on a deep sofa. Danielle closed her eyes. "You really have something going on here," she said.

"Especially since you're here."

"Your parents trained you well. You said you have sisters. Are you very close to them?"

"Very. They're great women. You know that Ashley is a gospel singer. My other sister, Annice—Neesie—is a psychologist. Her husband heads a school for troubled youth on Paradise Island and she heads the counseling unit."

"Fascinating. That's nearby. There was a murder there a year or so ago."

"Yes. They're preparing to go away, so I haven't taken you to meet them, but you'll meet them all after you wrap up this case."

"If. . . ."

"What's your closure rate on homicides?"

"Over seventy percent. Last year we had ten homicides. Seven solved."

Whit sat up straight, his eyes narrowed, thinking. "Knowing you, you'd have everything to do with the solving."

Danielle nodded. "I'm thought to be good. I do my best, but the whole department is top-notch. Chief Kellem runs a tight ship. Since you're so interested in law enforcement, you might want to know that most of the people killed are done in by people they know."

"Oh? I'd heard homicide of random strangers was getting more common."

"Not in Minden. Most cases are family and friends. Tension builds and someone says or does the wrong thing and someone else loses it."

He sat up straighter then.

"You're thinking of your ex-wife," she told him without meaning to.

"You know what I was thinking?"

"Not really. It's a matter of deduction. You're hurt. You're bitter. There must have been many things done and said. You'd think about that when the conversation turns to homicide, the ultimate bitterness."

"Do you like rhythm and blues?" he asked abruptly.

"I can't think of any music I don't like. Hard rock is at the bottom of my list. Would you sing 'Amazing Grace' for me?"

He looked surprised. "Of course I will. I'll do better. I'll play the guitar as I sing it."

He went to a teakwood cabinet and removed a case from which he took a guitar. He left the pick in the case and stood before her, breathing deeply. He had played that morning, so he didn't need to fine-tune it. He began:

"Amazing Grace, how sweet the sound that saved a wretch like me. I once was lost, but now I'm found, was blind, but now I see."

She let the old hymn fill her heart and she lay back and closed her eyes as he went through the other verses. His voice was incredible, a rich baritone laced with dark, velvet warmth. Then he played the tune on the guitar—softly, with heartfelt warmth and hope. As he played, he asked her, "Do you know the song?"

"Yes."

"Sing it with me?"

"I don't have much of a voice."

"It won't matter, but from your speaking voice, I think you *do* have a good voice. Let's try it."

He played a few chords. She cleared her throat as he began the song and she sounded surprisingly good to herself. Of course, she wasn't trained the way he was, but she sounded nice enough. They went through all the verses again and when they had finished, he bowed to her. "Brava!" he said.

"No. Brav*o*. My Lord, you're wonderful."

"Concert for Dani, number one. I hope there'll be many more."

She laughed. "There will if I have anything to say about it."

"I would sing more, but I have a slightly sore throat, and I take meticulous care of my throat."

"Your *gift.*"

"My gift, yes. God has blessed me, Dani, as he has blessed you. Do you like Marvin Gaye's music? 'Sexual Healing'?"

"I love it, as well as many of his other songs. His life was so sad for so many years, yet the music poured from his soul."

"Yes. I'm going to put on some of his music."

He pressed a button and an entertainment center was displayed. He sorted through the tapes and soon the dulcet, yet searing tones of Marvin Gaye and his song "Sexual Healing" filled the room. Coming back, Whit said, "He died too soon."

He paced in front of her, then sat down. "May I talk with you now, Dani? Only it's really *to* you since the story is mine. I want you to know *why* I can commit to no woman now and I suspect any time soon. Do you want to listen? If you'd rather I do it at another time . . ."

She felt his need as he sat beside her, a little farther away than he had been.

"I was in love with my ex-wife," he began tentatively, searching for ways to tell the whole, sordid story. "But there was trouble from the beginning. We married after knowing each other only three months. My parents thought we should wait. Annice counseled us to wait, but Ashley was on my side. She had fallen in love with her second husband swiftly, but they had known each other a long time. And they are happy.

"So, we married and before the first year ended, I thought it might be a mistake. I wanted, I still want kids and she wanted to wait a long time, she said. I travelled a lot and she didn't really like to travel. I found out we weren't operating on the same wavelength. There were frequent quarrels and I hate quarreling. I'm a peaceful man."

He stopped them, struggling to cool the pain he was reliving, the humiliation.

"I began to hear things, that she was running around. No one came to me directly. My family didn't know. She denied it all. Then the gossip all pooled around one man, Madison Bunks. He's a real estate dynamo, owns his own mortgage company. I asked again and she denied it again."

He paused for a long time and her slender hands caressed his back, feeling sympathy from the depths of her heart.

He ran his tongue over his dry bottom lip, then continued. "By the time she came to me, things had gotten out of hand. She was pregnant by him."

"Oh, Whit."

"She told me then she'd never loved me the way she loved him, that she wanted *his* child where she'd never wanted mine." Tears of remembered and present fury burned his eyes. "It was like a cyclone had torn through me. I wanted to hurt, to kill. I was in love. . . ."

Sympathetic pain flashed through Danielle, as she moved closer to him and drew his head down to her breast, stroking his beaverlike black hair. "I'm sorry," she whispered. "I'm so sorry."

He pressed his hot face into her soft bosom and felt her heart beating hard. It was a long time before he pulled away. This time, bitterness filmed his features. "It's a matter of trust, Dani. I trusted this woman. I put my life in her hands."

"And she betrayed you."

"She did. I know you're not Willo, but I have never been able to put aside that pain. Since I've met you, I have had my own share of bad dreams. You walk away from me, laughing, happy, but you're still leaving me and I can't stop you. It's not like we plan to fall in love with someone else, Dani. . . ."

Danielle sighed. "I think what hurt you so was the way it was done—the lying, the sneaking. My God, it was as if you didn't matter at all." She said again, "I'm sorry." It was all she could say.

The soft sound of violins came on then and she put her cheek against his as he said, "If only I could feel free, *be* free. Dani, you're young, beautiful. I want to keep seeing you, but I won't take it further, and I have something else to tell you—later. Wait for me, until I can get this miserable mess worked through. Can you do that?"

She thought about it carefully. "I honestly don't know, Whit. I've never met anybody I'm more attracted to, but I'm thirty-five. I want children, or at least one child. Kids mean a lot to me. I'm not going to rush into anything, but I appreciate your being on the level with me."

"I won't rush you. How can I?"

Her laugh was mirthless. "You keep saying that. It isn't all coming from you. I had a good marriage and it built up needs, desires I didn't know I had. Let's make a pact that we'll be adult friends and work on having a future."

"That sounds good to me."

In the meantime, in spite of the pain, he was going mad with wanting her under him, over him, surrounded by the hot walls of her inner body that he knew would be like nothing he had known before. She would give herself to a man in love and it would be a conflagration wondrous to behold. He wanted badly for that man to be him.

Danielle stroked his back with long, tender movements. "I'm glad you told me. I can see where you're coming from. Do you believe in God, Whit?"

"All the way. All the time. But at first I drew away. I had done everything right, had faith, lived with a loving heart. If there was a God, where had He gone? But my belief was too strong to let go. My faith was ruptured, not destroyed."

"Good. It gives you something to build on."

She wanted to tell him then that she loved him and it didn't matter that they had known each other such a short time. It was a *feeling* she had about him so that he filled her heart with joy and longing. Yes, it was a feeling, and feelings could be hurt. Whit would never intentionally hurt her, but he moved in a different world, surrounded by beautiful and attractive women, women who wanted him and were accustomed to getting what they wanted. He didn't seem to think too much about it, but what if *he* changed?

They ate their desserts, played shuffleboard on deck with the crew and very late that afternoon they headed up the Potomac. Standing at the rail with Whit, Danielle felt a sense of ease and contentment. It didn't matter that they couldn't be together the way they wanted to. But her heart said it *did* matter. What was she going to do?

They rode for a long time, spray stinging their faces, as the sun changed position. As the gorgeous red-orange ball that was sunset fanned out coral and gold rays, Whit lifted her hand and kissed it as they stood in the stern section of the boat. The crew was near the helm.

Her limbs felt heavy, golden as they stood together. He put his arm around her and smoothed her hair. "Gorgeous and natural," he told her.

"Thank you. I don't know where to begin complimenting you. I like the whole package."

"Sunset," he mused then. "A kiss at sunrise deserves a kiss at sunset. What d'you say?"

He didn't wait for her to answer, but drew her to him, intending to kiss her lightly and let her go. But liquid, honeyed heat filled her veins and she clung to him, her lips parting to let him in. His tongue teased her lips, then went into her mouth and ravished it. Her knees were weak as he held her up against him. What were they doing?

He drew his mouth away and murmured, *"Sunrise. Sunset."*

Time moved in a slow and wonderful metric cadence. She wasn't through with him. Like a magnet, she held fast. Both ached with desire. He shook her gently and feasted on the honey in her mouth.

Her lips were slightly swollen with wanting him. He thought her lips were like port wine and he couldn't get enough of them. Pulling her close, he felt her firm breasts agains his chest and it set him on fire. His loins ached with tension and with need. This couldn't lead to what they both wanted and he damned the reason that separated them. His pain that wouldn't go away. But he would wait, forever if that had to be. How much could he take? With ravening hunger, they kissed again and again and each groaned inside.

Then he thought that this was torment and this was madness, like starved people looking at a feast and unable to eat. Damn whatever reason kept them from making love, but he would never press her. She needed to be sure of his love and he respected that.

Still they clung with the fresh smell of the river and her perfume both hitting him where he lived, nearly sending him over the edge.

There were things he needed to say to her, but he couldn't let her go. They were drowning in desire and passion and her soft, soft skin, the deep curves of her body were driving him crazy. And Danielle was having her own hard time letting

Whit go. His muscular body was talking to her, begging for entrance to her secret place. She felt herself whimpering inside and touched his face.

Agonized with wanting her, he tore his mouth away, kept his hand in the small of her back. "Dani," he said gently, "I have something to tell you."

Reluctantly, she pulled away. "You said you did a while back."

"I'm going away to New York."

"But why? Are you visiting? I though you were on hiatus."

"It's been shot to hell. My agent, Mort Carrey, has got a great deal for me, but the CD's have to be cut now. They tie in with a promotional stint they want me to do in the fall. We can wrap it up by then."

Throat tight, she asked him, "How long will you be?"

He absolutely loved the longing in her voice. "A month. Maybe six weeks. Can you take off at least a week?"

Her heart leapt, but she shook her head. He had asked her and it wouldn't do. Away from here, things would happen and they couldn't stop them.

"No, of course you can't," he said. "You've got a case to solve. But if you solve it, could you then?"

"It wouldn't be wise, Whit," she said sadly. "You know it wouldn't be wise."

"The body has its wisdom, too," he told her, and she didn't deny it.

"When would you leave?"

"Day after tomorrow. Will I see you before?"

"Whit," she said hesitantly, "I don't think so. I've had a wonderful time today, better than I can remember ever having. Let's let you heal and pick up from there."

For a very long while they watched the heavily rippling waves and leaping fish.

He was silent, studying her in the twilight then, and after a while the captain turned the cabin cruiser around and headed back for the marina.

"I don't agree with you, but I'll go along. I want to call you, but it may not be too often. These sessions are hell; they exhaust me, yet make me very happy."

"That's because you're doing what you want to do."

"Aye. Aye. Is there a special time for me to call you? I don't want to wear out my welcome."

"You never could. Call anytime. You've got my home and my cell phone number."

"Thank you. Forgive me if I get to be irritable sometimes. My backup group will be recording with me and we have a new member."

The stars came out then in all their splendor. Planets and galaxies, stars upon clustered golden stars hung in a midnight sky. Nature in all its glory. Tonight she felt as one with nature. What had he said? *The body has its wisdom, too.*

Drawing her close, he kissed the side of her throat, then moved to kiss her breasts beneath the thin turtleneck. He rubbed his face across the tautened nipples that fought to get to him. His breath was scorching on her breasts under the cloth.

"Whatever it means," she said huskily, "I want you too."

He laughed then, a low throaty laugh. "One day," he said, "you and I are going to ride the crest of the waves and know *glory.*"

One day, she thought. *How soon would one day come?*

TEN

One week later

"*Buenos dias!*"

Sitting at her big oak desk, Danielle looked up and burst out laughing. Ed stood in the doorway with a brilliant red hibiscus behind his right ear. He spoke the Spanish greeting again.

"What's with you and the hibiscus and the Spanish?" she asked.

He ambled over to her desk and sat on the edge of it. "I picked the flowers up at Rhea's. I'm getting a late start with the Spanish. Just think, Dani, five more years, eleven months and twenty days and I'll be living in the lap of luxury in Mexico—a retired gringo."

Danielle tapped her teeth with her ballpoint pen. "Still going to settle near San Miguel de Allende?"

"No other place. Since it's a writers' and artists' colony, maybe I'll be a late bloomer and take up one or the other—or both."

"You never know who has talent."

"Maybe if I wear you down you'll go with me."

Danielle grimaced. "I like it here. Always have. I wonder if you aren't more attracted to the beautiful señoritas."

He shrugged. "That matters too." His voice got plaintive then. "You always slide away, Dani, when I talk about us."

She got nettled then and couldn't imagine why. Ever since

she'd begun working with him, he'd always teased her. She had never been interested in him in the least, except as a friend. And she thought then, with a delicious shudder, Whit and she called their relationship "friendship," but it was so much more.

She smiled a bit now. "Be real, Ed. We were never made for each other. You've got Shelley."

"I'll let her go if you say the word."

"You'll be out on your ear if she hears you say that."

"I couldn't get rid of that chick with a baseball bat. She loves me."

Danielle shook her head. "You're so modest."

She moved a stack of D-5 accident reports from one side of her desk to the other as her buzzer rang. It was going to be a slow day; maybe she could put a big dent in them. It was Jon asking if she and Ed could come in. Going down the wide hallway, Ed spread his fingers across the back of Danielle's neck and pressed. "You're a great gal, Dani. Don't ever change. By the way, where's the clown who was hanging around you?"

His comment disturbed her. Why was she so irritable today? Whit had called nearly every night. She enjoyed talking with him about the case she handled now and she enjoyed his description of his time spent recording. "I'm bringing you back something special," he had told her. "A surprise. You'll like it."

She couldn't help smiling as she thought of Whit and she answered Ed smoothly. "He left," she said, not wanting him to call Whit a clown. Then she teased, "I think you scared him off."

In Jon's office, Colin Matthews stood up as Danielle and Ed entered.

"I'm back early," the INS agent said. "I managed to snag a helicopter and I want to go over the countryside for about a ten-mile radius or more. I've explained to Captain Ryson . . ."

"Let's sit down," Jon said. "I've got plenty of coffee left

and some really terrific cinnamon buns my wife sent with me." He went to the kitchenette, got a coffee urn, paper cups, a tray of the buns, and brought everything back.

Before the conversation continued, Danielle bit into a bun. "Top-notch," she said. "I needed this." She got up and poured herself a cup of coffee. "I'll pour for anybody else who's too lazy to get up."

The men all laughed and asked her to pour for them. "Women's lib," she said, "is going to get me for this. Good ol' Dani—faithful servant."

"Yeah," Jon said, "and lightning-sharp detective. Fill us in, Colin."

Colin Matthews quickly told them what he suspected, that there was a safe house somewhere in a twenty- to fifty-mile area of the region, a safe house being a house where illegal aliens were brought before delivery to their final destination.

"We're on to something different," Colin said. "Illegal African aliens are becoming more plentiful. They come into New York City to safe houses there, then to various cities. Lately, more and more are coming from Africa, especially Zenia. Also from other countries in a state of unrest.

"What we've gotten lately is a professional class of illegal aliens able and willing to pay ten thousand or more for their journey here and a little help to get settled in a city of their choice. Green cards. Fake resumes. Fake professional licenses.

"We know what's going on, but we have to build an airtight case," the INS agent continued. "Our laws and the courts are lenient sometimes." He hesitated. "You've got a sterling citizen around here, Calvin Catlett. Know him?"

They all nodded.

"We think he may be tied up in this some way. As you know, he owns the mattress factory and has five tractor trailer trucks he sends his wares out on. We think he's bringing illegal aliens back from some of those trips. We just need to find out how he's doing it—if he is."

Ed whistled. "Ol' Cat, huh? I always knew he was a slick one."

"Yeah," Colin said, "I want you two to go up in the helicopter with me, show me the lay of the land."

Danielle raised her eyebrows and felt a rush of adrenaline. "We'd love to go."

"Right on, boss." Ed was always ready to rumble.

On the thirty-fifth floor of his hotel in downtown Manhattan, Whit lay on his bed half asleep. It was late morning and they had worked on a single record much of the night. He had finished a special song for Dani—"Life of My Life."

In the darkened room, he dreamed. Her beautiful face and body rose before him, not perfect, but always enchanting. She wasn't the only one who saw visions. He had her with him often. She curled around him like a gorgeous fairy flame, laughing, teasing, turning him on sky-high. "Dani. Dani," he whispered.

Was it possible he had known her for such a short time? He wanted to give her the world and he couldn't even give her his whole self. After Willo had left him, he had walked the countryside out from Crystal Lake, walked the city streets at night, mad with pain, his ravaged heart threatening to quit beating. He had been cold with fear. Love wasn't supposed to be like that, but its aftermath had been with him. He had stopped his fitness training. He drank too much and he was alienated from family and friends. They couldn't help him.

He felt a bit of the cold he had felt then, quickly covered over by the intense heat of his feelings for Dani—her warmth and loving spirit, her soft, fragrant body. He felt himself rise and harden with a passion that thrilled him and he drifted off into a light sleep. He blew kisses onto her lovely face and pressed his face into the valley of her beautiful breasts. Then bit by bit he lavished love on her, kissing, stroking, gasping for breath.

He jerked awake, his body tingling. It wasn't a good time to call her; he'd wait until late evening or night. He got a card of handy numbers the hotel had had made up and placed a call to the hotel flower shop.

Circling low over Minden and its outlying environs, Danielle, Ed, and Colin Matthews were chauffered by helicopter. The pilot zoomed in over Cal Catlett's two-hundred-acre estate—his resplendently big, redbrick home, with its magnificent grounds, his redbrick factory with its huge parking lot. A small woman stood in the backyard of the house playing with a big German police dog.

"We'd better not get too close," Colin said. The pilot lifted.

A little distance on, Colin asked, "Now, whose house is this?" He pointed at a big white country-style house with a wraparound porch and well-kept grounds.

"That's Annie Lusk's house." It was common knowledge that Annie and Cal were old lovers. Cal had set her up in business.

"The woman who runs Annie's Place?"

"Runs and owns."

"She and Cal are supposed to be tight," Colin offered.

"Hell," Ed said, "any tighter and they'd be a drum. It's like he's got two wives." He slapped his thigh. "Well, he can support a dozen wives. I like the way it's done in other parts of the world where a man can have any number of wives if he can take care of them. Irene, his wife, doesn't seem to mind."

"Pain can be quiet," Danielle found herself saying.

"Ask me," Ed said, "and I'll tell you I think nature set us up that way. One bull. Many cows."

Why did she keep getting irritated at him today?

"Don't put it on nature," she said. "It depends on how you look at it. When a cow *is* ready to mate, she doesn't need or want to choose that one special bull. We're humans, Ed. Why compare us to animals?"

Colin laughed. "I think she's got you there, my friend."

Ed shot her an amused glance. They spent over two hours pinpointing various houses and estates.

"Minden seems like a nice city," Colin said. "Is it?"

"It's great," both Danielle and Ed said.

"Any progress on the murdered man? At least you have time to work on it. We're swamped."

Danielle shook her head. "We're waiting for DNA results, although with a stranger, we don't yet know who to match it with. The man had a kente cloth and money taped around his chest. If what you say is true, Colin, there could be a tie-in, but what? Do you know Buck Lansing and Manny Luxor?"

"I've heard about them," Colin answered. "Made it my business to talk a bit to both. Think they're tied into the murder some way?"

"I think anything is possible with those two," Danielle said thoughtfully. "They're bad news on any front you care to consider."

"I'm going to be taking up a lot of your time," Colin said, "both of you. You might want to keep Luxor and Lansing under surveillance. . . ."

"They already are." Danielle pursed her lips. "If there is a smuggling ring going on around here, and with D.C. so close by, there's a likelihood, I think, that Luxor and Lansing can lead us to it."

"And Catlett?" Colin asked.

Danielle thought a moment. "Cal's a mover and a shaker. A first-rate pillar of this community—and rich. Why would he need to get involved in something like this?"

Colin rocked a moment in his bucket seat. "Just since I took this job, I've come to know that some people's greed is endless and for some nothing matters the way gold and jewels and lots of cold cash matters. It takes the place of blood in their veins and they'll let nothing come between them and their riches."

"Yeah," Ed said, nodding his head. "You've about got that summed up right. I think that what Lieutenant Ritchey is saying is that Cal is like some god here in Minden. He's handed out cash by the barrel and he's done more favors than a king. I can't see him indicted for anything, even if he killed his wife in cold blood."

"Yeah," Colin returned. "I know we've got our work cut out for us—if he's guilty and we can find out where he's coming from and where he's headed. Luxor and Lansing are tied in with the mob and Luxor is a way up the line.

"I can't stress too much to be careful. You don't come in contact with the depravity and danger we do, not to mention the bureaucracy. You're often just trying to do your job and we're trying to cover our behinds."

Back in her office, Danielle had hardly settled down when Jon sprawled in a chair near her desk. She told him how the morning had gone. "Looks like this could be something big," he said. Then with a light knock, florist Rhea Smith came in loaded with a huge crystal vase of peonies.

Danielle exclaimed delightedly, "How really beautiful." She stood up, as did Jon, and said, "Morning, Rhea."

"Good morning to both of you. You've certainly got your self an admirer, Dani. I was told to buy a crystal vase and exactly what kind of peonies to put in it—two dozen. The gentleman said they had to be beautiful like the lady they were going to. Whit Steele is a class act all the way."

"Oh," Danielle murmured. "He really is kind."

"I'd say he's *besotted*," Jon drawled, grinned.

Danielle blushed hotly to cover her embarrassment over the grand gesture. "Have some cinnamon rolls from Francesca's kitchen," she told Rhea.

Rhea grimaced. "Well, Lord knows I don't need an extra inch on my hips, but if Jon's wife made them, I won't even try to resist." She selected a bun and a napkin from the table and bit into it. She turned to Jon. "Tell Francesca if she ever wants to go commercial, mine will be the first request. I've got to run now. Mother's Day orders are fast and furious."

When Rhea had left, Jon turned to Danielle. "Things seem to be heating up," he said. Danielle went to the flowers, touched them. The colors ranged from pale pink to rose, then cerise. She bent to enjoy the delightful fragrance.

"He's like that," she said softly. "He brought me a dozen roses and a dozen gardenias the first day I met him. He's quite extravagant."

"He can afford it," Jon chuckled, then his face got somber. "You're good for him. We've been really worried about Whit. He's one tough hombre but once I was afraid we'd lose him; he was that shattered and it hasn't been too long ago. He slowly began to pick up the pieces, but he's been sad. Whit's a great guy. We were best friends at Howard and we've been best friends ever since. Be kind to him. Do you think he could grow on you?" For a few moments he was silent, then, "He seems happier since he's met you. He calls me from New York from time to time. In a few more years he's going to be a superstar."

"I think you're right. He calls me too, almost daily." She sat down. "As for whether he could grow on me, as you put it, it scares me how much I already like him. I could fall, but I'm worried about *him*. He needs to go into any relationship very slowly, don't you think?"

"Yes, I do. Whit gave his marriage his all and it tore him up when Willo just walked away with another man."

"It shows when he talks about her. What's happened to her?"

"I don't know. Her husband has a business in the Caribbean. They have homes in D.C. and in Trinidad. I suppose the kid's a toddler now. She was pregnant by the man she later married after she and Whit broke up."

Danielle shook her head. "He's talked a lot about it. I just listen—and hurt for him."

"So you like my buddy—a lot."

"Yes."

They were talking of other things when her phone rang. Danielle answered, "Lieutenant Ritchey." The voice on the line was soft, hushed, deeply accented.

"Danielle Ritchey?"

"Yes."

"I am Ada Appiah."

"Yes? How may I help you?"

"I saw a picture in the paper a few days ago. I couldn't decide at first whether to call, but I decided to. The man in the photo resembles my uncle, Cedric Appiah, my father's brother. The family has not heard from him in many months and we have wondered where he is. You said if anyone could identify him to call you. . . ."

"Yes. Thank you so much for calling. Where are you calling from?"

The woman hesitated. "Baltimore."

"That's wonderful. Could you arrange to meet me at the morgue sometime soon?"

"I can meet you as soon as you wish. Today. Any time you wish. I want to know, even if I did wait to call you."

"Would two o'clock this afternoon be okay with you?"

"Yes. That would be fine."

Danielle gave the woman directions to the morgue and murmured, "Thank you again for calling."

Hanging up, she formed her hands into a pyramid atop her desk and discussed the conversation with Jon.

"What do you think?" she asked him.

"If she's foreign, it would explain the kente cloth, the money. If the party is cooperative, we may find out lots more. Dani, you're off to a good start, but I have a hunch this will probably wind up a cold case. If the mob *is* in on this via Manny Luxor and Buck Lansing, they know how to kill and get away with it. Bigger, better police forces than ours have been foiled by them."

"You're right. Look, I'm going to meet her at two. Ada

Appiah. There's a lot to learn. It piques my interest to know how a man came all this way only to wind up under a giant oak—dead."

"Mine too. Let's hope we can solve this one."

They talked at length about Cal Catlett. "He'd be hell to pull in," Jon said. "This community loves him, although I think he's a lot rougher than he appears on the surface."

"He makes my flesh crawl. He's got a mistress, Annie, and Irene, his wife, but he looks at other women like a hungry dog or a sultan overseeing his harem. I don't like him, Jon. Irene's bruises are well known and he doesn't seem to care. She's a sweetheart, but she's got problems—masochistic ones, I think. Once, when he was away and I stopped by, her neck and arms were bruised and I asked her about it. She said he had fits of rage from time to time, but he never really hurt her. She kind of smiled and said, as she looked around that magnificent living room, 'I'm a lucky woman to have all this.' Can you imagine? But she also seemed very ashamed."

"It takes all kinds. Cal's got the best lawyers going in D.C. I doubt we could get any info from him. Let's keep trying to think of something to haul him in for and we'll concentrate on Manny and Buck. They're easy enough. When we *see* them, we know some law has likely been broken."

Ada Appiah turned out to be a small, very dark brown woman who carried herself with poise and dignity. She was tastefully dressed. Her hand shook as Danielle extended hers. The woman's hand felt cold in Danielle's firm handshake.

An assistant greeted them and took them to a short wall of drawers that held dead bodies—in police jargon, "the meat rack." *Corpses,* Danielle thought, *give me a hundred murdered corpses and I'll give you a hundred sad, sad stories.* She thought then of a Chinese town ruled by women in which there were no divorces, no word for war, *no murders.* How did *this* come to be her life? The answer, of course, was her beloved mother, Mona. Mona had lain in one of these drawers ten years ago—a cold case now.

Ada said something when the drawer was opened. "I'm sorry," Danielle told her, "I didn't hear you."

"I just said his name—Cedric Appiah." When the head of the corpse was uncovered, she stared at it a long time. "It is my uncle," she said. "It *is* my uncle."

She cried then and Danielle held her. The assistant handed Danielle a box of Kleenex and she took out a couple and gave them to Ada. Then, abruptly getting hold of herself, the woman stopped crying and closed her eyes as she stood there. "He was my favorite uncle, but he went away to the largest city in Zenia. . . ."

"You are Zenian?"

"Yes. My father is a farmer, an honorable farmer, but we were all so proud of my uncle when he finished at the university and became a police inspector. Things were wonderful for us once, but a new government came in and we were the enemies. My uncle often spoke of coming to America and sending for us. Instead, after years of waiting, I came last year as a person who would be killed as a political enemy. Most of my family were put to death. My uncle disappeared and we always wondered." And she added softly, "Now I know. He was trying to fulfill his dream."

"I'm so sorry. I want you to know that we will do everything possible to find who did this and punish them."

"It will not bring him back. Nothing will bring him back, and I have seen too much revenge and punishment."

Very gently Danielle said, "We have to punish them to keep them from doing this to others."

"I know. I was only speaking from the heart, not just about what is right. Of course you have to apprehend whoever did this. You are a detective and you are very kind."

They sat in the waiting room then and Ada answered many questions before she asked, "Do you think they will let me stay in this country?"

Danielle asked specifically what steps she had taken to come and it seemed she was well connected. Danielle told her she had every chance of staying and the woman seemed relieved.

"If only I could have helped him," Ada murmured. "He was my favorite uncle. I loved him so much. He wore a wonderful ring."

"Can you describe it?"

The woman described the ring in minute detail, including the engraved initials.

Reaching into her purse, Danielle extracted an evidence bag with a heavy gold ring set with small diamonds.

"Oh!" the woman exclaimed. "That is his ring my grandfather gave him when he finished the university."

Ada turned the ring, held it. "In my heart," she said, "I had a little doubt, only a little. Now I *know* it is him." She clasped her hands in front of her and said quietly, "Rest in peace."

ELEVEN

Three weeks later

Cal Catlett paced his study like a mountain lion before he roared, "Irene!" and his tiny wife came scurrying into the room.

"Yes, honey," she soothed him.

He cocked his head to one side as he studied her. "Don't 'honey' me. What the hell are you up to? Never mind, I know."

"What do you mean?"

Cal put his big hands behind his back and studied her. "I'm going on a little trip to New York tomorrow. Be gone a week. Maybe more. Think I don't know you can't wait to get over to my sister Edith's house and flirt with her dirt-poor stepson, Dave? Think I don't have your number?"

Irene sighed. She was such a small woman and he was such a large man, in countenance as well as body. Some bitterness came through as she defended herself. "I wouldn't cheat on you, Cal. I've got too much pride. Dave doesn't stay long after I come in."

"If Edith wasn't my sister, I'd stop the visits. Lord knows, you don't do much of anything else around here. Got somebody to clean your house. . . ."

"I do a lot of the cooking."

"Such as it is."

"I cook good food, Cal, and you know it." Her dander was up.

"Get away from Dave. How do I know you're not boinking him?"

At first, Irene didn't get the term, then she did and her pale yellow, calla-lily-rose skin reddened. "Edith is your *sister*," she said indignantly. "Do you think she would let something like that go on?"

Cal's eyes were steely on her. "Sister, my behind. Edith's always been jealous of what I've got. She lucked out and married a man with a little something, but he was never in my league. And he died young. Didn't have sense enough to live a long time like I'm going to do. And she was stuck with raising a kid that wasn't hers."

"She and Dave love each other. She and her husband loved each other."

Cal's laugh was harsh, short. "Now you're talking about *love,* a word idiots love to bandy about. You sure you ain't fooling around with Dave?"

"No," Irene said explosively. "I wouldn't. *He* wouldn't. . . And Edith sure wouldn't let us betray you in her house."

"You could go off in the woods somewhere. A motel maybe. It'd have to be cheap if he had to pay for it. For God's sake, Reeny, you gonna play the slut, get yourself a man who's got some money. That way he could lessen my burden. You spend enough of *my* money."

Irene was silent. It was true about the money. He was very lenient where money was concerned. He'd come in and she'd be sitting quietly or lying down and he would shower her with tens and twenties. "Pick them up," he'd always say. "They're yours. More where that came from. You lucked out. You didn't marry a poor man. I'm *rich!*" She never picked up the money. He did, laughing.

Now his wife looked at him obliquely, still silent.

"Tired of defending yourself? Maybe I ought to get you a chastity belt and no one but me would have the key. Think old Dave'd like that?"

"Don't tease, Cal," she implored him. "I don't deserve it.

I've been a good and faithful wife to you for fifteen years. You divorced your first wife to marry me, so you must have loved me some."

"Huh," he snorted. "I was a young fool. I didn't know then that women are all the same—strumpets."

Irene indignantly decided to defend herself further. "I'm a churchgoing, God-fearing woman, Cal, and I've been faithful to you every minute I've been with you." But it washed into her mind that she had long given up loving Cal and she did love Dave. She couldn't help it. *Was that why I let him abuse me?* Taking her punishment because she couldn't love him because he treated her so shabbily.

"Honey," she said softly, "I just came to tell you lunch is almost ready. I fixed the lamb chops and new buttered potatoes the way you like."

He mocked her soft voice harshly, then said, "I'm not sure I want lunch. Talking about old Dave has turned me on. Think we got time for a quick rocking?"

Irene felt her heart plummet to her shoes. It was becoming harder and harder for her to respond to him. Dave's face always rose before her. She had to make a decision and soon. More and more she felt that Dave was whom she deserved, whom she had to have.

"Well—" he prompted her.

"I guess it's all right if that's what you want," she said forlornly.

"Damned enthusiastic, aren't you?" he barked.

"It's just lunch will be overcooked or cold . . ."

"We got good warmers on that two-thousand-dollar special stove. What you say, Reeny? Be good to your only husband. Dave can wait."

Tears filled Irene's eyes and she felt so frustrated she could scream. She came up to his shoulder and he reached down and squeezed one breast, then the other. His touch was as hard, as punishing as the man.

"I have to put the food on the warmer," she said.

"No," he cackled. "What's a wife for but to give a man what he wants, *when* he wants it? Let the damned food ruin. It's not like we don't have plenty more."

"I used the last of the lamb chops." She was fighting for time, hoping she could stave him off.

"You can order in or go and get more. Come on, Reeny. I don't have all day. You don't want me, plenty of others do. Annie'd lie down and die for me."

Irene nearly choked. How dare he throw his girlfriend, his *woman,* up to her? Anger rose in her like wildfire, then she cooled. It wasn't like it was the first time. Annie Lusk was her rival in every way. Cal had a wife and a mistress, something all Minden and the countryside knew, and he was still very much Mr. *Rich* Cal Catlett. He was benevolent and always paid attention to people's needs, even if he didn't really care. And he had gotten more than one young son out of trouble, paid more than a few tuition bills. That he had done his share of hornswoggling and hurting wasn't talked about so much.

The two hundred prime acres Cal's estate sat on had been stolen from his arch rival's widow. Cal had courted her before he married his first wife. He was a young man and she had been a middle-aged woman who believed him when he said he loved her. She had signed over most of her worldly goods, believing he would marry her and then turned his back on her. She had died, heartbroken and he had gone on—to live the good life.

He reached out and caught his wife by her shoulders and she flinched. *Oh, dear God,* she thought, *not now.* She dreaded this and knew no way around it save to reach up to him and hug him. Maybe this would deflect what she knew he was going to do. He took her arms from around his neck and held her shoulders. Then he shook her violently.

"I just want to let you know your place," he said as he shook her. When he paused a moment, she begged, "Cal, please. I'm a little woman and you're such a big man. It takes my breath when you shake me."

His face looked evil to her then. "Just think," he gloated. "People shake babies and little children to death. To *death,* Reeny. I could kill you. Make your heart stop and even a doctor would think you'd had a heart attack. Hey, maybe . . ." His eyes sparked evil flashes as he considered his movements. He let her go for a moment.

"Think about it, Reeny. If you'd come to me like you wanted me, I wouldn't shake you."

Why am I arguing? The die was cast. At times, he *had* shaken her after they had been to bed because she hadn't been ardent enough.

"Honey, please," she pleaded in a last attempt to protect herself.

He caught her shoulders then in a maelstrom of shaking. Fast and furious. Tears streamed down her face. Would he kill her one day? He was threatening more often. Breathlessly, he said, "I'll be thinking about you and Dave Emlen while I'm gone. . . ." He licked his lips and didn't finish.

Something got into her then. "I don't say a thing about you and Annie."

"Because I'm a man and men got a right to the world's women. That's the world over. Ask your precious preacher. For all I know, you're shacking up with him too."

"Cal, don't," she begged again. "I've been faithful. I respect myself and I respect you."

"Yeah, that's what they all say. And don't talk to me about Annie. She's special to me the way you'll never be. Annie's an armful of golden tobacco leaves and you're just a pinch of snuff."

"You used to say you loved me."

"I was a fool, I told you. Now shut up."

He drew her to him roughly then, shaking and shaking until she thought she wouldn't be able to get her breath. Tears streamed down her face and it seemed like eons of time fled by. She was choking on her tears and the mucus in her throat and nostrils when he stopped abruptly, grinning.

Then he did something he did from time to time. He caught her arms in a vise, gripping them until she cried out in pain. In the midst of all that torment, she thought, *It is nearing summer and I will have to wear long sleeves.*

Strangling on her own body fluids, she felt herself beginning to pass out before he let her go and she stumbled. He picked her up then, grinning like a fiend.

"You can't fool me," he told her. "You like the rough stuff. Now, tell me it turns you on."

She got the strength from somewhere to sob. "No, Cal. It *doesn't* turn me on. You can't believe that. I hate it."

Had she really talked to him that way? She couldn't believe her own ears.

Putting her down, he struck her across the face with the back of his hand, bringing blood from her nose. Her blood looked good to him. Served her right for being so damned smart.

He looked at his watch. "Wash up," he ordered, "and meet me in our bedroom in no more than ten minutes."

Irene thought of running, hiding. Nothing Cal had held much appeal to her now. It was as if he *knew* how she felt about Dave. Maybe she deserved what she got. A man wanted his wife to belong solely to him even if he didn't belong solely to her.

In the bathroom down the hall from the study, she refused to look at herself in the mirror. He kept a gun in his top sideboard drawer in the study. She could kill him, but she thought, *Why now?* It was far from the first time, but this time had been more savage than any she could remember. She and Dave were innocent; they would not betray marriage vows, unlike Cal, who thought the world's women belonged to him.

She stanched the flow of blood with a towel and cold water and looked at the way it had dribbled onto her pale blue blouse.

In the master bedroom she shared with Cal, he lay in his undershorts. He didn't like being or feeling naked. She stripped to her bra and panties, which was how he liked her, and got into bed. He was all over her, pushing himself roughly into her before she could secrete sufficient moisture and she cried out. The friction was awful.

Inside her tight and dry labia and inner sanctum, he shoved relentlessly. "Move, woman, move!" he commanded and she strove mightily to comply.

"Give me a little time to get wet."

"I don't have time. I'm ready to go when I'm ready to go."

Lying beneath him she wondered when it would be over. She knew then that she *would* leave him. Or kill him. It was just a matter of *when*.

TWELVE

In New York City, the weather had turned nasty. For the past few minutes rivulets of rain had sloshed about in a deluge.

In midtown Manhattan Cal Catlett, Manny Luxor, and Buck Lansing lounged about Cal's luxurious suite. Cal picked bits of the delectable chicken dinner from his teeth. Eating good food always left him at peace with the world. He cleared the table of its good plastic plates. Now he turned to Manny.

"You enjoy the dinner?"

"Loved it," Manny growled. "You find the damnedest places. Best food. It's raining; I didn't want to go outside."

"Me neither," Buck chimed in. "Sometimes I think I hate rain, especially too much of it, which we've had."

Manny shrugged. "Don't question God."

Cal laughed. "Sounds funny, you talking about God. I didn't know you had a religious streak."

Manny bristled. "My mama raised me in the church. I just got sidelined somehow." He looked wistful. "Maybe I'll go back one day when I get really old."

Buck laughed. "Boss, I think you picked the wrong line of work to live a long life."

Manny looked at him sharply. "Don't talk like a jackass. I know my way around. I plan to *be* here."

Squabbles between Manny and Buck always amused Cal. He likened them to an old bulldog and a young terrier. Sometimes he couldn't decide if they loved or hated each other.

One thing was certain; Manny always got the upper hand. He was the boss and he never let Buck forget it.

Putting the heavy paper plates and the eating utensils in the large trash bag, Cal got on the phone and asked that the trash be picked up.

Manny looked around at the elegant cherry-wood furniture and the good art on the walls, the figurines, and the beautifully silvered mirrors.

"You got taste, Catlett," he growled.

Cal walked into the large living area and sat on the sofa. Manny and Buck came and sat near him. Cal lit a long, slender cigar and puffed on it for a few minutes before he spoke. "You checked out the Bronx and Marmion Avenue?" he asked Manny.

"Yeah. Everything's straight. A shipment of illegals will come in next week. They'll only stay overnight at our safe house on Marmion Street. One of your big rigs will pack all twenty to thirty of them in and drive them down to Minden and Annie's house. We've got all their papers in order. Green cards. Permanent resident cards. Damn, but I've gotten good at this kind of crap."

Cal looked at him shrewdly. "Don't call it 'crap,' Manny. It's making us all rich."

"I like the gambling and nightclub end of it better," Manny said. "How much time do we catch if we get caught with this?"

"Snowball's chance in hell of getting caught," Cal scoffed. "Annie's a God-fearing, churchgoing woman and her only sin is me. The money she shovels out to her church assures her forgiveness. Who'd ever think about her and illegal aliens? She won't even hire them in her restaurant." He smoked and blew small rings for a few minutes.

"Yeah," Manny said thoughtfully, "the major thing in our favor is INS is so damned busy. They're taxed to the gills."

"Good old Immigration and Naturalization Service, I-N-S, is making it real easy for us." Buck looked to Manny for approval and got it.

"Course," Cal said, "I bought the house for Annie with this in mind. We've been running it now for thirteen and a half years. Everything's always gone like fine silk." He knocked on the wooden table beside him. "Of course, we've played it slow, haven't gotten too greedy, and we've gotten filthy rich."

"Hell," Manny groused, "you've got a factory making you rich. I don't know why you came in on this. I didn't expect you to."

"Fooled you. Fact is I like excitement. Danger. I like putting it over on the law. Jackasses."

"Yeah," Manny said. "The other side's rolling in their kind of glory, and we're rolling in ours. Irene doing okay, Cal? She know about this?"

Cal looked at him a long while. "That's a fool's question, Manny. She don't know nothing. Never will. She's my wife, not my business partner."

Manny licked his lips, a bit nettled; he'd only asked. "I saw Irene in the park," he said. "She was talking to a good-looking guy younger than us. Black hair. Chocolate skin. Good-looking guy. They sat down on the bench next to my bench. I hid behind my newspaper. We was all there a long time."

Cal hated discussing personal business, but he had to ask, "Did you hear anything they talked about?"

"No-o-o, can't say I did. They was sitting fairly close. Seemed right comfortable with each other. That description fit anybody you know?"

"Yeah," Cal said shortly. Then again, "Yeah. Manny, how hard is it to contract out a clown?"

Manny grinned. So he had hit a nerve. Good old Irene. Like everybody else he had seen the bruises. He hadn't thought she was the kind of woman to play around. He thought a long moment before he said, "You got somebody you want whacked?"

"Maybe."

"The way I do it, it'll cost you ten thou and no one will ever be the wiser. When?"

"Don't press it. It just crossed my mind."

"Well, I like working with you, so I'll do the extras you want. Old Buck here would do it in a heartbeat." He raised quizzical eyebrows at Buck.

"Sure thing, Cal," Buck said. "You let me know who and when, and I'll decide how."

Manny was immediately ruffled. "I beg your freaking pardon," he told Buck. "Last I heard, *I* make the decisions as to *how*."

Buck sat forward. "No harm meant, boss. You make *all* the decisions. I'm just a pissant and you're the whole enchilada."

Cal smiled at the mixed metaphors. He wondered how Buck stood the scorn Manny sometimes heaped on him. Talk about keeping a man in his place.

"I talked with one of our top guys here in New York," Manny said. "He told me to be careful. This is a prize shipment. All professionals, paying fifteen thou a head for first-class treatment and edging into a strange land. Doctors, lawyers, university professors . . ."

Cal looked at him thoughtfully. "Last time we got half criminals and there was trouble. I'm sure you remember the guy you had to off."

"Yeaah. That was a helluva thing," Manny said. "He didn't have the rest of the money he owed and he got nasty. When we threatened to hold him, he said in Africa he had been a policeman and the police here would be sympathetic. Dude spoke good English. Too bad Buck here had to take him out. He was going to run to the police."

Cal looked at him with amusement. "You're telling me the story, Manny, like I wasn't there. I don't need to hear it again. Things've been quiet. Likely as not, nobody will ever know who he is."

"Well, I don't put much past that good-looking detective broad. She's a whiz."

"She can't do it on her own," Cal shot back. "Hell, law enforcement these days is on a budget and that's why we've got them coming and going. We've got plenty of money to run our end. We could be making over twice as much money as we make."

"Let's keep the numbers low," Manny said. "We get too greedy and we're liable to get caught with our pants down. This way, we finesse it. We're rolling. You guys want to take in a movie? I hear there's some great porn flicks off Broadway."

"Count me out," Buck said quickly. "I hate rain, remember? Only time I go out in the rain is when I'm starving."

"And when *I* say go." Manny shot him a furious glance.

Buck caught himself with a sickly grin. "Aw, boss, you know what I mean."

"Know what I'd like?" Cal asked the two men.

"I know what I'd like," Manny said. "Wine, women, and song. Let's order a few bottles and a few women and anticipate heaven. Forget the songs. Music don't mean much to me."

"None of that's what I'm talking about," Cal said. "That can come later. How about a crap game?"

Manny howled with laughter. "A *crap* game. Hell, craps is for guys who can only count to twelve."

Nonplussed, Cal said, "You choose your games; I'll choose mine. You two on?"

To mollify him, the two men agreed, with Buck throwing in, "I used to be a great crapshooter."

"Sure," Manny shot him down again. "Remember what I said about counting to twelve? Sometimes I think your mind stops at eleven."

Buck grinned sheepishly. "Aw, boss, everything's okay."

"It *better* be." As always, Manny had had the last word. "I got no damned dice."

"I've got a pretty pair. Pure ivory," Cal said and went to his bedroom bureau drawer to get the pair of dice.

Squatting on the living area floor, the three men hunkered down in their shirtsleeves. "Roll the bones," Cal called out.

Manny led off with a twelve and was out. "Damn," he complained. "Sure ain't my lucky day. Well, I'll give it time."

Cracking his knuckles, Buck was next. A pair of sixes. Twelve. "What the hell?" he fussed. "These damned dice loaded? Just kidding."

"Blame it on the dice," Cal came back genially. "I got better things to do with my time than load dice." He picked up the pure ivory dice and rolled them. A beautiful seven came up.

"You lucky stiff," Buck chortled. "But I'll get you."

They shot dice in desultory fashion then. His one win had left Cal sated and it was a high-stakes game. He hated to lose. Three games and the dice had lost their luster.

"Tell you want," Cal said. "The game was my idea. I won once and I'm satisfied. How about the wine and the women? What're you boys drinking?"

"Rum all the way for me," Buck said, feeling important in his choice. "Haitian gold if they've got it."

"Got you. And you, Manny?"

"As if you didn't know. Scotch and quarts of orange juice to drown it in. Might as well stay healthy while I'm drunk."

When Cal had placed the order, the men lolled about on the couches and Buck sat in a chair.

"Let me place a call for the broads," Manny bragged. "Three? Or four?"

"I don't feel like sharing," Cal groused. "Make mine a single. And send me a tall, leggy one with big bosoms. No little women."

Manny looked up with surprise, thinking, *Hell, the guy's wife is little. What axe is he grinding?* He licked his lips as he told Cal, "This is a night you'll never forget."

But Cal was lonesome. Annie had grown on him and sometimes he wanted her badly. He longed for her now. He spent nights with her and dared Irene to say anything about it. Hell, he was happy. Annie was happy. And Irene didn't matter. Dead men from Africa didn't matter either. He'd had his chance and blown it.

THIRTEEN

Dressed in stonewashed blue jeans and a cherry-red Ralph Lauren shirt, Danielle walked swiftly up the wide hallway of the station house from Jon's office to hers.

Jon was there and nodded toward the three other people seated around a big table in the room: Ed, Wink, Matt, and Adrienne. All of them, including Danielle and Jon, knew all the crime jobs well and interchanged their duties.

"I just wondered if you had any new ideas and I wanted to check with you all together," Jon said. "What have any of you gotten regarding the DNA?"

Danielle sat down in the chair beside Ed, who smiled at her.

"Well," Danielle began, "some bits of reports from the DNA have straggled in. We still have more to go. There's nothing we've been able to match it with. They've promised to have it all to us within the next two weeks. Jon, as you know, this is a mean one. This cadaver was wearing a thousand-dollar ring and he had two thousand dollars taped to his chest. It wasn't robbery, I don't think, but his wallet *is* missing. People aren't so stupid they don't recognize the value of an expensive ring.

"He's foreign. It could well be some kind of political murder. You know his background. . . ."

She broke off frowning, causing Jon to ask, "What's wrong?"

She drew a deep breath. "Something hit me a little while back with some force. Jon, I'm going to visit Cal's wife sometime when he's out of town. I called and she said he's out of town but he's due back tomorrow. And I'm going to visit Annie Lusk. I called her and she made me welcome to visit. So did Cal's wife."

"Want me to go with you?" Ed asked.

Danielle shook her head. "No. Adrienne perhaps, but no, I think I'll learn more if I go alone."

"You're probably right," Adrienne said.

Danielle loved her homicide team and they worked superbly together. Led by her, they were more a family than a team. People spoke of crime families, Danielle thought. They were a police family.

"I've been thinking," Adrienne, the crime analyst, said slowly, "if there is an illegal alien smuggling ring headquartered or simply operating in Minden, I think they'd need a good-sized house. Plenty of those around, but they'd need a leader. Has anybody noticed that Manny Luxor and Buck Lansing are around more these days?

"I spoke with Manny one day," Adrienne continued. "I mentioned that he was here often and he gave me what might be true and what might be a cock-and-bull story about getting the lay of the land to build a nightclub and hotel complex."

"You think he's lying?" Jon asked.

Adrienne pursed her lips. "He could be telling the truth. He's got great mob connections so he'd have the backing. He said he's looking for land and did I know of anyone who's got a good bit of it."

"Did he seem evasive at all?" Jon asked.

"No. Completely forthcoming. He might have been a minister chatting with one of his flock."

"Well, he's no minister," Ed growled. "Manny Luxor is a rough one and don't you forget it."

Wink had been silent for a moment. "Manny's been around a long time. He first came into town a little over thirteen years ago. He and Buck have land here and he owns that small garage and repair shop. Only that's too small potatoes for a bigwig like Manny, but it gives him a respectable facade."

Danielle grimaced. "Buck passes as a mechanic running the shop. They do a good business, but I think we'd all make bank that isn't all they do."

They talked then about other aspects of the case, the frustrating lack of fingerprints, the fact that the DNA report that had been forwarded held so little usable information. "It looks," Jon said, "as if we're going to have a cold case on our hands before the heat dies down."

"One other thing," Danielle said, "the man's niece has called and wants to know if she can get the ring and the money. I told her the evidence has to stay with us awhile—DNA samples and fingerprints—but we could release the body for burial."

"He must have had money to have a ring like that. You said the niece said he was a police inspector?" Ed asked thoughtfully.

"Yes," Danielle answered.

Wink lumbered up. "Thank God we've got time to spend on this case. Of course, money's always in short supply. I was going over to Howard University Library to check out Zenia and what their political situation is. There and to the embassy, where you can be sure we'll get no good info on political strife. The more I think about it, the more I feel it's a political hit—a man left dead under a tree in plain view. Think about it. . . ."

"I have," Jon said. "It's altogether a possibility." He sighed. "But is there any significance that it happened here in Minden?"

"Let's not forget Colin Matthews and the INS," Danielle said. "We got multicultural crime in this country, too. There may be a direct link running illegal aliens stretching from Africa to Minden and other larger and smaller cities."

Jon rocked the upper part of his body. "Excedrin headache number fifty."

* * *

By then it was twelve-thirty. Danielle planned to hold off going to get lunch for a few minutes until she checked her cell phone messages. There was only one. "Dani, please call me. It's Whit."

She dialed and his phone rang only twice before he picked it up.

"You wanted me to call you?"

"Dani! Thanks for getting back to me so fast. I've got a proposition for you."

"A *decent* proposition," she teased him.

"First rate. How's your case coming?"

"It's stalled. It's like someone dropped this man out of a helicopter and someone else murdered and sprawled him under the tree. Whit, we're stymied."

"No leads, huh?"

She told him about the niece, the ring. "I thought that was an expensive ring," he said. "So, it wasn't robbery."

"We think it may be political, but it may be a robbery. His wallet was missing."

"If anybody can solve it, you can. You're the best."

"Thank you. Now what's your proposition?"

"I was going to ask if you could come up for a couple or three days and then we could go back together. You could take a limousine up if you want to. That way you won't have the airport hassle."

A limousine? She laughed. "You make great propositions, Mr. Steele. I'm tempted, but, Whit, I just can't. When are you coming back?"

"Sometime next week since you can't come up. I was coming back sooner."

"How did the recording sessions go?"

"Like magic. I think you're good for me, Dani. I don't think I've ever sung like this before. I cut three singles and began my album to be released this winter. I have to come back in fall or winter to finish it, but I'm pleased with what I've done. Thank you."

"For what?"

"For being you." They were companionably silent for long moments before he said, "Oh, listen, I saw some people you know in a great restaurant in midtown Manhattan—Gina's."

"Oh?"

"Yeah. The two men you spoke with or who spoke to you in Annie's Place."

"Two men? Oh, you mean Manny Luxor and Buck Lansing?"

"Yes, those are their names. They were drinking a lot and talking a lot with a tall, dark red-haired man."

She thought a minute. "Cal Catlett."

"I think he's the one." You've mentioned him and one day when I was with Jon, he came up and began talking. Jon introduced me. Cal was drinking heavily when I saw him in New York. They all were."

"Hm-m-m," Danielle said. "I never thought the three were all that close. This is *very* interesting, Whit. Could I offer you a job? You're perceptive, on the *qui vive* . . ."

"Plus, I'm nuts about police work." He laughed, then added, "and police detectives, especially one in particular."

"I miss you," she said suddenly. It simply burst from her.

"Not the way I miss you. Dani, we're going to have to make some tracks when I come back. I'm not going to cower in my boots waiting to heal. I want us all the way into paradise, not half in, half out."

The passion in his voice took her breath away. Where was he leading? Wherever it was, she was tempted to go. "Come back in a hurry," she said. "Sprout wings and fly back. Now, I'm being silly."

"However you're being, I love it."

There was a light knock and Ed stood at the threshold with his girlfriend, Shelley. He began to dart back, saying, "Oh, sorry," pulling Shelley with him.

"Bye, love," Danielle said throatily. "I've got company."

Whit kissed her with a soft smack over the phone and hung up.

"Come back," she called to Ed and Shelley, who came back into the room.

"Never let me interrupt love and romance," Ed said.

"Ed!" Shelley remonstrated.

"Oh," Ed laughed, "Dani and I go way back. We can needle when we please."

An attractive woman ten years younger than Ed, Shelley wanted to get married, Danielle knew. A woman with short-cropped black hair, clear tea-brown coloring, and a good personality, anyone would have wanted to marry her. She had chosen Ed and stuck to him.

"I want you to talk to your cohort here," Shelley said to Danielle.

"If I can. He's not the world's best listener."

"I'm raking him over the coals because he went to New York without me. I'm still pouting."

"You grieve too long, toots," Ed razzed her.

"When did he abandon you?" Danielle asked. "Now, don't bring me into something that's not my business."

As if she hadn't protested, Shelley said, "The night you all found the man murdered. I wanted to go. He'd promised me a night out. We were going up on Amtrak and see a show and come back the same night."

Danielle's breath caught. She was about to say that Ed was in D.C. that night, but it was plain it was going to cause a fight. "Shame on you, Ed Ware," she said dryly. "You've got a good woman here. Take care of her."

"Yes, ma'am," Ed growled. He turned to Shelley. "Now, tattletale, you've shot your arrow, let's go."

Shelley flirted with him. "What if I want to stay and talk with Danielle? What if I've got other tales to tell?" She smiled prettily.

"You do that and I'll consider doing you in. I haven't been a girlfriend beater, but I could learn to like it."

Shelley turned a piquant face to Danielle. "Hear that threat? You'll be my best witness."

Danielle laughed. "Any time at all."

Danielle slipped off her pumps and wriggled her toes under the desk when the secretary announced over her intercom that Julian and Daphne were there to see her.

Daphne carried a big brown bag and Julian carried a smaller white bag.

"We hope you haven't eaten," Julian said. "We can't stay long. Daphne's job gets a little crazy around this time of day, but we wanted to do this."

Julian took a wide-mouth red thermos bottle from the bag and set it on her table. Daphne took a white-wrapped submarine sandwich from the bag she carried.

"We thought we'd fix it so you don't have to cook for a couple of days." In the thermos was a rich-with-cream New England clam chowder with oyster crackers in a waxed bag. Danielle licked her lips. "Oh, my."

She opened the wrapped submarine sandwich and oohed and aahed over the sandwich of ham and turkey, thin-sliced onions, and tomatoes. There was also a carton of salad greens and luscious-looking dressing.

"If I eat this, I'm going to die from sheer gluttony," Danielle said.

"Put a doggy bag in the fridge," Daphne said.

"I'll need two doggy bags. Where did you two hook up?"

Julian looked pleased. "Well, I went by the school to shoot the breeze with Daffy and we both thought about you around the same time. We know how hard you're working and we wanted to do something to help."

Danielle hugged and kissed each one, saying, "Bless you both." Then she grinned impishly as she said, "Looks like you two might be getting there." Julian flushed and ran a finger inside his collar while Daphne glowed.

"We love you," Daphne said. "This is just one way of showing it."

"And I love you both. Thank you." Her voice went fragile and she was reminded of Mona and Julian and the love they had all shared.

JULY 2000
A DREAM DEVELOPS

FOURTEEN

Whit was back from New York!

Danielle surveyed her freshly cleaned kitchen and sighed. Lord, how she had missed him. She waited in her ragged bottomed light blue denim shorts and her bare-midriff lavender knitted top for him to come. He had called earlier.

She felt she could have flown to the door when her chimes rang, but she made herself slow down. Carrying bags, he was all smiles. Suddenly, she was bashful as she took the bags, saying, "You're way too generous. You spoil me."

He grinned. "It's not nearly what I'd like to do. Stop protesting. Enjoy the loot. You deserve much more."

She wasn't going to hide her feelings. "I've missed you so much," she said.

He followed her into the dining room where she put the packages on the table. He looked pleased that she'd missed him. "That goes double for me," he told her.

The big bag held a giant loaded pizza. Taking the box out and opening it, she exclaimed, "My favorite!"

"Pure dumb luck. Open the little package."

With faintly trembling, anxious fingers, she undid the gold-foil-wrapped package with its crisp, cream-colored organdie bow and small spray of fresh flowers, saying, "It's almost too pretty to unwrap."

There was a black leather ring box inside a small white cardboard box. As she held it, she wondered what it was. Snapping it open, she gasped, "How beautiful!" A large perfect, oval, deep green jade stone banded by heavy shining gold with several small diamonds winked up at her.

Throwing her arms around his neck, she kissed him. Neither had meant for the kiss to go so deep, but each was starved for the other. Kicking off her shoes, Danielle stood on top of his shoes, giggling. The gesture sent wildfire racing along his veins and he crushed her to him. For long moments they clung, bodies blazing. He gathered the honey from her mouth before her tongue searched and found the hidden honey from his mouth. Half fainting, she whispered, "Whit. Oh, Whit."

Grasping her shoulder, he held her tightly a little distance from him. "Never do that," he said, "unless you're ready for action."

"Do what?"

"Stand on top of my feet. Dani, you don't know your own power. I'm putting an end to this. We're not ready to take it further."

To her surprise, she retorted, "You speak for yourself."

He took her face in his hands. "I said I'd never push you and I won't. Soon, but not now." And he groaned aloud, his loins, his whole body hurting with wanting her. "I dreamed about you last night. I dream about you all the time."

"What did you dream?" She slipped out of his arms and stood near him.

He chuckled shortly. "Want me to be honest?"

"Yes, I do."

"That those luscious legs were wrapped around me. That we were a wild tangle of arms and legs and bodies. Ah, Dani, I don't want to embarrass you."

"You don't embarrass me." She shook her head, remembering the bloody dream she'd had of Whit, wondering now what on earth it meant, and shuddering a bit. She hadn't dreamed it lately, but it was a special dream. She knew that.

"I've got my dreams, too," she said. Then shyly, "I know what you feel like inside me, Whit. I know your rock-hard body grinding against mine and it's as if I were a fragile cloud you were pressing into. . . ."

Again, he took her face in his hands and gently kissed her lips. "I've said it a while back. One day soon we're going to know glory the way we've never known it before."

Sadly then she said, "But I don't know how soon because I still see the pain in your eyes when you talk about making love and I know you're not free inside yet. . . ."

His eyes on her were haunted. "You're so perceptive. But then, I'd never try to hide it. I want you to know what's in my heart."

"I'm so sorry about what's happened to you, but don't you think it was the *way* Willo left that hurts you so. You were humiliated publicly. . . ."

"That, too, but I loved her. I built my whole life around her. Was I wrong to do that?"

"No. It's natural." She pressed an index finger to his face. "You'll heal, Whit. I promise you'll heal. Pray for healing."

"I do pray and it helps, but the pain just doesn't go away."

They cut the pizza and took it into the living room where they sat on the floor. Light-beer cans had been in one of the bags and the beer was delicious with the pizza.

"You say you like gardening?" she finally asked him.

"Love it."

"I'm putting out a very late bed of impatiens. Like to help me?"

"Point me in that direction."

Whit examined the ring on her finger and kissed her hand.

"You're a romantic clean through," she told him.

"Tell me something better to be, although I guess the way I've been burned, you'd think I learned my lesson."

"You were meant to have love, be loved."

"I'll talk with you sometime about what my father told me about love when I was a kid. I'm saving it for a special time with you."

"Sounds mysterious."

"It's one of the most wonderful things anyone ever said to me. It helps keep me going."

They went out on her sunporch and got the impatiens plants in a wide box, the charcoal, and the Miracle Gro fertilizer and took everything out into the side yard where a dirt bed had been worked and lay ready to receive the impatiens.

"My mother grew lots of these at home," Whit said. "I like the size of your bed. It's generous. Impatiens are such lovely blossoms."

"When you kept house, did you have time?"

"Willo didn't care for flowers, but yes, I planted them a couple of times."

He watched the sunlight on her delectable bare midriff and smiled inside. He had himself quite a woman. Her brown flesh was like brown cream, luscious, tempting. And her warm and gracious, caring spirit completed the package.

They were silent then, fine-grading the earth, crumbling the moist soil with their fingers. Both thrilled at the marvelous *feel* of it in their hands.

"I've always loved the feel of good loam." Danielle looked down at the rich, brown-black soil, her heart swelling with love of nature.

A bluebird lit on a limb of the big oak a short distance from them and stared at them. A red-breasted cardinal sang nearby.

With a trowel, she made short rows in the bed and sprinkled charcoal into the opened rows. Flexing her shoulders she said gaily, "Now for the planting. What do you say I take this side and you take that side? We'll meet in the middle. I'll water after sundown."

"Sounds good to me. At any rate now I know why you said to wear old clothes."

"Did you object?"

"No way. I already had on old clothes. I was practicing all yesterday. My backup group is coming over late this afternoon. I'd invite you over, but a couple of the members don't like anyone around when we're rehearsing new stuff."

"I understand." Carefully, they put the plant slips into the ground and lightly packed dirt around them. "Whit?"

"Yes."

"Your concert's on the eighteenth of this month. Did you notice the flyers in town? You said you went in town to gas up."

"Yeah, I did. They're great. This is going to be one of my best concerts."

"How can you tell?"

"*You'll* be there. You give me glory in my heart." He paused a moment. "When I said that, I felt something *new*. I'm going to lick this pain, Dani. Just give me time."

She went back on her haunches. "Take all the time you need."

"I keep being afraid."

"Of what?"

"That you'll fall in love with somebody else while you're waiting. It happens."

"I won't fall in love with someone else."

"How do you know you won't?"

"I just know." How could she tell him that she knew her own heart and that there had been no one else who filled her heart the way he already did. It was bone marrow, *soul* knowledge—and she trusted it.

They were so engrossed they didn't hear a car drive up to the curb or Cal Catlett walk over to them.

"Howdy!" he greeted them.

"Hello, Cal, how are you?" Danielle said as she and Whit stood.

"Fine, thank you." He looked at Whit a long moment before he asked Danielle, "Aren't you going to introduce me to the gentleman? Aren't you Whit Steele? Got your picture all over town. Boy, I wouldn't miss that concert even if I'm not crazy about gospel music. My wife's got a bundle of your CD's and tapes."

"That's always nice to hear," Whit said.

"Whit, let me introduce you to Cal Catlett, one of Minden's top citizens."

Cal looked at her sharply. Sure he was what she said, but Danielle had an edge to her voice. It wasn't like her to praise him.

"I'm happy to meet you, Mr. Catlett."

"Just call me Cal."

"Very well, Cal."

Cal grinned then. "That's some gospel-singing sister you got. And your whole family. Lord, how I remember the Singing Steeles. Like I said, I'm not much for gospel music, but I do like some of it."

"That's always nice to hear."

Cal cleared his throat and said to Danielle, "Actually I came by to bring you a check for five hundred dollars to use at A Literate Minden any way you see fit. You need more, you just tell me." He took the check from his shirt pocket and handed it to Danielle. He gave her money from time to time, but usually waited until she included him in the list of people who contributed to ALM.

"Thank you."

Cal seemed even livelier now. He turned to Whit. "I'll be taking a trip down to Mexico in a couple of weeks or less. You must like to travel yourself the way you go all over the world, Whit."

"I guess you might say I do," Whit answered.

Danielle wondered why Cal had so abruptly brought up the fact that he was going away. He went away often; he had a good second man in charge for his factory. It left him pretty free.

They chatted about gospel singing and Minden for a little while before Cal said, "Terrible thing about that man who was murdered."

"Yes," Danielle said softly. "A murder is always a terrible thing."

Cal moved closer and tapped Danielle on her arm, staring

at her bare midriff. He winked at Whit. "If anybody can catch the booger, our Miss Danielle can. She's the best."

Whit's eyes moved from Danielle to Cal. She didn't like this man, he decided. "Well," Cal said finally, rubbing his hands together, "we've got less trouble than most. Great police force. You want to be a devil, don't come to Minden. We've got the best police force there is. I got to be running along. You come by and visit my factory sometime, Whit. Make the lieutenant bring you. My folks'd be pleased to see you. I'll be at your concert and I'll introduce you to my wife. She'll faint with joy. Bye now."

After he had gone, Danielle was quiet, thoughtful.

"What are you thinking?" Whit asked.

"Funny. His being here made me think of A Literate Minden and that made me think of May Land."

"The girl you're trying to help."

"She's disappeared, Whit, and I can't find her. She was so distraught when I last saw her. I'm afraid for her."

"Anything I can do to help, I will." He was somber, then his eyes lighted. "Give me a chance to hone my law enforcement skills. I've always been interested in that field. Meeting you is pure lagniappe."

"Lan-yap?" she echoed him.

"A bonus, something extra. My mother's from New Orleans. It's one of her favorite words."

They were back on their hands and knees. She leaned over and kissed him on the mouth, then blew softly on his face.

He laughed shakily. "Don't make me take you in your side yard. It isn't seemly."

He touched her face gingerly and wanted to kiss her again, but he didn't. He was going to wait until they could go all the way through. Today and other days proved they were nearly too hot to handle, but they knew what they wanted and they were determined to wait for a full culmination of their dream.

FIFTEEN

In her office that morning, Danielle had hardly settled down when a call came from the medical examiner's office. It was a woman assistant.

"Lieutenant Ritchey?"

"Yes."

"We had a small glitch here. One evidence sample report was left out when we sent the last ones. We found several hairs on the shoulder of the cadaver's coat. Shall I read you a bit of the report, then send it on promptly?"

"Yes. Please do."

"The hairs were short, dark red and gray, coarse. Hair consistent with that of a middle-aged man in his fifties or sixties or a bit older. It's hard to tell. I'm sorry we slipped up on this."

"It's okay. Thanks for calling immediately. I appreciate it."

After she had hung up, Danielle leaned back in her swivel chair and mulled the information over. Hairs. Coarse. Short. *Dark red and gray*. Cal Catlett came instantly to mind. She picked up her phone and buzzed Jon, who answered right away. She told him about the hairs and he whistled.

"What in the world could Catlett be into now?"

"If it's him. There are other dark red-haired men."

"On the other hand, Dani, it could mean that he had something to do with it. He doesn't have to be the killer, but he may know something."

"I saw him yesterday. He says he's taking a run down to

Mexico to look over land for a factory. Do we care if we take our time on this?"

"I don't see that there's any hurry. We don't want to tip him off. Do you have anything in mind?"

"Yes. I want to get with Sam, his barber, and get some samples of Cal's hair. Sam's cooperated with us a lot of times."

"Sounds good to me."

The door burst open and a jubilant Ed ambled in waving a sheaf of bills.

"Congratulations are in order," he exulted.

"What on earth?" Dani said, laughing.

"I won five hundred smackeroos in the lottery."

His happiness was infectious. "Care to share the loot?" Dani teased him.

"Sure." He peeled off two hundred-dollar bills and came toward her.

"No, Ed. No way will I take your money. Take Shelley out on the town. That money can help pay for a trip to New York for the both of you."

"Maybe in the future," he grumped. "I'm still pouting with her for blurting out I went to New York when I'd said I was in D.C."

He sat on the edge of the big table. She got up and went to him, placed a hand on his shoulder.

"We all do things we'd rather not explain," she said. "Friends weren't meant to know everything."

Ed sighed. "You know, Dani, maybe the reason Shelley and I can't make it is I'm hooked on you. You're way ahead of any other woman I've known. I've been divorced ten years now and I've gone through at least ten women." He paused a moment. "I see the gospel clown's come back to town."

Danielle looked at him levelly. "Be kind, Ed. Don't call him a clown. He's a nice man."

"Okay, if you say so. But, Dani, you could be walking into hot water. You know what fame is like. Liquor, drugs, women coming out of their ears . . ."

"Didn't you just say you'd had ten women in ten years? And we're just plain old detectives. No celebrity, no glamour there."

"Yeah," was all he said. He took out his wallet and inserted the bills. "Guess this will keep me company a few days."

After he had gone, Danielle sat in one of the tub chairs and thought about Whit's upcoming concert this Sunday. She'd seen him perform several times before and admired him greatly. She wanted to wear the beautiful ring he'd bought her, but decided to wear it only on dressy occasions.

Since he'd been back, they had seen each other every other night. They'd taken long drives in the countryside and along the Chesapeake Bay. They watched the stars, a new moon, and seldom-seen meteors. And they'd avoided kissing too deeply or too long. They were simply rarely alone inside. They had grown closer and closer, but emotionally Danielle felt they still stumbled along.

They were on the *edge* of something new and both could feel it. Time wasn't everything. People had met, mated after a short time and lived happily ever afterward. And people had known each other all their lives, married and been divorced within the year. So much for time.

Getting up, Danielle yawned and stretched. *Was* Cal Catlett involved in a smuggling ring? And how were they going to find out what he knew? Cal was a close friend of Judge Lanier, whom they'd need to go to to get a search warrant. He was going to be on his friend's side. Old Cal was well protected with his good works and his largesse.

Snapping her fingers, Danielle remembered a call she wanted to make. She picked up the phone and called Jake, May's boyfriend. After a number of rings he picked up, his voice so thick with sleep that she could hardly understand him.

"I want to ask if you've heard anything from May."

"This got to be the detective."

"Yes. Have you?"

"Nothing. And I'll be blessed if I never do again."

Danielle drew a deep breath. "Jake, please be honest with me. I need to find her. . . ."

"Get off my case," he began, then relented. "Okay. She got a friend in Baltimore she prob'bly staying with. I ain't called. She run away. I'm willing t'let her. Plenty women out here. Eight women to every man."

"Oh?"

"What you mean, 'Oh?' "

"Nothing. Jake, please, do you have a number for this friend?"

"A number? Yeah, used to be one a' my gals. Gimme a minute."

He was back before she expected him to be and he gave her a number.

"Thank you."

"You got nothing to thank me for. I had my way, every cop I know be locked up in the county jail. Bye, Mama."

She was left with a dial tone and she called the number. There was no answer. She dialed it twice more and waited.

Where was May?

SIXTEEN

Washington, D.C.'s Constitution Hall was perfect for concerts. Onstage, Whit greeted his fans and exulted in their adulation. Looking out over the audience, he spotted Danielle and smiled. He caught her eye and as she smiled, he bowed and waved.

The announcer introduced Whit: "Ladies and gentlemen, I give you that paragon of gospel music—beloved, glorious. He has given the world his music and the world has given him its love. I give you *Whit Steele!*"

To thunderous, standing applause, Whit bowed and saluted his audience.

"I love you all," he said simply, "and you will have new facets of me tonight, for I am newly blessed and I am grateful. Tonight, I will give you a concert like no other. My heart is full and I want to fill your hearts."

The audience continued clapping wildly as Whit's five-person backup group of guitarists, tambourine player, and piano accompanist softly played their instruments. He announced the trio of songs he would shortly sing and led in his brilliantly clear baritone thrumming. He began to sing an old hymn:

Go down, Moses, way down in Egypt land.
Tell old Pharoah to let my people go!

His voice was liquid honey, pure molten gold. Love and years of practice had given it exceptional honing.

Whit closed his eyes and felt the music flow through him. He was on a roll from the beginning and his audience was fully with him. His strong voice rang out:

When Israel was in Egypt land.
Oppressed so hard they could not stand.
Let my people go.

Then again:

Go down, Moses . . .

He roused the crowd and from the beginning had them in the palm of his hands.

Danielle sat in a special box seat with Julian and Daphne, who looked stunning in lavender silk crepe, and Jon and his wife, Francesca, lovely in black chiffon. The men wore dark business suits. Dressed in a cream-silk chiffon gown with crystal iridescent beads and wide straps that fell across her upper arms and shoulders, Danielle felt beautiful, loved. Her heart swelled with pride and the words of ancient brutality known and overcome aroused her sympathy.

"He's never sung like this before," Jon leaned over to whisper. "And I've heard him many times."

"I agree with you," Francesca nodded.

When Whit had finished his first song, the audience thunderously clapped and cheered him. He smiled and went on to sing "Joshua Fit the Battle of Jericho," and "We Are Climbing Jacob's Ladder," both crowd pleasers.

Danielle looked around. Cal Catlett had said he and Irene would be here. She didn't see him and breathed a sigh of relief.

The backup group gave Whit a brief chance to breathe as he clapped his hands and moved joyfully about the stage.

"Who," he asked, "would like to do some lining?"

A great shout went up and he began slowly in a melliflu-ous voice:

Listen to the lambs,

And the audience echoed his words and his intonations. He went on:

All a crying—

Whit led again and again the audience followed:

All a crying.

Then:

I want to go to heaven when I die!

Whit felt the words deeply and closed his eyes, giving other words to the audience to line, which was simply the audience repeating after his words. This was a favorite. He began:

Come on, sister, with your ups and downs. Want to go
  to heaven when I die.
The angel's a-waiting to give you a crown.
  Want to go to heaven when I die!

The air was rich with words and music. They were led by a master who had never seemed so masterful. The audience was his and he was theirs. Whit had long held that one must *feel* spirituals to sing them, and he felt them in every fiber of his being. He wished for his parents' and his sisters' presence, but they were away on a trip around the world. He thought they would agree that there was a special element in his singing tonight. And Danielle was here.

Singing along with the lining, Danielle felt her eyes moisten. "Listen to The Lambs" was one of her favorite spirituals. Her great-grandmother had taught her the old, old songs.

Danielle looked down at her hands lying quietly in her lap, studied the lovely oval jade ring with its diamonds winking. Listening to Whit sing, she felt his body pressed hard against hers, felt his kisses and the warmth he showered on her. Her body trembled with aching memory as she wondered when they would know each other in the biblical way. She had known the constant touch of a man's love and she missed that touch.

Whit finished that set of spirituals and the announcer said there would be a brief intermission. The musicians moved offstage.

"Should we go backstage to congratulate him on a stellar performance?" Francesca asked.

Danielle shook her head. "I don't think so. The intermission is going to be so brief. Let's wait until after the concert."

"Good idea," Jon said, squeezing his wife's hand.

"I've heard him many times before," Daphne said, "and he's simply never sung like this. Pat yourself on the back, my fabulous girlfriend."

"He's really *hot*," Julian said and Danielle smiled at his use of a word he normally didn't use.

"I'm sure I have little or nothing to do with it," Danielle murmured.

Jon's eyes crinkled in laughter. "Don't be modest. My friend's in love. He's just got a few hurts to get over. I've got faith in him. You have it too, you hear?"

"I hear," Danielle said, wishing she felt his certainty.

They stood up and moved around in the box, but did not leave it as others went out for refreshments.

The curtain opened again. This time Whit bowed and moved into his signature song, "Ev'ry Time I Feel The Spirit." He was accompanied only by the pianist, and Danielle listened carefully to the words:

Ev'ry time I feel the spirit
    moving in my heart, I will pray!
Ev'ry time I feel the spirit
    moving in my heart, I will pray!

And its three verses:

Upon the mountain, my Lord spoke.
    Out of his mouth came fire and smoke.
I looked all around me, it looked so fine,
    I asked the Lord if all were mine.
Jordan River, chilly and cold.
    Chills the body, but not the soul.

After each verse he swept into the rich chorus and there
was the deep rustle of recognition from the audience. He
took three bows on that song and sang it again to deafen-
ing applause. When the applause had died, Whit announced
the wildly popular ring-shout, which was his backup group
rhythmically stomping to the spiritual muses. He had long
ago learned that the voice was an instrument that simply
could not completely carry the deep feeling of spirituals.
It would strip the vocal cords. So someone had begun to
work out the meaning of the songs with their feet and called
it ring-shouting.

His sister, Ashley, had popularized the old ring-shouting
and he had followed close behind. Now, he worked with his
group ring-shouting through three songs, ending on "Hallelujah!" from the song of the same title. He began:

Been down to the sea and done been tried,
    Been down to the sea and been baptized.
Been born of God, I know I am,
    Been purchased by the dying lamb.
Hallelujah!

That song finished, Whit bowed and took the microphone. "This is one of your all-time favorites," he said. "My Lord, What a Morning!"

The hall was hushed, listening and absorbing the beautiful meaning of the words:

My Lord, what a morning.
My Lord, what a morning.
My Lord, what a morning
   when the stars begin to fall.

The feed-in words were:

You can hear the trumpet sounding,
   and
You can hear the sinners moan,
   then
You can hear the Christians shout.

The song ended in a haunting chorus:

My Lord, what a morning
   when the stars begin to fall.

The crowd went wild with passion. Shouts went up. "More! More!" they cried and Whit thanked them. Whit cleared his throat and spoke to the audience. "Tonight, I want to introduce you to someone special to me. A special friend. A special person. Please stand up, Lieutenant Danielle Ritchey!"

Danielle's mouth flew open with surprise and her heart thudded with delight. What was he doing?

Daphne nudged her. "On your feet, girl!"

Danielle stood on trembling legs and waved to the audience, which stomped and cried out their approbation before she sat back down. He blew her a kiss. It was as he said, he was on the cusp of something great. She was in love. Was he truly in love?

Whit and his group took four curtain calls. The applause only died down somewhat when Whit began to speak. "A voice can be a fragile thing," he said. "It must have rest. Yet, I love your loving of my songs and I will sing one more, then I must rest. Who would like me to sing again 'Ev'ry Time I Feel The Spirit!'?"

Again, the laughter and the shouts, "Yes, brother!" and "Sing it, man!"

And Whit did sing it, softly at first, then crying out. He looked triumphantly at Danielle, who blew him a kiss, making his heart lurch. Then he blew both her and the audience a kiss before the curtain fell.

Backstage, Danielle and her group found Whit sipping champagne. He pulled her to him, grinning.

"How'd I do?"

"You were wonderful," she told him.

Waiters served them champagne as Julian and Daphne, Jon and Francesca all offered congratulations. "You're getting there," Jon said, looking from Whit to Danielle. "Don't wait too long."

Whit nodded and a shadow crossed his face. He couldn't lose her; he had to get on the ball.

"I'm going to change, then I'll sign autographs and we'll go out to eat," Whit was saying when Cal Catlett and a group came up. He introduced his wife, Irene, who was as bashful as a church mouse, his sister, Edith, and her stepson, Dave. And he added a surprise: Annie Lusk and his factory manager, Ted Keys, who was apparently escorting Annie.

"I said I'd come and I did," Cal said. "That was some concert. I'll have to come see you more often. You're really good." He looked at Danielle and licked his lips. "You're in fine form tonight, Detective."

"Thank you," Danielle said dryly.

Annie said quietly, "I never realized before what a beautiful woman you are."

"Thank you."

"I always did," Irene said.

Irene was surprisingly attractive in a draped navy jersey dress with gold jewelry. Annie wore black silk-crepe and emeralds, which set off her red hair and her florid complexion. The men were nicely dressed in business suits.

Cal's eyes owned both women as well as Danielle. To the rich man, he felt, belonged the spoils.

"You people planning on eating afterward?" Cal asked.

"Yes," Whit answered.

"Mind telling me where? I'd like to be around you as much as I can. Now, we'll have our own table."

"Downtown at the Rose Room of the Grand Hyatt."

"I've done it before. Watch me buy me a table." He laughed heartily.

Whit went behind the curtain with his dresser and shortly came out clad in a midnight-blue suit, a pale blue shirt, and a dark red foulard silk tie. Danielle caught her breath at the sight of him.

Then, a woman with long, silken black hair, sea-green eyes, and dressed in black peau de soie, swept into the room so imperiously that people fell back before her. When she reached their group, she stood in front of Whit, smiling disarmingly.

"Whit, I'm sorry to interrupt, but may I speak with you a minute?"

He took time to introduce her, but did not say she was his ex-wife. Her eyes on Danielle were frosty; Danielle's handshake was warm, friendly, but inside, her heart had cooled.

In a smaller room, Whit faced Willo, his face glum.

"How are you?" he asked.

"I wish I knew. I'm hurt, Whit, the way I hurt you."

"It's all right. Life's never easy. How is your husband? Your child?"

"My husband and I are divorcing." Her face went flat with pain.

"What happened?" Whit asked.

Willo stared at the floor for long moments. "Madison tried to make me get an abortion, but I refused. He mistreats my helpless, innocent baby and I won't take that! Whit, is there anything now for us? I know I was wrong. I know how I hurt you. Is there a chance for us?"

She was pleading now, and he tried to soften the blow.

"I'm sorry," he said gently, "but I'm in love with someone else."

"The woman outside who looks so happy? Danielle?"

"Yes, Danielle."

Her eyes filled with bitter tears. "Do you forgive me?"

"Yes, I forgive you."

"We all make mistakes. I made the biggest one of all."

"It's all *right,* Willo. At first I thought I wouldn't make it, but I did. Now, I have Danielle."

His voice on Danielle's name was tender and Willo flinched. "I won't keep you," she said. "Go back to your friends. I'll go out this door."

"Willo?"

"Yes, Whit?"

"Be kind to yourself."

She thought about what he had said a few moments, then answered, "I'm not sure I know how to be kind to myself any longer."

She left then and Whit watched her go. Once this woman had been like a flame to his moth and she had torn his heart from him, leaving him bleeding and starved for her love. Now he shrugged. He was changing; Danielle had done that for him.

* * *

In the Rose Room of D.C.'s downtown Grand Hyatt Hotel, Whit and his party of Danielle, Julian and Daphne, and Jon and Francesca were escorted to their table by the maître d'. The big room was beautiful with its twinkling white lights, snowy damask tablecloths, and multirose centerpieces.

As they walked in, each woman had been given a very long-stemmed deep red rose.

"Now that's what I call class," Daphne said.

"Um-m," Danielle agreed.

"What you're supposed to do is put it in your teeth and dance the flamenco for us," Whit teased Danielle.

They were seated. "Speaking of dancing . . ." Francesca began when their waiter came up. Whit ordered. They had decided they all wanted the same thing: prime beef ribs. And they all wanted the same dessert: chocolate carrot cake.

They were engrossed in small talk about the concert when Cal Catlett came up.

"I said I'd get a table," he chortled, "and I did."

Whit laughed. "Congratulations."

Cal lost no time. "You two will want to dance first, but may I have just one dance with Lieutenant Ritchey?" His voice sounded like a pleading child. Whit looked at Danielle.

"Is it all right with you?"

She hesitated before she said, "I guess so."

Cal's face lit up. "Thank you, ma'am. Now," he turned his attention back to Whit, "would you give a couple of ladies the thrill of their lives? Please dance with my wife and my friend, Annie."

A surprised Whit found himself agreeing to dance with the two women. "I'd be honored," he said.

"Thank you. You're a real gentleman. They're your devoted fans."

"And I thank them," Whit said graciously.

Their dinner came shortly. Roast prime beef ribs, green peas and onions, asparagus, a cheese-stuffed potato, spinach soufflé, and a crisply colorful garden salad. They drank pinot noir with an excellent bouquet from a very good year. Danielle thought she could fly with happiness; Whit's songs still lingered in her ears.

"I said it before," Danielle said to Whit. "You were marvelous." The rest of the group echoed her as Whit smiled modestly.

"I told you I would give you a *special* concert. Was I right?" They all answered that he was right.

Whit regaled them with tales of spirituals that had served to make hard lives bearable. Dreams of the future ameliorated then-present hurts. Emotional devastation had been turned into works of art. Music had served to overcome madness.

"You're headed to be one of the greats," Jon said somberly. "I'm talking Paul Robeson, C.L. Franklin, and Brother Joe May."

"Where'd you learn so much about gospel music?" Whit asked.

"My father was a devotee," Jon said, "and my mother couldn't have been happier when you and I became friends. I think she's got every record you ever made."

"Too bad she's away," Whit said.

"My mother and all your folks. Around the world and I'm sure loving every minute of it." Jon squeezed his wife's hand. "We've got to make that trip one day, honey."

"Just say when," Francesca told him.

"Dad, you're so quiet, and that's like you, but Daphne's quiet and only once in a while is Daffy quiet."

"I'm quiet," Julian said slowly, "because I've heard a magic voice tonight that gladdened my heart like nothing has in a very long time. Son, like that song 'He's got the Whole World in His Hands,' He's let you have the world's magic in yours."

"I am blessed," Whit said simply.

Saying they would take dessert later, Whit led Danielle onto the spacious dance floor with its dimmed rose lights and potted rose plants that perfumed the air. Julian and Daphne and Jon and Francesca followed them.

"I'd like to dance the night away with you," Whit said huskily as he and Danielle glided along. Then, "Your perfume is getting to me. What is it?"

"Shalimar bath oil. I've found the oil works better than the perfume."

"Lead on and I'll follow. I wish I didn't have the obligatory dances and could do them all with you."

"They're your fans."

"And I'm happy for them to be, but you come first with me."

She hesitated before she asked him, "Was your visit with Willo eventful?"

He didn't worry her question. "The marriage fell apart."

"Now she wants you back." Danielle knew she sounded bitter and Whit looked at her sharply.

"That isn't going to happen," he said.

Danielle relaxed then, curving in to him harder than she knew. A delighted Whit held her close to him and the softness of her body filled him with joy. Her breasts were straining against him beneath the beaded chiffon and her lips were just under his ear. Something strange was going on with them. It was as if they had long been lovers. As the orchestra played the old, old songs, "Deep Purple" and "My Prayer," Danielle grew lost in thought. They kissed then and a torrent of longing was unleashed in both just as the song ended.

Back at the table, they waited for the others, then took their delectable dessert. Jealously watching her as she ate, Whit wanted to taste her mouth with the carrot cake flavor in it. Her naked form rose in his mind and he felt his manhood strain against his jockey shorts.

"A penny for your thoughts," Danielle told him.

"They're worth diamonds and rubies. I'll tell you later."

Cal came back then. Danielle rose and walked a little stiffly onto the dance floor with him as Whit went to claim Irene. Dancing, Whit was surprised to find that Irene was charming, sophisticated. She smelled good and she looked good. He was delighted to have her as a fan, and he looked forward to dancing with Annie, but he wanted Danielle in his arms again.

Back at her table, Annie looked out onto the dance floor as she gleefully thought her turn was next. *Imagine dancing with Whit Steele, the handsome devil.* Rich as Cal was, Irene never knew what he was coming up with, but she, Annie, had to take any second best he cared to give her. Still, he had enriched her life and she loved him—most of the time, she amended.

Annie looked at Ernie, Cal's factory manager, and smiled. He smiled back thinking how cool he and Annie kept it.

"You want to dance with me?" she asked.

He sighed. "I'd love to, but I don't want to give old Cal any ideas."

SEVENTEEN

Danielle and Whit decided to stop by his cabin cruiser before he took her home. With a chauffeur and Cookie as bodyguard, they rode the short distance from the restaurant to the waterfront. All day long there had been alternate cloudy and blue skies. Now it was overcast, with rumbles of distant thunder.

Danielle shivered a bit in her midnight-blue silk wrap. "It's unusual for it to be this cool in July," she told Whit as they got out of the car.

"My arms could do a better job of keeping you warm."

"I'm going to take you up on that," she murmured. He drew her very close and squeezed her. Exhilarated, she kissed his cheek. "Let's walk a bit along the waterfront, near the apartment buildings. It's too beautiful to go in. I like gray skies sometimes. Cookie can keep watch over us from there. Harbor Patrol does a good job of policing."

"Okay. You've got it."

He told Cookie where they would be walking and they set out. "When we got out of the concert, the night was full of stars and there was a big moon," she said.

There were parking lots full of cars, and an occasional security guard or so could be seen. The Harbor Patrol was largely concentrated near the other end of the harbor.

"Whit," she said as they walked along slowly, "I don't think I've ever known anything as wonderful as the time I've spent with you. I'm grateful."

"I'm the one who's grateful," he said. "We always have so much fun together. My heart nearly burst with joy when I introduced you tonight. There's more to come."

She laughed shakily. "More?"

"Hold on for the ride. Spend a little while with me. Then I'll take you home."

"We cost each other a lot of sleep staying up late."

"We'll sleep later, in each other's arms. There are many years to come."

His words sent delicious shivers through her and he put his arm around her shoulders and drew her closer. They could see Cookie's bulky figure a little distance away and the lights of the Harbor Patrol.

They had walked a good distance up the waterfront before they decided to turn back. A man they took to be Harbor Patrol or a security guard came from the back of one of the parking lots. "Good evening," he said softly and they answered in kind.

In the same hushed voice, he told them, "Don't say anything. Don't scream. I want your wallets."

The man held a gun close to his side, pointed at them. "Now!" he barked. "Don't give me any trouble and you won't get hurt."

"There's enough money in my wallet to cover it," Whit said.

"Shut up and you *both* fork it over and let me see your hands at all times."

The man's voice was smooth, relatively cultivated. Whit handed him his wallet as Danielle thought about her gun in her specially fitted satin purse, but she reluctantly took out her wallet and handed it over.

After he had what he had asked for, the thug grinned. "I'm in a killing mood tonight. Maybe I'll take you both out." He waved his gun as a loud clap of thunder rolled and the man jumped, startled.

With her eyes glued to the thief, Danielle flung her body

onto his, knocking him over. "What the hell?" he screamed, as she wrestled him down. He was flabby, out of shape, and a sitting duck. Whit quickly moved in to help, picking up the gunman's gun, holding it on him.

"Get me the handcuffs from my purse," she told Whit.

He quickly snapped the purse open and in a few seconds was handing her the handcuffs, which she smartly snapped onto the man's wrists that she had twisted to his back.

Then they were surrounded by Cookie, who had seen what was happening, and Harbor Patrol and a couple of security guards from nearby apartments.

"I thought I shouldn't have let you walk so far from me," Cookie grumbled.

"Are you okay, Dani?" Whit asked Danielle anxiously.

"I'm fine."

"Well, well, well," a sergeant coming up to them spat. "If it isn't the little man who dresses up as a cop and robs people. You punk!"

"Your names, ma'am, sir?" the sergeant asked. "I'm mighty sorry for what you just went through. We try to keep it pretty safe, but as you can see, we don't always succeed."

"Lieutenant Danielle Ritchey, Minden, Maryland, Police Department," Danielle answered in a firm voice.

Camaraderie rolled in on them then like a soft cloud.

"Whit Steele."

One of the Harbor Patrol men burst out laughing. "I was at your concert tonight, man. You were awesome. I got your autograph."

The two men shook hands. Another patrolman said, "You live in this neighborhood when you're in town?"

Whit pointed out his cabin cruiser. "Because," the man said, "me and my buddies are going to be wanting autographs. We'll catch up with you. Welcome to D.C. this time. I've been going to your concerts almost since you got started."

The Harbor Patrol men and the security guards shook hands with Danielle and Whit.

The policemen hustled the handcuffed man off, hailed a passing squad car, and pushed him in as he snarled threats and curses. "Next one," he muttered to himself, "I kill."

"Be witness to this," one of the two policemen told Danielle and Whit. "He's adding to his troubles with his threats."

"I'm certainly glad you weren't hurt," the Harbor Patrol sergeant said. "We've had trouble with this guy all summer. Putting on a police uniform is a smart move, but thank God we caught him before he hurt or killed someone. You two certainly helped us out a lot."

Whit grinned. "I was anything but an alpha male here tonight. Lieutenant Ritchey handled it, and very well."

"With your expert help," Danielle said. "It would have been much harder without you, if possible at all."

Whit looked at her fondly. "You're way too modest."

EIGHTEEN

Back inside the living room of Whit's cabin cruiser, he took her in his arms and whispered huskily, "I have so much to tell you. You look so beautiful tonight."

"You're the one all eyes, including mine, were on tonight. Whit, I tell you again, you were magnificent. Do you *know* how good you are?"

He held her a bit away from him. "If you think so, then I'm magnificent." Drawing her close again, he smelled the fragrance of her hair and touched it, pressing the soft springy strands into her scalp. "I love your hair," he told her. "I love everything about you." He led her to the couch, where they sat down, and he went onto his knees.

"Dani, I love you," he said tensely. "Will you marry me?"

Electric shock waves flashed through her and she laughed shakily.

"Well?" he said after long moments passed.

Danielle shook her head. "No, sweetheart," she said softly. "Your eyes were haunted tonight when Willo was in the room. You're still hurting. You can't kill one love by taking on another. It would be a mistake."

"I want you to go with me to pick out a ring. At least I'll know we're getting there."

"No. I want you free from me, from anyone. Then and only then will you be able to love again."

He thought about what she said for a long while before he said gently, "I want you to have another ring. Even if we're never able to know what we think we can have, it will be yours." He kissed her hand, noticing the jade ring. She no longer wore her wedding ring. He didn't comment, but his heart felt full.

"You're a wonderful woman, all the way through."

He got up and sat on the couch beside her for a moment, then stood and pulled her to him. Her soft yielding body in his arms struck liquid fire in his veins and he knew then as he had known before that he wanted her more than anything or anyone. Even if he was not wholly free, there was so much they could have, *did* have.

For Danielle, his rock-hard body pressing onto hers filled her with rapture. His splendid tumescence aroused her greatly and the spirit of the night filled her. He had asked her to marry him. He had introduced her to his world and she felt she belonged there. That, and having proved her mettle tonight with the crook on the waterfront, brought her tingling with satisfaction.

She knew something then with all her heart: when a person is faced with death, with danger, it is one of the times he or she lives in the deepest part of life. She was trembling with wanting him and their kisses were drugged. Without realizing she would say it, she told him with tears in her voice, "Take me, Whit. I don't want to wait any longer."

He crushed her to him, but hesitated and loosened his hold. "I don't want you ever to be sorry about anything that happens between us."

Tears of painful desire filled her eyes. "I won't be sorry. I want you inside me. I want to feel your love all the way through. *Please . . .*"

She disengaged her arms and turned her back to him as he unzipped her dress that fell and pooled around her ankles. Stepping out of the dress, she flung it over a chair and took off her bikini. Then he undid her bra and she stood naked before him like a brown marble statue. But no, he thought, not like marble—hard; she was wondrously soft as he stroked her.

Gasping for breath, she unbuttoned his shirt as he unfastened his belt buckle and got out of his pants, then his undershirt and jockey shorts. She laughed with joy at the nakedness of his brown body that was like finely tanned leather. He flinched and shivered with delicious joy as her cool hands touched his shaft. He hardened then like a rock that pointed to the object of his desire.

He repeated then what he had said earlier, "I don't want you to ever be sorry for what we know with each other."

Overcome with passion, spinning with naked rapture, she told him, "I want you, Whit, more than I've ever wanted anything."

He lifted her then and she wrapped her legs around him and he hurried to the bedroom, where he laid her on the bed and leaned over her. The room shimmered with soft lights. Her breasts were stiff with desire and her protruding nipples crinkled with pleasure. "Whit, I—" she began, but he placed the edge of his hand over her mouth as her eyes sparkled.

"I'm going to do things to you that please you," he said, "that I hope make you want more and more. Everything in my life has been leading to you and this moment. Love me, Dani, the way I love you."

"I do and I will," she answered as he took his hand away and with his thumb stroked her jawline. As she lay on her side, waiting for him, he spread his hand over her waist and she thrilled with ecstasy. How could so simple a gesture, she wondered, arouse so much pleasure? Then she couldn't wonder any longer because he was kissing her from her scalp to her face, her throat. His kisses were hot and dangerous, dangerous because she could get lost in them and never be free again.

Before you was coming, I was I, she thought, a saying that Mona had explained to her that when you were alone, you belonged only to yourself. In love with someone else, you became a part of that person. Then it hurt terribly if they left you, the way Whit had hurt with Willo's leaving. Whit knew that quote too.

He leaned over and got a gold foil package from the night table.

"Let me," she murmured, and he lay back as he watched her concentrate on the task before her and felt her soft, slender fingers slipping on the condom.

His hot mouth left a trail of wet kisses on her upper body, then he sucked her breasts, ripe with longing, first one, then the other, and squeezed them gently. More wet kisses trailed down her stomach and to the hot core of her where the kisses lingered while she nearly went mad with ecstasy.

He took his time as he stroked her all over, his hands and his kisses on her inner thighs, then her calves. He sat up then and took one foot in his hands and kissed it, brushing his tongue over her instep. He did the same with the other foot as she arched her back and cried out.

"I want you to know what you mean to me," he said. "I want to give you everything you want. I don't intend to leave much out."

He bent, and his tongue found her pulsing secret female core and played it the way a virtuoso violinist plays his beloved instrument. No music he had ever heard had thrilled him more. Above him she almost fainted with rapture and continuing ecstasy. Threading her fingrs through his hair, she pressed him in to her body and bucked beneath him.

This had been a prelude. He needed more then, needed to be inside her for even more glorious pleasures, and his half-closed eyes caressed her. "You taste," he told her, "like ripe late summer fruit—sweeter than sweet."

He arched above her, then entered the nectar-sheathed path she made for him, as she cried out his name. With his swollen shaft securely throbbing inside her, she gave rein to bliss and wonder. Her womb welcomed him.

He laughed shakily, pleased at pleasuring her as she worked her hips in frantic concentric circles under him. He wanted to shout to the world, *This woman is mine!* A bit of sadness filled him then because she could never be his until he was completely hers. He was willing to take the chance now, but *she* held back. Still, she had let him inside her beautiful body and he knew that with that came letting him inside her heart and soul. He was deeply humbled.

Time seemed to move slowly as they curved in wondrous motion. Her wide hips bore him easily, fastened around his narrower hips, and her legs moved over his back. He pressed his face into her throat and working harder, swifter, felt the rush of his seed into her body as explosions like splendid Fourth of July fireworks set off in his body and spirit no less than in his loins. And she felt herself convulsing with a delight so deep it seemed she would go into a trance as her body shook to its core and her spirits soared. They were fire and water. Earth and universe. And they were together—at last.

They lay side by side, spent for the moment, and he caught her close again.

"Thank you," he told her.

"No, you're the one who deserves thanks. Whit, you were so *good*."

"*You* were so good."

He stroked her back as they turned on their sides. "Span my waist with your hand again," she said.

"Like this?" He did as she asked, and again the thrill shook her.

"That gives me a feeling I've never had before. It's wonderful."

"Anything you want."

"A repeat of the first act." She laughed.

"When you're happy, your laughter is musical. You're full of music. That's one of many reasons I love you. Dani, do you believe I love you now?"

"I think we've loved each other from the very first moment we saw each other. It's just that you have work to do on your emotions, Whit. Don't be afraid I'll fall in love with someone else. I'm completely tied up with you."

"I love you for saying it, but you can't know your mind forever."

He was quiet then for so long she laughingly asked him, "Cat got your tongue?"

He was somber as he pressed her cheek. "I'm thinking of something my father said to me more than once. A teacher had been unfair, unkind to me, and another kid had taken my girl. I was an emotional mess and I went running to my father; we talked a lot. He listened carefully and after a while he told me, 'Don't sweat it, son. No matter what the world throws your way, you were born to love and be loved and don't you ever forget it.' "

"That's beautiful."

He ran his index finger over her slightly open bottom lip. "I'm thinking about that now because I've come to feel I was born to love *you*. *Born to love you*—can you understand that?"

"I do and I feel the same way about you. You've said it before. We're getting there."

"The onus is all on me and I'm healing. If we got married it might go faster."

She shook her head. "I don't believe that. Give it time."

"Okay, but I'll be pushing hard every minute now. How about some Marvin Gaye?"

"You know he's a favorite of mine, along with Pendergrass and Luther Vandross, of course."

He got up and said, "Would you like a drink?"

"I'll take a piña colada if it's not too much trouble."

"No trouble because I'd like one myself."

When he came back with the drinks, they got up and he put on Marvin Gaye and Luther Vandross CD's. "I'm putting on 'Sexual Healing,' " he said.

"Have you something in mind?" she asked impishly. "You play this often."

"Yeah. I've got a lot in mind."

"Then that makes two of us."

"Dance with me."

Naked, Danielle rose as "Sexual Healing" came on in Marvin Gaye's haunting, earthy voice. As she had done before, she stood on Whit's toes and he laughed. "I've told you before what that brings on," he said.

"Then let it. I can take anything you can dish out."

"We'll see about that." And he squeezed her to him, sucking her bottom lip in his mouth and squeezing her soft buns.

"Don't neglect the breasts," she told him. "They don't like it when you do."

Whit laughed. "I'll never neglect the breasts. They're so beautiful, Dani."

"I'm glad you like them. They love the way you handle them."

He bent and sucked her breasts gently, then harder, then he led her to the bed.

Lying on his back, he pulled her astride him. She bent to kiss him and his hot breath fanned her face. "We've got the rest of the night," he said. "We've got a lifetime."

She didn't answer. He was going full speed ahead and she didn't think he was ready. For him the part of him that said Slow and Secure was silent. Full Speed Ahead raced on happily. Again he reached into the night table drawer and took out a foil-covered condom. This time, she let him put it on, watching, marveling at the rigidity and smooth beauty of his member. Then she stroked it and he shivered. Rising a little, she lowered herself onto him bit by bit until he was firmly placed.

She rode him then as he had ridden her and her very soul expanded at what they now knew together. Bending forward, she gently sucked a nipple of his flat chest and he moaned aloud. "My most tender spot," he said.

"Oh? Mine are tender, too."

"I've got a hunch that I'm all tender spots where you're concerned. Dani, don't ever leave me."

"I won't."

"Promise."

"I promise with all my heart."

For a long time they moved slowly, savoring each sensation. She nibbled the lobe of his ear and heard him gasp. "Keep that up," he growled, "and you'll bring me on."

She kept it up for a moment, then stopped. This was too good, she was enjoying it too much for it to end. Time itself seemed to have slowed to favor them. The world hung, suspended in glory.

Enthralled, she drew a deep breath. "You said one day we'd know glory. That's what we have in this moment."

"Lord, don't I know it," he said fervently.

Looking at her angel face, he knew he had come home for all time. "My love," he said softly, and Danielle felt the start of tears—she felt him so deeply. "Spend the rest of the night," he said.

"Yes."

He leaned up and hugged her tightly as her heart thrummed with passion and with joy. He turned her over on her back and entered her gently, teasing her as he did so. He was so tumescent and the walls of her nectared sheath drew him in and closed around him like a tight glove.

"Whit?"

"Yes, love."

"I don't want to finish now. I want to go on and on."

"We can go on and on *and* you can finish when you will. I can take you however many times."

"I want to see what it's like outside."

He withdrew then and opened the curtain over the port-hole. The night was hung with uncountable brilliantly twinkling stars, a galaxy to remember. She felt her heart nearly burst with splendor. "Since I've known you, I feel so much more beauty around me," she told him.

"So do I since I've known you. Would you like to slip on one of my robes and go topside?"

"Oh, yes."

He got up and got robes for them both. Slipping into underwear and robes, they went on deck and were greeted by Cookie. "The bad weather left in a hurry," he said. "Beautiful night."

Whit grinned. "You don't know how beautiful."

Cookie smiled broadly. Danielle thought there was so much camaraderie between Whit and his crew and she knew the same feelings with her group at the police department. They were both so lucky. The moon was waxing now in the very early morning light. She could sleep over since she was taking a day off.

"What are you thinking?" Whit asked.

"A whole lot of things," she answered. "How I still feel you inside me. No, not just that excellent part of you that gives me so much pleasure, but your spirit and, I think, your very soul. You're what I've waited for all my life."

He pulled her to him and kissed her long and deeply, then harder as if he would go into her, meld with her. His big hands pressed her in to him until their bodies seemed to have fused.

"Dani, Dani," he murmured, his breath catching. "If I die tonight, I think I will have known the best there is, except for us continuing along this path, maturing, growing old." He stopped then, considering. "But I'm leaving out a part of the best, babies from your womb and those great hips, watching you give birth and suckle them. We're going to have it all."

She didn't want to stop him now; this time was too precious. But she knew he had healing to attend to and she knew it even if he didn't seem to. His face in the moonlight was full of wonder now, but earlier when he was in the concert hall room with Willo, he had been full of perceptible pain. Yet, in a small part of her, she began to feel hope as deep as faith and she kissed the corner of his mouth, flickered her tongue in that corner and teased him.

"I see you're ready to go in," he said. "You're making all the right moves."

"I wouldn't mind going in." She watched the wind-driven waters slap the sides of the cabin cruiser and she shivered a bit.

"Cold?"

"A little."

"Let's go in."

In the bedroom, he told her, "I'm writing a love song for you."

"How wonderful. When will you finish it and can I hear what you've composed now?"

"Other business comes before songs. I want it to be a surprise. That was what I had in mind when I talked with you from New York and said I had a surprise."

"I thought it was my ring." She stretched out her hand and he kissed it.

"That, too."

"You spoil me so outrageously."

"I've got money to spoil you and as I've told you before, you've only seen the beginning."

She hesitated a long moment before she said, "Whit, let's not rush things."

Somberly he said, "The warning comes a little too late now, don't you think?"

Reflecting on what he said, she told him levelly, "We care about each other, deeply. I wanted you and you took me. . . ."

"I wanted you more than I've ever wanted anything, even my music. What we're experiencing tonight just makes it deeper. I haven't hurt once since I've been here with you. I know it won't last entirely, but you help take the pain away, Dani. You're like my psychiatrist here, the way you're helping me heal. That's something that psychiatrists and yes, my sister, Annice, the psychologist, my family, and myself were unable to do."

"I'm glad. You don't know how much this means to me."

"I think you know what it means to me."

He walked her over to the CD player and loaded a single

CD he had set aside. Music filled the room. Gina Campbell's gorgeous voice filled the room:

Come here and lie down beside me.
Cross the room as I watch you
    in the candlelight
While a warm mist drifts in on
    the shadows.
Love, be good to me tonight.

They were in the bed then, lying side by side, listening to the soothing words:

Come here and let me stroke you,
Toast you with kisses and hold you tight.
We'll feed every hunger and quench
    every thirst.
Love, be good to me tonight.

"I love her," Danielle said.

"My sister, Ashley, knows her very well. You're going to meet a lot of people you'll like. Just as soon as my parents and my sibs get back from their tour, I'm taking you to meet them. Annice may be away a while longer. She's going to attend seminars in London in her field."

Danielle shook her head in wonder. "You do all the right things. How could anybody let you go?"

"As long as you love me, that's what matters, because I love you, love you, love you."

They grew silent then, enraptured with fresh kisses, both fleeting and deep. With the thin, latex sheath on Whit, he and Danielle blended together. On her back, she opened her legs to let him into her body, then wrapped her legs across his back and pressed. It was a path they had taken shortly before, but this time thrills shot through the length of her body, much deeper thrills. What was happening to her?

Barely moving, they lay there, willing this splendid time to last. He worked her gently, then harder. She worked with him. led by him and following his lead. Then, she led as he followed. Her nectared sheath twinkled with delight at the wonder of the guest inside it—the *beloved* guest. Gina Campbell's song, "Love, Be Good to Me Tonight," played on and on as they both paid special attention—as best they could—to the final verse:

We are so close to heaven.
With you the world seems right.
I could die happy, but I'll live happy.
Love, Be Good to Me Tonight.

Finally, Whit said, "I put the song on repeat. 'I could die happy, but I'll live happy,'" he quoted. They were silent again, then moving with fluid grace. He struck a deep spot and worked it and she came, with tidal waves of wonder sweeping her entire body, shaking her to the core, leaving her as limp as a rag doll.

He felt her delicious spasms and a siege of thunderous glory shot through him that brought his seed flowing. And he quickly thought that one day—soon—they would be entirely spiritually naked, seeking a child, then children, knowing the best life had to offer. His lips fastened hungrily on hers then and they were transported to some heavenly spot.

One day, he had said, *we will know glory,* she thought. And this was the first of many times when that would happen.

As a rose and gold dawn fanned out beyond the open porthole, Danielle dreamed of walking along a woodland area. She saw Whit ahead of her. He ran toward her, crying out her name, "Dani!" There was blood streaming down the front of his body. She screamed, "Whit, *no!*" as he collapsed. Breathless, she ran to his side, but before she could reach him, she woke up to Whit, who was holding her close.

"You were having a nightmare," he said.

"Whit?"

"Yes, baby."

She began to say, "You're all right," then stopped. She didn't want to frighten him. Instead, she said, "I had a nightmare, but I don't remember just what it was. We were in danger. There was fog everywhere. Whit, be careful, as I'll be careful. Will you?"

"Sweetheart, I'm always careful. You're the one who could be in danger at times, like tonight. But you were great. Try to remember the dream so I'll know just how to be careful, what to be careful of."

"I will." She felt it was a necessary lie.

Pulling the curtain over the porthole, he threw the room in darkness again and continued to hold and cuddle her.

"My Dani," he said tenderly. "With you, I have everything."

NINETEEN

In her bed, Danielle groggily awoke the next morning to the sound of the telephone ringing. Whit's voice came over lively and vivid.

"Did I wake you?"

"You did, but it's fine with me. Whit, I had such a wonderful time with you. I can still hear you singing in the concert."

"Then you'll feel good about keeping up our relationship."

"Yes, but I am pretty busy. We seem to be on to something going on in Minden that, as far as we know, we haven't had before."

"Oh? Remember, I'm interested in mysteries."

"How could I forget?"

"It's one of the things that ties us together, along with fate."

"You think we're fated?" Danielle asked him.

"I *know* we're fated. Don't you feel it?"

"Yes, I do. Our relationship is marked with a strange wonder."

"And I love that wonder."

"Me too."

She hugged herself with her left arm and felt the hardness of his muscular body again. Trembling, she drew a deep breath.

"When will I see you again?" he asked, then, "Oh look, I almost forgot. Jon invited me to come to headquarters and look around. He's well aware of my interest in mysteries."

"Will you be coming by soon?"

An Important Message From The ARABESQUE Publisher

Dear Arabesque Reader,

I have some exciting news to share....

Available now is a four-part special series **AT YOUR SERVICE** written by bestselling Arabesque Authors.

Bold, sweeping and passionate as America itself—these superb romances feature military heroes you are destined to love.

They confront their unpredictable futures along-side women of equal courage, who will inspire you!

The **AT YOUR SERVICE** series* can be specially ordered by calling 1-888-345-BOOK, or purchased wherever books are sold.

Enjoy them and let us know your feedback by commenting on our website.

Linda Gill, Publisher
Arabesque Romance Novels

Check out our website at www.BET.com

* The **AT YOUR SERVICE** novels are a special series that are not included in your regular book club subscription.

A SPECIAL "THANK YOU" FROM ARABESQUE JUST FOR YOU!

Send this card back and you'll receive 4 FREE Arabesque Novels—a $25.96 value—absolutely FREE!

The introductory 4 Arabesque Romance books are yours FREE (plus $1.99 shipping & handling). If you wish to continue to receive 4 books every month, do nothing. Each month, we will send you 4 New Arabesque Romance Novels for your free examination. If you wish to keep them, pay just $16* (plus, $1.99 shipping & handling). If you decide not to continue, you owe nothing!

- Send no money now.
- Never an obligation.
- Books delivered to your door!

We hope that after receiving your FREE books you'll want to remain an Arabesque subscriber, but the choice is yours! So why not take advantage of this Arabesque offer, with no risk of any kind. You'll be glad you did!

In fact, we're so sure you will love your Arabesque novels, that we will send you an Arabesque Tote Bag FREE with your first paid shipment.

Call Us TOLL-FREE At 1-888-345-BOOK

* Prices subject to change

"Tomorrow morning as a matter of fact. Will you be there?"

"I'm there in the morning. I have visits to make both tomorrow and the next afternoon."

"Okay, then. I'm not going to crowd you, but I've got so many possible plans for us. I'll go along with any program you have. There is one thing. You *must* meet my family soon."

"They're back?"

"In a few days. Can you make it one Sunday soon or on an off day? I'm anxious for you to meet them. Dani?"

"Yes?"

"I love you." His voice was hushed, deep.

She blushed and stroked her throat. "I love you, too."

They talked about the concert then and the time he would spend in New York later that fall. "This time you'll come up, spend a few days. It gets lonely."

"I'll come, keep you company."

"And I can show you around, show you off. Name the celebrity you'd like to meet and I can almost certainly set up a time for you."

She chuckled. "Whit, you're the only celebrity I want to meet. I'm a plain woman—a small-city detective who loves her life and what she does, and oh, yes, with a new person coming into her life finds joy without end."

"I said we'd know glory."

"You said we'd know glory and we know it, all right."

"I'm not going to push you on this," he said, "but if you change your mind, any time you change your mind, we can tie the knot."

Very gently she told him, "Don't push yourself. I'll be here waiting until you feel you're entirely healed, then we'll go on with the rest of our lives."

"You're going to get tired of my saying I love you."

"No, I'll never get tired of hearing you say it, or saying it back. I love you."

"And I love you more."

They talked of many things then, but the subject kept coming back to the love between them. Finally, reluctantly, they hung up, with the night after the concert bubbling over in each other's mind. It seemed like a heady dream, the way they had made love, separate entities coming together in ecstasy. Finally, Danielle got up. Today, she would finish her flower beds and go over her new investigation manuals and case studies. The next afternoon, she would visit Annie, try to find out what secrets her old house held. She raised her arms over her head, beginning a set of stretching exercises she did each day.

She thought about calling May's aunt's house again, then decided she'd do it from the office the next day.

Annie Lusk rubbed sleep from her eyes and got out of the bed, her heavy body fighting her every step of the way. At a shrill ringing of her doorbell, she slid her feet into pink mules and padded to the door. That should be Ted. This was her day off and she had intended to be awake and prettied up when he came.

She brushed her red hair back from her face, unchained and unlocked the door. Ted stepped inside, his slender, wiry body thrumming. He hugged her and tried to kiss her as she pulled away. "You got on no girdle or bra, so that makes it easier for me to get to you."

"I haven't brushed my teeth."

"I don't care. Your breath always smells like those little breath mints."

"Have a seat. You had breakfast?"

"Yeah. I didn't come for breakfast." He grinned waggishly.

"Gimme a minute," she mumbled, went into the bathroom and closed the door.

Ted looked around him. Nice country house. Annie made money, but probably Cal bought her the house. He had heard stories about Annie and Cal since he'd come to Minden fifteen years ago. He was Cal's manager, second in command, a job he'd held for three years. He thought Cal liked him as much as he liked anybody, but he wondered what Cal would do if he knew about him and Annie. They'd been carrying on over a year. Well, they kept it quiet, hushed. If Cal knew, would he invite him to go places with Cal and Irene? He didn't think so. He was long divorced and Annie was the only woman he saw. He had no wish to marry again. He stood up when Annie came back out.

"I ought to get dressed," she said. He liked her without makeup; she wore too much eye makeup and rouge, and she painted her mouth like a model.

"You look good the way you are." He went to her, hugged her fervently, pressing his wiry body into hers. "How about us pitching a little woo?"

"Did Cal get away? He was going to Memphis." She was restless, nervous.

"Hell, I guess so. Who knows where and when Cal goes and comes. You'd know that better than me."

"Ted, we haven't talked about it for a while, but if Cal comes when you're here, you know what to do."

He grinned. "Go right through that passageway into that little dark pantry-room and lock the door behind me."

She nodded. "He's got a key to the front door, but he knows I keep the chain on all the time, even if we don't have much crime." The way he was looking at her made her lick her lips, feeling his kisses before he began.

"Let's go in the bedroom." His voice was hoarse, raspy.

Quickly, he stripped her of her robe and gown and pushed her heavy body onto the bed. Her skin glowed reddish and he was mightily turned on. He had no pet names for her, needed none, and he wondered if Cal had a pet name for Annie.

He worked her over carefully, his hands cupping her big breasts, sliding down the big hips, squeezing and patting. He took his sex straight, with none of the side things. He didn't particularly care for the taste of a woman's breasts. His mother had told him she never breast-fed him; without realizing it, he was still a little angry about that.

Annie liked her sex long and slow and Cal always accommodated her. Ted never could; that was one reason she didn't cut Cal loose. That, and his generosity with money. It hardly mattered that Cal bought people with his money. He didn't repay love with love, but with gold. He knew he couldn't love and it didn't matter to him.

Ted pumped furiously and came with a strangled cry, clutching her to him. She felt keenly disappointed. She kept hoping that one day they'd finish together. It had never happened. He didn't need second go-rounds either. She wondered why she kept fooling around with him. If Cal caught them, she thought, he'd kill her, or have her and the man killed. Cal didn't fool around. He wasn't friends with Manny Luxor and the clown, Buck Lansing, for nothing.

Ted got a pack of cigarettes from the night table, tapped out one and lit it. "You want a smoke?" he asked her.

"Yeah. Light me one. The more they keep telling me how dangerous it is, the more I get addicted. Ted," she asked slowly, "how do you feel about danger?"

"Danger? What about danger?" His stomach felt queasy. Maybe he should have let her fix him something.

"You know, like us playing around on old Cal, them saying cigarettes can kill you—danger."

Ted rubbed his chin. "I don't have much use for it. Why d'you ask?"

Annie's reply was almost dreamy. "My brother who I loved so much went to prison for killing a man in a crap game. He was a heller and I worshipped him. You name it; he did it. I think I've got a lot of him in my blood."

"Where's he now?"

"Dead. Killed in a prison riot. But it's like he never left this earth when I'm feeling what I think he felt—the thrill of the danger."

"Annie," Ted said, exasperated, "you made a good life for yourself. You're not living like your brother you say's so wild.

You give up looking for danger. You're too good a woman to be courting trouble, you hear?"

"Yeah," she mumbled, "I hear you, but danger turns me on, makes my blood race. You ever wonder why I took up with Cal Catlett, why I let him use me as his back-street woman?"

"Stop calling yourself names. If I wondered, I know the answer now. You keep fooling around and you're going to ruin your life. You ought to get away from Cal."

They lay side by side, smoking. Dreamily, Annie thought, *What if we fell asleep drunk and the mattress caught fire? We'd go up in flames, die before anyone could get to us.* The thought thrilled her in ways she didn't understand. It was a gift from her brother to feel this way—a morbid gift. Lying there, she felt alienated from Ted once the sex was over. Cal understood her moods, her lust for danger. It was what kept them together.

"You hungry yet?" she asked.

"Tell you what, I'd be grateful for a fried egg sandwich. Now, let the yolks get hard. I can't stand all that yellow running. You might nuke me a big piece of sausage, too."

He was flat on his back and she leaned over and kissed his lips. "You in a hurry to go? Coming right up, one egg, one hog-sized hunk of sausage."

"Well, it's not like I'm ever comfortable here. Cal pays me well and I guess he trusts me; I don't know."

"Well, I can tell you. Cal don't trust nobody. If he's just letting us get by with this, he's got his reasons. He ain't friends with Manny Luxor for nothing. Maybe one day they'll find us both dead."

"Oh, hell's bells, Annie! Knock off that kinda talk."

"You look cute when you get scared," she said and leaned over and kissed his face. "It puts some life into you."

In the kitchen, Annie leaned on the sink looking out the window. That nice detective woman, Danielle Ritchey, had asked to pay her a visit and she'd said yes. She would be there around one o'clock.

Annie wondered why Danielle wanted to visit. She'd said she was trying to get some ideas about fixing up her house and that she liked Annie's house. With some bitterness, Annie felt she liked her house, too, but not so much any longer.

The stink of too many human bodies permeated the air, even though she paid an industrial deodorizing company to cleanse the house. She'd always thought that after thirteen years, one day the human traffic would end. Had someone found out? Cal seemed certain he had everything sewn up. She shrugged. Maybe danger was closer than she knew. The thought thrilled her. There was something about Danielle's eyes that drew her. She had seen too much, knew too much. Her mother had been murdered and nobody had ever found out who did it. She'd always liked Mona; she was so respectful and warm. So, danger had been a part of Danielle's future ever since her mother's death and what Annie saw in Danielle's eyes was what she, herself, felt in her heart.

"I guess it's like you, but you came right on time. I'd be glad to get you coffee or something to drink and a light snack." Annie sat on the edge of her sofa beside Danielle.

Danielle smiled at the older woman. "I had a heavy breakfast," Danielle said, "and I drink too much coffee sometimes. Thank you anyway. I try to be punctual, especially when people are kind enough to invite me to visit."

"Oh, I'm proud to have you here. You wanted me to show you around my house, give you ideas for redoing your place."

"Yes, and I thank you for letting me visit and look around."

"You're welcome. We can get started right off if you care to." Annie was far from comfortable with Danielle. Was her only reason for being here that she wanted to renovate her house and wanted ideas? Well, she didn't see any way she could have said no.

Danielle tried to put Annie at ease. "Mrs. Catlett has

agreed to let me visit her home and so have a couple of others. I like your house very much. It's warm, homey."

"Countrified," Annie scoffed. "I'm no kind of decorator, but I know what I like." Her furniture was chintz covered in the living room. Eggshell-colored ninon curtains draped the windows in full length and deep swags. It was all quite charming, Danielle thought.

A radio in another room blared the morning news. Annie excused herself, changed the station to Francesca Worth-Ryson's show and came back. "She's good," Annie said. "I listen to her most days, even when I'm in my restaurant."

"Yes, I like her."

Breathing deeply as they toured the living room, dining room, the three bedrooms, kitchen and three baths, each tastefully furnished and decorated, Danielle became aware of a pervasive smell and frowned a bit. One bathroom was more rumpled than the other two.

"You look puzzled," Annie said.

Danielle shook her head. "I've got a lot on my mind."

"Like that man getting killed back in April? I guess if anything had come of it, if you all knew who did it, it would be on the news. We'd have heard by now."

"We don't know yet, maybe in time . . ." Danielle's voice trailed off.

Annie's skin was flushed and her pale eyes glittered. "It ain't like we have too many killings around here. Thank God for that."

As they passed a room near the back of the house that Annie neglected to show, it seemed to Danielle that the odd smell grew stronger. It was as if someone had tried to cover a basically bad smell with disinfectants, only it wasn't a necessarily *bad* smell, Danielle reflected, just an *odd* smell. Annie looked at her sharply. "You look like you're spooked. I been hearing a long time you know things the rest of us don't know."

Danielle laughed heartily. "Don't believe everything you

hear. I'm a bit psychic, but I feel everyone is. I just pay more attention to my hunches."

"You ever solve a murder that way, I mean using your psychic powers?" She sounded anxious.

Danielle thought about that. "I can't say I have." She started to speak of Mona, but changed her mind. And she didn't tell Annie, but two years after she was on the force she had a hunch that someone committed a murder and her suspicion turned out to be true. Why didn't she know who killed her mother?

Danielle felt her attention riveted to the room she hadn't been shown. What was in that room? She thought of Colin Matthews and his helicopter trips over this house and Cal Catlett's. *Any house with plenty of space. A safe house.*

Back in the living room, seated, Danielle said she thought she'd go since she had a lot to do. Annie remained seated, reluctant to let her go. She liked this woman and wished they could be friends. "You come again any time you want," she told Danielle. "You're always welcome here."

"Thank you and, any time you wish, stop by and see how my renovation is going."

Annie flushed crimson. "I really appreciate that and believe me, I will. I know you were with Whit Steele at his concert. You looked beautiful and you two make quite a couple."

Danielle felt her mouth lift in a smile. "Thank you. You looked lovely, too."

"Well, I . . ." Annie began. She had been going to say something about the gossip regarding Cal and her, but she thought better. Let sleeping dogs lie.

In the deepest part of herself, Danielle knew she had gotten some kind of information by coming here, but what? Probably the room she hadn't been shown was just a junk room, but possibly not. Colin had spoken of safe houses and human bodies crowded in narrow rooms. It was part and parcel of human smuggling. Out the kitchen windows, she had seen the tall fence that surrounded the backyard and came up to the center of the house. She had noted a couple of Cal's big rigs parked there. He was the kind of man who'd use a friend's house to do his dirty work. And this was perfect. The feeling she got that this was a possible place for the smuggling was so strong that she was nearly overwhelmed.

"You look like you're going to pass out."

Danielle shook her head. "I do feel a little faint. Too many aspirins, but I'll be all right."

"Well, if you're sure. You could lie down a few minutes."

"Thank you for being so kind, but I really am all right. Any aspirin over one makes my head spin." She extended her hand. "I really appreciate your help."

"I haven't been much help. You just looked around a little."

"You'd be surprised what I can absorb on a short visit. The way you've treated your windows. These marvelous chintz covers . . ."

"Well, you come back now, anytime. Just let me know when."

"I'll do that and I can't thank you enough."

Outside, as Danielle walked across the porch, aware of Annie standing in the doorway behind her, she hesitated a moment, then turned around. Annie had gone back in. Walking slowly, she went down the steps and down the walk. At the gate she heard it—the sounds of *drums* rolling, like the drums she had heard the night Cedric Appiah had been killed. She stopped to listen and realized that the drumming was coming from Annie's house. She walked on.

A couple of hours later, Annie answered her doorbell to find Cal standing there. "Hi, sweetie," she said, hugging him. "I thought you were going out of town."

"That a thought or a wish?"

"Oh, honey," Annie cooed.

Cal listened to the drums on the stereo and screwed up his face. "Cut that crap off," he barked.

Annie laughed. "I've been playing the whole album. I put it on just after Lieutenant Ritchey left."

"Danielle Ritchey was here? This afternoon?"

"Well, yes. I told you she was going to visit me. She wants to get ideas about fixing up her house, and I was flattered. I like her."

Cal pursed his lips. "I hope that's the only ideas she was looking for. It would have been better if you put her off."

"But I told you . . ."

"You said you were *thinking* about letting her come here."

"You've been so busy, honey. I didn't want to bother you."

Cal strode over and cut the stereo off. He came back to where Annie stood and gripped her arms the way he did Irene. "You're not a stupid woman," he said, "but you sure as hell can act like one. We're running *people,* Annie, the way other folks run drugs or other contraband. Every week I bring twenty to thirty unwashed, stinking humans, if you could call them that, I bring them here and others come and pick them up, ferry them to their destination. We've gotten rich, all of us. Twenty to thirty thou a head adds up and we're thinking of expanding . . ."

"Oh, Lord," Annie said wearily. "I've got all the money I need. I'd like to quit, go to some other place. You ever think of leaving Irene, marrying me?"

Cal laughed harshly. "Two damned wives in my lifetime are two too many." He relaxed his grip and Annie rubbed her bare arms.

The way he gripped her arms enraged her. She faced him as he let her go. "Cal," she said evenly, "we've talked about this a lot. Okay, so you don't want to marry me. I can understand that, but you're the only man I ever wanted."

"Aw, baby, that's sweet."

"I'm not finished. We've talked about it, how I don't want you to ever manhandle me and you haven't until today. I'm going to be honest. If you take it further, I could hurt you. I was beaten by my folks and I ran away before I killed them." She shuddered. "Not one time since then has anybody beat me or manhandled me the way you just did. Likely I'll have bruises the way Irene gets bruises. I don't want that to happen again, you hear?"

Cal looked at her, astonished. They never quarreled. "Big Red," he said slowly, "what in the hell has gotten into you?"

"I'm like an elephant—long memory."

He was stung by her mention of Irene and he resented it, sought the offensive. "What in hell is wrong with you today? You got another man and trying to get rid of me?"

Her heart hammered. "I never wanted nobody but you."

"You swear?"

"I swear."

Cal licked his dry lips. "I guess I get to thinking sometimes how good you and I are together. Big Red, you sure you ain't got a way of letting someone out the back way as you let me in the front? You keep the chain on the front door, so I can't come in unannounced."

His statements were too close for comfort. She understood then that Cal might well be on to Ted and her. Cal was not a man who brooked betrayal. He would toy with her when he *knew* what was going on. A lump rose in her throat. He would toy with her as a cat does with a mouse, then he would strike. Manny Luxor's ugly face rose before her.

"Honey," she said, "don't talk trash. Let's go in the bedroom. I've got some fine new scotch. Or, some beer. I know you like beer in the middle of the day."

Cal opened his mouth, but said nothing. He caught her roughly to him and kissed her.

"Now you're talking," she said. Then her mood changed. "You can't blame me for wanting to get out of the smuggling business. My house *stinks,* Cal. All those sweaty, scared bodies. Sometimes I think they haven't had a bath in weeks. The deodorizing man comes out and he can't fight it."

"Relax," he said. "Nobody noticing but you. I don't smell a thing."

"I wonder if Lieutenant Ritchey didn't smell something

strange. I'm beginning to think like you that I shouldn't have let her come."

"Now you're talking. You run everything past me from now on and I'll keep you straight." He kissed her then, but not deeply.

"The bedroom?" she asked him.

"No, baby, I've got to go. When I left, Ted hadn't come in. He had a doctor's appointment this morning. I don't know if he's coming in, so I've got to get back. Then I'm leaving."

He looked strange to her. Was he looking at her strangely? It bothered her that she couldn't read Cal better. He was too dangerous a man not to understand.

But she thrilled with pleasure at the danger in the situation between them. Still, maybe she ought to cut Ted off. Danger was one thing. Being a damned fool was another.

TWENTY

"Looks like we've hit pay dirt," Danielle said thoughtfully. Sitting at her desk, she studied the extra report from the crime lab as she talked with Jon.

"The hair matches Cal Catlett's?" he asked.

"Unless modern science lies. Are you surprised? I'm not."

He sighed. "How in the hell is he mixed up in this? The man's got everything he needs. Why screw it all up?"

"Well," she said, "there's the law-abiding and there's the law-defying. I think Cal likes to think he's above the law."

Jon frowned. "I don't think anything surprises me anymore. Dani, I suggest we go slow on Catlett, smoke him out. Visit him a couple of times. A few hairs don't add up to murder, but we've got him in our crosshairs and we'll work with Calico."

Jon ran his finger across his chin. "We've got to get the meeting on, Dani. Whit's coming by and as you probably know, he's going with me to Baltimore. He's always been interested in law enforcement. Now you've come into his life and the interest is growing. The world spins on love."

He grinned at her as she blushed.

Jon glanced at his watch. "Colin's late. He said he has some important news."

As if summoned by his name being called, Colin Matthews came in. "Ready for me?" he asked.

"Yeah." Jon waved him in. "Have a seat. Grab some trail

mix and you've been around enough to get your own coffee."

Ed came in then, looking glum. "I could use some action," he grumbled.

"You may get what you wish for," Colin told him. Ed's eyebrows lifted as a smile spread across his face. "You don't say."

The four of them sat at the table in Danielle's office.

"I've got to leave early for Baltimore," Jon said, "but I want to hear your news. Danielle's handling this, with Ed's help and a couple of others. Tell her everything, Colin, and work it through. Now, what's your news?"

Colin blew a stream of air before he began. "Our informant in New York is one of the best. He tells me there's a shipment of illegal aliens coming in tomorrow night from New York. I've been monitoring it. You and Ed have been with me, Danielle, so you know we've got helicopters working overtime. They've traced a shipment of aliens almost certainly being let out of one of the big rigs and into Ms. Annie Lusk's side entrance. As I told you, infrared devices gave us a *lot* of bodies in one section of the house after the rig parked. Twenty, maybe thirty. We've checked on houses in this area big enough to hold this kind of contraband. This is the only one where there's activity of this kind.

"We're set up on our part and we'd like to move against them with their next shipment, which should be tomorrow night. Can you handle this?"

"No problem," Jon said quickly. "We're going to have to be careful, though. As we've talked about, Manny Luxor's mixed up in this. Together, he and Catlett have some of the best legal minds in the country, maybe the world. We can't afford a lot of huge lawsuits."

Colin's mouth tightened. "We're pretty sure of this one. I think we're right on the mark."

"Okay," Jon said, "get it together with Dani and we'll roll tomorrow night. Now, I've got to run." He grinned at Danielle.

"We should be back around three. Please put the report you got this morning on my desk."

"Well, well, well," Ed said after Jon had left. "Some more action. I'm ready. What about you, Dani?"

Colin looked keyed up. "We'll handle most of the action. You'll do the arrests for the people in this town who're involved."

"Sounds like a breeze," Ed said.

Colin shook his head. "You'd be surprised at the things that can go wrong."

Danielle called in Wink, Adrienne, Matt, and a couple of other policemen and briefed them on what was going on. They listened quietly, ready for action.

"Still no word on who killed Cedric Appiah?" Colin asked Danielle.

She told them about the niece. "Things may be coming over to our side."

"That's always good," Colin said slowly. "I feel sorry for the poor devils who get caught in this. From Africa, we're getting teachers, professors, formerly well-to-do salt-of-the-earth people fleeing political persecution. For Mr. Appiah, it was out of the frying pan and into the fire."

He stood up. "Good company excepted, I've got to run. I'll be in very close touch with you all, Danielle. Tomorrow night, we roll."

Ed stayed a few minutes after the others left.

"You ready for this?" he asked her.

She nodded. "As ready as I'll ever be."

She told him then about the matching hair and his mouth opened. "Damn!" He hunched his shoulders. "There's got to be some other explanation for this."

"*Why* does there have to be?" she asked gently. "You like Catlett, don't you?"

"A lot of people do. I just admire the way he's lined all his ducks up. I think he's richer than any of us know."

"And being rich makes him a good guy?"

"I never said I thought he was a good guy. I guess I tend to admire the renegades. The Astors and the Rockefellers weren't angels. Hell, Dani, you came up on one side of the tracks; I came up on another. Give old Cal and me a break."

"Okay. Now, you tell him to give himself a break—stop being so friendly with Manny Luxor and—"

Ed laughed shortly. "Hell, Cal's friendly with *everybody*. He's a diamond in the rough. I've been told he gives away hundred-dollar bills, and on occasion, thousand-dollar bills. He helps support ALM."

Danielle nodded. "And I'm properly grateful. Okay, I'll cut him some slack."

"That's my girl. How about lunch?"

"I'd love to, but I'm visiting Irene Catlett. I want to see her house."

"On police time?"

"Well," she drawled, "there's a bit of police work involved here, so I kill a business and a personal bird with one shot."

"Later then," he said. "We're losing touch since that clow . . . since Whit came along. Sorry, Dani."

She put her head to one side. "We've been friends a long time, Ed. I don't think much could spoil that." She held out her hand and he shook it, squeezed it a bit. She was grateful he said nothing more about having a deeper relationship.

An hour later, most of her paperwork cleared, Dani got up and watered her African violets. The newest one was drooping. Her buzzer rang and the receptionist announced that May Land wanted to see her.

May knocked quickly. She and Danielle both ran to close the distance between them and there were tears in their eyes.

"Oh, May," Danielle said, holding the young girl close. She brushed the brown hair back from May's face and kissed her cheek. "Oh, Lord, I'm so glad to see you. Where have you been? I called and called everywhere I could think of."

They sat down. "I had to come," May said. "I'm sorry I didn't tell you where I was going. I left . . ." She shook her head. "I can't talk about it now. I went to another aunt's house in Baltimore, but she moved away and didn't want me to go with them. I'm staying with a friend. . . ."

"Have you eaten?"

"I had an early breakfast, but that trail mix and the doughnuts look good. May I have some?"

"You help yourself."

May got herself food and some coffee and came back. She and Danielle sat in chairs, side by side.

May smiled wanly. "You served me food at ALM one night when I was so bummed out I almost couldn't stand it. You care about me, don't you?"

"Yes, I care about you. You know that."

"And I *love* you."

"Then come back. Stay with me. Are you still with your boyfriend?"

"Not really. He still wants to marry me, but we're not together. He calls, but I don't call him." She bit her lip. "He fights me when we're together. When I leave him, he gets nice. He'd be a mess in your life."

"I can handle him."

"No one can handle him. He's a devil, like that man who was two people."

"Dr. Jekyll and Mr. Hyde."

"Yes." A small smile lit May's face.

"What are you doing about school?"

"I'm in summer school. I took today off. Look, Detective Ritchey, this is a pop call. I have to baby-sit this afternoon for the lady I'm staying with and I've got to get a bus back. I work part-time. You know I'm not lazy."

"You're a wonderful girl and I want all the best for you."

A lump rose in May's throat until she couldn't talk, then it cleared. "I know you do. Leave me be awhile, let me get myself together. I've got a whole lot to tell you that I just can't right now." She shook her head.

"Then promise me you'll keep in touch."

May reached into her drawstring bag, took out a small pad and a pen and wrote a number down. "If I'm not there they'll know where I am and take a message." She handed Danielle the paper.

May sat a long time after talking, then she got up slowly. "You don't know how hard it is to say good-bye." Danielle stood up and they hugged tightly with tears streaming down May's face. "Good-bye," May said. "Don't walk me out. I love you."

"And I love you. I hope you know how much."

Danielle stood for a few minutes in the middle of the floor after May left. May was the child she'd never had. She smiled a bit to herself. She was seventeen years older than May, old enough to be her mother, and she wanted this girl.

Her cell phone rang; she picked it up from her desk.

"Hello, beautiful!"

"Whit, aren't you traveling with Jon?"

"We are and I'm having a ball. I didn't stop to say hello because I was running late."

"It's all right. I know when you don't call there's a reason."

"How about a late lunch, early dinner?"

"Sounds good. I think early dinner. I sat here in a meeting for a while with Jon and scarfed up too much food and chocolate milk. I'm not going to have much of an appetite for lunch."

"Annie's Place?"

"Why not?"

"I'll meet you there around five. I'm really being given the grand tour."

* * *

Outside the medical examiner's office, Whit grinned as he snapped his phone off.

"Can't go without talking to her for a few hours?" Jon teased. "I remember when Fran and I were like that. Hell, we just about still are. Am I doing this tour right?"

"I'm enjoying this." Whit glanced around at the tables with their morbid burdens both covered and uncovered with sheets, their toe tags sticking out, and at the drawers that held still more sad burdens—a morgue. Sad as it was, it was a part of Dani's world and he wanted to know everything he could about it.

When the door chimes sounded, Irene jumped. Lord, she was nervous these days. Passing a hall table, she paused, wondering if she should open the table drawer and put her dark glasses on. The mirror showed her blackened eye. It should be that nice Lieutenant Ritchey at the door. Grimly, she decided against the glasses. The lie she had in mind was cover enough. She had domestic help, but she answered her own door and her own phone. Cal liked it that way.

"Danielle!" She hugged the younger woman.

"Hello, Irene. Am I too early?"

"I like it when people come early." She made herself giggle a bit. "Now, you're going to wonder right off about my eye." She placed her hand over the eye for a moment. "I'm so clumsy. I ran into the edge of a door last night. When I woke up, I had this." She laughed hollowly.

"It's a beauty," Danielle commiserated. "You tried beefsteak?"

"Oh, yes. Cal insisted on it. By the way, he's here. He was supposed to drive down to Richmond, but he's a few hours behind. Lord, I'm forgetting to invite you in. Cal's upstairs getting ready to leave."

By this time, they were out of the black-and-white-tiled foyer and into the beautifully decorated living room with its heavy and expensive mahogany furniture and its gold-leaf glass tables. The living room and dining room walls were jade green.

"Everything's so beautiful," Danielle complimented her, "but then I've seen it once or twice before when you've had parties."

"Yes," Irene said thoughtfully, "it *is* beautiful. Cal insisted we get a decorator. We've had it redone several times." She held up her hands. "I'm going to take you around the house. Now, can I offer you refreshments?"

"It's early and I'm pretty well stoked up. I can't stay too long. As I told you, I'm trying to get ideas for my place."

Irene cocked her head to one side. "I always liked that old house. I'll give you any help I can."

The house had many rooms. Downstairs there was a living room, parlor, dining room, den, guest room and bath, plus one powder room. Upstairs were four bedrooms and four baths. Spacious. Like something out of *House and Garden*. When she had been there before, Danielle had not seen the upper rooms. She was full of admiration and she could not imagine unbathed human bodies, a lot of them, smuggled into any of these wonderfully fresh rooms.

"My husband is in the bedroom," Irene said. "He's rushing to get out of town, so he isn't coming out. Do you travel?"

"Rarely. I go down to Quantico for police seminars. That's hardly travel."

"I've always thought you have such a thrilling job." She gasped a bit then. "Not that murder is thrilling, but, well, I guess you know what I mean."

Danielle smiled. "I think I do." A slightly hard edge came into her voice. "Someone's got to do it. We've had murder since Cain and Abel. . . ."

"And I wager we'll have it as long as any human is on earth. Why can't we do what's right?" From time to time, Irene's hand strayed to her face, as if to call attention to it. Looking at Irene, Danielle wondered how much she knew about her husband. She felt that any man who took his wife and his mistress out on a double date left a lot to be desired, but that didn't add up to murder.

Irene paused to talk about each beautiful room and Danielle reflected that the furniture alone was worth much of what she had paid for her house. But, she thought her own house was beginning to be a warm home, and this house, by contrast, was a gorgeous mausoleum.

They wound up in the kitchen where a small woman prepared lunch. "Oh," Irene said delightedly, "have late lunch with me. Cal has said he doesn't want lunch. You'd be company."

Danielle smiled at her. "I wish I could, but I've got to move on. I've already taken up so much of your time, and I really appreciate your showing me around."

"Any time at all. Do you have to go?"

"I'm afraid I do. I've got a couple of other stops to make. Tonight is my night for ALM and I've got to pull some stuff together."

"I think it's so wonderful you work with ALM. You *keep* the peace with battling couples, too."

"I certainly try."

Irene looked somber and said no more.

They stood in the foyer then and Irene involuntarily moved closer to Danielle for protection and for comfort. She had often thought of going to the police when Cal shook her, slapped her; the abuse just didn't seem severe enough to warrant a warning or arrest. But with the two recent blows, her own anger was beginning to frighten her. The night before, she had dreamed of plunging a knife through Cal's heart. She shuddered, thinking about it.

"Nothing about the man who was found dead?" Irene asked.

Danielle shifted her stance. "Well, we've got some info, some leads, but no, we haven't found the perp yet. I think we've got a good chance."

"I saw that article in the *Minden Journal* on him. Funny thing, that he used to be a policeman in Africa."

Danielle nodded. What would Irene think if she knew the hairs found on the man's suit matched Cal's head hair?

"The paper said he had a niece, that she was torn up. He was a distinguished-looking man. Poor soul. You used the term 'perp,' I know that's a *perpetrator*. Lately I've been reading a lot of true crime. I find I like them. Cal thinks it's dreadful literature. 'Why focus on the negative?' he always says."

"I guess there are lots of ways to look at it. If you enjoy reading them . . ." She shrugged. "I like all manners of mysteries and crime fiction."

Irene smiled then, glowing in the corroboration of her taste in literature.

"I really do have to go now," Danielle said. "I've enjoyed talking with you so much."

Irene touched Danielle's arm. "Do come again. Once can't be enough to guide you in your decorating. Come next week for dinner, or on your off day for brunch. You've given me so much happiness today, talking with you." What she didn't say was that she felt safe and secure with Danielle.

When Danielle had gone, Irene leaned against the door. Cal was supposed to have gone by now. She fretted nervously.

"Irene!" Cal squalled and Irene stiffened. He called again. Her throat was closed and she couldn't answer. She scurried up the stairs and to the bedroom. The door was locked. She rapped softly and he flung the door open.

"Cal, Lieutenant Ritchey might have heard you yelling."

"Hell's bells, I saw the woman go down the walk. Besides, in my own house," he muttered, "I do whatever the hell I want."

Irene sighed. "What did you want?"

He caught her by her shoulders and she cowered, weeping inside, afraid he would hit her again. He had shaken and slapped her many times, but hit her only the two times lately.

Now there was the blackened eye to lie about, but she thought she carried it off well with Lieutenant Ritchey. Had she believed her? Probably not.

"Why in the hell didn't you put on your dark glasses?"

"I . . . I said I ran into a door," Irene stammered. "She didn't seem to pay it any mind."

"Cops get good covering up their suspicions. Anyway, she doesn't know you deserved it."

"Cal, I try to please you . . . a black eye is so humiliating and it *hurts*."

"Woman, back *off,*" Cal roared. "You're my wife. You live under my roof and I give you every comfort. So, I hit you now and then. It couldn't hurt much and it's nobody else's damned business. So, don't come whining to me. I give you everything a woman could want."

"Except love," Irene mumbled under her breath.

"What's that?"

"Nothing, honey. It's all right."

"Don't I give you plenty of money, this fine house? Go look out the window. Looks like a majestic park on these grounds. Clothes. Status. When I feel you don't appreciate it, it makes me hit you. Maybe you'd rather have that piccant Dave Emlen who ain't got a pot to piss in. Maybe you'd like him to crawl into your bed."

"I'd never cheat on you," she said quietly. "You know that."

He looked at her long and hard. "If I didn't know better, you'd be a dead woman. Maybe I ought to stop you from going to visit my sister."

"Please, Cal. Edith and I love each other. It's like she is my own sister."

"She could come here."

"I stay in too much as it is. Please don't stop me. Dave's an honorable man. There is nothing between us."

"There sure as hell better not be. You stay in with that shiner I put on you. I'm right proud of myself. Didn't know I had it in me. I've been coddling you, and even then you've been complaining." He walked to the bed and picked up a large black briefcase. "I packed for myself while you were lollygagging with that detective. You take care now and think about what I said."

He kissed her cheek. "Yessir, hung me a shiner."

Irene's mouth felt as dry as dust. "Have a good trip. When will you be back?"

"I'm coming back tonight, or maybe in the morning. Not that it's any of your business."

"I'm sorry," she said.

"Yeah, you're sorry," he said. "Sorriest woman I ever met." He left the room and she murmured to herself, "It's going to be all right." A few minutes later, standing at the window of their bedroom, she watched him pull out of the garage in his big black Cadillac, and again she murmured, "It's going to be all right."

Two hours later, Irene sat in the backyard of her sister-in-law Edith's comfortable gray house. She always felt peace the moment she neared Edith's. How could a sister be so different from a brother? Edith was a fairly tall, bird-like woman with chocolate skin and glossy black hair. Under an oak tree, Edith set a big pitcher of excellent lemonade on the yard table and sat down, pulling up a chair near Irene.

"Cal gone on to Richmond?" Edith asked.

"Yes."

"Is he staying a few days?"

"No, he's coming right back, probably tomorrow morning."

Edith squinted at her. "You got red eyes? You've got the sunglasses on."

"Well, my eyes have been hurting. I've got to see a doctor."

"You don't take good enough care of yourself, for what it's worth."

"I'm all right."

Edith sighed as she poured two glasses of lemonade, handed one to Irene and sipped from the other. Another glass was on the table. Irene's heart jumped. That meant Dave was home.

Edith took a mint sprig from her glass and inhaled the aroma. "I've been meaning to talk to you. Irene, it's just going to get worse. I'll bet you've got on the dark glasses because he's given you a black eye. Cal's my brother, but he's mean. He's always been mean. My mother used to say he'd go to jail one day, but instead he got smart and he got rich, but he's kept on being mean. It's like there's a devil locked up in him, no, not locked up, running his life.

"He's hooked up to that Manny Luxor somehow. I go by Annie's and they're there. He's dog enough to try to have you and Annie, too. I got nothing against Annie, but she knows he's a married man. You ought to get away from him, get a man for yourself. My stepson's a good man. He doesn't make much money, but money can be cold comfort, and Dave would belong to you. He wouldn't run around on you. . . ."

They both looked up as the back screen door slammed and a lanky, cocoa-colored man came across the yard. Without saying anything, he came to Irene, lifted the glasses from her face and stared at her. "Damn it to hell!" he sputtered. "Come inside. We got to talk."

He took Irene's hand, pulled her up and she felt his tears fall on her arm.

"I'll go in, too," Edith said, "just in case that no-good brother of mine takes it in his head to double back to try to catch you or something. If I'm inside, too . . . well, he knows I don't run a room-by-the-hour motel." She put the pitcher of lemonade and the glasses and a plate of cookies on a tray and turned to them. "You two go on ahead. I'll be along in a bit."

Irene thought she looked so grim. These were her friends, her only friends in Minden, and she didn't want to get them into trouble.

* * *

Irene and Dave sat in the sunny living room side by side. He took her hand, then put his hand on her cheek.

"I can't stand much more of this," he said. He was tense with anger. "No, I'm wrong. I can't stand *any* more. I love you, Reen. I've loved you right from the start. Leave him and come with me. I'll protect you."

She had to stop him. "We'd both be dead inside of a day. You think he'd let us be together, you don't know Cal. Oh, *he* wouldn't do it, but he'd see it was done." She sounded as bitter as gall.

Dave leaned forward. "He's got you scared to death of him. I figure he's all bluster, mostly bark and little bite. I can best him, whip him."

Irene's heart was soaring and plummeting back and forth. She knew then how much he loved her and God knows, she loved him.

"We've only stolen a little kiss or two," he said, "but God knows, I *want* you. I want to make love to you, show you what a man's love can be, what *my* love can be. You're still young enough to have my children and I can make more money than I do. It just never seemed to matter.

"Say yes, Reen. I know you feel the way I do, and we can't go on like this. I'll kill that son of a bitch if I have to to protect you. Don't sell me short. I'm not a mean man, but I don't take a lot. Please, honey."

When Irene looked at him through her tears, she thought she loved him more than she had ever loved anybody or anything. Why shouldn't they be together?

"All right," she murmured. "I'll take the chance, but expect trouble with a capital T. Give me a little while to get used to this, to knowing that I'm going to have a life like other people." Her heart felt light, thrumming with joy.

Dave kissed her then, the way he had never kissed her before, and her soft body opened out to him. *Delicate little flower,* he thought. *His* flower that he would tend to for the rest of his days.

And, sitting there, transfixed with love, Irene thought it was going to be all right. *It really was going to be all right.*

TWENTY-ONE

Around eight o'clock the next evening, Minden Police Headquarters was humming. Tonight would be the night of the raid. Cops in plainclothes milled about and coffee flowed. Then it was ten o'clock and the helicopter had signalled that a big rig had pulled up to the side door of Annie's house. Danielle felt a stream of pure adrenaline course through her. Danielle, Jon, Ed, and others waited patiently for a further report.

Ed touched Danielle's hand as she sat beside him at her table.

"Are you ready for this?" Ed asked.

"As ready as I'll ever be."

Jon laughed as he looked at Danielle. "You're practically wired. Are you all right?"

"I'm fine," Danielle said as other team members filed into the room.

"How's it coming?" Adrienne asked.

"Pretty much on schedule," Danielle answered.

Danielle's cell phone rang. She answered it, talked briefly to a cop stationed outside. "Let's do it now," she said and stood up. "They've got infrared that tells them some part of that house is holding a whole lot of warm human bodies. Let's go!"

Even with the task before them, Danielle thought about how she hadn't been able to sleep for a couple of nights. One night she had been with Whit and he had held her. She had dreamed crazy dreams of chaos and confusion. There had been blood and madness and she had cowered along a wall. She had been alone the way she had felt alone after Mona died.

"Sweetheart," Whit had crooned after she had told him about one of the dreams, "it's your life and you love it, but I worry about you, and about your safety."

"I'll be all right."

"You'd better be. I pray for you, Dani. Always know that."

She had smiled. "And I pray for myself and for you. Don't worry about me."

In a little while the neighborhood that held Annie's house buzzed with police and Immigration and Naturalization Service traffic: unmarked cars and pickup trucks, shadowy figures along the countryside. Two paddy wagons were parked near the house. Danielle was with Jon and Ed as others covertly got to the front door of the house and, with a pole, rammed it open. Annie and Buck met them in the hallway.

"What the hell!" Annie exploded.

Buck's mouth hung slack, then he got himself together. "I sure hope you got some good explanation for this. We're in America, not some damned fascist county."

Danielle, Jon, and Ed flashed badges. "We're coming in," Jon said and the others crowded in behind them.

They went past Annie and Buck and Danielle stopped in front of the door to the room. It was locked. Ed kicked it open and inside they found a group of fifteen to twenty men cowering just as Danielle had cowered in her dream. They all seemed to be African, some with carvings on their faces. They seemed frightened and intelligent—and they were silent.

"Does anybody here speak English?" Danielle asked.

A number of hands went up. Danielle pointed at one man near her. "Why are you here?" she asked.

The man shrugged and looked downhearted. "We come to this country to save our lives. We are dead men at home."

Danielle felt her heart go out to the man, to all of them, because she felt that in more cases than not, this was the truth for all of them.

As Annie and Buck tried to wrench away from the cops who held them, Danielle said brusquely to Ed, "Read this man and this woman their Miranda rights and cuff them." Buck was defiant, but Annie looked scared.

One man tried to bolt for the door but the police caught him. Danielle wondered if Cedric Appiah had, for some reason, bolted for the door and been shot for his trouble.

Annie paused before Danielle. "This was what the visit was all about, wasn't it? And I trusted you."

"I'm sorry," Danielle said, "but you're operating outside the law." She now knew where the strange odor came from. These men, unwashed for too many days, smelled, and the odor of their suppressed fear was sickening.

"Hold up a minute," Danielle said, looking at one of the immigrants. "*When* were you to move on?"

"Don't tell them anything," Buck yelled. "Don't talk. You've got rights, even as illegal aliens." In an effort to communicate with the men who didn't speak English, he shook his head and pointed to his mouth before he could be fully cuffed.

It was quick work as the twenty men were loaded into paddy wagons. A helicopter landed on the spacious lawn and a couple of men got out while the pilot stayed in the cockpit.

Buck muttered half to himself, "Ten years down the damned drain, but Manny'll get us out of this."

Not much could be done by the Minden cops that night other than to arrest Annie and Buck. The illegal aliens were arrested by the INS. Jon drove Danielle home.

"I want to talk over the case a bit with you," Jon said.

Danielle felt her bones screaming with tension, but she agreed. As they drove along, he talked. When they reached her home, he came in with her.

"Coffee?" she asked.

"Yeah. I need it. So do you."

He took out his cell phone and called his wife, and Danielle answered the phone message from Whit; he wanted her to call him back.

Quickly, she called Whit and told him about the raid. "It's over," she said, "and we got the perps. Whit, everything went off without a hitch."

At first he said nothing, but his heart ached with fear for her. "I'm glad it's over."

"I'm really tense. Jon's here. We're mapping out how we'll handle the rest of this."

"Good luck." He hesitated and then his concern burst from him. "Dani, I need to see you."

"Then come over. We've cost each other enough sleep to last a lifetime, but it's been worth it."

"Do you want me to come? Won't I interfere with what you have to do?"

She smiled. "I'm your lover and Jon's your friend—you won't interfere with us. We'll have it under control by the time you get here."

The next morning the station house was busier than it had been in years. The illegal aliens would be held until they could be questioned. They were held temporarily in the Minden jail. Only INS had the authority to arrest the aliens; Minden police couldn't. Annie was defeated and deflated and looked ashamed to her bones; Buck held his bluff. They both asked to make telephone calls and were given permission.

Cal Catlett came in early with a high-powered and expensive lawyer, Quincy Tyler. He asked to see Jon.

"Seems like you got two friends of mine in here," Cal drawled, as jaunty as usual.

"It's news to me that Buck Lansing is such a good friend of yours. I knew about Annie," Jon retorted.

Cal reddened. "I'm friends with both of them." He introduced his lawyer to Jon and Danielle and the lawyer laughed. "Captain Ryson and I are old friends—ah, well, acquaintances—and I know Lieutenant Ritchey."

A bail bondsman met them at the desk and filled out the necessary papers to set Annie and Buck free on bail. Cal grinned from ear to ear.

"See you in Sunday school," Cal said and put his arms around Annie's shoulder. Buck couldn't wait to get to the door.

Danielle called out, "Both of you see to it that you don't leave town."

Danielle and Ed were somber. "I know Annie doesn't pose any flight threat," Danielle said, and Ed finished for her, "but God knows what Buck will do."

"As long as Manny's here, he's not going anywhere. He's Manny's boy all the way," Jon said. "What do you think about Catlett? Think he's involved? His big rig brought them in."

Danielle thought about it a moment. "Well, if his love, Annie, set the city on fire, he'd be here to put out the flames, but Buck, well, I didn't know they were so close. Cal at least knows about it."

"I think he's doing it as a favor to Manny," Ed said. "As far as I've found out, they're not buddies, and maybe not even good friends, but they probably do each other favors. Manny can help him with labor problems and Cal probably owed him a few. I told you Whit saw them together in New York."

Ed laughed. "The phrase 'thick as thieves' comes to mind. Manny is a small-time mobster through and through, with *ties* to organized crime big time. He likes being a big fish in a small pond like Minden. But he's got plenty of connections to the New York and Vegas mob."

"Annie was scared," Danielle said slowly. "I think she was mostly dragged into this." She turned to Jon. "You don't really think Cal's a part of the team?"

"What team?" Jon answered. "Manny, most likely, Buck, then Annie as accomplice."

"That's a team," Danielle pointed out. "Although I can't see those two paying Annie what she's worth."

"Maybe," Jon said, "she's Cal's way to be in it and out of it at the same time."

"I feel," Danielle said, "as if I could sleep a couple of days. I was up late."

Jon looked at her sharply. "Why don't you give yourself tomorrow off? I know you were up later than you expected last night. We're all going to have to stay alert." He gave her a conspiratorial wink and went out into the hall.

When Jon had gone, Ed turned to Danielle. "I'm dying for a cigarette. Go with me outside."

"Sure. As long as you promise to blow the smoke away from me."

Outside they found Adrienne and a couple of others smoking busily.

"I don't know why you asked me to come with you," Danielle fussed. "You know I'm going to carp at all of you about putting your lives on the line."

"Gotta go some time," Ed countered.

"I watched a heavy-smoking uncle die of emphysema. It was not pretty. He really suffered. You keep on and you'll never retire to Mexico like a rich king."

Adrienne looked at Danielle and smiled. "Give yourself credit. With your nagging, I've decided to give it up; just not today. Next week, I'm going to get started for sure."

"Coward," Ed said. He turned to Adrienne and the others. "What do you think of the raid?"

"Stunning," Adrienne answered. "Who would have thought

something like that could happen in a sleepy little city like Minden? Buck now, I'm not surprised about, but Annie? She's no little Miss Muffet, but I swear I gave her more credit."

Danielle's cell phone rang. "Daffy!" she said.

Daphne chuckled. "Your voice tells me something red hot's going on. Whit?"

"Saw him last night, but he's not the red-hot thing this time. Have you heard the news?"

"As a matter of fact, I haven't. Julian and I were out late. I didn't even turn on the radio for the news. I'm rushing to get to school."

Danielle told her about the raid and she whistled. "So you had double excitement in your life. Whit *and* the raid. Well, I'll tell you, I've got excitement, too." She paused a moment. "But who am I kidding? As much fun as your dad is, I don't think he'll get serious any time soon."

"He likes you a lot. I know that."

"I know he likes me, sweetie, but I want much more and I don't think I'll ever get it from him. He had a real thing going with your mother and maybe he'll never get over her. He hasn't so far."

A small pain lodged in Danielle's throat. "You and I are in the same boat," she said.

"Whit's in love with you."

Danielle's heart lifted with the words. "He said he is and I believe him, but there can be varying degrees of love."

"He asked you to marry him."

"He did and he meant it, but you don't see the pain in his eyes sometimes when he mentions Willo or I ask about his life with her. Humans are strange creatures, Daffy. Sometimes we never manage to get it together."

TWENTY-TWO

Irene Catlett awoke cramped and frowning. She glanced at the clock on her night table: four in the morning. She sat up abruptly, throwing the covers back. What was that noise? It sounded like a dog was scratching at the front door and howling. It must be Girly, and how long had it been going on?

She blushed, thinking she'd had a bit too much to drink before she went to bed. She had pretended to be asleep when Cal came to bed and also when he got a phone call and left the house. She had suppressed her anger the way she always did as she thought, *That bitch, Annie Lusk, is getting him out of bed with me, his rightful mate.* Her eyelids had felt like lead.

Swinging her legs over the edge of the bed, she sat up, slid her feet into mules and pulled on her robe. The scratching and the howling got louder. She went out into the hall and stumbled down the steps.

"All right. All right. I'm coming, Girly. What in the hell is wrong with you?" The dog had her own house, but sometimes slept in the big house where she had several doggy beds.

Unfastening three locks and opening the door, Irene snapped on the porch light and was treated to a woeful sight. Girly ran back and forth frantically, whimpering and howling. She came to Irene, then ran a bit away, again and again. Irene tried to pat the dog, but Girly couldn't be still; she was agitated beyond belief. It became plain then that the dog was trying to tell her something.

It was also crystal clear that Girly wanted to lead her somewhere. Was Cal hurt? Maybe he had an accident? He could be so careless. "All right," she said calmly, "you stay here and I'll be right back."

Inside, she hurriedly threw on some clothes, got a hunter's flashlight, picked up her cell phone and put it in a tote bag. At the last minute she threw in a small phone book and a first-aid kit. When she went back out she found Girly in the same state of frenzy.

"All right," she said, "lead me to wherever, and if it's too far to walk, I'll come back and get the car. I can call someone if there's trouble."

As they moved along the country road, Girly kept running on ahead. Irene had visions of Cal lying beside the road or in a ditch, his car mangled. He drove while drunk all the time and she had warned him about it. At least it was in the opposite direction from Annie's house.

Stars and the moon were packing it in, saying good-bye to the night, as Irene and the dog walked. Girly kept running, looking back anxiously. Finally, she came close enough for Irene to pat her head. "We'll be there shortly," Irene said. "Or I'll go back and get the car."

They had walked well over a mile and Irene thought she'd better turn back for the car when Girly sharply urged her on. The only building in this quarter-mile stretch was the ALM house. Cal frequently came here and she sometimes came with him to help. When they reached the building, Girly flew around to the back and barked furiously.

"What on earth?"

Irene held the flashlight in her hand and beamed the powerful light all over the backyard and the near wood. She saw nothing amiss. Yet Girly's behavior said something was badly wrong. Then the dog stopped at the wide, latticed door of the crawl space and hunkered down, whimpering piteously.

Trusting her instinct, Irene knelt and opened the door of the crawl space and holding the flashlight looked inside. There was a man sprawled there on his back. These were Cal's clothes and this was Cal. She was too stunned to scream. Laying all caution aside, she crawled in. Had someone robbed him? Knocked him out? Girly crawled in with her, her mission accomplished. Why had whoever did this left him there?

Her eyes were so clouded over she didn't see the blood on his chest and the puddle of blood on the ground beside him. Then she screamed, but she kept her presence of mind. Quickly gathering her wits, she thought he'd need help. But he looked so still. Girly howled once again, then was silent. Irene felt for a pulse and could find none. If she put her hand in his blood on his chest, she probably couldn't feel a heartbeat. "Oh, my God," she wailed.

Putting the flashlight on the dirt, she knew what she had to do. She took out the cell phone from the tote, fought herself to be calm as she sought a number, and with fingers that had suddenly become icy cold, pushed 9-1-1.

Danielle awoke very early and lay in bed, stretching. She always turned the air-conditioning off at night and slept with open windows. It was very warm in the room, a hot July night. The excitement of the raid the night before still exhilarated her, but she was sad too. She liked Annie Lusk and hated the criminal activity she was mixed up in. *What Annie did for love,* she thought—Cal's love, because she was certain he was mixed up in this somehow. He had the best lawyers and would probably get off scot-free, leaving Annie and Buck Lansing holding the bag. But Buck was Manny's man and Manny had even better lawyers.

Now she threw back the covers and stretched long and luxuriously. Mischievously, she thought of waking Whit and decided against it. She was poised to get up and brew coffee and drink a very early cup when the phone rang. Thinking it was Whit, she picked it up and Irene's voice came over the wire, trembling so much that she could barely understand her. Danielle managed to get where Irene was located and told her to hold on, that she would be there immediately.

"Please try to stay calm," Danielle told her. "I know that's really impossible, but do the best you can."

Hanging up, she quickly called Whit and told him what had happened.

"Shouldn't I come over to your house or go to ALM?"

"No. Unless you want to come here, use your key and just stay until I can stop back. I don't know yet if Cal's dead or just badly hurt. Irene's devastated. Whit, please call my dad and Daffy. Tell them what's happened. I may not get a chance to call any of you for several hours. It's going to be a madhouse in any case."

Her mind moved quickly then. She placed calls to Jon, to Ed, and the rest of her team and she began to prepare to leave. Everyone said they'd meet her there.

Danielle pulled into the driveway of the ALM house and drove around the back. She found Irene kneeling on the ground still peering into the crawl space, the flashlight burning bright, vying with the early sunlight. When Irene saw her, she turned the flashlight off.

"I brought a thermos of water and some Tylenol," Danielle said, handing Irene a paper cup and two tablets. Opening the thermos, she poured the water. "I want you to swallow these before you go into shock."

"I'm not going to conk out on you. Is he dead?"

"Oh, sweetie, how do I know yet?"

Danielle moved into the crawl space then with her own powerful flashlight and felt for a pulse and like Irene, found none. It was a large space and she squatted on her haunches. A heavy gold ring glittered on Cal's hand and a gold Rolex wristwatch ran on his wrist, so it wasn't robbery. If, indeed, he was dead, his features were relaxed, soft, peaceful, unlike the Cal she thought she knew. She took evidence bags and thin plastic gloves from her tote and slipped the jewelry into the bags.

Breathing deeply, Danielle got up and went out to Irene, who sat on the back steps.

"I didn't want to leave him, but now you're here. Danielle, I need to know. Is he *dead?*"

"We'll know in a few minutes."

It seemed a long while to Danielle, but it was only fifteen or so minutes before her team—Ed, Adrienne, Wink, and Matt—pulled in, sirens silent. Jon came next. Then an ambulance. The ambulance crew went to work immediately, probing, examining.

"He'll never go hungry again," one of the ambulance technicians said tiredly.

"Be careful," Danielle said quietly. "It's her husband."

The technician nodded.

Jon called the specially equipped funeral home that handled dead bodies for the police department.

Shaking so badly she could hardly breathe, Irene told them as best she could how Girly had awakened her and how she had dared to walk down a lonely country road in search of help for her husband. She wrung her hands and her face was wet with cold tears.

They secured the death scene, roped it off with yellow tape and made a chalk outline of how the body lay, except for the part of the dirt floor that was covered with Cal's blood. It seemed a long time before they heard the sirens of the body wagon and the black van pulled in.

"You offered us a good, used body?" one heavyset attendant joked.

Adrienne took Irene's hand. "Don't you have a key to the building?" she asked Danielle. "I thought I'd go in and make Mrs. Catlett a cup of coffee."

Irene tried to smile and her face crumpled. "I don't want to bother you," she said, "but God knows I need *something*."

Adrienne nodded. "I'll make some in the big coffeemaker. I certainly need some." Adrienne was also an ALM volunteer.

By then a rosy, pink dawn suffused the sky. It was one of the prettiest dawns Danielle had ever seen and she thought: *It's like my life, so much joy and beauty and so much* pain.

The crew of the special funeral home loaded the body on a stretcher and put it in the special hearse. The jocular man was more subdued now. *God, I hate death,* Danielle thought. How did she come to deal with it on such constant, intimate terms?

Finally, Adrienne came to the door. "It's ready," she said. "Coffee, cream, sugar. I found some cinnamon rolls in the fridge and put them in the oven. I fixed a cup of coffee for Irene. She's really a basket case."

The group filed into the kitchen for the coffee and quickly came back outside as if it were necessary to watch the body being transported. Girly lay mournfully with her head on her paws. She had done what she could.

And inside, clutching a cup of coffee so hot that it nearly scalded her mouth, Irene was sick with guilt. Had Cal really believed she was having an affair with Dave? And Dave's furious face rose before her. "I'll kill him," he had said more than once. What had gotten into Cal to make him begin to strike her so hard where he had formerly cursed, shaken, and slapped her? This had aroused Dave's wrath more than anything. She wanted Dave's love, needed his love, but she didn't want Cal to have to die for it.

Whit didn't go back to bed after Danielle called him. He was going to drive over to be there for her and to talk with Jon, who, along with Danielle, was drawing him more and more into crime scenes.

He watched the same dawn Danielle watched and thought about her. He had been so impressed at the way she and others had handled the murder of the African man. And the night she had thrown the holdup man. He couldn't talk to her about his fear for her safety. It wasn't like just any other job, but she certainly could take care of herself. He knew, too, that something in Danielle *liked* danger, maybe even craved it, and he had to live with that.

What worried him more than anything these days was the deep sympathy he felt for Willo. He had loved this woman once with all his heart and she had crushed his heart *and* his manhood. Now she had changed, he thought, and wanted him back. He knew he wouldn't, he couldn't go back, but he still felt so much for her. Not what he felt for Danielle—that was rock solid. But he wanted to go to Danielle with a heart that was just for her taking, not tattered with deep, leftover feelings for a woman out of his past.

TWENTY-THREE

At the police station, Danielle reflected that in her thirteen years on the force, there had not been a case like this. She had gone home, changed, and talked to Whit for a while. He had driven from D.C. to be with her.

"It's going to be a three-ring circus," she told him. "Cal Catlett was an important man in this city."

"I can imagine." He had brought in the morning paper. Photographs and news of the raid and the illegal aliens covered the front page.

"Sorry I couldn't talk with you about it. We had to have top secrecy," she said.

"No problem. I don't want you to compromise yourself. The man who was killed was part of a group like that?"

"Almost certainly."

He had wanted to fix her breakfast, but she never could eat after a murder. His kisses had been warm on her face and lips as she left him. Now she sat down and waited while Jon, Ed, Wink, and others filed into the small room off from her office. A green board was on the wall and she walked to it with chalk in her hand. When the last person had come in, she began.

"We've got a live one this time. When a man like Caleb Catlett is murdered, everybody comes to attention." She shrugged. "Yet to me, one life is like another and all life is precious." She wrote *Suspects* on the middle of the board, then the number *one*.

The widow, Irene Catlett, she wrote with good penmanship. "Now I hardly think she'll be the perpetrator," she said, "but as you know when a person is murdered, we look first at those closest to them."

She wrote down other names: *Annie Lusk, Dave Emlen, Manny Luxor, Buck Lansing.* She paused a while then, and last, but not least, *Keith Janey.* Numbers preceded the names and Danielle's face was grave.

"I've been in touch with Judge Lanier and he's being kind to us. We'll get search warrants signed today as soon as we take them over. I'm going to say again what I always say: The first forty-eight hours are the most important. Every hour after that makes the crime more likely to go unsolved. But we don't ever give up. We've got no cold cases, just lukewarm ones. Are you with me?"

The group answered, "Yes."

"Good. Because Mrs. Catlett is the closest to him, I'm going to begin with her. I'll interview her, go to her home and talk with her. I have a hunch she'll be more at ease with me than with anyone else."

"Sure," Ed said.

Danielle tapped on the board. "I put Keith Janey last, but actually I want him searched first. He could be a flight risk. Let Manny Luxor and Buck Lansing be among the first searched too."

The receptionist stuck her head in the door. "Lieutenant, you have a visitor. Mrs. Irene Catlett."

Danielle looked up sharply, her eyes narrowed. "Please seat her in my office and tell her I'll be with her in a very short while." She turned to Ed. "I guess now I can just interview her in my office."

On her way to talk with Irene, Danielle stopped by the small, crowded squad room. Desks with jumbled file folders were pushed close together and several detectives greeted her. "Hello, Loo." It was not a term they used as often as big-city cops used it. Smiling narrowly she went to the part of the room where her team had their desks pushed together.

"Got something for you," Adrienne said as Mark nodded.

"Oh?" Danielle responded.

"Yeah. Luminol showed blood on the floor of the darkroom at the ALM house. And a very small amount of blood in the hallway. We figure Mr. Catlett must have been killed in the darkroom."

Danielle nodded. "Anything else?"

Adrienne shook her head. "We're working. I'll let you know the minute we find anything else."

Danielle did her best to put Irene Catlett at ease. That was *so* important. Irene had no objection to taping their conversation.

Her body trembling, the small woman said, "I had to come."

They went into a room off Danielle's office, where she seated the woman and asked if she'd like coffee. Irene shook her head. "I'm so nervous." Her hands were tightly clasped in her lap.

"Try to relax. I have to tape our conversation."

"That's fine with me."

Danielle sat quietly as Irene gathered her thoughts.

"Why did you come?" Danielle finally asked.

"Because I wanted to tell someone that Dave Emlen is not guilty. He didn't kill Cal. He couldn't."

"Why would he want to?"

"Because he loves me, as I love him. He's been beside himself since Cal began hitting me. . . ."

Danielle sat up straight. "I've seen the bruises so I won't be coy about it. He's been hitting you for a long time, hasn't he? Why would Mr. Emlen get so furious about it now?"

Irene expelled a harsh breath. "He's always shaken me so hard I could hardly get my breath. I've always been afraid I'd die when he shook me. He slapped me often, but only in the past two months has he struck me so *hard*. Cal had things on his mind, I think. The paper is full of the raid on Annie Lusk's house. Everybody knows she was his woman."

"I've heard."

"He thought a lot of himself and he loved Annie. I was just for outside show. A man like him needs a wife."

"You think Ms. Lusk killed him?"

"Most likely hired someone to have it done. She's pretty thick with that Manny Luxor and Buck Lansing. They're said to be mobsters. I know you have to question Dave. There's a little light gossip about me and him, but there's no hanky-panky going on. I'm a God-fearing woman and I wouldn't fool around, but if I did . . ."

Irene's mouth opened in a slight smile and her hands in her lap relaxed. "Well, just forget I said that. I talk too much."

"Did you ever want to kill Mr. Catlett when he struck you, squeezed your arms so bad it hurt? Did he curse you?"

"He called me names sometimes. I didn't pay it any mind. I know I'm a good woman. He knew it too."

"Did he ever mention Mr. Emlen to you?"

"Oh, yes, all the time. I guess I feel it's God's punishment to me for loving Dave when I had a husband."

Danielle bowed her head with sympathy for the woman before her. "Tell me about your relationship with your husband. I know you're shocked and hurting, but we want to solve it quickly if we can, and anything you can tell us will be helpful."

"Well, you're a volunteer so you know Cal and I worked together for A Literate Minden. That's about it. We lived together and slept and ate together, but we seldom went out. You remember the Whit Steele concert. You were there with Mr. Steele. He's your beau, yes? He seems to be a fine man and you're a fine woman."

Danielle's face warmed. "Thank you. I've always thought you were a good person. Did Mr. Luxor and Mr. Lansing visit your husband often?"

Irene shook her head. "They've only been there once or twice that I can remember. Cal used to go to New York all the time. They probably met there. Why would Cal be mixed up in something like smuggling illegal aliens?"

"Money?"

"Cal had money to burn. The mattress factory is thriving. He's got a good product." She put her hand to her face. "How am I going to run a mattress factory? What do I know?"

"You could go back to school and learn. Take business courses. I understand he's got a good manager. He could help."

Irene hugged herself. "I can't believe he's gone. Come to my house and visit whenever you want to. I'll tell you anything you want to know, but the reason I came was that I'm afraid for Dave—not that I'm not upset about Cal, because I am."

"Has Mr. Emlen ever struck you?"

Irene looked surprised. "Oh, no, he'd never . . . Why do you ask that?"

"Just curious. I'm glad to hear that."

"Dave loves me. He'd never hurt me. He'd got so mad when he saw the bruises." She sat up straighter. "If you're through with me, I'll go now. Am I a suspect?" She sounded bitter for the first time. "I certainly had reason."

"We have many suspects until we solve the murder. Just be open and aboveboard with us. Do you have a good lawyer?"

Irene looked alarmed. "Why would I need a lawyer?"

"To look out for your interests."

"I like Cal's lawyer. He treats me with respect."

"Good. He'll probably call you. If not soon, you call him. Now, any time you have something you'd like to ask, call me or Ed." Reaching into a box on her desk, she took out a business card and handed it to Irene. As she stood up, Irene rose and offered her hand.

"Who can you depend on to help you through this?" Danielle asked.

"Cal's sister, Edith—and Dave." Her voice sounded husky when she said his name.

"That's good. Please take care of yourself and if you need me . . ."

"You're so sweet. Believe me, I'd never lie to you. I'll tell you anything you want or need to know."

As Irene left, Danielle cut off the tape recorder. She sat thinking *No, I don't see Irene killing Cal, but Dave Emlen might have done it on her behalf.* Her psychic waves were silent about Irene Catlett. She had set off no warning bells, but then her psychic gift was incomplete. It consisted of vivid dreams, visions and hunches, the dreams and visions more dependable than the hunches. It was a gift she shared with many who cared to exercise it.

It was strange, she thought now, that beginning with seeing Cal's body this morning, she had begun to feel bits and pieces of a vision flutter through her mind. There came a growing certainty for the first time that one day she *would* know Mona's murderer.

Keith Janey's house was just short of a hovel. Set back in the wood out from Minden, he had never lived well and since Cal Catlett fired him, he had lived in partial squalor, eating little, drinking a lot. It was eleven o'clock in the morning when Danielle, Ed, and Wink knocked on his door. A bleary-eyed, unshaven-for-three-days Keith drank the last from a fifth of bourbon, set the bottle on the table and answered the door.

"Yeah," he said hoarsely, taken aback.

"Mr. Janey?" Danielle began.

"Yeah. I was Keith Janey last time I looked in the mirror. Who the hell are you?"

Danielle identified herself and showed Keith Janey the search warrant.

"Well, I don't guess there's no way I can keep you from coming in, is there? So, come on in. It ain't much, but it's home."

"Did you know Mr. Caleb Catlett was murdered last night?"

Keith Janey's mouth fell open. "You don't say. Well now, it

ain't no point in me lying. I heard it on the news in the liquor store an hour or so ago. He had it coming if anyone did. Excuse the shape my house is in. He fired me a couple of months ago. Fired me when I was sick with heart trouble."

"I'm sorry. I'll need to question you a bit and I want to tape it," Danielle told him.

"What about? Oh, hell, you don't think I did it, much as I wanted to. Go ahead—tape."

Danielle snapped on her recorder. They remained standing. Every chair was filled with articles.

"Where were you all last night and yesterday afternoon?"

"What time was he killed?"

"Please answer my question."

Keith Janey coughed. "I don't reckon I got no alibi. I drank a fifth and crawled into bed, got up later and ate sardines and crackers. I didn't go back out until I hit the liquor store this morning. A man like me, the world's against him."

In the meantime, Ed and Wink were turning the house upside down. On sudden impulse Danielle said to them, "Be as careful as you can. We don't want to mess things up more than necessary."

Ed gave a hoarse laugh, but said, "We'll be careful."

"Thank you, ma'am," Keith Janey said.

Wink searched and took photographs of the two-room hut. Papers were strewn everywhere; old aluminum pie plates on the table and stove were crusted with food and flies buzzed.

"Mr. Janey, we're going to have to ask you to come down to the station."

"What in hell for? I didn't kill the bastard."

"Cooperate with us, please. It's in your best interests."

"You can question me here."

"No, we need to question you both places."

Keith Janey stuck out his mouth, pouted. "Well, if I got to, what time?"

"Well, well, well," Ed's provocative drawl came from the closet and he came out with a gun on his handkerchief, his hands encased in thin plastic gloves. "What have we got here?"

"Everybody needs a gun in the house," Keith Janey said fretfully. "I'd forgot about that raggedy old thing."

"It shoots, I'll bet," Ed said as Wink took pictures.

"This is your gun?" Danielle asked.

"Don't nobody else live here."

"Then we're going to have to ask you to come with us now," Danielle said.

"Like this? I ain't had a bath in a week."

Ed was feeling a bit mean. "You can go to the liquor store," he said, "but you can't come down to the station house?"

Then Ed relaxed as he looked at the gun: a .22-caliber. Janey had been all over town threatening Caleb Catlett. He had gone further downhill lately. *Keith Janey,* Danielle thought. Maybe they weren't going to need the full forty-eight hours.

TWENTY-FOUR

"Lieutenant!"

Danielle slowed her pace and turned around as Ted Keys came down the hall.

"Mr. Keys," Danielle acknowledged him. She fully intended to question Cal's factory manager, but it would come later. She knew of no reason he would want Cal dead, but in this business, you never could tell.

Ted Keys reached her, looking rumpled and harried. "Could you talk with me?" he said. "I've got something that might interest you."

They were near her office and she invited him in. Seated, Ted frowned and clenched his hands, but said nothing. Danielle waited him out, then turned on the tape.

"Listen," Ted finally said, "I don't want to get a poor fool in more trouble than he's already in, but I think you need to know this."

"Yes, what is it?"

"Well, it's Keith Janey. I think you ought to know he came to see Cal yesterday. You see, Cal gave Janey a couple of bad recommendations and he hasn't been able to get a job. Of course, in time someone would hire him, but there's his drunkenness and his plain orneriness. . . ."

"Did they quarrel?"

"Did they quarrel? You couldn't really call it that. Cal called me in and I thought Janey would burst a blood vessel.

Cal seemed to be enjoying the whole thing. He was a strange dude. . . ."

"Go on."

"Well, as the security guard was coming in, Janey yelled, 'Call the cops and you'll be dead before they get here.'"

"Did he display a gun?"

"No, but he kept putting his hand in his pocket. God, Cal was so cool. I don't know how he did it. He told Janey he wanted him out, *then,* and that he'd kick his rump and he really would call the police. He gave him five minutes to cool down."

Ted was silent, reliving that time.

"What happened then?"

"Yeah, it got flat, believe it or not. Janey cried. I got him a box of Kleenex off Cal's desk. He blew his nose and shuffled out. Cal told the security guard not to bother him, just let him go, and Cal laughed and yelled at him, 'Don't forget you owe me, Janey. Kleenex doesn't come cheap. You damned crybaby.' The guard said he left the grounds in his old, beat-up car and that was the last of that, or was it?"

"You think he killed Mr. Catlett?"

"Cal sure pushed him hard enough. Hell, I had a mind to give him a recommendation myself, but Cal would've gotten mad and he could be vindictive. Do I think he killed Cal? I sure think it's possible. He's a desperate man."

"Cal was a big man and Janey's average build," Danielle said. "Drunk and all, I think Janey would have had a hard time handling him."

"Not really. Remember, Cal drank, too. Enough fury, enough hurt, and anything can happen. Was I wrong to come?"

Danielle smiled. "You know you weren't. This info is going to be useful to us. We searched Mr. Janey's house and found a .22-caliber gun. Mr. Catlett was shot with a .22-caliber gun. Motive, opportunity, both are present. We've arrested Mr. Janey for the murder of Mr. Catlett."

Ted Keys's eyes lit up. "Oh, *man,*" he breathed. "Any additional help I can give you, I'm more than willing."

At the large beige bungalow with the black shutters where Manny Luxor and Buck Lansing lived, both men stood in the living room. A woman cleaned once a week and cooked for them when they didn't order or eat out. Buck's thin shoulders were hunched as if he couldn't believe what he was hearing.

"You look at it my way, you may yet live to be a rich man," Manny told him.

"Yeah, more like a jailbird. Listen, I never stayed no time in jail. You saw to that."

"I kept you out, with the help of hotshot lawyers. Look at it my way, Buck. There's no point in both of us serving time. You swear you were running this smuggling scam by yourself. You're smart enough. Annie was your accomplice."

Buck grinned in spite of himself. He loved it when Manny complimented him.

Manny patted him on the back. "You're the son I never had. Sure, the cops may not *believe* you handled the whole thing, but if you say so, they can't prove squat. They'll have to take your word."

"I don't know. Lots of slipups are possible. What about Annie? She could spill the beans."

"Listen, Annie loves money and I'm offering her a half million to do this for me. Each one of you may, *may* get ten years or less, with time off for good behavior, that is if she didn't kill Cal or likely hire it done. That's a lot of money, Buck. And I'm offering *you* more."

"More?" Buck's eyes glittered. He breathed rapidly through his mouth.

"Well, how about it?"

Buck thought about it. "I dunno. I seem to feel I'd die in

jail. Prison. I'm a good-looking man; I'll kill anyone come trying to get me to be his wife."

Manny threw back his head in a guffaw. "We got people on our side in prisons. You'd be safe. I'd see to that."

Buck hung back. Manny began to get hot under his collar and he tugged at it. Buck was changing, beginning to flex his muscles. When Buck was still silent, Manny lost his temper.

"You're a boneheaded young punk," Manny yelled, taking advantage of Buck's sensitivity about being accused of being gay.

"You never gave a damn about me," Buck yelled back. "For all I know, I'll rot in the pokey and you'll be out living high on the hog. If I go down, I'm taking you with me." That last statement just slipped out.

Manny looked at his young friend. "Well, I'll be damned. At last you're showing me what an ingrate you are. *If* my lawyer can't get you off, and that's a big if, you'd spend less than ten years in jail. You still wouldn't be forty-five and you'd be *rich*. Plus, if you play your cards right, I'm your friend for life. Think about it, Buck, and see it my way."

Manny turned on his heel, stalked out, and Buck slumped into a chair. Prison, and what folks said went on there, scared him to the marrow of his bones. It came in floods of thought now how Manny always belittled him, playing the upper hand and never losing the opportunity to make him look like a stupid fool. His heart was flooded with bitterness and he wanted to hurt his mentor the way his mentor had hurt him.

He was settling in to think about Manny's proposition when the doorbell rang and he surlily greeted Danielle and Ed.

"We have a search warrant," Danielle said evenly. "May we come in?"

* * *

A half hour later, the search had gone smoothly. They found one major thing of interest. A small arsenal of guns was stashed in a small room. Ed carefully and quickly examined each gun. Suddenly, he spied a picture that hung on the wall and moved it aside to display a safe door in the wall.

Ed called Manny and barked, "Open it."

Manny took his time, then flung the door open and Ed searched as thoroughly as he had searched the arsenal until he said, "Well, well, well."

Danielle was still checking the other guns cursorily when Ed crowed, "Well, we've got us one. A .357-magnum. Dani, I'll call the station. We need the crime van to pick up this gun factory." He slipped the .357-magnum into an evidence bag.

"You're taking all my guns with you?" Manny's voice was hoarse.

"Yeah, and we'll have them until we check them out. The smuggled guy was killed with a .357. Who knows but maybe we'll find a .22-caliber like the one Cal Catlett was shot with?"

At the station house, Jon picked up his phone and spoke to the sergeant at the holding cell section. "Release Janey," he said tersely.

"Mind telling me why?" He and the sergeant were old friends.

"Yeah. The gun we found in his house, the .22-caliber, hasn't been fired in at least a couple of months. Hey, wait a minute, maybe I'm going too fast."

"Want to hold him?"

"Yeah. Threatened assault. Disrupting the peace. Someone just told me he burst into Cal's factory the day he was killed and made a lot of threats. This guy who told me just left and he'll testify. We can book Janey on that. Keep him a day or so. I doubt he can get a lawyer."

"Good deal. I'll go back to sleep," the sergeant teased.

* * *

After work, Whit picked Danielle up; she left her car in the police garage. Ed would stop by and take her in the next morning. On the way home, Whit noticed that she was quiet, somber. They didn't talk much. She looked so tired.

"What's in the bag on the floor?" she asked.

"Chinese food. Just served up hot. Beef 'n broccoli, sweet 'n sour shrimp."

"I wasn't hungry, but that aroma is making me hungry." She looked at his craggy profile and moved closer to him.

Going into the house, she leaned on him.

The food was good and Whit opened a good bottle of cabernet. He put on an album of romantic pop tunes and listening to it seemed to give her even more of an appetite.

She told him then about the case, what they had done all day.

"Forty-eight hours," she said. "We thought it was Janey. Now, as far as we know, it's not. But it could be Lansing and Luxor, and if it is, guess who goes to prison and who stays out? Manny's lawyer is an old-fashioned mouthpiece who always wins. Whit," she asked somberly, "God gives life. Why, except for self-defense, does anyone feel free to take it?"

She insisted that he let her load the dishwasher, then they went back to the living room where she lay on the sofa with her head in his lap. Suddenly, his big hands closed around her shoulders. "Tell you want I'm gonna do," he said. "Massage time."

He led her into the bedroom and pulled off her top clothes. She was glad she'd worn the leopard-print silk bra, bikini, and half slip. He breathed harder but held himself in. "Wait," she said. She got up and got a bottle of Tahitian monoi oil from the shelf and opened it. The lush and sensual odor of exquisite gardenias filled the room and he felt himself slightly reeling.

She lay facedown and, pouring a little of the oil in his palm, he spread it onto her smooth brown back. He kissed her lightly, his hot breath fanning her as he traversed her body from scalp to toes, kneading gently, massaging with his fingertips and the heels of his hands.

"Where did you learn to do this?" she murmured.

When he was silent, she asked, "Willo?"

She wished she could see his face and when he spoke his voice was strained.

Finally, he said, "After Willo and I broke up, I went to Tahiti. Alaska. China. Hell, I went everywhere. Running. I kept running until I realized I took myself with me no matter where I went."

She turned over then and propped herself on her elbows. "I'm sorry," she said softly. "Your father was right. You were born to love and be loved."

He kept massaging her, wanting her so badly the ache in his body was palpable, but she was bone weary and kept dropping off. There was something he had to tell her.

"Dani, my folks are all back in place and I want to take you to meet them this Sunday. Can you go?"

"Can I go?" she murmured sleepily. "Try to stop me. I'll really look forward to that." Then, as he lightly and alternately stroked and kneaded the front part of her body, he took special care of her breasts, bending to kiss them.

"I'll need a rain check on this when I can do full justice to it," she said, groggy by now. And by the time he reached her toes, she was fast asleep.

Her sleep was deep and he watched over her for a few minutes, then he got up and slipped off her undergarments from her body. Dani and he slept naked. He brushed the springy brown hair back from her brow and kissed her forehead, then lightly touched his lips to her. She did not awaken.

Lifting her, he got her under the covers and turned off the lamp on the night table on her side.

"Good night, my love," he whispered. "Sleep well." And he thought of Danielle's dreams and the danger she dreamed of. What did she dream when she was too worn out to guard against dreaming of danger?

TWENTY-FIVE

The next day was Friday and as she walked up the hall to Jon's office, Danielle reflected that over half the forty-eight hours had passed since they had found Cal Catlett. Sid, the firearms expert, called to her and walked swiftly toward her.

"I've got the results from that .357-magnum you found at Manny Luxor's," he said. "I thought I'd tell you now and send you the report sometime today. It's positive, Lieutenant. That gun fired the bullet that killed Cedric Appiah."

Danielle felt her breath catch in her throat. "Thanks, Sid," she said and touched his arm. "I really appreciate your quick work on this."

He walked on toward the front door and she went into Jon's office and told him the news about the .357-magnum.

Seated behind his desk, he rocked in his chair. "This is quite a break, Dani."

"We'll need all the evidence we can get. That one thing may not be enough. Juries are demanding more and more . . ." she said.

He looked at her thoughtfully. "What do you want to happen here?"

"I think a confession along with this would be very useful. Now that we've got blood samples from Buck when we booked him, we can compare the gob of saliva and DNA with what we found on Mr. Appiah. His clothes were swarming with DNA but we had no one to match it with. Good old DNA."

"Yeah."

She went over the past day with him as he nodded, saying little.

"Who're you and the team taking on today?"

"Several people. I'm going to let Adrienne and Ed talk with Irene at her house. I'm going to talk with Annie and with Dave Emlen and, while I'm there, with Cal's sister, Edith. I want to talk with those three alone and at home."

"Because you believe that at home people loosen up, reveal themselves in ways they don't intend to."

"Yes. Jon, Buck Lansing wants to talk with me. The jail sergeant called this morning."

"I'll be damned." He cocked his head to one side. "Dani, if the department had a Medal of Honor, I'd give it to you. Why do you suppose you're so successful at getting people to come clean?"

"Thank you." Then she was silent for a long while before she answered. "I think it's because I respect people, Jon. The worst person in the world is a precious human being and I believe in the biblical admonition to hate the sin but love the sinner. Especially since what was a sin to one generation is not a sin to another."

Jon nodded. "And you care. You really care."

"I do. People have always cared about me. Buck's being arraigned Thursday afternoon if you want to sit in. I think there's almost zero hope of getting a confession, but I think the jury will go hard on him with what we have. He's not exactly Mr. Personality."

"Okay. You know I'm working very closely with you on this one. Chief Kellem's getting flak from the city. They want answers and they want a perp, pronto."

Jon placed his elbows on his desk and made a pyramid of his fingers, then laughed. "Such pyramids as I've made here are said to indicate a lust for power. Don't I wish I had some right now."

"You do. You're a powerful man."

"And you're a great woman. Thirty-five, going on ninety in wisdom. Your mother was like you, Dani. She'd be so proud. I loved that woman. She trained me."

"I loved her too."

"What're you doing on the weekend and how's Whit?"

"As you possibly know, he's rehearsing a lot with his backup group this week. Sunday he's going to let me meet his family."

"Great! You're all going to love each other."

"I certainly hope so." She paused. "Jon, neither of us is saying what we hope for, that Buck killed Cal. We've heard all along that he's a hired killer for Manny Luxor. We just never knew anybody he killed."

"You're right. I've been hoping. Think he did it?"

"I don't know. We can work with DNA and fingerprints again. Fibers, everything we can get our hands on. There wasn't one .22-caliber in the gun collection we confiscated, but that doesn't mean they did not have one. They could have weighted it, thrown it in the bay or somewhere."

"Yeah," Jon said. "I've got to be in the chief's office in a few minutes. I know how you drive yourself, Dani. Relax this Sunday and enjoy the Steeles. They're a wonderful set of people."

"You wanted to see me?" Danielle coolly asked Buck Lansing as he sat dejectedly on his jail cot. She sat on the cot opposite him. He had no cellmates.

"Yeah, I did. I've got some info I think you might need."

"What I'd like from you is a confession that you killed Cedric Appiah."

"Cedric who?"

"Don't play games, Mr. Lansing. It won't help your case."

A warm shiver ran down Buck's spine. He liked her calling him "Mr. Lansing." Who else ever did?

"Oh, you mean the guy in the paper that got whacked? Can't help you there." He got scared when he said it. *Was* Manny going to hang him out to dry? He was on edge waiting for Manny's lawyer to come and really talk with him.

"I think you can help me and I think I may be able to help you," she said.

His head jerked up. "Help me? How?"

"We may—and I emphasize *may*—be able to make things easier for you. We caught you and Annie in the midst of the smugglers. That's certain prison time. . . ."

"Hell, I was just there visiting. Anybody can be anywhere."

Danielle made a move to get up. "Well, if you're going to insist on playing games, Mr. Lansing." She had quickly seen and assessed the grin on his face when she gave him the title.

"No, please. Don't go. Tell me what you can do for me."

"Less time and even less for good behavior. I need to know everything—about the smuggled aliens and how Mr. Appiah was killed, even if you didn't do it. But I warn you about lying. DNA results are light-years ahead now and if there's enough of yours tangled with Mr. Appiah's, you'll go up for the crime."

"The electric chair?" And his voice came out squeaky like a child's voice.

"I don't know. The more you cooperate, the better it will be for you."

Buck cradled his head in his hands, looking at the floor, then looked up. "Give me a little while to think it over."

"As I told you, you'll be arraigned Thursday. You don't have much time. I'm away Saturday and Sunday. You could be left holding the bag. You're too smart a man to be that stupid." Her voice was so gentle, pleasant.

His head jerked up. She had said he was *smart*. He was going to try to be as smart as she thought he was. He *liked* this woman, really liked her. And Manny was selling him out. Did she know or just guess that Manny was selling him out?

Danielle rose to go then, remarking to herself on how much friendlier Buck seemed now. She almost felt sorry for him, always living in someone else's shadow and under someone else's complete domination. But she thought of Cedric Appiah and his proud, cold, rigid body and she didn't like the life Buck lived. She was close to hating the sinner *and* the sin.

She had planned what she would say as she rose. "The evidence points to you as Mr. Appiah's killer, Mr. Lansing. Did you also kill Mr. Catlett?" She was on her feet and he was still sitting. A bit of intimidation.

"Oh, hell, I *never* killed Cal," he exploded. "I don't even know who did."

"Which means you *do* know who killed Mr. Appiah?"

"I might know if I rack my brain."

"You do that over the weekend and let me know what you decide. Your lawyer has left word that he'll see you later this morning."

"Good old Quince," Buck said sarcastically. He sat, breathing hard. "I hate the thought of prison," he burst out. "I've never been in."

"Without coming clean, you're going to have a long time to hate it." She was cool again.

"Look," he said, emotionally clinging to her, "I'll do my best to help you, if you'll help me save my butt."

"I'll do my best if you'll do your best."

"Listen," he said.

"Yes?"

"I didn't tell you what I said I would."

Danielle sat back down. "I haven't got much time," she said.

Buck licked his lips. Would she believe him? "Well, I—

hell, you probably already know, but most folks don't. You know Annie's been carrying on with Cal's factory manager?"

Danielle looked at him sharply. "No," she said. "I didn't know that."

"Well, I think you'll want to question that dude. I followed him to her house a lot of times. He sneaks in the side. I never told Cal or Manny. I never liked Cal that much. He and Annie were maybe cheating Cal in the money department, too. Maybe Cal found out and they fought. Maybe Ted didn't mean to kill him, then got scared and tried to hide the body.

"You got a whole lot of people wanted Cal Catlett dead. He was a skunk straight out of the woods. Now most people talk about his wife, Irene, and Dave Emlen. Dave's so righteous. Big act, if you ask me. Don't hang me, lady, until . . . and there's Janey." He shook his head. "I could go on . . ."

Back in her office, Danielle took a quick call from her dad. "Listen, sweetie," he said, "I just want to touch base. How's it going?"

"We're getting some breakthroughs, but not the one we want."

"Well, you hang in there. You're still going out of town Sunday?"

"Yes."

"Don't be nervous. Your future in-laws have got to love you and I expect you'll love them."

"Dad, we're not engaged. Whit's got a ways to go to get over the hump."

"But he's willing to risk it."

"I know but I'm not."

"Well, you fill me in as soon as you can. There's my other line. It's probably Daffy."

"Give her my love."

* * *

"What've you got in store for me, boss lady?" Ed purred as he came in.

Danielle told him about her conversation with Buck Lansing and he whistled. She filled him in on the .357-magnum that had killed Cedric Appiah and he whistled again.

"Think he killed Catlett?" he asked.

"I don't know. It's certainly a possibility. They could have thrown the gun away."

"You say 'they,' meaning Manny Luxor."

"Meaning Manny Luxor. They're practically Siamese twins. I don't think Buck likes being the fall guy, and it's plain to me Manny is going to try to leave him holding the bag. Ed, I'm going to question Annie at her house. She's going to meet me there. And I'm going to question Dave Emlen and his stepmother, Edith. I want you and Adrienne to talk with Irene again. She hasn't got an alibi and she could conceivably be in on this, although I don't think so. I don't see her as a killer."

"She sure had reason. All black and blue on a weekly schedule. She could have hired a hit man."

"Fooling around with Luxor and Buck, Cal may have crossed the mob line somehow. They don't play around," she said.

"Look," Ed said wistfully, "I sure would've liked to have been with you when you talked with Buck, and I think maybe you ought to consider taking me along with you to talk with Annie and Dave, especially Annie."

"Why?"

The abrupt question startled him. "Well, in cases like Buck's anyway, a rough man's hand might get more done. Dani, you know I think the world of you and couldn't ask for a better cop, but some parts of some jobs call for a man's rough hand."

She grinned inside. Good old sexist Ed. He only rarely showed this side of himself, so she forgave him.

"What I really need you to do is check the DNA and work with the forensic pathologist to understand the matches they make. It's going to be two weeks or more before they can get it worked out and give us results. Fingerprint matching you can do in a couple of days, working with Matt. Give this your best shot, Ed. You're the one I trust for this."

Ed bowed his head. "Whatever you say, boss. Whatever you say." He leaned across the desk, patted her arm and went out.

Later, at Annie Lusk's house, Danielle sat in an over-stuffed chair in Annie's pleasant living room, across from Annie, who sat on the sofa. Annie's face was puffed, swollen, as if she'd cried for days. She smiled crookedly at Danielle.

"Well, Lieutenant, you still looking for ideas for your house?"

"I really was, you know."

"Come off it. You were casing the joint. You weren't looking for ideas when you came back to raid us."

Danielle's expression was cool. "Annie," she said gently, "you were breaking the law. We have to live with laws."

"Sounds good," Annie growled. "You think everybody does it? Live by the law? My brother was in prison most of his life."

"You can be different. *If* you go up for your part in this, you could lead a clean life when you come out."

"And what if I don't want to? I loved my brother . . ."

"As you loved Cal."

"Yeah. Cal came along when I had stopped hoping for a man I could love, other than my brother." She rubbed her forearm across her brow. "But you're not here to talk about what I'll do once I get out of jail, *if* I go to jail. You want to know if I killed Cal, or had a hand in it." Her voice was flat, weary.

"Yes, that's why I'm here."

"At least you're honest this time. No," she said slowly, "I

didn't kill Cal and I don't know who did. The way it's hurting me, I'd kill whoever did this myself." She looked as if she would cry, but didn't.

"Do you know who might have killed him?"

"Do I know there's a heaven—and a hell? Look, Lieutenant, I shouldn't be talking like this, but you know Cal wasn't loved by everyone. Irene gave him plenty of grief. . . ."

When she didn't go on, Danielle asked, "About what?"

"Me for one thing. Irene was plenty jealous. Cal told me his sister's stepson was hot for Irene. Maybe he was changing his will, cutting her out of anything extra. A whole lot goes on."

"Did Cal say anything definite about his wife being cut out of his will?"

"He talked about it a little sometimes, said he ought to, but he never said he did. Sometimes he talked about a divorce, but he never got around to it. He was chicken," she scoffed, "in a lot of ways. He always said a man like him needed a certain kind of wife. He often said he wished he'd married me. 'Big Red' he called me." She put a hand to her hennaed curls and smiled sadly. "I'd like to kill myself. With him gone, I'm going to catch hell."

"I'm sorry."

Annie's head jerked up. "You're sorry? Why, ma'am, I broke the law, helping people get to this country who would've been dead if they hadn't got here." Her voice went low. "The way I see it, I deserve a medal."

Danielle was silent.

Annie sighed. "I'll tell you one thing. I'm too hurt to be mad at you, at anybody. Anything I can do, *anything* to help you find out who killed him, I'll do it. You just say the word."

And Danielle thought: *Murderers seldom proclaim their guilt.* "You know Mr. Keys. Ted Keys?"

Annie's lips parted and her breath came faster as she shrugged. "I've seen him around. He comes to my place from time to time."

"Were you having an affair? Had Cal found out? He's his factory manager."

Annie got up. "You want to question me, I want my lawyer there. You can call me into the station and I'll bring him."

"Is Quincy Taylor your lawyer, as he was Cal's lawyer?"

Annie stood up, rigid. "I want you to leave now."

Danielle got up. "Are you still willing to help me in any way you can to solve Mr. Catlett's murder?"

"I'm willing, but I want you to go now."

Danielle nodded. "Very well, but I will need to question you at the station house. Thank you for seeing me."

Annie was like a zombie walking to the door with her. The woman was really hurting. At the edge of the walk, Danielle turned and saw that Annie still stood in the same spot. She opened the car door and got inside, feeling the sweltering July heat.

Turning on the air conditioner, she leaned back. Taking her cell phone out of her tote bag, she quickly dialed a number. A man's gruff voice answered.

"Quincy," she said, "you were Cal Catlett's lawyer, or one of them?"

"I had that honor."

"I'm going to need to see a copy of his most recent will."

"Not a problem. I'll fax it over to you right away."

"Thank you."

Hanging up, she started her car. None of this had taken very long. She remembered the drums she thought she'd heard last time at Annie's. Now, on to Edith Emlen's—and Dave Emlen's.

At Edith's house, Danielle smiled a bit at the quaint, old-fashioned living room with its antimacassars and heavy mahogany furniture. It was like something out of a distant past.

"Thank you for seeing me," Danielle said.

"You're welcome, I'm sure. It's a sad thing about my brother. I thought you'd be liking to question me. Only thing is I thought you'd like me to come to you."

"Anything to make it easier for you to deal with. I thought you'd be more comfortable here."

"That's real kind of you. I'll tell you anything I can."

"I'm going to need to talk with Mr. Emlen, too."

Edith Emlen scratched her cheek. "Well, now, that isn't going to be possible. Dave's not here."

"Oh? Will he be back soon?"

"Not for a few days. He said one to four days. He's real upset." She looked up, alarmed. "You don't think my stepson killed Cal? He wouldn't harm a fly."

"I certainly hope not. You're very close to your stepson, aren't you?"

"It's like I'm his mama. He's never really known another mama. Why do you ask?"

"I just wondered. How close were you to Cal?"

Edith thought about this a long time, then finally she spoke. "From being children, we were never close. Cal always felt our parents loved me best. He was wild, but he worked hard, saved his money, always had some money-making scheme going on. Our parents were God-fearing, plain folks and Cal drank. He was a heller, but he *always* made money, and he didn't care how he made it. And he saved money.

"I don't guess it's no secret that he beat Widow Crandall out of the mattress factory her dead husband left her. He promised to marry her and he didn't. She died, I guess of a broken heart. She'd deeded the factory over to Cal, thinking he'd marry her. It was a real small outfit and he stopped drinking and built it up. Cal's smart, that way. I guess you could say he was brilliant.

"But he had a mean streak a mile wide. Truth to tell, I always thought Cal would be the one killing somebody. He led Annie Lusk a dog's life, but I think he loved her. . . ."

"I don't want to interrupt you, but how about Irene and Mr. Emlen?"

Edith's mouth curved into a slow, fond smile. "Irene," she said. "Now, she's like a sister to me." She stopped, trying not to say too much.

"There's been some mild gossip about Mr. Emlen and your sister-in-law."

"Oh, folks're always going to talk. But I'll tell you, those two love each other. Dave would kill for Irene and he was plenty mad when Cal began to hit Irene harder. . . . God only knows what got into him. He never should have been manhandling her at all. Dave's cried many a time. . . ." She broke off, shaking her head. Then she looked up suddenly. "Now, I don't want you to think there was any hanky-panky going on. Irene is a good woman and I was always here with them when she visited. Cal, of course, having an evil mind, thought otherwise."

"Maybe Dave lost his temper in a quarrel with Cal," Danielle suggested. "Maybe it was an accident."

Edith's face looked stricken. "Oh, Lord. What if it *did* happen that way?"

"Was Dave here with you the night Cal was killed?"

Edith seemed perplexed at the question and Danielle saw she was trying to marshal her thoughts. "Well, he was awake when I went to bed, but I couldn't sleep, so I heard him when he went to bed. His room's right next to mine."

"And he didn't get up and go out? Or you didn't hear him go out?"

"No. I can't say as I did." The woman was hiding something now, suddenly hiding something, and Danielle felt it in her bones.

"Does Mr. Emlen call you when he's out of town?"

"Every day."

"Please tell him I need to talk with him. If he can come back, fine. Otherwise, please call me. I'll write the number and leave it for you."

Edith nodded. "Cal and I were so different. I think he married Irene because she is so much like me, and I think he also mistreated her because she is so much like me. He was a mixed-up man in a lot of ways. He was my brother, but God forgive me, I hated him for the pain he put Irene in. You don't really think Dave. . . ?" She crossed her arms over her chest and was suddenly terribly afraid.

Back in her office, Danielle paced back and forth, working through the case in her mind. From all she'd found, Cal's murder carried plenty of suspects, but she went with Buck Lansing as murderer. He had killed Cedric Appiah. He had the opportunity and heaven only knows what motive. He would kill *for* Manny Luxor. It felt good to have found the answer to the puzzle of Cedric Appiah's death. But it wasn't going to be easy to send Buck up for it. A confession would be valuable, and she had a snowball's chance in hell of getting it. Buck liked her, looked up to her. Could she use this in any way? DNA and fingerprints were going to help a lot. They seldom failed, but sometimes they did.

She sat at her desk bent forward, and put her head on her arms. Day after tomorrow, she would meet Whit's family and though she looked forward to it keenly, she was also nervous. In the midst of going over her case, she thought about the outfit she chose to wear for the meeting—a cream-colored silk and linen pantsuit with a navy-and-cream-striped shell. Not too bold, not too mousy. Whit had admired it extravagantly.

Opening a large dictionary, she flipped to the open page and looked at the giant peony she had dried there. Touching a finger to her lips, she touched the flower and looked at it a long time. "Whit, my love," she murmured. One more day and they would take another step on the journey to whatever future they might know.

Ed knocked and came in, frowning.

"You look frazzled," she said.

"I am, but I'm also feeling we're getting somewhere with the Catlett thing. Adrienne and I went over the floors at the ALM house with Luminol, searching for blood. Only when we got to the darkroom and the hall did we find blood on the floor. Someone had tried to clean it up. So, he was killed there and someone cleaned it up. A whole lot of people volunteer at ALM, so it could be a lot of people. Dani, doesn't your psychic side give you any clues?"

"If it's giving me clues, I'm not reading them right. I'm dreaming of a lot of people, especially Buck Lansing. But, Ed, I'm not going to be foolish and *depend* on dreams; they're useful, but dreams can't give the whole story. I'll mostly stick with DNA, fingerprints, Luminol, and the like. . . ." Frustrated, she let her voice drift off. She wanted to solve this crime.

"Well, one down, one to go," she said.

"I'm happy about Appiah." Ed patted his shirt pocket and she knew the signs by now. He would shortly go out for a cigarette.

"So am I. Sometimes his face haunts me. I wonder why."

"You're haunted by a lot of things, Dani," he said softly, "and I'm sorry you have to be." He laughed shortly. "Now don't close down on me. I'm not going to hit on you or get maudlin. How's Whit?"

She was surprised. He made comments about Whit, but seldom asked about him. "He's fine." She started to tell him she was meeting Whit's folks Sunday, but she didn't. She didn't want to hear some sarcastic remark; she would mention it when they got back.

"The chief's treating us to dinner next week in celebration of the Appiah case being solved," she said. "Forty-eight hours is well on the way to being up. . . ."

"My money's on Manny Luxor by way of Buck Lansing."

"The trouble," she said, "is proving it. And for all we know,

Quincy Taylor can get him off for the Appiah murder. I sometimes wonder how some defense lawyers live with themselves."

Ed cocked his head to one side. "Oh, didn't you know? They spend their spare time sifting through their many, many piles of gold coins, like King Midas. I guess old Cal's counting his in hell."

TWENTY-SIX

"Happy?"

"I'm flying. Can't you tell?"

Danielle stood against the white side wall of Whit's parents' wraparound screened front and side porch, facing Whit. He placed an arm above her head and splayed his hand as he bent and kissed the corner of her mouth, then ran his tongue lightly over her lips. She shivered slightly in the hot July air.

He lifted his head. "Yes, I thought you were happy. My folks love you."

"It's too early to tell," she scoffed. "It's ten o'clock in the morning."

"They *know*. The way *I* know." He patted his heart, then his stomach. "After knocking back the buckwheat cakes and a waffle, the ham, the bacon and the sausages, to say nothing of freshly squeezed orange juice, I may never need to eat again."

Danielle laughed. "By four, when your mother says they're serving dinner, you'll have forgotten all about breakfast. It was a scrumptious meal, Whit. You flip a mean pancake."

"They're sourdough pancakes. Got the recipe from Del and Val Craig."

"Oh, yes, the couple who're visiting. They're nice. I wouldn't mind living in Alaska, their home state, right now, with this heat and all."

Frank and Caroline, Whit's parents, strolled up, arm in arm. They beamed at Danielle. "I see you've been royally entertained," Caroline said. "You've made our son a happy man."

"Oh," Danielle said, laughing. "I'm the one who's floating on cloud nine. Congratulations, Mr. and Mrs. Steele, on the wonderful son you've raised."

Whit got a lump in his throat as he looked at Danielle, the woman he loved so much. And at that moment, a car horn sounded outside and a well-rounded and lovely woman got out of a Mercedes Benz.

"Come on in, Ash."

Ashley walked over to them, kissed Whit, and Whit introduced her to Danielle. Ashley smiled roguishly. "You've certainly made a difference in my favorite brother."

"I'm your *only* brother."

"Whatever," Ashley teased him. "Has Neesie come yet?"

"She's going to be a little late. She had a spell of morning sickness," Caroline said.

"We could use some more grandchildren." Frank rubbed his chin.

A very attractive man and woman came in the side back screen door. "We were out strolling, enjoying the trees and your great garden," the woman said, then extended her hand. "You're Danielle—Dani."

Whit introduced Del and Valerie Craig. "I was just telling Whit I wouldn't mind being in Alaska today," Danielle said.

Valerie put her head a little to one side. "Why not come up in this beautiful season of the midnight sun? Do it soon," she urged, "then come back for the aurora borealis." Her husband joined in the invitation.

"I'm game," Whit said. "The sooner the better. Dani?"

"I'd love that," Danielle said enthusiastically. "Right now, I could only stay a short while. I'm a detective and I'm working on a case."

"Oh, we know all about you," Ashley drawled. "Whit never stops singing your praises. The poor man is besotted, and am I glad!"

Danielle smiled, thinking "besotted" had been the phrase Jon had used describing how Whit felt about her. *She* was the besotted one.

"How are you, sweetie?" Frank asked his daughter.

"I'm feeling on top of my rainbow," Ashley said. "Of course, I'm still resting from that long, long trip. Danielle, be good to us and let us show you our travel pictures."

"I'd love to see them," Danielle told her.

Caroline clapped her hands. "We're milling about out here in this heat when we could be cooler. Who'd like a brief songfest? I think my son has a song he wants to sing, and we'll join in afterward."

Whit grinned. "A mother after my own heart." He put an arm around Danielle's shoulder.

Inside, the group went into the living room and gathered around the magnificent grand piano. Frank sat to serve as accompanist, and the others stood nearby. "Whit?" his father said.

Whit closed his eyes and said, "This one's for Dani."

He began then in his mellifluous voice:

Love lifted me. Love lifted me.
When nothing else would do,
  Love lifted me.

He sang to Danielle, and everyone in the room knew and sympathized. Their beloved son and brother and friend had come out or was coming out of the shadows at last.

He sang the other verses and when he had finished, Frank played a few chords and began the song again. This time, they all joined in joyfully. Then there were other spirituals, other songs: pop and country-western, some old rhythm and blues.

They sang for over an hour, then Caroline announced that she, Frank and Ashley would help Minnie and King in the kitchen to prepare dinner.

"This is going to be a lavish dinner, so it's going to take lavish preparation," Caroline said.

"I'd love to help," Danielle offered.

Caroline shook her head. "Frank, Ash, King and Minnie, and me, that's all the kitchen needs. Now I wish for Derrick, Ash's husband. That man is a fabulous cook."

Frank pretended to pout. "You always said I'm the best."

Caroline laughed throatily and went to kiss him. "Sugar, you are the best at everything."

Frank grinned from ear to ear.

Ashley nodded to Danielle, saying, "You'll meet my husband a little later. He had an emergency with his horses, so he couldn't come. Yes, he is a fabulous cook."

"Of course, we're willing to help," the Craigs said.

Caroline demurred. "Now what I want you two Craigs, Whit and Danielle to do is fan around. Look the place over some more, Val, Del, and for the first time, Danielle. We've always loved it. I can guarantee you will, too. Don't stay out more than an hour. It's too hot. Scoot!"

"My daughter, Eleni, would love this," Ashley said. "But today, she wanted to help her new dad. Lord, am I glad they're so crazy about each other!"

On the back porch, the two couples found wide-brimmed straw hats with ragged edges, as well as long-sleeved cotton shirts. The housekeeper, Minnie, a tiny woman, and King, her king-sized husband, came onto the porch. "Now you be careful out there," Minnie said to them. "The sun'll scorch you in a second."

"Aw, Minnow," King said, "they know when to come in outa the sun." Both couples smiled at his use of the diminutive for his wife.

The Steeles' place was lovely by any standard. Moss-hung giant oaks and a grove of sycamores graced it. They had taken pine seedlings from the South and transplanted them. Weeping willows lined the very large man-made pond that was edged by varicolored water lilies. Catfish leapt occasionally and a big turtle lazed on the shallow edge. Ashley's old home, now leased to a couple, sat across the way.

"Whit, it's beautiful," Danielle said.

"Yes, it is," Valerie agreed. "But you've got to come and see our beauty, too."

"Count on it," Whit said.

They walked into the woods. A jackrabbit and a squirrel skittered and a deer flashed in front of them.

Whit laughed and looked at Danielle. "We began with a deer," he said.

Back inside, the four who'd gone walking took half-hour naps, then got up and played cards. Bid whist and poker were Frank's favorite, and he stopped and joined them for a while.

"Scrabble anyone?" Danielle asked.

"Now, that's a game I love," Caroline said. "I've done most of my part, so I'll join you in a few minutes."

"Let me tell you about your son," Danielle told Caroline. "Whit forgets he knows how to spell when he sits at a Scrabble board. You've got to think for him." She expelled a long breath. "But he builds mile-long words and worse, he *always* wins."

"Ah," Whit said, "Scrabble and I are great buddies."

Annice, the other sister, came then, honking lightly outside as Ashley had done. She came in, moving slowly, and there were hugs and kisses all around. She held Danielle's hand a long while. "I love what you've done for my brother," she said.

Danielle blushed. "He's done a lot for me," she said somberly.

"I'm sorry Luke couldn't make it," Frank said. "What's he up to?"

"It's proposal time again. He's in New York."

"And you, Missy, how's my grandchild coming along?" Frank was fiercely protective of women.

"Dad, I'm doing fine. You worry too much."

"Just protecting my future," Frank said softly as Caroline looked at him, smiling.

Dinner was a superb affair. The table, set with cream damask, Waterford crystal and heavy silver that was an anniversary present from the Steele children, was beautiful. Gladioli and purple dahlias from the garden had been fashioned into a grand centerpiece by Ashley. A small table with a single display of flowers sat near the larger one; in the middle stood the large and lovely green jade vase Danielle had brought to the Steeles. In what time she could spare, Danielle had scoured the countryside for something special and she had found this. On impulse she had bought it and had it appraised at a price far higher than what she had paid, and it had not come cheap.

"You're a doll of a young woman and that's for sure," Frank said, as Minnie placed a gift-wrapped small box at Danielle's place.

They rang a dinner bell for laughs and sat down. Danielle was told that sometimes Minnie and King and the family took turns serving. King Johnson and Minnie were family, as well as servants.

They began with clear tomato consommé and oyster crackers. The bowls were frosted and the consommé was tasty. Small dishes of freshly chopped celery and parsley sat beside each dish. Iced tea and iced coffee, and wine were the beverages offered. The main course consisted of a choice of roast rack of lamb, prime beef rib roast, and a spiral ham. An extensive array of vegetables from the garden, brown rice and satiny gravy, and candied yams all blended in to make a memorable dinner.

They ate slowly—laughing, talking, enjoying the camaraderie. Time seemed to Danielle to pass so swiftly. She felt wistful about being here. This aura was something she had had with both her parents and she missed it. Minnie sat at the table now and she beamed. "Don't forget to open your present."

"Yes, do," Caroline urged her.

Finishing a final morsel, Danielle unwrapped her package, remarking on the beautiful wrapping.

"Minnie's handy that way," Caroline said. "I'm a klutz when it comes to gift wrapping."

"Thank you," Danielle told Minnie.

Danielle lifted the flat box top and held her breath at the creamy cultured-pearl stud earrings. "I love these," she said. "Thank you all so much."

Her pleasure was Caroline's pleasure. "Everybody pitched in. All the Steeles, including King and Minnie. Whit said your ears are pierced. Maybe this will tell you a little about what we think of you." She waved her hand a bit. "Oh, I know you and Whit haven't known each other a lifetime, but you *fit*, you belong together. That's plain to us, and to him."

And Whit sat thinking that Willo never did fit in.

After Ashley, Annice, King, and Minnie did the dishes, the whole group gathered in the family room. Frank operated the slide projector and photographs flashed on the wall. First footages were of the Steele place; Frank had done a journeyman's job of shooting. There were special shots of the strawberry patch and the large grape arbor.

Next came shots of the Craigs' beloved Alaska and those were fantastic. Caribou and reindeer roamed the tundra—the spongy earth beneath the natives' feet. Danielle marvelled at the many varieties of birds circling and the leaping fish of many descriptions. Big salmon wove in and out of the crystal streams and bears fished for their daily meals. Suddenly a gargantuan bear loomed onto the screen.

"Methuselah!" Val exclaimed. "He's a big one. Nine feet high."

"I imagine he strikes terror in your hearts," Danielle said.

Del shook his head. "We stay out of his way, but the townspeople aren't afraid of him. He's been around since he was a cub many years back."

A laughing, live-wire girl of seven danced on screen, playing with a baby seal. Her flyaway black hair and soft brown skin made Whit think of Ashley's daughter, Eleni.

"Anna, our daughter," Valerie told Danielle.

"What a beautiful child," Danielle said.

"She's a handful." Valerie smiled widely. "She takes after her father." She gave Del an arch look.

"She's between the two of us," he said quietly. "Proof of our love."

Next came the huge stack of photos of the Steeles' recent world trip. From the Great Wall of China to the verdant rain forests of Brazil to the gorgeous flowers of Mexico, they had captured it all. Whit and Danielle sat, entranced.

Frank cleared his throat. "I thought I was a good photographer, but Caroline took so many of these."

"Don't underrate yourself," Caroline said gently.

They were there the better part of two hours and finally Frank finished the last group of photos and Caroline said, "I could use some dessert about now," and the group agreed with her.

On the glassed-in and air-conditioned back porch, they all watched the sun preparing to set and both Whit and Danielle thought about the times they had made love on his boat to setting suns, and the first time they had kissed at her house to a rising sun. A quick, hard rain began and soon eased.

Peach cobbler. Blackberry cobbler. Carrot cake with cream cheese icing. Those were the desserts, topped with vanilla- and peach-flavored ice cream made in two big, hand-cranked freezers.

"We had these machines specially made, copied after an

old one from my parents," Frank said. "We usually make two flavors, or more."

Danielle thought she had never tasted anything so good as she dug into her generous helping of both peach and vanilla. She sampled everything and ate as she had eaten her dinner, with a hearty appetite. Did everything really taste so much better than usual? Or was it the company of these loving people?

Whit slid into an empty chair beside Danielle. "The earrings are fabulous," he said. She had put them on earlier.

"Yes, they are," she agreed.

Danielle looked out on a startlingly spectacular rainbow. "Glorious," she murmured.

"Few things are more beautiful," Whit said. "You're one of them."

Frank and Caroline and the rest laughed delightedly. "Did I raise my son to be a lover," Frank chortled, "or did I raise my son to be a lover?"

Where did the time go? It seemed they had been there only a few hours. They asked Danielle about her job and she told them about Cedric Appiah and Cal Catlett. They listened intently.

"Sounds dangerous," Frank finally said, "but it also sounds as though you've got the best of training to handle that danger."

"I do have the training. And no, it isn't really dangerous, although, sometimes, things do happen." She thought she saw a flicker of concern cross Whit's face, but he didn't mention the robber on the waterfront.

"The *world* is a dangerous place," Danielle said gravely, "and getting more dangerous every day. But I love my work." She told them about Mona then and they sympathized.

Whit said, and the group agreed, that they'd like to sit up all night, but they had to leave. And Danielle sat thinking that not since she lived with her parents had she felt more at home.

The Steeles packed boxes and bags of food for Whit and Danielle to take with them: vegetables from the garden, strawberries, jams, and even an ice-pack of ice cream plus dishes of the cobblers and carrot cake.

"I'll be *waddling* back to see you," Danielle said, laughing.

"You *do* come back and soon." Caroline hugged her, then the others hugged her. Whit grinned and told Danielle, "Bringing you here, I feel more successful than at any of my concerts."

At her house, Whit and Danielle backed his car up to the side porch and they unloaded it and put the food away. "I won't need to go shopping for food for a while," she said. He insisted that she take all the food, save for portions of some of the desserts.

Once they were finished, Danielle checked her house phone. There was a message from Julian and one from Daphne, both just checking in. No need to call. And there was one from Jon. "Dani," he said, "call me on your special line tomorrow morning after nine. I want you to be on top of something before you come in at one."

Danielle hung up, wondering what that was about. The special line operated just between her and Jon's office. No one could intercept their conversations on those phones.

She turned to Whit. "I had a wonderful time, but then I've said it before."

"Doesn't hurt to say it again. You look so beautiful today. Come to Papa!"

As they stood near the refrigerator, she went into his arms and something caught in both of them, sealing them in with each other. "How about that rainbow?" she said throatily.

"Wondrous, but then the whole day was magic. Dani?"

"Yes, love."

His voice went husky. "You feel it, don't you, the same pull I feel? A wonderful drawing together from the very soul."

"I feel it. Oh, *how* I feel it."

It was as if they were alone in the world. Who was the

magnet and who the filings? Both were magnetized beyond the telling.

He took her in his arms and murmured into her hair, "Dani, I think the attraction between you and me is one of the most magical things that could ever happen. I enter your body and it's paradise."

"Whit," she whispered, "you *are* going to stay?"

"Try sending me away."

In a hurry now, they walked into her bedroom, hugging, and disrobing hastily. Danielle turned on the lamps on the night tables and in the soft, rosy glow went into his waiting arms. They stood locked together before he bent his head and ran his tongue over her nipples that tautened and crinkled under the beloved attention.

"The end of a perfect day," he said.

"Wait a minute," she told him and disengaged herself. Going into the bathroom, she took a small vial of French lavender perfume from the shelves and put a few drops onto her wrists and behind her ears. Then she carried the vial into the bedroom and sprinkled a few drops onto the bed.

"You smelled delicious as you were." Whit's mouth had curved into a teasing smile. "Your natural smell." She put the stopper back into the bottle and set it on the night table.

"Come here," he murmured.

"Come and get me!" Frolicking now, they laughed like happy children as they played tag about the room. Then, soberingly, he caught her close and thrilled at the softness of her body pressed against his rock-hard frame.

"Tonight, I'm going to make you cry with passion," he whispered. "And I'm going to cry along with you."

Still standing, she bent her head and raked her teeth lightly and unexpectedly over his flat nipples as he jumped with surprise. "You little devil!" He laughed and crushed her in his embrace. "You want to burn me, you've got it."

His breath was hot on her face and body as they stood, and finally he kissed her long and ardently, sucking the honey from her tongue and licking the corners of her mouth until she moaned.

"Ready?" he asked her.

"I'm more than ready. Don't play with me anymore."

He lifted her then, his sinewy-muscular arms bulging with their burden. He laid her on the bed and straddled her.

As he stroked her face, passion that was as timeless and deep as an ocean engulfed them. She reveled in his masculine beauty as she stroked the hot, hard and throbbing length of his shaft and whispered, "Aren't we forgetting something?"

He shook his head. "No, I haven't forgotten." He got off her, leaned over and got the gold foil packet from the night table drawer that held the rubber shield. She usually helped slip the shield on the first time; the second time, he would do it alone.

"I'm getting to be expert at this," she said.

"One day in the near future, we'll be making a baby," he said suddenly. He placed his hand over her belly and spread out his fingers; then he put the side of his face on it.

"How can I properly shield you when you keep doing things to me? Keep still." And she smoothed on the length of the sheer rubber and squeezed him lightly.

"That feels wonderful," he said. "Everything you do to me feels wonderful."

"Come inside me," she murmured, "and I'll show you what wonderful is."

He began to kiss her slowly on the lips, nibbling as he went. She made a small fist and tapped him with it. "I usually want a lot of foreplay," she said. "Tonight I'm ready. Don't make me wait any longer."

Her softness and the fragrance of the French lavender combined and together with love driving his passion, he entered her. As she flung her legs over his back and locked them, he moaned deeply in his throat. "You're asking for a quick resolution of this trip, aren't you?"

"You told me once you could take me as long as I wanted to go. Shall I take you up on that tonight?"

He laughed. "It may be in the end I'll make you cry 'Uncle.'"

His love for her buoyed him, filled him. He sucked her breasts gently as she bucked beneath him, every cell of her yearning toward him, even as he yearned for her. Turning him over onto his back, he thrilled as she sat astride him, a gentle rider at first, then she pressed him harder.

"Think I'm a wanton woman?"

"No. I think you're an angel and a woman I can't get enough of. Hang in there, sweetheart. We've got a long way to go."

A high wind blew up and whistled around the eaves and Danielle felt as wild as the wind. Whit worked her now, pushing from beneath, strong and powerful. Each time they made love, she thought now, they seemed to get better and better. Inside her, Whit felt her tremble and felt her clutching him, holding him tenaciously with powerful muscles of her own.

"What is it you do to me?" she murmured. "How can I feel so good?"

"Tell you what," he told her. "If you'll figure out what you do to me to set me on fire, I'll figure it out from my side. We're good together, Dani." He was still a few moments. "We've been good together right from the beginning, and I don't mean just the lovemaking. There's something about us that blends, fuses, although we're not needlessly dependent. Dani, I love you, love you, love you."

Neither could last. The passion was too vivid. She had been on the edge when they began. Now he paused and thrust a bit and came back in harder and she went over, trembling with sweeping love and fulfilled desire. She trembled as if in the eye of a hurricane and wept tears of joy, and he saw the salt tears on her face and kissed them. She pressed him closer and his body plunged into a storm that flashed wildfire into his loins as he came with her.

"Finish?" she asked him.

He laughed shakily, teasing her. "No way. This is just the beginning."

"Oh, you," Danielle said. "You know what I mean. Whit?"

"Yes."

"That rainbow this afternoon."

"Beautiful. One of the most beautiful I've seen."

"I think it's an omen that tells us we're going to make it together."

Lying in his arms, she thought of Willo and knew he had not wholly gotten over her. And she wondered about something else. She had not dreamed the nightmare lately where he had called her name and she had called his and his blood had run down his body.

She shuddered involuntarily and moved closer. He was drifting into sleep, but he woke up and eyed her lustily. "Ready for another magic trip?" he teased her.

She propped herself on her elbow and smiled at him.

"Whit?"

"Yes, love."

She touched his male member, stroked it. "I'm going to call him *the wizard*."

"Oh?" He grinned at her affectionately.

"Yes, because he casts magic spells. When you're inside me, my body's here on the bed with you, but my spirit is floating on high. Can you understand that?"

Whit placed his hand over hers on his male member. He loved her with everything in him as he told her, "You're the sweetest woman. We like what you're calling us. We'll *take* it."

Leaning over, he sucked her bottom lip slowly, voluptuously until she pulled away to say, "From you, the heart of a master magician."

TWENTY-SEVEN

Promptly at nine o'clock the next morning, Danielle called Jon.

"What's up?" she asked.

"Lansing wants to see you."

"Oh? Do you know what about?"

"He wouldn't say. He *does* say you may be pleased."

"Pleased?"

"Those were his words. He asked to see me to tell you this. He didn't have much else to say."

"Did you want to talk with him?"

"I'd thought about it, but who wants to talk to a hard-leg like me when the likes of you is available?" he teased her.

"I don't much like Buck Lansing. He gives me the creeps. Likewise Manny Luxor, his lord and master."

"You're an expert at this questioning business, Dani, and—"

"So are you."

"Yeah. I think he killed Catlett. Like I said, a falling-out of thieves. Or maybe he killed him for Luxor. Play him along. Pick his brains. We haven't got much else yet, but the field is wide open. You coming in on regular schedule?"

"I'm coming in early. I've got a lot on my plate."

In the Minden jail, Buck Lansing fretted; he had a short fuse. Why in hell hadn't the lieutenant paid him a visit?

Didn't she want his information? He alternated between despair and hope. He had questions he wanted to ask her. Lieutenant Danielle Ritchey. He mouthed the words. Pretty name for a pretty woman. *He* could use a woman like that. He rubbed the side of his face and grinned. He wasn't bad looking; many a woman had worshipped at his shrine. But the same looks that got him what he wanted were going to be his downfall if he got to prison.

The guard tapped on his cell door and growled that he had a visitor, and Buck's heart leapt. He couldn't see where a visitor would stand before coming to his cell, but he brushed his hair back and smiled, preparing his lead-in sentence in his mind: *Good morning, Lieutenant Ritchey.*

But it wasn't Danielle and his heart fell as Quincy Tyler rounded the corner. The guard let him in. "I didn't send for you," Buck said belligerently.

"Happy to see you, too," the rotund Quincy Tyler greeted him. "I've got a lot to talk with you about." He sat on the bunk bed by Buck, put his briefcase on the floor, and dug in.

"Buck, you've been playing games and I've got to get some straight answers. And I need them now. Manny's told you before. You take the rap and you're over a million dollars richer. . . ."

"And if I don't?"

"If you don't, it's almost a certainty that you'll go up anyway. They've got you for the murder of Cedric Appiah."

"You can get me off, Quince," Buck said, suddenly pleading. "You always have. Listen, with the murder *and* being a front for the smuggling, I haven't got a chance in hell. Why can't Manny take a share of this? Lighter on both of us."

Quincy Tyler settled back, patting his foot, nervous now. How to put this to this fool? Quincy Tyler was a rich lawyer with rich clients and he spent a lot of time and a lot of money finding ways to defend them. He'd lost few cases and his oversized head seethed with ideas about defending those who could pay for it, sometimes through the nose.

"Buck," he said slowly, "let me put it to you straight. Manny's a wealthy man who's also smart. He's popular with the mob, as you very well know. He's got businesses to run and he hasn't got *time* to go to prison. You, now, I'm not trying to be cruel, but you're little more than Manny's lapdog. You go in and in five or so years or maybe less with good behavior and you're out, a wealthy man. You'll never have to work again for Manny, for anybody. Doesn't that appeal to you?"

Buck sighed, hiding his fury. He was tender to being called a dog and he wanted to smash Quincy's face in, but he was cool. Quincy and Manny needed him; he no longer needed them.

Buck sighed. "It's going to prison worries me," he said. "I talk to people and they tell me how it is. I've been in jail a couple of times. You always get me out. Why can't you get Manny *and* me out of this?"

"Because times are different now. Smuggling's on people's mind. The country's being overrun with illegal aliens. Now you cop a guilty plea, tell it like it was about the murder. He was trying to take you down. . . ."

"It wasn't that way."

"You can say it was."

Buck put his head in his hands, then put his hands in his lap. "I shot the dude and, yeah, I can say he was gunning for me and I took the gun away and it went off. We don't have to bring up about him being a policeman in his home country. I'm straight on that part. But, Quince, I don't want to say Annie and me *headed* the smuggling. I don't know a damned thing about smuggling. I just do what I'm told."

"The police don't have to know that."

"They can guess."

"They can't prove a damned thing if you say you're the main man."

Buck laughed dryly. He'd been called dumb often enough to have it stick. "You and Manny're pretty thick," he said.

"You got it all mapped out. Manny's never spent a night in jail and he brags about it. Where am I? Sitting here in this pissant jail. You keep me out of prison, Quince. You can do it."

"Only if you plead guilty to running the smuggling ring."

Buck shook his head. "I don't want to do that. If I do, they can throw the book at me. The killing I'm goin' to say was in self-defense. What defense have I got for smuggling? None. I'm not going to be some gorilla's *wife* so Manny can walk the streets a free man."

"Not even for a million bucks?"

"Not even."

"Maybe Manny'll sweeten the pot. A million and half. You could live high on the hog right here in the States and like a king in some foreign country."

"I'm not gonna be emas—" He groped for a word and Quincy caught him up.

"Emasculated?"

"Yeah."

"You worry too much. We've got men on our side in prison; guards we've bought. Knowing you're Manny's boy, you'd be as safe as in your mother's arms." But Quincy frowned, thinking Buck was changing since he'd talked to Danielle.

And Buck thought: *She made me think of settling down, of having a respectable life in keeping with the way my mother raised me.* The detective probably wouldn't give him the time of day, but he could *dream*. She was the reason he wanted to kick this one and be free. That and his morbid, soul-wrenching fear of rape. He couldn't even think about it without turning as cold as a corpse. He would kill if it happened; he knew that much. And this time there would be no getting away.

"Are you thinking it over?" the lawyer asked.

Buck shook his head. "I don't have to. I can't pull your and Manny's chestnuts out of the fire this time."

"You'll get some time even if you're just a party to this." Quincy was getting hot under the collar. What a stubborn fool. Buck was different lately, changing, had changed. What had happened? Were he and Manny falling out? He knew that Manny depended on the slim, physically attractive man as much as Buck depended on him.

"I've gotta run. You think about it long and hard," Quincy said. "Believe me, being rich is better than being poor. You like women. You can have your share of them. Don't cheat yourself, son. Go for it."

Buck sat, thinking, a long while after Quincy left. He liked it when older men called him "son." His hands hung between his legs and he was sick with disappointment. He'd thought she'd come running, but she hadn't. Well, the day was still young. He thought with surprise that he had changed without realizing it. If she came to talk with him, he had what he figured would be a surprise for her. A slow grin of anticipation spread across his face. He'd been Manny's fool long enough. Time now to get out on his own.

In the drugstore a few blocks from the station house, Danielle collected her face creams and started to the check-out counter.

"Lieutenant?"

She turned to see Keith Janey. "Yes?"

He scratched his head. "Ma'am, I got some information you might want and I long been hearing about informers. . . ."

"Informants," she said quickly, then thought she shouldn't have corrected him.

"Well, whatever. In-for-mants." He drew the word out. "Could I be one? I go everywhere all hours of the night and day. I hear a lot . . ." He twisted his gray knitted cap in his hands.

"You want to be an informant?"

"I do. And I got a bit of news I should've told you when you questioned me."

"Okay. Shoot."

"Can you hire me as an in-for-mant? God knows I need the money and Cal Catlett gave me bad job write-ups every-where."

"Maybe I can. Tell me your news." She led him to a cor-ner spot.

"Well, the night Cal was killed, I saw Dave Emlen parked near the ALM house. I was over that way. He got in the car while I watched him and he just sat there. He hadn't stayed there more than a couple of hours when he left and I went into the woods. Know something else?"

"What is it?"

He looked strained now. "Once I sat near him and Irene Catlett in the park. I don't think Cal knew about them being together from time to time. I heard Dave tell her—and he wasn't talking soft—'I'll kill the'—excuse my language, ma'am—'*bastard* if he hits you again.'"

Danielle breathed a little faster. "How long ago was this?"

"A few days before Cal was killed."

"If it comes to that, would you swear this in a court of law?"

"Yes, I would. Can you hire me?"

"Yes, I'll hire you. The pay isn't all that good."

"It's something."

Opening her bag, Danielle took out a pad and a pen, scrib-bled her number at the station house on the pad, and gave it to him. "Call me every day," she said, "with whatever you see and leave out nothing. Come to the station house this after-noon and I'll get you—do you have a cell phone?"

"You mean those little things people talk on?"

"The same. Come to the station house and I'll get you one. It'll take a couple of days to set you up. Mr. Janey?"

"Yes, ma'am?"

"You'd better be on the level. No games. No tricks or I'll come down on you." He was surprised at the flint in her eyes. She wouldn't do to mess with.

He grinned from ear to ear, stuck out his hand, and she took it. "I'm gonna be the best informant you ever had," he told her.

* * *

Danielle picked up the fax from the machine room and took it to her office. She sat at the long table and leafed through a legal document. She glanced at the boilerplate at the top and the captions delineating origin and subject: *Last Will and Testament, Caleb Norman Catlett.* She hunched forward and began to read.

The first bequest went to Irene, and Cal was Cal in death as in life. Irene was to get a widow's lawful share, but he had more to say. She imagined she could hear Cal's voice.

> *This holds only if she doesn't marry Dave Emlen. Save, for this one man, she has been a good wife, and if I didn't love her, well, I gave her everything and she had status as my wife she would never had had otherwise.*
>
> *Irene gets my share of the restaurant I owned with Annie, to dispose of as she pleases. But she cannot sell her share to Annie and must keep it as long as she lives.*

The next bequest was to Annie Lusk, and Danielle sat up straighter. The words seemed to jump off the page. Again, she could hear Cal's voice.

> *To Annie Lusk I leave my undying love and little else, because Annie betrayed me and it hurt, although I am a tough man. Annie, I strike back by giving Irene my share of our restaurant that everyone thinks you own outright.*
>
> *Did you have fun with Ted Keys, Annie? I surely hope you did. All this time, you thought I was in the dark, but I'm never in the dark. I had you followed from the time I knew I loved you. Big Red, you had me going in more ways than one.*

I thought about having the both of you wiped out, but I couldn't get you out of my heart and I didn't want you dead. You brought me too much pleasure.

I expect to be an old man when you read this and we'll laugh about what I wanted to do to you. I think you'll be tired of other men by then and realize we belong together. It's natural for a man to roam and a woman to stay close to home. You flouted that law as you flout all laws. You're a dangerous woman, Big Red, and I love every inch of your cheating, treacherous, outsized body. I leave you no money in punishment for your betrayal. Get a man like me and don't fool around with the likes of Ted Keys. He isn't worthy of you.

There were a few other bequests. His church was bequeathed a quarter of a million dollars. ALM got a quarter of a million dollars, "to keep it going a long time." This was to be matched with money Danielle and others raised. Sighing, Danielle put the will copy down and stared at it, thinking about Annie and Irene as coowners of Annie's Place. Had Cal and Annie quarreled? Did she know what was in the will? Danielle thought Annie would surely be hurt at the contents of the will. But he declared his undying love for her and that was worth a lot.

Ted Keys and Annie—lovers. She thought of the day Ted had come in to give her information about Keith Janey. Did he have some grudge against Cal? She needed to talk with him again.

Ed swung through the door, knocked on the table, and grinned. "Afternoon, Lieutenant. It's for sure you've been touched up around the edges."

Danielle couldn't help smiling. "Don't let me have to bodily throw you out of here."

"What's up?" he asked.

She shoved the will copy across to him as he sat down. He read it carefully and looked up, smiling. "Old Cal likes to play hardball. Imagine having a mistress followed. I never heard anything about Ted and Annie."

"They seem to have kept it well hidden. He speaks of thinking of having them both killed. Maybe they got to him first. Do you think Annie somehow knew about the will?"

"I doubt it. Quincy plays it close to the vest. If you ask me, Cal was kinky enough to *like* feeling he bested his woman's lover. But Lord, was she ever living on the edge. I think little Annie's going to be in for a shock. Big Red, huh? I never would've thought Cal was romantic enough to proclaim his undying love." He seemed so keyed up as he broke off and asked, "Have you talked with Buck Lansing yet?"

"No, but I'm going to a little later. I'm trying to digest this will. What do you think?"

"I think we've got reason to talk with Annie and Ted Keys again. Cal mistreated a whole lot of people. Ted never said how he and Cal got along, except that Cal was a hard man. He told you that when he came in just after Cal was killed."

"Yes," she said, "about Keith Janey." She told him then about meeting Janey in the drugstore.

Ed thought about it a minute. "He could be a big help, I think, bringing up odds and ends from the neighborhoods. *If* he can stay sober."

"I'm going to talk with him about that, get him in detox and rehab. I've seen worse men go straight, get ahold of themselves."

"Maybe. You want me to talk with you when you see Buck?"

"Not the first time. I want to wing it alone. Next time, yes, I want you there."

Ed's sigh was prolonged. "Thank heaven for that. You've taken too much of this whole thing on yourself. You don't want to burn out."

"I'll watch it. How's Shelley?"

"Running me ragged, as usual. I'm about ready to try on another woman for size."

"Stick with Shelley. She's crazy about you. You ought to be grateful."

He laughed. "Yes, Mama Hen. Shelley and I aren't going anywhere. But she *does* know me. Maybe she doesn't want to get married either."

"She probably does."

"Do *you* want to get married?"

"The idea is growing on me."

"You took it hard when Scott died. Think you're over it?"

"I'm getting there. You were so kind when he died. I'll never forget it."

"We could be . . ."

Danielle looked up, frowning slightly.

"Okay! *Okay!* I won't hit on you any time soon, but don't rule me out, Dani. I think we could be good together. You consider it."

He got up and left as Jon came in. "Was a good time had by all yesterday?" he asked.

"Jon, I had a wonderful time. The Steeles are people after my own heart. I love them."

"And I'm sure they love you. Whit called me this morning. Poor besotted fool," he teased her.

"Whit's nobody's fool," she defended. "He had it all together, or will have when he gets over Willo completely."

"I think he's just about there. He talks more now about being willing to take a chance. Dani, I don't want to meddle in your business, but he told me he asked you to marry him and you didn't think he was ready."

"That's true. I think he needs more time of not hurting so much."

"Let me caution you. I know how much you love him and God knows he loves you. Don't hold off too long."

"You think he'll turn to someone else?"

"I've seen it happen. He needs someone badly. Whit's not a man to go it alone."

Danielle opened her mouth, but no sound came. Whit

had pursued her so ardently she hadn't thought too much of him and someone else. Willo was free now and in full pursuit. She could lose him and it hurt thinking about it, but she felt strongly that he wasn't healed yet and that needed to happen.

She sighed deeply. "Thanks for that advice." She mulled it over a little while before she said, "I'm going to talk with Buck Lansing in a few minutes."

"What do you anticipate he'll say?"

"Oh, Lord, who knows? Quincy was by to see him this morning. He didn't stay long, I understand. The jail sergeant told me about the visit."

Jon pursed his lips. "Dani, I think Ed's got a real crush on you. I feel sorry for him. He's had it for you ever since Scott died, and I think he's badly disappointed that you turned to Whit."

"Why do you mention it?"

Jon shrugged. "I don't know. He's looking a little more ragged emotionally. Shelley doesn't seem to be what he needs. . . ."

"Well, I'm certainly not what he needs. I'm very fond of Ed, but there's never been any deeper attraction. Some people simply want what they can't have."

"That's true."

He sat down and read the will then and cupped his face in his hands, his elbows on the table. "Hell of a will," he said. "This is going to cut Annie deep."

"Yes. Buck Lansing's arraigned tomorrow afternoon. Annie's time is Thursday." Her eyes on Jon were fond. "I'm glad I work with you, Jon. It's so much easier that way."

Danielle had gathered her purse and tote, was ready to go to the jail to see Buck Lansing, when her buzzer rang and the receptionist told her she had a visitor—Dave Emlen.

"Bring him on back," Danielle said, "and please hold my calls."

Danielle greeted the man warmly. She could remember seeing him from time to time and he had brought his stepmother to ALM infrequently and picked her up. She got up and met him midway in the room. "Mr. Emlen, thank you for coming by."

"Yeah," he said. "My stepmom said you asked me to call you. I was going to stay away until after the funeral, but I decided to come back. Irene needs me."

"I see. Please sit down."

He sat opposite her at the table.

"Mr. Emlen, I'm going to be blunt. You were overheard threatening to kill Mr. Catlett a few days back."

Dave's mouth fell open. "Threatening to kill—" He broke off, frowning. "Who told you that?" he demanded.

Danielle shook her head. "Sorry. I can't divulge my sources. I'm sure you understand."

The man frantically tried to recall. Sure, he'd said that to Irene more than once and as far as he knew, he *meant* it. But they had been in Edith's house.

"Do you deny it?"

No use to lie about it, he thought. Cops had a way of finding out things. And these days with all the electronic stuff, they had a great head start. Then it hit him: sitting with Irene in the park the day Irene had the bruised left eye and had wept with pain.

"No, I don't deny it. I said it to Irene. It wasn't meant for the world to know."

"Did you make good on that threat?"

"Did I kill him?"

"Yes."

"No. I swear, but God knows I wanted to. If he'd come by the park or by my stepmom's house demanding that she go home with him, I don't know what would have happened. I *love* Irene. Maybe she don't want the world to know it, but I do. I want to marry her, and her money since he's dead doesn't mean a damned thing to me. Course I guess she'll be too rich for a poor fellow like me."

"I understood you're good in electronics. The sky could be the limit for you."

"Thank you, ma'am. I never wanted a whole lot until I started falling in love with Irene. No, I didn't kill Cal, but if you want me to take a lie detector test, want my blood and fingerprints for testing, I'll be glad to cooperate. And I wasn't running away, save for a few days. Thank you for leaving that message with my stepmom. It made me stop and think."

She liked this man and hoped he wasn't guilty. Still, it was a question she had to ask.

"You were seen in the vicinity of the ALM house the night Mr. Catlett was killed. You were walking around, staying close to your car. The person who saw you said you seemed agitated."

A crestfallen Dave Emlen looked at her steadily. "I went there, all right. I knew Cal went by at odd hours, but I stopped a few hundred yards short of the ALM house. And that's God's truth."

"Thank you. I'd appreciate it if you'd stop by the sergeant's desk and set up for fingerprints and a blood sample. If only everybody were as cooperative."

Dave smiled bitterly. "Maybe others have something to hide. I don't."

She glanced at him and the cop in her made her wonder. She had seen heinous crimes committed and the perps had steadfastly proclaimed their innocence to the end.

TWENTY-EIGHT

It was later than Danielle had intended before she got to see Buck Lansing. Whit had come in to talk with Jon and he came by to visit a bit with Dani. Because she was busy, Whit and Jon had lunch out and brought her back a big slice of sausage pizza and a carton of iced tea. The flavor of the food was still on her tongue, and the three of them had talked, discussed the visit to the Steeles.

Now on her entering Buck's cell the good feeling vanished, but he was smiling broadly, looking her over. She sat on the bunk bed opposite him and got her recorder from her tote, snapped it on. He sat hunched on his bunk bed, as she said, "You asked to talk with me."

"Ah—yeah, Lieutenant—do they call you 'Loo'?"

"Never mind what they call me, Mr. Lansing. I've got a lot of work to do. Don't waste my time."

"This won't take long."

"Good, because if it's going to take a while, we'll talk in the interrogation room with a couple members of my staff."

He seemed momentarily alarmed. "No, please, I just want to talk with *you*."

Had he forgotten what he said to Jon? she wondered. "You told Captain Ryson I'd be pleased. . . ."

He chuckled then. "Oh, yeah. Lieutenant, the words just don't come out right. I'm skittish. I haven't completely thought this through. I'm nervous. They won't let me smoke except outside. It's killing me. Can you give me until tomorrow morning? But ask me anything you want to know."

"Did you kill Mr. Catlett?"

He drew a deep, ragged breath. "No. I never did."

"But you *did* kill Cedric Appiah. Your fingerprints were on a pen in his pocket and I think we're going to find your DNA all over him when the tests come back. I think we're going to find threads from your clothes . . ."

He might as well have not heard her as he sat staring. "You're a good-looking woman, Lieutenant. Are you married?"

"It won't do you any good to know that."

He grinned with apparent pleasure at discomfiting her. "You could do worse. I may be a rich man one day . . ."

"Or in prison."

"Ouch! That hurt. Give me until morning and I think you *all* will be pleased. I want to sleep again on what I've got to say."

"Very well, but next time there'll be others with me. If you don't feel comfortable talking to several people, you're out of luck."

"Forgive me," he said softly in an apparent about-face. "I play the fool when I'm scared and I'm scared now. You ever been betrayed by someone you trusted?"

She nodded. "Rarely, but yes, I've been betrayed." It had been a minor betrayal in high school when a friend had lied on her to a teacher, saying she had cheated on a test when she hadn't.

"I'll bet," he said, "you've never known it the way I'm knowing it now. Oh, you'll be pleased, Lieutenant," he repeated. "You'll all be pleased."

Instinct told her not to rush him. He looked as scared as he said he felt. She looked at him with a modicum of sympathy until she thought of Cedric Appiah—and Cal Catlett. He slid to the back side of the bunk bed, dismissing her.

"You're being arraigned at two o'clock on Thursday," she said. "I think you'll be wise to talk with me as soon as you can."

"They said you were on the afternoon and night shift."

"I'm coming in early, and I'll be at your arraignment."

"Maybe it won't be necessary. Lieutenant?"

He slid back forward to the edge of the bed. "Yes?" she said, her patience worn thin.

"You haven't said much about the smuggling ring. What if *I* ran the ring? Would I get much time for that?"

"Enough. *Did* you run the smuggling ring?"

"Maybe." He wrung his hands. "There's just still a few wrinkles I haven't ironed out. What if I killed Cedric Appiah because he attacked me?"

"Too many what-ifs, Mr. Lansing. Are you confessing? Or playing games?"

He thought a long moment. "Both, I guess. Please be patient. I don't want to make you mad. If I'd had a mother like you, things would have been different."

Danielle thought of nothing to say to that. She shut her recorder off and started out. When she reached the doorway he said, "Tomorrow morning, then, any time you want to talk, I'll be ready then."

She turned. "Let's get this straight, Mr. Lansing. I'm not going to play games with you. You're the one who's going up."

He kept talking and she got her recorder from her purse and turned it back on.

"Can you make a deal?" he asked. "If I confess, will I get less time? Or if I'm just a small part of the smuggling ring, does that make a difference?"

"You could plea-bargain. You need to talk with your lawyer."

She thought he said "that bastard" under his breath, but she couldn't be sure.

"I'm leaving now. Think everything through. Tomorrow's going to be very important to you, Mr. Lansing." Again, she snapped her recorder off.

He nodded, loving it when she called him "mister."

* * *

Danielle found May waiting for her in her office. They hugged delightedly and she reflected that May looked drained.

"Pumpkin," she said, hugging the girl again. "What's up? I'm so happy to see you."

"And I'm so happy to see you." May looked apprehensive as she said, "I've got something I want to talk to you about. I've been wanting to tell you, but I couldn't. I'm so ashamed."

"Let's go in my little conference room where I can lock the door and we'll talk."

A leaden May got up and went with Danielle. Behind the locked door, the girl's sobs suddenly shook her young body, but they cleared as Danielle stood beside the chair and held her, stroking her back.

"Just cry. Don't try to talk."

"No, I've got to. I can't stay long. Rhea needs me back and I've got to catch a bus. I'm running late. She's going to deliver soon, but I had to come. It's eating me up. Mrs. Ritchey?"

"Yes, sweetheart."

"My aunt's husband—you met him, John?"

"Uh-huh."

"He tried to take me down. You know, tried to rape me."

"Oh, my God, that's why you left."

"Yes, ma'am. I fought him off, but I didn't want to hurt him. I thought about hurting him. He said I enticed him, threw myself at him. I've been feeling like God is punishing me for coming on to him, but now I don't think I did."

"I don't think you did. He's the adult; you're still a child."

"You're with homicide," May asked in a small voice, "but can you help with this?"

Danielle patted the girl's back. "You bet I can help. I'm with Homicide, Sex, and Robbery. Come back soon and I'll introduce you to Mrs. Lord, our juvenile person. She's off today. Do you want him to do jail time?"

May shook her head. "It would kill my aunt. She doesn't believe he tried to molest me."

Danielle's heart hurt for the girl. "I still want you to stay with me."

May looked up, bursting with gratitude. "And I want to, as soon as Meena's baby is born and I can help her a while longer. She's a nice person, but her life is not what I want. I love you, Mrs. Ritchey."

The girl stood and flung her arms around Danielle, as Danielle told her, "I love you, pumpkin, very, very much."

As Danielle unlocked the door and she and May stepped outside the conference room, Whit came in. Danielle blew him a kiss and turned to May, introducing them.

"The elusive Miss May Land," Whit said. "I'm glad to meet you."

May blushed and stuck out her hand, which Whit took.

"You're the gospel singer and you're great. The lady I stay with loves you to death, and"—she gave Danielle a shy look—"you're Mrs. Ritchey's beau."

"Guilty as charged," Whit said, laughing.

"I wish I could stay and talk, but I've got to get a bus back to Baltimore." May looked rushed now and, getting a handkerchief and a few Kleenex from her purse, blew her nose. "I'm a mess, I know," she said.

"You're a lovely, young girl and I'm glad to have met you. Wait a minute." He smiled widely at Danielle. "Baltimore's not that far away and I've got time to kill. Why don't I run her home?"

A sunburst of smiles lit May's face. "That would be so wonderful. You don't mind the traffic on the beltway?"

"I can take it."

Whit caught Danielle's hand. "Is this okay with you?"

"It's more than okay. You're a wonderful man, Whit Steele. I never stop saying it."

His lips touched her cheek and he left with May. But he came back into the room. "Listen," he said, "I'm going to bring you one of Arnold Bakery's fantastic lemon meringue cream pies. Like the thought of that?"

Danielle laughed. "I'm beginning to think I like anything you do. I admit it. I'm your slave."

"No. I'm *your* slave and I'm happy to be."

By ten o'clock the next morning, Buck Lansing had sent word that he was ready to talk. Danielle and Ed were seated at a table in one of the interrogation rooms when a jailer led Buck in. He sat down stiffly and Danielle thought he looked as if he hadn't slept at all. His face was drawn, his eyes red and watery. Danielle decided not to press him too hard at first.

"Would you like something to drink?" she asked him.

He looked at her paper cup of hot chocolate and croaked, "Yeah, I'd love a cup of chocolate." Ed looked at him sharply and said, "I'll get it." He pushed his own mug of black coffee aside.

Danielle shook her head and picked up her half-empty cup. "I want a refill and it's better when I mix it myself, so I'll get it. Ed, more coffee?" Ed shook his head.

"Thank you," Buck said, a grin tugging at the corners of his mouth. Ed sat forward and put his elbows on the table. He silently studied Buck, who met his stare without flinching.

Danielle was back in short shrift. She carried two paper cups of hot chocolate and a glass of water on the tray. A pitcher of water sat on the nearby table. She placed one cup of chocolate and the glass of water before Buck as Ed looked on, saying nothing.

"Thank you, ma'am. I didn't know I wanted water, but I sure do." He lifted the glass of water and gulped it down without stopping. Then he took a sip from the hot chocolate. "Good," he said.

Danielle had already switched on the recorder. They sipped their drinks in silence until, after a short while, Buck said suddenly, "I'm a little fish in a big pond." Buck had the floor. He tugged at his collar. "I did what I was told to do. Whenever I complained, I was told if I didn't like it to bail out. I knew I couldn't make the kind of money I make there anywhere else, so I went along. But I'm a small fish . . ."

"You know all about the smuggling operation, don't you?" Danielle asked.

"A whole lot," he answered, "but they didn't tell me everything. I figured out a lot for myself. Manny and Cal had been quarreling lately."

"Do you know what about?" Ed asked.

"I know it had to do with money, but I don't know what."

"Would you be willing to go state's evidence?" Danielle asked.

"Yeah," he answered without hesitation. "That's one of the reasons I needed to talk with you. I couldn't do it yesterday. I just didn't have it all together. Can you cut me a deal? Less time or something like it?"

Ed looked at Danielle and narrowed his eyes, then turned to Danielle. "We can talk about it. We have other questions to ask you. What do you know about Mr. Appiah? Cedric."

"He was a mean man," he said in a low voice.

Danielle's head jerked up, but she remained calm. "Were you ordered to kill him?"

"And were the two of you—you and Annie—alone at the time?" Ed brought up.

"Whoa!" Buck said. "I can't field too many questions." His eyes were glued on Danielle.

"Okay," she said softly. "Why don't you just tell us how it happened?"

Buck clenched and relaxed his fingers again and again, then he sighed. "He didn't have all the money to pay he was supposed to have. He'd paid five thou and needed five thou more. He'd said he'd have it, but he didn't. He said he had no relatives over here. The paper said he had a niece.

"Anyway, he got mad when Manny said he'd knock him out and fasten a note to his back that he was an illegal alien and dump him near a police station. Manny left me alone with him, and when we were alone he turned to me and said he'd been a policeman in some little country. He spoke English okay and the others were watching. I laughed and he spit in my face and ran out the door. Annie had gone to her car to get sandwiches and beer.

"God, he was fast. I took time to wash the spit off. He was an older guy and I was sure he couldn't get far. I was right. I saw the back of him diving into the woods across from Annie's and I went after him. I'm a good runner. I had my gun in my pocket. The .22 Manny didn't want to let go of because it was a gift from a buddy who'd been killed. I'd sneaked it out."

He paused and after a minute, Danielle urged him on. He expelled a harsh sigh. "He kept running and when I got to him, I turned him around and he called me an American dog, spit on me again. This time I hit him and spat back. He brought a little gun out of his pocket and shot once. The shot went wild and I held him, got my gun out of my belt and shot him twice in the chest. I meant business. He tried to say something and I shot him again.

"He slumped then and I was pretty sure he was dead. We were near the side of the road by the highway under that big oak tree and I dragged him over, propped him against the tree, and went back."

He was breathing hard. "Annie saw what was happening and yelled to me not to let him get away when I first started out."

"You and Annie were the only ones there other than the illegal aliens?" Ed asked.

"Yeah. We'd never had any trouble before and we've run a *lot* of *ilimmies*."

"Illimies?" Ed asked, then answered himself. "Oh, that's short for illegal immigrants."

"Yeah. That's Annie's word for them."

Buck seemed more loquacious now. "I wasn't looking to kill him. I felt sorry for him. I'd be scared to death of being in a strange country with no friends."

"Did you know he had two thousand dollars strapped to his upper body?" Danielle studied Buck as she asked the question.

Buck's mouth fell open. "Hell, no, I didn't know," he said. "He probably could have borrowed the other three thousand from Manny or Cal. He'd have had to work it out doing whatever they said to do."

"Then Cal *was* very much a part of this?" Danielle finally brought out.

"He and Manny were the top of the gang. I was a pissant. The gofer."

Ed smiled a little at that.

Buck scratched his face. "Annie'd die for Cal, so she's going to tell you *she* was one of the top people, along with me. I told her cops weren't stupid."

"She doesn't have to die for him anymore," Ed growled.

Remembering the will that was going to break Annie's heart, Danielle said thoughtfully, "I think she's in for a very big surprise."

The tape spun on and in a room next to that one, Jon Ryson smiled grimly. One murder solved. And he wondered if they didn't have two murders solved with Buck Lansing at the wheel.

Buck seemed to be preparing to get up when Danielle asked, "Did you kill Cal Catlett?"

"Hell, no!" Buck exploded. "I'm a company man. Was I wrong to confess? You gonna try to pin Cal's whacking on me too? No. No, you can't *do* that."

"Calm down, Mr. Lansing," Danielle said soothingly. "Somebody killed him. We have to find out who."

Ed's eyes narrowed, set hard on Buck's face and body. God, he hated crooks.

"You have an alibi for the night Cal was murdered?" Ed barked.

"I was home with Manny that night," Buck said hurriedly.

"We've checked," Danielle said, "because we thought he'd be your alibi and you'd be his, but Mr. Luxor was at the gaming tables in Atlantic City that night. He was there until two-thirty in the morning. Mr. Catlett was killed around twelve."

Buck's face went ashen. "Okay. I was alone, but I got drunk, went to bed, slept like a log." His eyes beseeched Danielle. "Look, I believed you'd be fair and help me. I can't stand a long time in prison. I'd die there." He was close to blubbering.

Danielle was touched in spite of herself; she often was, but Ed's face was grim. "You know what they say, old buddy," Ed told him sourly. "If you can't do the time, don't do the crime. Are we through with him, Lieutenant?"

"For the moment," Danielle said.

TWENTY-NINE

Cal Catlett's funeral was held Wednesday, the week following his murder. Danielle went early, taking Whit with her; she was somber and Whit caught her mood. The church was filled with funereal flowers; their scent and the odor of incense lingered in the air. Ushers led them in and the minister came down from the pulpit to greet them.

"It is a sad occasion," the minister said. "Your presence is welcome." His eyes were moist.

Danielle thanked him and chose a seat near the back. She wanted to see everyone who came and went, wanted to study the expression on their faces. She quickly identified Annie, Manny Luxor, Irene, Dave and Edith Emlen, and Ted Keys. In a few minutes, Keith Janey slid into a seat behind her and smiled as she turned around. She returned the smile. She hadn't expected him to come.

Organ music played softly, "Rock of Ages," and she thought, *Let me hide myself in thee*. Whit took her hand and squeezed it lightly.

It was the most expensive funeral she had ever known. The funeral home estimated it cost one hundred ten thousand dollars. Since it was the same funeral home that worked with the police department's and the medical examiner's office, Danielle had been able to access the financial information easily.

Danielle had talked to Edith, who had told her that Cal left a separate long-standing will outlining what he wanted at his funeral. Quincy Tyler had not sent that will along, but she would ask to see a copy.

Jon and his wife came in, sat behind her on the bench with Keith Janey. They quietly greeted Whit and Danielle as Ed entered with Shelley. He grinned and slid onto the same bench. "Howdy," he said to Danielle and Whit. She had already seen him at the station house. Shelley was pensive.

"Hello again, Ed." Danielle's smile flitted across her face. Ed seemed in a very good mood, unlike Danielle, who always knew a moment of sorrow at any funeral.

At last, the church was filled and the organ player began in earnest with soft chords swelling gently. "Amazing Grace" was one of Danielle's favorite hymns; Whit sang it often. Now his mellifluous voice blended with the others and she closed her eyes, letting the sweetness and the joy of the song wash over her.

Irene turned around and caught her eye, smiling nervously. Danielle saw her look at Dave and smile. He flushed vividly and Danielle studied the others who had a role in this drama, including herself. She was surprised at how grief-stricken Dave looked. *Why did he seem so upset?* She thought then that she would ask him again why he was parked a bit down the road from the ALM house the night Cal was murdered. She had asked him before when she questioned him and he had given an evasive answer. Cal's sister, Edith, seemed calm, well rested.

Manny Luxor was one of the reasons she had come early. She wanted to see his reactions. He sat with Annie and his expression was cool, sober. Turning around, he looked directly at Danielle and nodded. She nodded in return, but a small chill shook her. He and Annie and Buck would be arraigned the next day on charges of smuggling illegal aliens. Somehow, Manny seemed more threatening in this social setting. He was an outsider, she thought, always had been and always would be. She was certain that he fit very well into the world he inhabited.

She was ready to question Manny now. She knew Buck would be his alibi as he was Buck's. Manny didn't need to kill; he could always find someone else to do the job. But she intended to find out what he knew.

The minister's sermon was richly beautiful and benevolent.

"Caleb Catlett was not a man to stand on ceremonies," the minister began. "He loved life and he loved a lot of people. But as it is with all of us, he had friends, and he had *enemies.*"

Members of the choir were gathered back from the pulpit and their devout faces mirrored rapt attention.

"Cal was a man who spent his time and his money wisely. He gave lavishly and he lived lavishly. He supported many causes and I am certain that nothing he did warranted the death dealt him. Therefore, we deeply mourn his passing.

"He was a man of warmth and humor and he leaves a beloved and loving wife, Irene, who mourns him deeply." Danielle observed that Irene looked down as the minister continued.

"'Amazing Grace,'" the minister said, "how sweet the sound, that saved a wretch like me, but Cal was not a wretch, but a prince among men." He spread out his arms. "This splendid altar and the beautiful stained windows of this church were two of many of his gifts to us and we are grateful.

"Cal Catlett bore his own amazing grace. He lived a life of honor and generosity. And we are grateful. He was my friend; I was his friend and he had a host of other friends who loved him dearly. He frequently came by to talk with my wife and me. Mrs. Catlett sometimes came with him. I never knew a sweeter couple."

Danielle's head jerked up. This was stretching it pretty thin. Everybody knew about Irene's bruised arms and throat that she sometimes refused to cover with long sleeves and high neck-lines, as if defiantly displaying her injuries. They say money talks, she reflected. Cal's money was brilliantly *orating*.

The minister's voice swept on. "We will never forget you, Caleb Catlett. You will live on in our hearts. Our city and its people were yours and you belonged to this city and its people. Rest well. Sleep well. I gave you a brief sermon because I have a long prayer. Oh, I know, God, Cal does not need my humble prayers. You have blessed him from the beginning. Now, he has gone to be with you forever."

Danielle and Whit looked at each other, and Danielle thought, *We're at the wrong funeral. The man he speaks of was light-years ahead of the poor sinner I think I know a little about.* This oracle this funeral grieved was nothing like the Cal Catlett she knew.

Suddenly, Annie stood up and fled swiftly down the aisle, her face a burning red, drenched with tears. Danielle rose to follow her, but she looked at Ted Keys, whose eyes had followed Annie from the time she got up.

Annie raced to the lounge and collapsed on a couch. Danielle went to her, saying softly, "Let me help you."

She expected the big woman to pull away, but she didn't. She sat up as Danielle put her arms around her. "I'm so sorry," Danielle said.

To her surprise Annie gave a twisted smile. "I thought you'd be happy since you've caught us."

"I'm never happy at another's misfortune," Danielle said quietly. "Cal's death is hurting you terribly, isn't it?" She thought about the will that Annie would not have seen. *You've got more hurt on the way, lady, and I feel this is really going to hit you where you live.*

"What hurt you so bad, so suddenly?" Danielle asked.

Annie thought a moment. "I was thinking ahead. I thought about viewing the body and I got sick. I knew he wasn't really dead to me until I thought about that. I've got to look at him one last time and never again. I knew then that he was really gone and I don't know how I'm going to live without him. Prison doesn't matter to me now. I don't care anymore."

Annie's body was wracked with sobs for a few minutes, then she stopped abruptly and wiped her face on the Kleenex Danielle gave her.

"I'll wait while you do your makeup," Danielle told her.

Annie shook her head. "No. I mean it when I say I don't care. Ted Keys is my lover. Did you know that?"

"I've heard."

"Oh. Who told you?"

"Someone. We get a lot of information."

"He thinks Cal is going to leave me a lot of money, *has* left me a lot of money, and he's sniffing around already to marry me. Lieutenant, you don't know what hell is until the man you love dies. You asked me if I killed him. No, I love Cal too much to hurt him. I've wanted to die since his death."

"You told me you have a brother you love."

"Yes, but not like I love Cal. It's like a butcher knife blade in my heart, Lieutenant. I breathe and the damned thing twists. It's killing me and I don't think it will ever stop."

And the worst is yet to come, Danielle thought glumly. Annie's tears had stopped and she looked at Danielle. "Thank you so much. I want to stay a little while longer."

"Very well. I'll stay and walk back with you."

Back inside the church, the two women went to their seats. The minister's long prayer was over.

The bier was beautifully arranged, surrounded by flowers, fern, and baby's breath. The choir sang and hummed as the minister announced that they would now view the body. The bronze casket was magnificent, much wider than usual, with a foot-wide inner rim of mother-of-pearl. The handles were gold plated.

Irene and Edith went first and Irene's poise was remarkable. She seemed sturdy, dry-eyed. People arranged themselves in a line around the edge of the rows after Irene had come back and sat down. Whit and Danielle, Jon and his wife, and Keith Janey all stood near each other.

It took a long while for people to view Cal's body, but when Danielle and Whit finally reached him, Danielle studied the body in death as she had in life. He was resplendent as always. His entire body, from the close-clipped gray-flecked reddish-

brown hair and wonderfully well embalmed face to his dark
navy Armani Italian silk suit with its red-patterned silk rep tie
to his navy socks and Gucci shoes, said his death mattered.
He was the last word in elegance. His tie clip, fashioned of
gold and diamonds, winked at the viewers.

When Annie got to the bier, she stretched out her hand,
touched Cal's stony face, and said in a choked voice, "Sleep
well. I love you. I've always loved you."

In her seat, Irene thought bitterly, *Even in death, he belongs to you.*

After the funeral, the cortège made its way to the cemetery
where Cal would be entombed. The expensive white marble
crypt was waiting to receive the body. The cemetery was
crowded in the hot, muggy August air. Danielle and Whit
stood a little back from the crowd and Irene stopped on her
way to the crypt. Only a few people would go inside. Dave
walked with Irene and held an umbrella over her head.

"I want to keep you updated," she told Danielle. "Cal
wanted his body to lie in state for a month after the funeral.
There'll be two guards night and day, but only those with special permission can come in. Visit me sometime, Lieutenant.
I've come to really like you. You have class. God only knows
what Cal's will gives to me; it might put me out of house and
home. . . ."

"No. That would be against the law," Danielle assured her.

Irene shrugged. "It's been a long row to hoe, living with
Cal. He wasn't always kind, but I think he hurt bad inside.
Maybe he's at peace now."

She and Dave walked on then and Danielle was happy for
them. She hoped they would find a life together.

Whit drove Danielle back to the station house and they
talked awhile in the car. "We go to a murdered person's

funeral," she told him, "because by watching faces, we often get information that wouldn't be otherwise available. Things happen at wakes, at funerals. People display feelings they've hidden. At the M.E.'s place we get a chance to fathom sometimes how the murdered man or woman came to die. A body in that place is the most naked it has ever been: sans wine, sans song, sans singer and—sans end. Remember the *Rubaiyat*?"

"I've got it at home. I read it every so often. Danielle, we're psychic twins. Don't you know that by now?"

"I've thought I did."

Lifting her hand, he brought it to his lips. She smiled at him.

"I'm very pleased at the way Keith Janey has turned out in the short run," she said.

"He's certainly a changed man."

"He swears he's going back to school. He's not drinking. I don't know how long it will last, but, Whit, it lets me know I'm right to feel that we should never harshly judge others. People can change. They *do* change. Sometimes veins of solid gold lie far beneath the surface of rot and slime. People are just unbearably *hurt* so often it drives them crazy."

"I know, love," Whit said slowly. "Lord, how I know."

"You were hurt, but you didn't strike out at others."

"I turned it in on myself. Now I'm not doing much of that anymore, thanks to you."

"No. You're the one who's done the work. I think you're almost there, sweetheart. I think you're almost there."

In her office later that afternoon, Danielle placed a call. Manny Luxor would have had sufficient time to get home from the funeral and she had decided it was time to question him.

His voice came low and growly, "Manny Luxor here."

"Mr. Luxor, this is Lieutenant Danielle Ritchey. I wonder if you'd come in to see me this afternoon?"

"Hell, Lieutenant, I'm just getting back from the funeral.

This is hardly the time." He hesitated. "Is this a summons, or an invitation?"

"It's an invitation. You don't have to come, but I think it would be to your advantage. I have some questions I want to ask you."

"I been wondering when you'd get around to it. My lawyer comes with me."

"That's not a problem. Would you prefer this afternoon or tomorrow morning?" She would come in early, she thought, to talk with him.

"Tomorrow morning. You know my arraignment is tomorrow afternoon. Don't keep me too long."

"I'll be brief." Even in trouble with the law, Manny was having his own way as far as he could.

Hanging up the phone, Danielle spread her hands on her desk and looked down at her long, tapering fingers. Getting up, she walked to the copy room and picked up two faxes. One copy was from Quincy Tyler, Cal Catlett's will addendum that delineated what he wanted done with his body, and the other was a two-page profile from Dr. Art Little, a forensic psychiatrist she used in murder cases. She needed to read that one first.

Back in her office, she sat at the table and read the profile. Dr. Little felt the perpetrator was cool, methodical, and capable of deep rage. The fact that he hid the body, albeit in a place it would be easily found, was indicative of some degree of caring and a fear of being caught.

Dr. Little was a deep man and he wrote:

Forgive me my idiosyncrasies, but I have always be-
lieved that the way a person is murdered tells us a lot
about the murderer. Thus, a gun or a knife to the heart
may very well tell us that the killer has had his or her
heart broken by the victim.

Danielle looked up, somberly reflecting on this. Whose heart had Cal broken? Certainly Irene's, but perhaps she had grown beyond him. Annie. He had certainly hurt her. He had helped and he had hurt a lot of people. And had he hurt Manny Luxor or Buck Lansing? She anxiously awaited the DNA lab results from all the blood samples.

Buck had confessed to killing Cedric Appiah. He was a likely suspect for killing Cal Catlett. And if he did, he would rot in prison. Even Quincy was not likely to successfully defend him, for Cal had friends in high places.

Dr. Little wrote that he would send her a full-length profile in a few days. She looked forward to it. His profiles had been instrumental in helping her and the team to solve several murders.

Putting aside the profile, she picked up the copy of Cal's will addendum that was devoted solely to what was to be done with his body. Irene had already told her a part of it at the cemetery. Now she read the rest. She was deep in thought when Ed came in. She looked up and slid the profile across the table to him.

Ed read and seemed deep in thought.

"See anything you think may be useful?" she asked.

"Doc Little's a character. Trust a psychiatrist to get psychology into everything."

"You're referring to the part about broken hearts?"

"What else? Some guy runs a hot temper and loses it. I think it often doesn't matter a damn what drove him to it." He drew a couple of deep breaths. "Give me DNA and fingerprints, not psychological drivel. I doubt any shrink can say what a murderer's characteristics are unless they talk to the person."

Danielle shook her head. "He's got a believer in me. He's been right on the mark several times, Ed. Don't you remember?"

"I know you thought so. But I won't argue with my boss."

He was all charm now and he seemed upbeat. "I'm glad Mr. Scumbag Lansing confessed. That'll save the taxpayer a little money and us some time and trouble. We're at the top of our form, Dani. Now, if we can just get him to come clean on Cal's murder."

"Then you think he did it, too."

"Hell, yes, I think he did it. We found Cal's hair on Appiah's clothes. He was mixed up in this. Lansing's told you he was. He and Luxor were getting rich transporting bodies. Buck was a minnow swimming in a pool of sharks. He knew they were ready to eat him and he turned tail and turned them in. We'll never know the whole story, Dani, but I'll bet it's a good one."

Manny Luxor and his lawyer, Quincy, came at nine o'clock the next morning. They sat at the table across from Danielle.

"Let me get you coffee or whatever you wish to drink," Danielle said.

"Manny?" Quincy asked, "what's your poison?"

"I'll take coffee, black with sugar. Big cup."

"Have you any orange juice on hand?" Quincy asked.

"Sure. Orange juice, grape, pineapple."

"Is your budget big enough for me to have a big glass of the o-juice?"

Danielle smiled. "For you, I think I can handle it, Attorney Tyler."

Quincy leaned back in his chair and smiled at Danielle. He liked women, all of them, but he had sharp favorites; Danielle was one of them. As he looked from one to the other of them, Manny's brow creased into a deep frown. He, Manny, was coming in to be questioned on what he knew about a murder and maybe to be tricked into saying he killed Catlett. And here his lawyer had time to flirt with a woman who could put a noose around his neck. He shot Quincy a hard look and got a cool glance for his efforts. Quincy could read his client's mind.

Danielle came back to the table, sat down, and lost no time. "I wonder if you'd be willing to give us a blood sample, Mr. Luxor?" she asked him.

Manny looked up quickly at her, then at his lawyer. "Why, I guess so."

"It's okay," Quincy said soothingly.

But Manny was edgy now. "I don't need a lawyer to tell me that."

"Mr. Luxor, where were you the night Mr. Catlett was killed?"

"Home. Buck's my alibi and I'm his."

He was lying. She knew he'd been gambling in Atlantic City.

"You could have gone out. Either one of you could have gone out without the other knowing it. Did you?"

"Yes, I could've, but I didn't. I slept like a hibernating bear the whole night. It was on the early morning news Cal'd been killed. No blood on my hands. As for Buck, who knows what that scoundrel was up to? I sure didn't hear him go out if he did."

She was silent and the two men fell in line. Then Manny cleared his throat. "I'm being arraigned today at two-thirty for the smuggling deal. . . ."

"Yes, I remember."

"How long is this going to take?"

"You're early. You've got time. I have only a few questions to ask."

"I need to talk to Buck. I hoped you'd trade favors here. You got nothing on me. I never killed anybody."

"Mr. Luxor, don't you wonder why I haven't asked for your fingerprints?"

"A little, maybe."

"We have your fingerprints from New York. Before you moved here you were a suspect in a murder and they have your fingerprints on file. We got them. You did time for manslaughter."

"That was twenty years ago—you mean to say—"

"The arm of the law is *very* long these days. We've got

DNA, a world of cooperation between law enforcement agencies, more expertise . . ."

Manny laughed shortly. "And you still don't know all the answers. I didn't kill Cal Catlett and a wagonload of DNA can't prove I did."

"Very well. Then thank you for coming. Thank you, Attorney Tyler."

"You're very welcome," Quincy Tyler said.

"I want to talk with Buck," Manny demanded.

Danielle shook her head. "I'm afraid he doesn't want to talk with you. He's left word to that effect."

Manny's mouth fell open. "The hell you say. I just about raised that kid."

"Well, apparently he doesn't need you anymore."

Danielle thought now that they didn't know that Buck had confessed to the murder of Cedric Appiah. They didn't know he was going to refuse to be the fall guy for the smuggling operation. They didn't know that Buck was no longer one of them.

THIRTY

Ten days later the final DNA reports were in for Cedric Appiah and Cal Catlett. The reports on Mr. Appiah had struck a snag, so they were late. In her office, Danielle leafed through them. Buck's DNA was all over Cedric Appiah. It had been there all the time, but they hadn't had his blood sample. Cal had been there, had talked with the African illegal immigrant, had left hair samples, so they had known this. Buck had confessed to killing Mr. Appiah, but he'd vehemently denied killing Cal Catlett.

Buck and Annie had been duly arraigned for illegal alien smuggling. Both refused to acknowledge that Manny had been at Annie's house that night, and Manny had denied his own part in the smuggling ring. A convened grand jury had indicted him. All three trials were set for October of this same year.

Leaning back in her plush swivel chair, Danielle pondered the case. They were no closer to finding the Catlett killer than they had been when the first forty-eight hours had passed. A knock sounded and Jon Ryson entered.

"Captain Ryson," Danielle said, teasing him.

"Lieutenant Ritchey," he responded.

Theirs was an easy relationship and they worked well together. "Isn't it about time you went home?" he asked.

"I'm tying up some loose ends, to coin an old cliché. In fact, I think I'm leaving a bit early."

"It's a beautiful day. I went to the park for lunch. Fran and I had a picnic lunch."

"I'm envious. I'll have to try that on Whit."

"You've got nothing to be envious about." He sighed then. "Dani, the Catlett case is coming up against one brick wall after another. We know from his own confession that Lansing is a hothead. My scenario says that Cal insulted him or short-changed him in some way, maybe laughed at him, and he killed Catlett, maybe without intending to. It keeps playing out in my head."

She nodded. "He steadfastly denies it. I think he's the likely suspect, but there are others. The DNA reports tell us nothing we hadn't already gathered. Mr. Appiah's clothes swarm with Buck Lansing's DNA, but then he's confessed to that murder."

"The mayor called me in this morning. The business people, the movers and shakers of Minden are demanding an early resolution. We're getting frazzled, all of us. Ed's like a zombie, he's working so hard."

"They may have to get used to a long-in-solving-if-ever case. It has happened before. We have a seventy-five percent solve rate and that isn't one hundred percent."

Jon stroked his chin. "We all have said Minden is a great place to be murdered because your killer *will* be found."

"That doesn't seem true anymore."

"If it ever was. We've been cocky. This is pulling us."

Jon's eyes were warm with concern. "Dani, you're looking a little stressed, too. You might want to consider taking a few days or at least a couple of days off."

"Murders always stress me, Jon. They hit me where I live. In thirteen years, I've done a poor job of getting over my mother's murder."

"Sometimes we never do. I often think now it was a stranger and it was robbery. Her purse was missing."

"I've come to think you're probably right."

He sat down at the head of the table and she pushed the DNA reports toward him. "I've seen all I need to see at the moment if you'd like to look them over."

"I would. I'll return them."

"What does your second sight tell you?" he asked.

"Nothing really. It works at times. Dreams told me who killed the Wiggins boy and I was right. It's the only time that's ever happened. I *saw* Whit just before I actually met him. It's a sometime thing." She stretched then, saying, "I really am leaving early."

He got up and left and what he had said about taking some time off swept over her. Whit loved short trips away. She would call him this afternoon.

A half hour later, she pulled into her driveway and parked near the side porch. Lazily, she sat stretched out in the butter-beige leather seat of her Mercury Cougar when her cell phone rang. She dove into her tote bag and answered.

"Dani, this is Val Craig. Alaska."

Danielle chuckled. "You don't have to identify your home state to me. Those gorgeous photos are still burned on my brain. I've never been to Alaska."

"Then come soon, you and Whit. Could you come within the next couple of weeks or even a week? The wildflowers are stupendous, the spongy tundra soil is like velvet beneath your feet, salmon are running, and animals of every description bless us. Don't mention the midnight sun. Come now and come back when the aurora borealis holds sway. Please don't turn us down."

"I don't need to be sold. All I need is a little block of time."

"You could come up on a Friday and go back the following Monday. I'm not setting time frames for you. We just want you to rush getting here."

"Let me call you back in a few days and set a definite time."

"Make it soon now."

"I will."

They chatted then about Alaska and Minden, the Cedric Appiah and the Cal Catlett murders, touching briefly on other topics.

"It would be good to get away. These murders bring back a lot of unpleasant memories," Danielle said softly. "I pray we can put them behind us soon."

"So do I, Dani. We all need prayer these days."

"Prayer has always been the backbone of my life. I prayed to meet a man I could love the way I love Whit, and God sent him to me."

"You're a perfect pair. His family adores you. You adore each other."

"You and Del are the perfect pair. I love the Steeles. And we *will* see you soon."

When Danielle hung up, she dialed Whit, sitting up as she did so. There was no answer. She left a message.

Tapping the side of her head with her fist, she thought about the fact that she had wanted to pull weeds from the big Japonica bush back of the ALM house. She had intended to go there before coming home. Now she sat up on the sun-warmed seat and switched on the ignition.

In a short while she had parked behind the back of the ALM house. Her eyes and her mind went swiftly to the crawl space where they had found Cal's body. A chill ran through her and she shuddered a little thinking about it.

The house was quiet and she thought of the quarter-million bequest Cal had left. He had been more wrapped up in their work than she had dreamed. Getting out, she opened her car trunk and removed some gardening tools. There were men and boys who would be glad to deweed the Japonica bush, but it was her favorite of the flowers the yard was planted with. She wanted to do it.

She thought wryly that she should have changed clothes, but she got out, retrieved a large plastic leaf bag from the trunk and began. She thought about going in just to check around the ALM house and decided against it. She wanted to get back home. She craved some fast food from Popeye's. And everything seemed to conspire against her getting to take a short afternoon snooze.

With her gardening knife, she cut six Japonica rose flowers and set them aside. They were for Whit, who loved flowers. Putting the blossoms on the grass, she began to weed the bush in earnest. She was well into the tall weeds when something gleaming caught her eye. Bending, she picked up a beautiful gold object—*an Egyptian ankh.* A small key lay beside it and she picked that up too. Ed's face and body sprang to her vision.

There were other ankhs and other keys that might belong to other people, but the pit of her stomach felt cold and tremors took her before she steeled herself. There had to be an explanation. As fond as Ed was of his ankh, *if* this was his, why hadn't he mentioned losing it? And the small key? It wasn't a door key. No, experience and her own safe deposit key told her what such a key looked like. Her heart felt leaden as she thought about the possibilities of these two articles belonging to her coworker and friend.

Her mind swiftly made deductions. At the moment, she didn't feel her fellow detective and friend had killed Cal Catlett, but he might know what was going on, might be mixed up in it in some way. Ed was no saint, and didn't pretend to be.

There could be no further weeding. With a heavy heart, she slipped the ankh and the key into an evidence bag from her purse. She picked up the leaf bag and put it into her car trunk, then got into the car and drove to Minden's police station house.

Jon was still at work when she walked into his office.

"Dani, what is it?" he asked. "You look stunned."

Quickly, she told him she needed to talk with him about something urgent. "Let's go into the safe room," he said.

The station house had one small soundproof room. They went in the double doors and he locked the doors behind them. Sitting down, she told him what had happened and he whistled.

"*Could* he be mixed up in this?" she asked.

Jon shrugged, hunched his shoulders. "He wouldn't be the first rogue cop. We once had a guy on the force before you came on who was a robber baron. He hit half the houses in Minden, only he had a gang working for him. He went up for fifteen years. He was a knowledgeable, gutsy cop, but a crook. It happens, Dani. Maybe there's an innocent explanation, but I hope it doesn't hurt you too bad if Ed is mixed up in this."

"Jon, I'm thinking of something that seems simple to me. What if I wear a wire, ask him to meet me at the ALM house and confront him with this? Ask if he killed Catlett or if he knows anything about the murder. What could it hurt?"

Jon thought it over and nodded. "It makes a lot of sense. One thing he's not is a hothead. In fact, he's a pretty cool customer. I'd surveil you all the way over and be outside the ALM house just outside the old darkroom. There's an inverted corner there and bushes we could hide in. We'd hear everything that was going on and if anything went wrong—"

"Another thing," Danielle told him, "I'm going to get a warrant to search from Judge Lanier. If this key *is* to a safe deposit box, I want to know what's there."

"Seems an excellent idea. You're hitting on all cylinders, as usual."

"Let's just pray that nothing goes wrong," she said softly. Hot tears sprang to her eyes. "When my mother died," she said, "my father was a rock, you were a rock, and Ed was a rock. Without you three, I don't think I could have made it."

Jon reached over and pressed her hand. "You're strong, Dani, you would have made it. Mona was a wonderful woman."

"Wonderful," Danielle said bitterly, "and somebody took her wonderful life."

"You're sure you want to do this? Once you were inside the ALM building, someone would be inside the house by the darkroom door. There's a little danger, but there's always some. There may be a side to Ed none of us know about."

"And if we're wrong," she said, "may God forgive us. I'm not sure Ed ever will."

She was home when Whit returned her call. She told him the parameters of the situation and he was silent. She didn't tell him what she would do. One unwise and unintended word could snarl up the whole plan. She felt her heart beating too fast. He had hated the thought of linking her to danger. She knew that he would hate hearing about possible danger.

"Guess what?" he said. "I'm riding with one of your cops tonight. I understand you've got a cop-citizen friendship campaign going. Well, I'm not a Mindenite, but I've got jewels who are."

"Jewels?"

"You. What if I come by when I'm done ridding Minden of crime?"

"You have a standing invitation. My house is your house."

"And my heart is yours."

Smiling, she hung up and began to prepare red clover tea and a grilled cheese sandwich. Gone was the appetite for Popeyes' best.

THIRTY-ONE

Everything was set! Danielle stood in the darkroom of the ALM house facing Ed.

"You wanted to see me, babe?" he drawled. "Tell me what this is all about, but you got to rush it, I'm afraid. I've got promises to keep and miles to go before I sleep."

It was nine o'clock and fast growing dark outside. "Let's sit down," Danielle suggested.

"Sure." They sat across from each other in the charged air. "Ed," she began, "we've been friends a long time. . . ."

"Yeah. It's been good."

She had chosen the ALM house for her questions because Cal Catlett had been killed here. Luminol had shown he was killed in this room and taken outside. People resonated to places where they had done dark deeds.

How to begin. She decided to just dive in. "Do you know *anything* about Cal Catlett's death that you're not telling us, anything you *can't* tell us?"

Ed's mouth fell open and he snorted. "Do *you?*"

"Please level with me. A man is dead and we've been unable to solve it. If you know anything . . ."

"What do you *think* I know, Dani?"

"Only you can tell us this."

"Hell, you could have asked me this over the phone. Why all the cat-and-mouse games?"

She still hadn't decided to tell him she'd found the ankh and the small key. Now she decided she would.

He hunched his shoulders and was silent for a while after she spoke; then he expelled a harsh sigh. "I lost both items. I haven't been sure where. You brought them with you?"

"No."

"Dani, you didn't rat me out without talking to me first."

"No," she lied.

"We've been friends," he began, then stopped.

"Lord, don't I know it," she told him. "If you know anything, Ed, I'll be lenient. I promise you that. You can't be hung for what you know."

Ed spoke slowly then, his eyes half closed. "If you got the key, you're a cop and you'd go after what that key fit. You'd guess in a heartbeat that it's to a safe deposit box at the bank. Dani, hear me out so you can help me when the time comes.

"I've always gambled, but I'm *really* gambling now. Atlantic City, the lottery; every time I've said I was going to New York on a long weekend, I was mostly in Vegas." He licked his bone-dry lips. "If you looked, you found a lot of money in my safe deposit box, upward of two hundred thou. For a while now, I've been mostly winning. I discovered a partner, a Mexican multimillionaire who doesn't mind losing. He wants me to head a security force for him back home in Mexico. That's where the money's coming from for almost a year now."

"Gambling's forbidden to us except in small amounts," Danielle said evenly.

"Lord love you. You're acting like Little Miss Innocent."

"You're not answering my question. What do you know about Cal Catlett's death?" Her voice was gentle.

"You know what I know, which is nothing. *I* sure didn't kill him, Dani. I'll swear to that on a stack of Bibles. Cal and I got along pretty well, but we weren't close by any means. I'd have no motive. Are you asking because you found the ankh and the key?"

"It did cross my mind."

"You're a great cop, Dani." He smiled crookedly, "And I

don't blame you for suspecting me. If the shoe had been on the other foot, I'd suspect you too. Does Jon know about your suspicions or did you come to me first? I'd have come to you first."

"He doesn't know." The second lie came effortlessly.

"You wearing a wire?" He didn't believe her. Small fingers of alarm clutched her brain cells.

"No," she lied yet again. "I've got plenty of doubt about your being deeply involved. As far as I know, you didn't know Cal that well. Now, I'm asking, do you know anything, anything at all that might be helpful?" She was pleading now. "This case is running me ragged, Ed. I'm not sleeping well and the pieces aren't coming together. They keep pulling at my mind."

His glance at her then was warm, friendly.

"Join me, because I'm not sleeping well either. I hate crime; that's why I joined the force, and I hate a murderer worse than I hate the devil. I'm sorry I lost the ankh and the key and put you through this. No, baby, *I didn't kill Cal Catlett* and I don't know who did, but I'm working on it, along with you and the others."

She felt a deeper sense of relief then, and thought she recognized sincerity when she encountered it. She put out her hand. "Friends still?"

"Always. I love you, baby. It can't be any other way."

She engaged him in small talk then, giving Jon and the others a chance to get away from their places by the outside of the darkroom and inside the house. Ed no longer seemed anxious to leave. He got downright loquacious.

"You've gone after Lansing and that's smart," he said. "He's a sometime hit man, used for ultra-special jobs. I've told you that."

"Yes."

"I figure Cal crossed them up in some way, shortchanged Manny Luxor, and Luxor sicced his hit pit bull—Lansing—on him. It would mean nothing to Lansing, killing Cal. He's killed at least one mideastern head of state and lived to tell it."

"I believe it's Lansing," she said slowly, "but we've got no evidence."

"Hit men learn not to leave evidence. Dani, I got to go now, but look, don't feel bad about this. I tell you again, I'd have done the same thing."

"You're not upset?"

"Hell, yes, I'm upset, but I've been a cop long enough to know the game and play it well. We've got a killer on our hands. Somehow, I think we'll nail the perp. We all think it's Lansing and we're almost surely right, but if we don't come to prove Lansing guilty, we're still friends, Dani." He stuck out his hand. "Twine your little finger in mine."

She held out her hand and they intertwined their little fingers. "Care to make a blood exchange?" he asked, grinning.

Danielle smiled. "I don't feel like giving blood," she said, "but I don't think I'll doubt you again."

Back in the safe room that night, Jon rocked in a swivel chair. "Everything's recorded. Ed seems to be on the level, but we were right to check. You did a great job, Dani."

"Thank you. If he's guilty, he's not admitting it. I think he's innocent."

Jon smiled. "Innocent. Ed Ware doesn't have an innocent bone in his body, but his story seems to ring true to me. I've got to ride him about the gambling, though. It opens you up to all kinds of blackmail and can get you killed. Welsh on a bet to the wrong mobster and you're an alligator's tasty supper."

"What now?" she asked. "I said you didn't know."

"That's fine. He'll never learn from me. One thing I know. You and Ed and the rest of us are still frazzled. City Hall and the mayor are still coming down on us for action, but I don't believe in driving myself and my people into the ground. Ed can fill in for you for a couple of days on the investigation."

"He complained of being frazzled, too."

"I think he can hold out a bit longer. You've been working harder than anybody else. Take a break, Dani. Go away somewhere."

She told him about Val and Del's invitation to Alaska.

"Then *go*. Make it next week. You're already in love with Whit and you'll fall in love with Alaska. Who knows? You may well come back married."

LATE SUMMER 2000
PASSION, DANGER, AND THE CULMINATION OF A DREAM

THIRTY-TWO

Val and Del Craig met Danielle and Whit's plane that afternoon. There were warm hugs all around. Del asked if they were tired and Whit replied that no, they weren't; instead they seemed energized. Del proposed a short sight-seeing trip, and driving out from Nome, Danielle thought Alaska was more beautiful than any photograph could depict.

The deep blue waters of magnificent Norton Sound stretched out before them and they marveled at the terrain stretching from Nome where Del and Val lived. Del parked his Porsche and they walked out onto the spongy summer tundra to a marvel of wildflowers and wild berries.

"Watch out for mosquitoes," Val cautioned. "They're the rough side of paradise."

"There's nothing they love more than human blood." Del reached into his knapsack and brought out bottles of insect repellent that Whit rubbed on his face and arms; he wore a short-sleeved shirt. Danielle rubbed the lotion only onto her face and hands. She wore a long-sleeved gauzy cream blouse over a dress.

Before he could finish smoothing on the lotion, Whit growled an "ouch" and slapped himself.

"They win the speed record every time," Del said, laughing.

"Are you two hungry?" Val asked. "Because we can either eat in town or go home and let Womenga fix us something special."

Both Whit and Danielle said they weren't hungry. "The

food on the plane was far from special, but it squashed the hungries," Danielle explained.

They drove along Norton Sound, and back from it was a woodland stretch. "These are man-planted trees," Del pointed out. "This section of Alaska was treeless save for a few blue spruce. Now we have a fair sampling of trees."

"Oh, good Lord!" Danielle explained and pointed to a spot many yards away from them where a giant grizzly stood on his back legs.

"And there you have Methuselah," Del told them. "He's supposed to be thoroughly tame, but I don't trust him. I stay my distance and he stays his. All the households in Nome and the surroundings keep Craig rifles and shotguns. If he ever does choose to misbehave, he's a goner."

Salmon ran swiftly in Norton Sound and other fish abounded.

"Am I right, or is it my imagination," Danielle asked, "that the air in Alaska is fresher, cleaner than that in most other places?"

"You're right," Val answered. "It's good now, but in winter it's fantastic. Let's go in now. We've got two whole days to traipse about the countryside. I want you well rested when you return home."

Val and Del's house in Nome was a very large, cream-frame house with dark blue shutters. It was beautifully landscaped with evergreens and two large blue spruce trees in the front and one in the backyard. A round structure of cream stucco stood in back.

"I'm going to show you to your suite and leave you to rest for a while," Val said. As she spoke a middle-aged Inuit woman came in the door bearing a large basket of wild berries. Del introduced her as Womenga, the woman who helped them and was part of their family.

Val sighed. "Anna, our daughter, is visiting friends in Anchorage. She told me when I talked to her yesterday that she hates missing you, but I told her you'd come again when the aurora borealis comes due. Was I right? I hope so."

"We'll come," Whit said. "Just set a date."

Val showed them the round house where they were to stay. A beautiful structure done in aquamarine and cream, with touches of scarlet and pale yellow, it had one large room and a smaller bedroom. But it was the bath that took their breath away: a huge aquamarine-colored sunken tub with plants growing along the back side, gold dolphin-shaped spigots, and a narrow shelf of scents and bath gels that adorned one corner.

Danielle smiled. "We may not need to come back. I'm going to have a hard time tearing myself away."

"My husband's a tinkerer and an inventor." Val pointed out the overhead clear acrylic shields over the bed and the bathtub. They were set to automatically open and close at will. Val quickly showed them how to operate the shields.

Then they noticed the small slick brown bird in its cage, seeming to ignore them. A nightingale.

"This is Mr. Music," Val said. "My late mother-in-law left him to us. He sings in fits and starts. If you're lucky, he'll sing for you."

Val left and Danielle and Whit quickly unpacked their bags. She stood before him in a beautiful beige silk and nylon slip with lacy borders. He wore a tank top and abbreviated boxer shorts. Her silken brown skin and the sudden look she gave him almost took his breath away. Would he never get used to the loveliness of her?

"Come here," he said suddenly.

She shot him an arch look. "Are you speaking to me, sir?"

"Don't be coy. I mean business."

"Should I be afraid?" she whispered, going to him.

"Yeah, you should be afraid. One day I'm going to just gobble you up and there's nothing the law can do because I couldn't help myself."

She placed a slender hand on each side of his face and

lightly grazed his lips. "You're a madman," she told him. "You know that, don't you?"

"I'm mad for you."

Slowly, he stripped off her undergarments and, bending his head, suckled her breasts, first one, then the other. She slipped out of his grasp for a moment and removed his top, then his shorts. Drawing in her breath, she devoured him with her eyes. "You're a mighty specimen, Mr. Man," she murmured. "You turn me on without half trying. Be careful you don't catch my fire."

"Too late. I'm already burning."

He thought now that nothing he had done in his life had made him deserve this woman, but she was his for the taking. And standing there, he knew he was going to make her his, press her, ride and be ridden by her. She was the championship game he was going to win.

His engorged, hard shaft rose mightily against her and she moaned aloud.

"What's wrong, sweetie?" he said, a smile tugging at the corner of his mouth. "Can't you take a little foreplay?"

"What if I want the *real* play?"

"Ask me nicely for it and I might give it to you. Or I might make you beg."

"Meanie."

"After all, if it's as good as you say it is, I need to protect it. Not give it away so easily, wouldn't you say?"

Danielle looked at him levelly. "Don't play games. You're giving it to me because you *want* to. I can hide my fire; you have no such luck."

"I can put my jockey strap on. That'll hide my craving."

"I think that the wizard will burst the jockstrap. Am I right?"

"You know you're right." Whit laughed gleefully. "Okay. When? Where? How? I'm going to give you the time of your life."

"The bathroom," she said gently. "I could float in that huge tub the rest of the day and half the night."

She turned on and tempered the spigots in the bathtub, selected bath beads perfumed of lemon verbena from the shelf, and sprinkled water on her body. They lay on the bed then, close to each other, silent, still.

"Saving it?" he teased her.

"Aren't you?"

"You know me. You look my way and I have a powerful erection. One day you've got to tell me, Dani, exactly what it's like for you."

"If you'll tell me what it's like for you."

"Agreed. No better time than tonight."

The big tub was full in a short while and they climbed in. They drew the crinkled plastic enclosure tight and settled down. Whit looked up at the sky, proclaimed it gorgeous and bent his head to suckle Danielle's breasts again.

"You keep giving one more attention than the other," she said. "I've told you it doesn't like that. One day, it'll bite back."

"I don't bite."

"No, but you suckle so hard. As if you're starved, famished . . ."

"Hell, can I help it if you turn me into a raging animal?"

"What do you think you do to me?"

The water in the big oval tub swirled around them then, caressing their bodies with its fluid warmth. They bathed with cold cream soap and loofah sponges and each rubbed the other's back. Mischievously, Dani scooped up water and doused him with it. "You're getting it," he chortled.

"Promises. Promises."

They let some of the water out and got down in the tub. "Hell, I *would* forget," he said.

"It's okay," she said soothingly and reached onto the floor to the pocket of her white terry-cloth robe. Laughing, she held up a condom. "What would you do without me?"

"Probably die of grief. Thanks. Will you do the honors, or should I?"

"Let me. It's such a thrill feeling it, stroking it. Come to

Mama, sweetie." And bending her head she lovingly smoothed on the filmy shield until it was fully on. He hugged her then, their slippery bodies enthralled and intertwined.

"In just a little while, we're not going to need these. We'll be hell bent on making a baby."

Danielle's heart leapt at his words. Oh, happy day!

Leaning her against the back of the tub, he entered the nectared sheath of her slowly, slowly until he was fully in. She closed around him like a tight glove and her muscles nibbled at his swollen, throbbing hardness. Gasping for breath, she cried out, "Oh, my God, Whit, what are you doing that makes it feel so good?"

He slipped into a deeper place, touched her womb, and shuddered with joy.

"Making love to you," he whispered. "And, baby, you're sure making love to me."

Her wet breasts thrilled him as he laved them. Their naked bodies had a feel of glory itself. He scooped water from the tub and dabbled it onto her face and she laughed as gleefully as he did.

"We're children," she said, "playing at love."

He shook his head. "No child ever knew what we know now." Her wet sheath surrounded his engorgement and he stopped suddenly. "I don't want it to end right now," he murmured. "Help me make it last."

So she grew still again and felt the violently throbbing rock-hardness of him lingering inside her. His heavily muscled body was leathery smooth, rippling with power and strength and she wanted him, wanted him with desire that was scorching her. After a few moments, he began to move again, sliding delicately, but even this was too much. "I can't last," she gasped. "You're too good at what you do to me. Help me to last, Whit."

But, intent on what he was doing, he drew out, then slid all the way in swiftly, suddenly with burning smoothness and she was undone.

"Whit!" She called his name, and his mouth fastened on hers, his tongue darting feverishly in her mouth. Wildfire swept madly through them both and with her an oceanic tide of fervor swept her loins, then quickly her whole body. He felt the stormy shaking of her body and his heart leapt as he clutched her to him and his seed surged forth.

"I'm sorry," she said softly. "I didn't want to finish so fast."

"This is heady stuff," he said. "Besides, there is time for a whole lot of this. Let's take advantage of it."

THIRTY-THREE

Dinner was served by candlelight at six. "How beautiful!" Danielle said when they saw the pink damask table linen, the Wedgewood china and the Steuben crystal. Fine silver tureens and silverware gleamed. "You set a magnificent table."

"It's so great to have you here," Del told her. "We're pulling out all the stops to see that you come back."

They began with shrimp and crab cocktails in excellent hot sauce. The main course was a choice of ptarmigan bird stuffed with wild rice and mushrooms, baked reindeer steak, and grilled fresh salmon. The vegetables and the salads were from the king-sized vegetables displayed in the kitchen this afternoon. The lettuce and cabbages were a foot in diameter and the tomatoes were stupendous. To Danielle and Whit, each bite seemed better to savor. Womenga joined them at the table when she had a break in serving. A quiet, devout woman, she contributed greatly to the conversation with her tales of old and new Alaska.

By the time dessert was served, everybody was in a gay mood. Cabernet wine soothed and nourished the palate. Val helped Womenga clear the table and bring out the wild berry pie with its rich, flaky vanilla crust. Danielle groaned at the generous servings and at the delectable whipped cream and rich vanilla ice cream.

Val grinned. "Of course Whit will recognize this ice cream as an old family recipe."

"Each time I eat it," Whit said, "it seems better than the last."

Rachmaninoff's Second Piano Concerto, recorded by Andre Watts, pealed over the CD system and made great music to dine by. They lingered over their coffee, laced with fine brandy. When Womenga finally got up to clear the table, Danielle asked if she could help.

"No way," Val told her. "We're treating you two like the king and queen you are, and we have one command: Enjoy yourselves to the fullest."

Del suggested that they jog a few laps in the jogging path out back to work off part of their dinner. The five of them set out to do so. It was seven-thirty and the sun was high, radiant in gold and red.

"What an absolutely fascinating place to be," Danielle said. "Thank you so much for inviting us."

Back inside they listened to music and talked about Alaska, about Whit's coming album to be released in the fall, and Danielle's work. Finally Val said, "Turn in as early as you like and sleep as late as you like. Your time is ours."

In their lovely round bedroom, Danielle and Whit lay down in their clothes. The air had refreshed them and they weren't a bit sleepy. "What a journey," Danielle said. "Who needs sleep?"

She was aware of his eyes on her, slumbrous and warm, but sleeping was not on his mind. She sat up, crossed and rubbed her arms.

"Here, let me do that," he said, hugging her and stroking her lovingly.

She smiled. "Let me get out of my clothes and you get out of yours. I can see where you're headed."

"Why, Lieutenant Ritchey," he teased her, "I do believe you're accusing me of being a sex maniac."

She laughed. "A fact that warms me where I live."

"Don't you feel a smidgen of desire?"

She grinned impishly. "No, not really. I feel a big, round, fiery ball of desire and all of it is for you."

They undressed then and Danielle put CD's they had brought with them on the CD player. Soon Marvin Gaye's incredible voice flled the room—entreating, cajoling, leading them on. Naked, they faced each other and Whit took her in his arms. "Wrap your legs around my waist," he said gently. She did as he asked and felt the stiff, hard wonder of him caress her.

He walked her to a wall, propped her there against him, and after putting on a condom, he entered her with leisurely thrusts as she kept her legs wrapped around him. Lowering his head, he took her breasts in his mouth one at a time and gently laved them. Then he suckled them harder, tonguing the nipples. She felt as if she would go under, but she stayed alert and ravening for his touch.

Inside her nectared sheath, he took it easy, pulling out to the edge, then thrusting back in deeply.

"You're so good," she murmured, "so good."

"I mean to give you whatever you want."

"I want *you*." Her voice welled from the depths of her.

"You've got me, body and soul."

For a long moment she was silent. Then she had to say it. "I love you, Whit. So much."

"And I love you. Let's be together, Dani, really together. Let's get married—soon. I've said it before. I was born to love you. How can you deny me when I would deny you nothing?"

"We're getting closer all the time. Soon, love," She gently squeezed him with her sheath muscles and he gasped.

"You're an asking-for-trouble woman, Dani. I'm going to start giving you multiple orgasms if you keep fooling around."

"Oh, I have those with you."

He leaned forward and kissed her on the mouth. "You've kept it from me. Why?"

Tenderly, she said, "I didn't want you to get a swelled head. Besides, I thought you knew."

"I thought I felt you coming around more than once, but I wasn't sure. You feel so fantastic to me, I rarely know what's going on. I just know I'm in heaven with you, inside you or not."

Soft sunlight filtered through the skylight, spilled onto their loving bodies and warmed them with stated brilliance.

"It's nine o'clock," she said. "Doesn't the sun ever go down?"

"It sets a little around two or so, or a little later. But two or three hours and it's as bright as ever. I'll bring you back for the aurora borealis, Dani. I want to make love to you all night under one of those."

"Okay, but I certainly can't last. I just go on and on with you. My legs are tiring, sweetheart, and you must be getting tired of holding me."

In answer, he unloosed her legs and set her down. As they stood there, smiling at each other, they became aware of Mr. Music watching them, his head to one side. Suddenly, he ruffled his feathers and came to the edge of his perch nearest them.

"He knows when the good stuff's going on." Whit leaned over and kissed her again, then took her hand. He led her to a big aquamarine velvet, armless chair.

"What are you up to?" she asked his retreating back. He went into the bathroom, brought back one of the huge bath towels and spread it over the chair. Then he got a condom from under his pillow and smoothed it on.

"Sit down, my love," he told her. "But first, let me sit down."

Once seated, he pulled her onto his lap facing him. He teased her with his shaft, rubbing it against her, and she almost fainted with joy. Positioned onto his manhood, she couldn't get enough of him, but then it wasn't time to get enough. She loved this man with blinding insistence, with surging wonder that he was hers. Inside her. Giving her joy like nothing she had known before, he came into her life.

On the bed after a little while on the chair, he sat on the edge of the bed and looked at her closely. "You're glowing," he said. "Is it because of me?"

"Who else?"

"Then we should be married. Dani, don't make me beg."

"I'm not. I'll marry you, Whit, but I want you to be certain. You've had a nasty blow that takes time to get over."

"I'm as sure as I can be that I *am* over it. I want to buy three rings no later than the end of next week. Two for you and one for me."

"Very well, my darling, if you think you're sure."

"I don't think, I *know.*"

Looking at her satiny brown body, he lay down and put her astride him, then went inside her. Her inner muscles were throbbing, keeping time with his.

"The wizard's working overtime," she told him.

He laughed merrily. "The wizard *likes* his work. These are his glory days."

She stroked his face. "I don't think I've ever laughed so much as I do with you. Did you bring enough condoms? We're working overtime."

"I packed a lot of them and I can buy more here. This is a land of romance and I've got the queen of romance with me. I won't be caught short."

"Good, because I'm going to run you ragged."

"Go ahead." He grinned. "Make my day."

She balled up a mock fist and tapped his chest with it. "The nightingale's giving us the once-over. Think he's envious? Pets get jealous of their humans."

Whit turned to face the nightingale. "Knock it off," he growled to the bird. "This woman belongs to me."

Lying down, he pulled her back astride him and let her si on his shaft. "It's going to force me off you. Tell the wizard to behave."

But he was looking at her beloved face, going crazy with wanting her again. What in hell was the matter with him Couldn't he get enough? Still, she had said she was going to run him ragged and her words set off joy in his very soul.

Pushing him aside, she slid to the edge of the bed and for

dled his shaft, rubbing it lightly over her cheek. His face lit up and his eyes got sleepy. "The wizard is your slave," he told her. "Your wish is his command."

She was too choked with passion to answer and she sat astride him again as his wizard burgeoned under her. "Whit," she murmured as he slid expertly into the channeled nectar of her wonderful body. "Sweetheart, please. Let's make it last. I feel so hungry for you, hungrier than I've ever felt before."

He felt his heart leap at her words and he knew he would and could do her bidding. "I can make love to you again," he said, "because for this round I'm on the edge of a major explosion."

He felt her soft walls close around him then, grasping, clutching, singing a gorgeous song of passion unleashed and to be satisfied. Not even the beloved songs he sang and the fervor he sang them with could compare with this. They came together in a burst of glory that brought them a world of splendor. His loins were bursting with what seemed to be master fireworks on a hot, lazy Fourth of July. And Danielle felt the familiar hard trembling she knew from an orgasm with Whit. Then in a few minutes another monumental orgasm.

"You're the man," she told him. "My darling, you're the man!"

"And you're the woman for this man."

In the still, sunlit room, Mr. Music ruffled his feathers and lowered his neck. Then, like Whit in concert, he faced his audience and burst into magnificent song.

They didn't make a night of it. Instead, they slept deeply after the nightingale finished singing. Danielle came awake to the sound of wolves singing a howling song. They had closed the windows' blinds and the room was dark as she reached over and switched the light on. She touched Whit's beloved face, but he did not awaken, so she lay back down and slipped into sleep again.

And no sooner did she sleep than the dream came. Whit faced her, blood streaming down his body, and his hoarse cry of, *"Dani!"*

She screamed, *"Whit, no!"*

THIRTY-FOUR

In her office the following Tuesday everyone teased Danielle about how happy she looked. Jon lifted her hand and said, "I'm looking for the ring. You look wonderful, Dani. The trip did you a world of good, but I have a hunch it isn't just Alaska."

Danielle blushed as her team gathered around her. She laughed with them before she asked, "Where is Ed?"

"Oh," Jon said, "he took the day off. He had something to attend to. I signed off on him for you."

Dani had brought back and now distributed pound boxes of wild berry jam hunks dipped in heavy, dark chocolate. Adrienne opened her box, took out a piece of the candy and rolled her eyes. "Giving me this is signing my death warrant. I don't think I can stop until I go through the whole box."

"Then *share*," Danielle told her, smiling. "You've got a whole lot of coworkers. They'll save your life."

"Somehow I hadn't thought of that," Adrienne came back. "Well, anyway you tried. This candy is delectable, Lieutenant, and thank you very much."

Danielle spent the rest of the morning going over old cases and working on Cal's case. They were at a standstill, with no perpetrator except for Buck Lansing, who denied he had killed Cal. But no, they were *not* at a complete standstill; there was Manny Luxor. He was a long shot, but he and Cal were in business together. Both men were edgy, with a vivid love of doing things their way. Both men were dictatorial. If they crossed lances, who could tell the result? She was going to work on Manny again, beginning tomorrow morning. Call him in or go to his house; she couldn't decide at the moment.

May came to Danielle's around one. She hugged Danielle tightly and accepted her box of chocolates, put it in her tote bag.

"Have a seat."

May hugged herself. "I've got such good news. My friend's mama is coming to stay with her for at least a year, help her out. That frees me up so I can move in with you this September. I'm going to enroll in school in Minden while I'm still living in Baltimore. I'll just give your address. Is that okay?"

"That's fine and it makes me happy."

"Me too."

"How's your friend's baby doing?"

"Fine and cute as a button. Do you ever think of getting married, Ms. Ritchey?"

Danielle nodded. "I do. It's a future thing."

"You'll make a great wife, and a great mother. Listen, like always, I can't stay long. I thanked Mr. Steele for taking me home that afternoon and I've mentioned it before but he's da bomb!"

"I hope you told him that."

"I was too bashful. I know a lot of people who have his CD's and his tapes. He's fabulous. Are you marrying him?"

"Maybe."

May burst into peals of laughter. "Don't say maybe, say *yes.*"

Danielle got up, stood beside the chair May sat in and tweaked her ear. "So I'm going to have my very own teenager."

"Looks like it." May grinned. "And I'm going to have my very own mama again."

Jon came in after May left. "What are your plans for today, Dani?"

"I've got a late afternoon appointment with Dr. Little, on

of the profilers we work with. So I'm driving down to Quantico, then I'm going home and work on the Catlett case. Something keeps worrying my mind, Jon. Knowledge is trying to get through and I'm blocking it. Why? My dreams are blurred, foggy. People move in a mist." She told him about the dream in which she called to Whit and he called to her; both voices were frantic.

"Have you mentioned this to him?"

"No. I just keep warning him to be careful."

"Maybe you ought to. From what you tell me, the dream comes when you two are very happy."

She nodded slowly. "Maybe you're right. I'll tell him soon. I just don't want to upset him unnecessarily."

Danielle always enjoyed her visits to Quantico. She spent a couple of hours in their vast library studying case histories like the Catlett case, and was disappointed to find nothing particularly helpful. They had Buck; maybe they had the answer. She made copious notes and studied manuals on DNA interpretation so she could at least be even with some of that knowledge.

She visited from time to time and knew the librarian. "How's the law enforcement business?" the librarian asked, smiling.

Danielle shrugged. "Sometimes it's very good and sometimes it's horrible."

"You're not talking about law enforcement, you're talking about my life."

Both women laughed.

She met Dr. Little at five; he had said he had meetings until then. A good-looking bald man, immaculately attired, he greeted her effusively. "We'll talk," he said, "and I now admit that I wanted a late appointment so I could beg you to go to dinner with me. I'm a widower and my children are scattered. Have pity on a lonely old man."

Danielle laughed. "You're about ten years older than I am."

"I'd guess fifteen. Is it a yes? I went ahead and made reservations for six-thirty at La Martinique. They have superb food and a great wine list. They're highly regarded and they deserve it."

They settled down to talk about the Catlett case. "It looks like you've got one of the messier cases here," Art Little said. "As for Manny Luxor, in the past I've studied mobsters since one offered me a king's ransom to work for him. They're a different breed."

She laid out the case for him again, verbally this time because he asked her to, then he consulted his notes.

"I've just about got this down from memory," he told her. "What a case. A man who was held in high esteem in the community. Rich. A philanthropist. Involved. But bruises showed he mistreated his long-suffering wife. Had a flaunted mistress on the side. Owned a thriving mattress factory. Connected to the mob. Then, someone killed him. You'll hardly find a snarlier case."

"That about sums it up." Danielle drew a deep breath. "Dr. Little?"

He smiled, pursed his lips before he said, "I've been Art to you for so long."

She chuckled. "Okay, Art. My question is a loaded one and I was just going into the therapist-therapand mode, I guess."

"Take your time."

"I *see* things."

"Second sight? Psychic? Many, many people are."

"Sometimes it brings me joy, then again I hate it."

"What has happened?"

"There's a man I'm very fond of. We're close and sometimes when I feel we couldn't be closer I dream that we're in a chaotic situation. He is bleeding profusely. I cry out, 'Whit, no!' and he yells my name and his voice is agonized, as is my own. I guess you'd have to know me better than you do to give me your opinion. It's driving me crazy. I'm scared, Dr.—Art. Really scared." Her flesh had cooled. Her head hurt.

Art Little looked at her carefully. "You're in love with this man. Is he in love with you?"

"He's asked me to marry him."

"I see. Have you told him the dream?"

"I've thought about it. Should I?"

Art Little thought a long while. "Psychiatrists aren't God, although a great many of us would like to be. I'd hazard a guess and say tell him. He may understand something about the situation you don't."

As they finally walked out of his office on the way to dinner, Danielle breathed a sigh of relief and thanked him profusely. They had talked a long while and she was grateful to him for his help.

"I think I put on the report I sent you that Cal Catlett comes across to me as a thoroughly sadistic man. Such men frequently bring about their own death."

Later, in her car, Danielle patted the box beside her, which held a wine cake from La Martinique. She was going to take a longer route and go by Whit's, surprise him. He loved wine cake. She switched on the stereo and "Love, Be Good to Me Tonight" came swirling through. Gina Campbell never failed to move her. She glanced at the dashboard clock: eight-thirty and fast getting dark. She was less than two miles away from the marina and Whit's boat. She would tell him about the dream tonight.

It had been a long day and Danielle found herself a bit tired as she pulled into the parking lot of the marina. Going up to Whit's boat she walked faster than usual, wanting to see him, turned on by the song. Only Cookie was in view.

On deck, she greeted him. "Cookie, how are you?"

"Why, Miss Danielle," he said fretfully. "Lieutenant."

She placed a finger to her lips and spoke in a low voice.

"I'm going to surprise Whit. I have something for him, a wine cake. Make certain he shares."

The big man couldn't seem to get his breath. He sputtered, "Well, I . . ."

She patted his arm and walked swiftly on. "Not a word," she said over her shoulder.

There was no one on the second deck, but she heard the murmur of voices below. A woman's voice. Perhaps one of Whit's sisters. Then going to a lower cabin level she faced the couple outlined in the open door. Willo sat on the back side of the bed in Whit's arms.

"Oh, my God," she whispered. She wanted to call to him. There had to be some explanation. She didn't tarry. With her heart breaking, she raced up the flights of stairs and somehow got to the top deck where Cookie stood, looking miserable. She thrust the cake into his hands.

"It's likely not what you think," Cookie said. And she thought, *Even you qualify it.*

"I'll ask him to call you," he said.

"No, don't. Enjoy the cake. Don't even tell him I was here. I'll talk to him later."

She left then in a haze of hurt and violent anger. She had seen what she had seen. What explanation could there be? She had a wild fantasy of getting into her car and running them both over. She thought of Ed's warning about celebrity lifestyles and the women followers of celebrity men. Had Whit been lying all along?

She all but ran to her car, opened it, and got in. Willing the steel in her soul to come forth, she drove recklessly for a few minutes, then thought that wasn't her no matter what had happened. She slowed down.

Looking for some excuse not to go home, she was aware of her cell phone ringing; she didn't answer it. The twenty-mile trip to outer Minden seemed the longest in her life, yet it wasn't long enough to cool her rage and hurt. She accepted the rings he would buy, glad she hadn't made a fool of herself by saying yes to Whit's marriage proposal. If she had come across him in such a situation after they were married, she thought she would have killed him.

A soothing thought crossed her mind. She had left a packet of accident report forms she had to sign off on at the ALM house. She would finish them tonight. Now she turned off the highway and onto the road that led to the house. The last time she was here she had worked in the darkroom, summoning visions. None ever came that she could decipher.

Now, she let herself into the big house gingerly and went straight to the darkroom, switched on the light and closed the door. She had plenty of time now. She could summon psychic fantasies for the rest of the night. Going into her purse, she cut the cell phone off.

She stood for a long, long while, then walked over to the back of the room where the accident form packet lay on a filing cabinet. Picking the packet up, she put it back down immediately. She was here for a purpose far beyond a bunch of accident reports. She thought she might find something she had missed about Cal's death, about Mona's death, and her own life. She forced herself not to think about Whit. It had been a chimera after all. He wasn't real and she was a fool.

She stood with her back to the door ready to pace the floor, getting visions if she could, when the voice came through slow and measured, "Hello, Dani."

THIRTY-FIVE

Danielle felt an almost painful sense of relief. She laughed shakily. "Don't scare me like that, Ed. I didn't hear you come in."

"Put your bag on top of the file cabinet." His voice was guttural, compelling.

"Don't tease me. Something just happened and I'm in a bad way." For a moment she wondered if she should tell him about Whit and Willo. He'd be pleased.

"Go on, Dani. I'm not teasing."

He held a gun as she looked at him then and saw his eyes were flint hard. He lurched over to her and she smelled the liquor on his breath.

"Oh, my God," she cried suddenly as certain knowledge washed over her. "What are you going to do?"

"I killed Cal Catlett, which I assume you've guessed about now."

"But why, Ed? You hardly knew the man."

"Oh, we were *secret* friends. I was his friend, but he sure wasn't mine. We were all in the smuggling game for a long time and I found out from a New York informant that Cal was cheating me big time, had been cheating me; lying about how much they collected from the illegal aliens. When I confronted him, he laughed at me, said I could get out if I didn't like it. I thought I was on a high level with him. It turns out I was on a low level with Buck. I wasn't going to take that.

"He and Manny Luxor played me over, but he was the chief

offender. He threatened to turn me in, cost me my job and send me up for the smuggling. He was going to swear he had little to do with it, that Buck, Annie, and I ran the operation."

"But it wouldn't have worked. We had samples of his hair on Mr. Appiah's body."

"He didn't know that. And it wasn't enough evidence. I lied to you. I've been gambling and I'm heavily in debt now, thousands of dollars. The hombre from Mexico helped Cal double-cross me. Cal was going to have one of Manny's men work me over. I wasn't going to stand for that. Dani, I'm sorry I've got to take you out, and you deserve to know I killed Mona."

Shock waves of horror struck Danielle's body then. "Why?" was all she could croak.

"She found out somehow, so you see this has been going on a long time. She was going to turn me in and I couldn't let her do that, just like I couldn't let Cal do that."

His words were like bullets piercing her brain. "That was a sharp ploy you and Jon pulled to smoke me out. I knew then you'd found my ankh and my safe deposit key. The money in that box was my getaway money. I wasn't going to spend it to pay gambling debts."

Her knees were like jelly now and she closed her eyes. The lump in her throat threatened to choke her.

"I trusted you," she said bitterly.

"Yeah, we make mistakes like that sometimes. Didn't your gift ever tell you these things?" He seemed gently mocking now.

She shook her head. Her throat was dust dry. "I *believed* in you. And I thought there was a limit to evil; now I know I was wrong."

He laughed then. "I came up the hard way with a father who believed in nothing and nobody except his ox whip that he liked to use on me. I became a cop so I could arrest people like him. I didn't really think about killing Cal or Mona until they were going to take being a cop away from me."

"Now you're taking it away from yourself."

"Give me a good-bye kiss, Dani? And don't try any fancy stuff."

"You're crazy."

"Am I? I'm going to put your body in a body bag and roll it up into a rug. I've got both waiting outside. I'm going to put it into the Chesapeake Bay. I'm really sorry. They'll know you're gone, but there'll be no body."

She was fighting for time now. "After a while the bag and the rug will rot. My bones will float to the surface. Have you thought of that?" She damned the shakiness in her voice.

He shook his head. "You're going into a metal case I also had made up. I've thought of everything. I didn't give a damn about killing Cal. I've killed men before and gotten away with it. I hated killing Mona and I hate killing you, but I've got to protect myself."

"Then don't do it. You can't live with yourself if you do."

"I can," he said calmly. "I'm my own God, Dani. I found that out when I killed Mona. I can reward and I can punish. One way or another I can get the things and the people I want."

His eyes narrowed then, glittering evilly as he raked her over.

"I'm going to have that kiss, you know. You can't stop me, even if I have to knock you out first."

Her brain was on fire now, working smoothly. She kneed him in the groin and he struck her with his gun. She screamed and the door burst open with Jon standing there.

"Drop the gun, Ed!" Jon commanded.

Instead, Ed grabbed Danielle and held her against him. He jammed his gun into her side. The policemen stood at wary attention.

"One move and I kill her!" Ed thundered.

Her vision was blurry, but she saw Whit move almost imperceptibly across the room, then he lunged across the room for Ed crying, "Dani!"

"Whit, *no!*" she screamed. Ed's gun went off and Whit's

blood spurted, but he kept struggling with Ed, forcing his arm toward the ceiling. Then Jon's gun took over and dropped Ed in seconds. The bullets struck him in the head and chest and he sagged to his knees, groaning. "Damn you," Ed snarled, lurching, "for taking her away."

Jon kicked the gun aside and bent over Ed's body. "He's dead," he said.

Danielle went on her knees to hover above Whit, her tears wetting his face. Jon called an ambulance as Danielle crouched by Whit. It seemed Whit had been struck in the chest. Frantically, she and Adrienne fashioned bandages as best they could from their shirts, cutting the strips with scissors from her first-aid kit.

All they could do then was wait as Whit murmured again and again, "Dani." There were sirens screaming then as her team and two other policemen came in. The short time until the ambulance arrived seemed the longest Danielle had ever known.

Later, at Minden's excellent hospital, Danielle and Jon sat in a private waiting room. Her body felt heavy with depression. Next to Mona's death, she thought it was the saddest moment of her life. What had gone on between Whit and her today no longer mattered. *He has to live.* She put her head down on her knees. She had long trained herself not to break down, but she was breaking now.

She sat up and Jon took her hand, squeezed it tightly.

"I'll want to know how you came to be at the ALM house," she said, "and thank God you were. But right now I can't talk, I can't listen. My brain is frozen. . . ."

"It's all right," he said. He looked at his watch and she looked at hers. It had been over an hour.

A somber doctor came into the room, "Captain, Lieutenant. You'll be glad to know that Mr. Steele is coming along nicely. His wounds are non-life-threatening. Just a deep flesh wound. You'll be able to talk with him for a short while when he comes out from sedation."

Looking at him, Danielle felt a hysterical desire to hug him tightly. Instead, she choked, "Thank you so much."

"Yes, thank you," Jon said.

"I knew you'd want to know his status. Now, I must warn you not to talk too long. He's lost a lot of blood and will be here for at least a couple of days. Is your name Dani?" he asked Danielle.

"Yes."

"He called it often. What he feels for you is probably making him come through faster because he's coming along much better than we expected even for a deep flesh wound. These can be dangerous at times. Captain Ryson, I'll be seeing both of you soon."

Frank and Caroline had been called. They were on their way.

Jon and Danielle frequently came in with crime victims. It was an added touch to make the victims feel more cared about.

Tears streamed down Danielle's face and Jon blotted her face with his fresh, white handkerchief.

"Tell me now what happened tonight," she said.

"Okay. I know what happened between you and Whit, but he's guiltless. I'll let him tell you."

"Very well."

"Now, as to how Whit and I came to be there. Thoughts kept nagging my mind about Ed. I felt he knew something he wasn't telling. When he asked for time off while you were in Alaska, my alarm bells went off. He's usually hell-bent to take care of things when you're not there.

"As you know, the ALM house has been electronically wired since we tried to set the trap for him. You and I have the listening device, as well as the one at the station house. Wh came to me and told me what had happened between you two He had been by your house, by the station house, and h couldn't find you. He was crazy with worry. I check from time to time to see if I can hear anything. I tuned in this time and heard nothing. On a hunch, I kept listening. Then I heard you call Ed's name and everything clicked, even before I heard him threaten you and confess.

"Whit drove up and insisted on coming with me. I radioed for help. Your team drove up. We snaked in, jimmying the back door locks and placing ourselves in strategic positions. We were buying time; we couldn't know when he would abruptly try to kill you and we couldn't let that happen."

He patted her back. "You've been through hell tonight. Your decision to let the recorders stay on at the ALM house paid off. Those tiny little things. You're one of the best, Dani. I'm very, very proud of you."

"And I'm so proud of you and Whit. Ed killed Mona."

"I'm not surprised. I couldn't listen to everything he said because I had to get on top of his movement, but I'm assuming he said that. Or did you just know?"

"He said it and I knew. My gift has come in full force. Jon, I always dreamed of Ed when I dreamed of Mona. He was there, sorrowful, helpful, grieving, and he was *there*. I didn't put that together; it didn't seem strange. He was her friend, *my* friend. I didn't *want* to know that he was her killer."

She clenched her fists, some of the agony filling her again.

"We hide things from ourselves when they hurt too bad," he said. "Forgive him, if you can."

"It will take a lot of time."

"You've got a love he'll never know. Think about that."

Her heart soared again. Whit was alive! And he was going to be all right.

It was well after eleven that night when Whit could talk. Jon grinned down at him. "Are you bucking for a medal, my man? Yelling Dani's name might have been a stroke of genius. . . ."

"I was trying to surprise Ed, throw him off."

"And you did just that and we thank you," Jon said.

"I'm never going to let anything happen to Dani." Whit grinned crookedly.

She stood beside Jon. "Can you be hugged? No, I think probably not."

"I've got an uninjured side."

She bent over and stroked that side. "I'm so sorry, Whit."

Jon went out then and they were left alone. A nurse came in, took a small white tablet and a glass of water from her cart and gave it to Whit, who took it quickly and swallowed the pill.

"I'm going to leave you alone, Mr. Steele." And she nodded to Danielle. "Doctor's orders are he shouldn't talk more than twenty minutes or so."

She sat down and he smiled at her.

"Beautiful Dani," Whit said. "I love you."

"And I love you. It doesn't matter if you want Willo. I just want you walking the face of the earth for a long time."

"You should have come on in." He drew a deep breath and winced.

"Whit, if it hurts you to talk you can tell me at any time. I'll understand."

"No. I've got to tell you now. Willo came unexpectedly. She looked terrible. Her baby was smothered in his crib a week ago and she blamed herself. She said she intended to kill herself, that she had nothing to live for . . ."

"I'm so sorry."

"I tried to do what I could to help her. She asked if she could stay awhile. I told her she could spend the night and called you, but got your answering service. Cookie told me you had been there and I knew what you must have seen. He stayed with Willo and I set out to find you. You know what happened then."

"You saved my life. If you hadn't yelled and thrown yourself at Ed, he would have killed me."

"Still think being a police person isn't dangerous?"

She smiled. "It's a once-in-a-lifetime thing. In thirteen years, it has never happened before. Life gives us no guarantees. I still love it."

He smiled widely then. "I'm groggy, but I'll remember your answer. Dani, you've got to marry me. I can't stand it if you don't."

She got up, went to him and kissed him full on the lips, her tongue going into the corners of his mouth. With surprising strength he kissed her back, a flaming kiss.

"Hey, you really *are* going to be all right," she teased.

"You haven't answered what I told you."

"About getting married?"

"Yes."

"Hm-m-m, how about as soon as you get a bit better, then a gorgeous, wonderful wedding within a year. Does that tickle your fancy?" She caught his hand and held it. "I'm going to copy a sheet full of my lipsticked kisses and bring it to you to keep you company while you're here."

"Great!"

"Meanwhile . . ." she murmured and bent forward to receive another passionate kiss just like the first one.

EPILOGUE

September 2001

Danielle—now heavy with child—felt a wave of happiness sweep over her as she mingled with the people gathered in Whit's and her backyard. Caroline and Frank Steele were there and so many others: Annie and her husband and baby; Ashley, her husband, her stepson and her baby; May, who lived with them now.

Frank Steele came to Danielle as Whit reached her side. "What's the occasion for this great little party?" Frank asked, smiling. Caroline Steele came up in time to hear the question. "Yes, what is it?" she asked.

Whit grinned. "I guess you could say it's a *pregnancy party*. I'm about to take off with happiness. I wanted to spread the joy."

Danielle looked around her. Their house was newly renovated, with beautiful patterned redbrick and a gorgeously landscaped yard. Their life was rife with the meaning of giving and having so much.

The year and five months since she'd fatefully met Whit had flown by. So much had happened. Annice and Ashley came up, kissed her. Then her father, Julian, and Daphne, who had been married to each other for six months.

Daphne whispered to her now. "You'd never guess, but Julian wants a baby. Am I too old, Dani?"

"Absolutely not," Danielle said staunchly. "Don't che

yourself. You and Julian love each other. You deserve a baby." Daphne laughed and began to sing, "I've got my mojo working."

Jon and his wife, Francesca, were there, along with Danielle's police team and most of the people at Minden's police department. The former Irene Catlett and her husband, Dave, were a happy couple; Danielle strolled over to them.

"Wonderful party," Irene said before she impulsively took Danielle's hand. "I'm so glad you agreed to be my friend," Irene continued. "I never dreamed life could be like this." Dave smiled from ear to ear.

"And I never dreamed a woman could be like you," Dave said, his eyes shining as he looked at Irene.

"You're really getting there with that baby," Irene said, and her expression went somber. "I might have had a child . . ."

"You still can," Dave offered. "Others take the chance."

"Maybe." Irene's face was sad.

Cameras were out and clicking at the yard decorated in paper lanterns and gay balloons. The impatiens bed was showing off its beautiful best. Several movie cameras recorded the gay scene. Danielle caught Irene's hand. "You and Dave will decide what's right for you. You're happy now and I'm so glad for you." Irene's eyes filled with tears.

There was something missing here, Danielle reflected—Ed, who had been at every gathering Danielle had planned since she knew him. As his face rose before her, she felt sad, yet angry. He had killed Mona, planned to kill her, Danielle, and he had cost Whit months of suffering.

She saw someone slap a mosquito and walked back to the deck to pick up more mosquito-repellent spray. Once there, she decided to go inside to the kitchen. Standing at the window, she thought long and hard and deep about the pain of the past months.

She had gone to Ed's funeral and comforted Shelley, who had loved him so. "He always loved you," Shelley had cried.

"Shelley, don't," she had responded. "Love doesn't kill. Ed was a man who didn't know how to love."

Shelley was all right right now, with a new man she cared about. Annie and Buck had gone to prison; Buck for murder and smuggling and Annie as an accomplice in smuggling. Manny Luxor had drawn ten years for smuggling aliens. Abruptly her thoughts rechanneled, and she smiled.

What she remembered was the first morning she and Whit had spent at this window with a dawn, then a rising sun. They had kissed that first time with a passion both knew with some inborn knowledge would last. They were made for each other and wise enough to know it.

She heard the screen door open and Whit came to her side. "Dani? Are you all right?"

"Oh, Lord, I'm fine." Tears of happiness moistened her eyes.

He spread his fingers on her stomach and laughed as the baby kicked. "I know we don't want to get an ultrasound because we don't need to know the gender, but this kid's acting like a boy. Rough and rowdy."

"And loved," she amended. "He or she will be okay. Whit, remember when we kissed in here that first early morning?"

"I've never forgotten it. I never will." He brought her hand to his lips, glancing at her sparkling rings. *"Scientists are finding out,"* he said, *"that love is real, romance is real, no just some figment of our imagination."*

"I know," she told him. "Whit, if you could have just one characteristic, what would it be?"

Surprised, he studied her a moment, then did not hesitate. "I'd choose to be *trustworthy,* all the way through."

"God knows *I* trust you."

"And I trust you."

Thoughtfully, she said, "I'm glad Willo's made it through. Just think, she'll be getting married again soon and she seem happy. I'm proud we helped her."

"I'm glad, too. Sweetheart, let's make a pledge to commer

orate our first kiss in this window each anniversary year. What are you thinking?"

"That that's a great thought and something else . . ."

"Yes?" she murmured.

"That I was born to love you."

She chuckled. "We were born to love each other." He kissed the corners of her mouth and her heart soared with a happy, passionate, and lasting love.

Dear Readers,

Thank you so much for your kind comments and your many encouraging letters. I deeply appreciate them all and hope you'll keep writing. If you wish a reply, please enclose a stamped, self-addressed envelope.

I finished this book the day before the first anniversary of 9-11-01, a sad, sad day for our country. I have wept and I have prayed for those who died and those who were injured. But we know God grants us hope in the midst of the most devastating circumstances, and He is with us always.

My very best wishes,

Francine Craft
P.O. Box 44204
Washington, DC 20026
www.francinecraft.com
francinecraft@yahoo.com

ABOUT THE AUTHOR

Francine Craft is the pen name of a writer based in Washington, D.C., who has enjoyed writing for many years. A native Mississippian, she has also lived in New Orleans and found it fascinating.

Francine has been a research assistant for a large nonprofit organization, an elementary school teacher, a business school instructor, and a legal secretary for the federal government. Her books have been highly praised by reviewers. She is a member of Romance Writers of America.

Prodigious reading, photography, and songwriting are Francine's hobbies, along with baking truly yummy chocolate chip and oatmeal cookies. She lives with a family of friends and many goldfish

More Sizzling Romance From
Francine Craft

__Betrayed by Love	1-58314-152-9	$5.99US/$7.99CAN
__Devoted	0-7860-0094-5	$4.99US/$5.99CAN
__Forever Love	1-58314-194-4	$5.99US/$7.99CAN
__Haunted Heart	1-58314-301-7	$5.99US/$7.99CAN
__Lyrics of Love	0-7860-0531-9	$4.99US/$6.50CAN
__Star-Crossed	1-58314-099-9	$5.99US/$7.99CAN
__Still in Love	1-58314-005-0	$4.99US/$6.50CAN
__What Matters Most	1-58314-195-2	$5.99US/$7.99CAN
__Born to Love You	1-58314-302-5	$5.99US/$7.99CAN

Arabesque Romances
by *Roberta Gayle*

__**Moonrise**	**$4.99US/$5.99CAN**
0-7860-0268-9	
__**Sunshine and Shadows**	**$4.99US/$5.99CAN**
0-7860-0136-4	
__**Something Old, Something New**	**$4.99US/$6.50CAN**
1-58314-018-2	
__**Mad About You**	**$5.99US/$7.99CAN**
1-58314-108-1	
__**Nothing But the Truth**	**$5.99US/$7.99CAN**
1-58314-209-6	
__**Coming Home**	**$6.99US/$9.99CAN**
1-58314-282-7	
__**The Holiday Wife**	**$6.99US/$9.99CAN**
1-58314-425-0	

COMING IN DECEMBER 2003 FROM
ARABESQUE ROMANCE

__LOVE IS NOT ENOUGH
by Marilyn Tyner   1-58314-290-8 $6.99US/$9.99CAN
After her marriage collapsed, Kendall Chase decided that she would rely
only on herself. It's difficult for her to believe that Ben Whitaker is the
warmhearted man he seems. But when they uncover a dangerous plot,
Kendall and Ben must face down their misunderstandings and distrust
if they are to truly fulfill the love they've found.

__TREASURES OF THE HEART
by Jacquelin Thomas   1-58314-348-3 $6.99US/$9.99CAN
Kemba Jennings has spent years trying to recover the diamond that re-
sulted in her father's death. When she finally gets a chance to reclaim it,
she witnesses a murder. Despite finding refuge in the arms of handsome
minister Eric Avery, she embarks on a quest to discover the truth . . . and
finds a love that may be the greatest treasure of all. . . .

__GUARDED LOVE
by AlTonya Washington   1-58314-408-0 $5.99US/$7.99CAN
The success of her magazine has eased Selena Witherspoon's painful
memories of her last relationship. While in Miami to promote her newest
venture, entrepreneur Darius McClellan offers her friendship with no
strings attached. . . . But a series of threats could jeopardize Selena's happiness with this special man who has transformed her life.

__TAKE ME TO HEART
by Deborah Fletcher Mello   1-58314-473-0 $5.99US/$7.99CAN
Marguerite has had her heart broken too many times. So the charm and
good looks of this latest prince don't faze her when they meet on the job.
Her days of trusting men are over, no exceptions. But this one's already
moved in on her professional life, and now he's looking for a spot in her
personal life. If only she could trust him. Maybe just once. . . .